Books should be returned or renewed by the last
date above. Renew by phone 03000 41 31 31 or
online *www.kent.gov.uk/libs*

Libraries Registration & Archives

Martina Reilly, formerly known as the author Tina Reilly, lives in County Kildare with her husband and two children. Catch up with Martina on her website www.tinareilly.info, on Facebook or on Twitter @MartinaReilly

Previously by Martina Reilly

martina reilly

PROOF

HACHETTE
BOOKS
IRELAND

First published in Ireland in 2016 by HACHETTE BOOKS IRELAND

1

Cataloguing in Publication Data is available from the British Library

ISBN 978 1 4736 3669 9

Typeset in Bembo Book Std by Bookends Publishing Services
Printed and bound in Great Britain by Clays Ltd, St Ives plc.

Hachette Books Ireland policy is to use papers that are natural, renewable and recyclable products and made from wood grown in sustainable forests. The logging and manufacturing processes are expected to conform to the environmental regulations of the country of origin.

Hachette Books Ireland
8 Castlecourt Centre
Castleknock
Dublin 15
Ireland

A division of Hachette UK Ltd
Carmelite House, 50 Victoria Embankment, London EC4Y 0DZ

www.hachettebooksireland.ie

My twentieth book is dedicated to Colm with all my love.

EXTRACT FROM *PLACES OF INTEREST IN IRELAND*

The Orchard and Monastery at Applegate

In 1895, in Drom Rí (now Applegate), a tract of land, measuring approximately one acre, bordering the Eden River was in dispute. Four landowners laid claim to it, among them Jacob Hanratty, the local mayor. After many bitter disputes in which one landowner was allegedly killed, though no body was ever found, the courts decided that the land should become common ground. In an act of generosity, Jacob Hanratty provided funds to plant five hundred apple trees on the land and thus make free fruit available to all the inhabitants of Applegate. The orchard is still there and is an asset to the town.

Just sixty miles from Dublin, Applegate has approximately eight thousand inhabitants and is run by a local council. High above the town, on a hill, lie the extensive and well-preserved ruins of an ancient monastery. Tours are on the hour every hour in the summer months. This attraction brings a lot of business to the pretty town, in which all the shopfronts are painted vibrant summer colours. The town has a hotel, Hanratty's, owned by Charles Hanratty, a descendant of Jacob Hanratty, two schools and a number of pubs, among them Daly's, which serves excellent food.

Recommended as a place to visit? Yes.

Recommended as a place to stay? Yes.

EIGHTEEN MONTHS AGO ...

As Charles Hanratty lay dying, blood pooling around his head, his attacker began to cluck.

Charles, from his supine position on the floor, glanced up. His vision was dimming now, but just in case he made it, he wanted to remember this person. It was hard to see properly, but the attacker appeared to be tall – tall-ish, he amended. Strong. Dressed all in black. Face covered. Charles opened his mouth to speak but he couldn't form the words. Who are you, he wanted to ask. And why. Though he might not have liked the answer to that question. There were a few people who might like him dead. He was a businessman and in business hard decisions had to be made. He'd made a lot of tough decisions in his time. He'd also done a lot of things he shouldn't have.

The realisation made him shiver. Or maybe it was death creeping in.

He wondered if moving here, to Dublin, had caused this. Or was this some hangover revenge from Applegate.

A shower of glass fell on him. The glass of a photo frame, the picture drifting down. He'd treasured that picture. It was a symbol of all he had. The frame thumped down on top of him but he barely felt it. Now it was really broken. Just like him.

He watched, through a blur, as his attacker clucked again before saying, 'Your chickens have finally come home to roost'.

Charles Hanratty suddenly understood. He tried to speak but his voice wouldn't work.

Then, his attacker froze, for just a second, and listened, before peeling off the ski mask. 'I want mine to be the last face you see.'

And it was.

WEEK 1: DAY 1

Marcus

I'm innocent, it's important you understand that. I'm not sad the guy's dead and maybe, given a few more months, it could have been me standing over him brandishing an iron bar or whatever it was he was killed with. That's what I told the police, only I shouldn't have. I was already chief suspect: I had no alibi, I had plenty of motive and I was in the area the night he was killed.

It's mostly circumstantial, though, as my perky barrister, Melissa, keeps telling me.

'Marcus,' she says, her ponytail swishing and her teeth, in braces, gleaming up at me, 'they've got very little.'

I think they've got plenty.

I guess I'd better introduce myself a bit. It's polite, isn't it? I'm Marcus Dillon and I'm thirty-two years old. The first eighteen years of my life were spent in a small town, in the middle of Ireland, called Applegate. It's a pretty kind of place, bright shops, the kind of place where bunting flutters all year round and big urns of tumbling flowers sit on the paths. The kind of place where people used to know each other, or thought they did at least. The left-hand side of the main street of Applegate is dominated by Hanratty's Hotel. Charles, the man I allegedly murdered, owned that hotel and a pile of shops and houses besides. In fact, he owned Applegate.

I left there with my mother when I was eighteen after I'd lost my full-time job in Charles Hanratty's newsagent's and she'd lost hers in his hotel. I knew then that we'd have no hope of making the rent payments on our house, which was owned by Charles Hanratty, and so we'd left, in the middle of the night, still owing a month's rent. It gave me a small bit of satisfaction to get one over on him. After Applegate, Dublin was a shock to us both. We lived in council housing for a while until I started to make money as a comic-book creator. I live in Malahide now; my mother lives in Wales with her husband, Alan. I draw most days. And here is the confession, the one that might make you decide you don't like me. Or make you think I'm guilty. When I wasn't drawing, I was sitting in my car, stalking Hanratty. For the last year of his life anyway.

Thinking about it now, it seems bonkers that I would have wasted my time doing it. I look back and think, how can that have been me? But it was me and I was obsessed. It's like a nasty version of being in love with someone and not being able to stop thinking about them. Only I hated the guy. I hated him so much, my heart squeezed whenever I thought about him.

Now that he's dead, I feel free but also bewildered that I spent so much energy on hating. I feel like I never want to feel like that again.

'The prosecutor will make his speech first.' Melissa slides in beside me and the junior counsel, a thin, twitchy guy called Josh, with a pale face and hair that sticks out all over the place, starts hefting files from her trolley onto the desk in front of us. I give them a hand. Melissa is tiny; she's young but I reckon she looks younger than she is and she has a scary way of speaking when she's cross. She didn't much like me at first – some people don't. I think it's because I never say much. I don't see the need. I'm one of life's observers – I just sit and watch. I guess that's why I was good at stalking. Anyway, she likes me now. I tend to grow on people. 'There's no need to do that, Marcus.' She flashes me a smile full of glittering metal. 'Josh has it.'

Josh grins and continues to pull files out of the trolley.

'All you need to remember,' Melissa says to me, 'is that when the prosecution is speaking you have to keep calm and look innocent.'

'I *am* innocent,' I remind her.

'I know that,' she says, 'but the jury won't. How are you holding up?'

I shrug. I'm wrecked. I haven't slept right in weeks. 'Good.'

'Two weeks from now, you'll walk out that door an innocent man.'

I love her optimism. Even if I am acquitted, will I ever be innocent? They'll have to catch someone first before people will believe it. Mud sticks, just like it did in Applegate all those years ago. No one trusted me after what happened in the shop; no one trusted me because of my mother. Still, I give Melissa a smile, like I believe her.

'Marcus!' A loud whisper. My mother waves up at me. She's just come in with Alan, her husband of two years. I wasn't sure what to make of Alan when my mother first told me about him – older, lover of cardigans and gardening – but on their wedding day, when he looked as if he couldn't believe his luck to be marrying my mother, he earned enough brownie points to last a lifetime. He's taken all the adverse publicity about me in his stride. His 'No fucking comment, you fuckheads,' to the media is now quoted daily on TV. YouTube is full of celebrities saying it. None of them can pull it off like Alan, though, his soft Welsh accent making it sound almost endearing.

They've been great, putting up bail for me, agreeing to all the bail conditions that were set out. Their life in Wales has been turned upside-down this past eighteen months as we waited for the trial and they've never complained or made me feel bad about it. But I do. I owe them big time.

Alan comes over. 'Keep calm, Marcus,' he says, likes he's a courtroom pro.

'I will.'

He turns to Melissa. 'And how's the best barrister in the world?'

'Top form.' Melissa nods as she scans her notes. 'I was just saying to Marcus, it's important everyone keeps a cool head when the prosecution gets going. We'll have our chance later.'

'Cool is my middle name.' Alan pats me on the back. 'Good luck, son.'

My mother blows me up a kiss. She's dressed soberly in a black suit and white blouse. In fact, she looks like she's going to a funeral. Mine, most likely.

Melissa turns to talk to my solicitor, who is behind us. It's like I've brought my own private army into the courtroom, like I'm some kind of a celebrity. Which in a perverse way, I sort of am. This trial has received wall-to-wall media coverage.

I spot Sash. I haven't seen her since all the stuff about her and Paddy splitting up hit the papers. That was about sixteen months ago. It's funny how Paddy was news even though he never got elected to the Dáil that time. But he's memorable, that's the thing – he's like my polar opposite. He attracts love and attention like gravity. And Sash, she's another person you can't ignore – even the watered-down version of her that she was when she was with Paddy was pretty spectacular. Their relationship was another casualty of my arrest. Sash's dad, looking a lot older than I remember, follows her in and slides into the seat beside her. Sash glances up at me and offers a brief smile.

It cuts my heart. Even after all this time, she can still do it to me.

Sash

He's there, all dressed up. A man off either to the gallows or a wedding. He's lost weight, which doesn't surprise me. I've lost weight too. All my life, I've wanted to be thinner, hating my strong arms and thighs. And now, though I've lost a stone, it seems to have fallen off my face. Who knew I carried fourteen pounds on my face?

Marcus glances at me and I smile. It's a reflex. I want to kill him. Why did he have to fixate on Charles Hanratty? If Marcus had stayed away, like I'd asked, he'd never be in this mess. I wouldn't be in this mess. Neither would Lana. Or Paddy. I try not to think of Paddy. He of all people did not deserve this. But yet, I'm here, at the trial, because I understand why Marcus did it too. I came forward for the defence because, Marcus and me, we're in it together. We've always been in it together. I've coaxed Lana into giving evidence too, though hers could go either way.

I'm sitting behind a woman wearing a bright pink jacket and an older bald man. My dad joins me and he catches my hand and gives it a squeeze. He tries to smile but his eyes are sad. He's looked like that ever since he found out, sixteen months ago. I wonder will he ever smile properly again. I wonder will any of us. Rachael, my boss, who's been brilliant, told me that this was just an episode in my life, that it will pass and that one day I'll look back and it'll be over. I want so much to believe that but what she doesn't realise is that it's an episode that began fifteen years ago and it hasn't ended yet.

I'm Sash, by the way. I'm thirty, almost thirty-one. I've got short black hair, cut tight. It suits me better than it did, because my face has lost so much weight. I'm brown-eyed, freckle-faced and I have a tiny scar on my foot that no one ever sees.

My mother left us when I was fourteen and Lana was

twelve. I have to admit that I've never really got over it. There was no hint that she was thinking of going – we just got up one morning and she was packing as Dad stood by, begging her to reconsider. I remember how he followed her out to the taxi, how when she came back to get her final bag, Dad started to cry. She hesitated in the doorway for just a second before saying, 'I can't do it, Kevin, don't ask me to keep doing it.'

At that my dad just nodded, a granting of permission or something, I think. Then she wrapped her arms about me and Lana and said she was sorry she wasn't stronger.

A few months after she left, Dad applied for promotion to sergeant, got it and brought me and Lana from our home in Dublin to Applegate. It was just a way for him to escape my mother's absence, I think now. And it was a huge absence, a gaping hole at the centre of our lives that no amount of tears could fill.

For a long time after we moved to Applegate, I was afraid that one day my mother would decide to return to us and arrive at our house in Dublin only to find us gone. But Dad said that he'd never have moved if there had been any possibility of that. It made me realise that she was out of our lives for good and I grieved for a long time. We haven't seen her since, and after Dad divorced her I finally accepted the fact that it was going to be a part of my life I'd just have to live with.

I don't miss her like I used to.

I do miss Paddy, though. And feel guilty about ruining his life for him. Sixteen months since we broke up and it's like a wound that hasn't healed. I had thought, once I moved into the cottage in Applegate with Paddy, that everything would roll out before me, like a shining carpet stretching into the future. I should have known from that very first picture I had taken with Charles Hanratty that things would go like this. I should have known that Marcus would go apeshit and that Hanratty financing Paddy's political campaign for election was bound to end in disaster for us. I think back and I don't know how I did it, those photos, that smile. I think back and it's as if everything that's happened to me since my mother left happened to someone else. All I have now is the truth and I have to share it with a room full of strangers next week. The thought makes my stomach heave.

Marcus is talking to his solicitor now, his dark head bent towards her fairer one. Or maybe it's his barrister – I get mixed up even though I'd researched court appearances and what to say and all that before coming here. Anyway, whatever she is, she's squashed in beside him, whispering away, and he's nodding and she pats his arm and he flashes her one of his rare smiles before pulling back and heaving a sigh.

For a tiny second, I see that he is scared, before the mask is back on.

I think it's my fault that we've ended up here.

All my bloody fault.

Lana

It's just me and Mona at home in Applegate now because my dad and Sash have gone off to the trial. It's a big deal, Mona said, but her and Dad agreed that it's best if I don't go to see it. I have to go one day to give evidence but that's all. The trial is about a boy, Marcus, that Sash used to be friends with being accused of murdering the man who used to live up the road from us. Only he didn't get murdered up the road from us because he doesn't live in that house anymore. He got murdered in Dublin. Loads of people get murdered in Dublin. He was a rich guy too, I never really liked him – though now he's dead, it seems everyone else liked him.

In case you're wondering, Mona isn't my mother. She's a woman my dad met when he went to a conference on Dealing with Adult Asperger's or something. Mona ran the course. My real mother isn't here. She left when I was twelve years, two weeks and a day old. No one really talked about it, not Sash or my dad, and if someone did, Sash would just end up walking out, so I learned to keep my mouth zipped. Before my mother left, I thought nothing would ever change. I don't like change. I like getting up at nine, having cornflakes and milk, getting dressed from my socks upwards and, back then, if it was a weekday, going to school. I liked school loads in the beginning but then we got a teacher who had a high voice and when she talked it made my ears jump and I would try to think of other things but if she kept talking I would rock to get her voice out of my head and then I would scream really loud to move it out of the room and then Sash would have to be called and then my mother would have to come and take me home. Then my mother would have to teach me at home and I liked that and so did she because she would say, 'You're killing me, Lana,' which is what people say when they are enjoying a joke. On weekends I would watch all my programmes on TV until three o'clock. After three, I did puzzles and coloured. Every day the very same. I always liked that.

Then my mother left and Dad moved to Applegate. I screamed and screamed and two neighbours had to put me into the car and then Sash gave me Lana, who is my favourite doll to play with, which is one I've had since I was only two and who has the same name, colour hair and eyes as me and Sash told me that moving would be fine, that she was my big sister and that she would always be there and that that would never change.

Then nine years and four months ago, I asked Sash why our mother had left. She was surprised that I asked I think, because it had been years and years since our mother went away. But I like details. They make up a picture. You have details, you have a story, something to hold on to. Sometimes the details that you have tell one story and sometimes they tell another, even though they're the same details. That's scary and confusing. My memory of our mother is of a nice lady with medium dark-brown hair like mine and a face like Sash's who made me all my favourite foods and taught me letters over and over again when I wasn't in school. She loved doughnuts, like Homer Simpson, and every day or night after his shift in the police station, Dad would bring home a bag of doughnuts for her. One time I heard her say to him that it would take more than a bag of doughnuts to make her happy and Dad never bought doughnuts after that. I think maybe if he had bought two bags of doughnuts she might have been happy and, who knows, she might have stayed with us.

The day I asked Sash about our mother leaving was just after Sash had failed her art college final exams and had come back home from Dublin to live with us. She had brought me for an outing. She likes to do that to give me new experiences and I don't mind new experiences once they are with her. She always explains in advance where we are going and what we might see and she always says if I don't like something to tell her and for me to explain why I don't like it. I try to do that but sometimes I just get soaked in a feeling and I can't breathe and I just have to do something to make myself feel better like throw knives or rocks. Anyway, this day, we were up the hill, beside the ruins of the monastery, and tourists were walking in and out of the ruins and a guide was telling them all about the monastery that looked down upon Applegate and that Applegate existed because the monastery used to give the people of the town food and stuff. The guide had a voice that made my head hum and I had to put my hands over my ears for a bit until she went around the other side and I couldn't hardly hear her anymore.

Sash had her camera with her. She was taking pictures of Applegate so she could paint them for Dessie Daly. In case you get confused, Dessie and his mother, June, own Daly's pub in Applegate. Dessie is Marcus's friend and Sash's friend. Dessie wanted Sash to paint some landscapes for the pub. Sash thought that he only asked her to do them because he felt sorry for her because she had failed college and had no job and when I asked Dessie if this was true, Dessie looked all annoyed and said that of course it wasn't so I told Sash this and she got all annoyed. I thought she'd be glad.

Anyway, it was a sunny day and there were four sheep of medium size in the field beside us. One of them had a black spot on its back. I was sitting on the stone wall that is right on the edge of the mountain, only it's a safe stone wall – that's what the notice says in blue letters. Blue and red flowers were planted along the side. Possibly about one hundred and six red flowers and eighty – sorry, that's not an important detail, I don't think.

Sash was taking pictures and peering at them through the viewfinder and pressing buttons. I like to look at Sash when she does stuff like that. Her brow creases up and she sticks her tongue out the side of her mouth and she reminds me of the Sash she used to be when she drew the cartoons. Before our mother left, she drew cartoons all the time and she made me laugh with them. When we moved to Applegate, she just read comics a lot. Then she stopped. Sorry, that's not important either. Anyway, because she looked like the old Sash, I asked, 'Why did Mammy leave us?'

I kind of wanted to know for a long time but I didn't want to ask Dad as he might not want to answer. I think he might feel guilty about the doughnuts and anyway there are some questions you don't ask, that's what my teacher in school once said. Sometimes it's hard to figure out the questions though. Or what 'don't ask' means. You can ask any question you want, it seems to me, but once Sash told me that 'don't ask' means there are some questions that might upset people if you ask them. That made a little more sense.

Anyway, I sort of thought this was a question like that because Sash didn't move for three seconds, she just kept the camera held up to her eye and then she let it go and it bounced on its strap around her neck. She turned around. She had a smile on her face so I guess she was OK with me asking her. 'You know why,' she said. 'She had places to go. She needed to go to them.'

'I don't think so.' I spent a lot of time figuring this out and I know that when people go places they normally come back.

Sash didn't look so smiley now.

I rocked back and forward three times. That's a lucky number. Then I count to three in my head and on my fingers. I've added my fingers recently because that's three things counting to three. Nothing bad will happen then. 'I remember it was sunny when she left.'

'It rained.'

'It was sunny.' I remember stuff like that. I see it in my head like a film. 'The flowers in the garden all died in the heat and that made Mammy cry when you and Dad were gone out.'

Sash came and sat beside me. Birds chirped. 'It did?' She sounded like she didn't know that.

'Every day that summer she just cried when she saw the dead flowers. Is that why she left? Or was it because Dad didn't buy her doughnuts anymore?'

'Why do you want to know now?'

'I always wanted to know.'

Sash smiled. Sighed. Ran her fingers over the top of my

head. I don't mind Sash doing that – no one else, though.
'Our mother left because she was sad and tired,' Sash said.

'Could she not just go to bed?'

'No.' She was careful how she talked, like she was thinking hard about the best way to say stuff. 'It was a different sort of tired. She was tired of being a mother.'

'Tired of us?'

'Yes.'

Sash sounded upset but I thought that at least it made sense. It's easy to get tired of things. I get tired of Sash not being there or tired of Mona and Dad watching the quiz shows, though Mona is very bossy and won't let me turn them off. She makes me wear headphones instead. 'Could she not wear headphones or anything like that?'

Sash laughed though I wasn't being funny. 'I love you, Lana,' she said and she squeezed me. 'No, she couldn't wear headphones. Apparently she just told Dad that she couldn't take it anymore, then she told me and you, do you remember?'

'I didn't understand.'

'I know. Then she packed her bags and left.'

Sash was quiet for ages and ages after that. I left a pause because when someone tells you something sad or important, it's not right to jump in with another question. Like when our teacher told us her husband had died and I asked her if she could get a dog now. She used to tell us she always wanted a dog but as her husband had asthma she couldn't get one. But apparently that wasn't an appropriate question. So I left a five-second pause. Then I asked, 'Where did she go?'

'I don't know. She just left.'

'No one knows where she is?'

'No.'

'It took her four hundred and eighty-nine seconds to pack her bag. Fifty-one steps to the car. She did that three times. Ninety seconds to get out of sight.'

'Really?'

'You told me to count, remember?'

'Yes, I told you to count and that if you did you'd be OK.'

'I counted for ages.'

'Ages and ages.'

'Thanks,' I said to Sash then, because I had the details. 'You helped me out.'

'I will always help you out,' she said. 'You know that, right?'

I do. It's always good to help people out.

'Why did you never tell me she was sad and tired before?' I asked.

'I guess I wanted to protect you,' Sash said.

I liked that.

Marcus

'All rise for Judge Wayne Conroy.'

We all stand and I think what a weird name for a judge Wayne is. He sounds like he should be on a skateboard, wearing a baseball cap. I have a sudden flash of a cartoon kid wearing a judge's cape. Some kind of a skateboarder-judge superhero.

The judge is a small guy with a bald head. He reminds me

of someone who spent all his life trying to be cool, the way he walks with a sort of hop. Cartoon gold.

'Stop smiling,' Melissa hisses and I realise that I'm grinning like an idiot.

I do that from time to time. My thoughts skitter about all over the place when I think about drawing cartoons. I'm always on the lookout for characters and when I hit on a good one, I grin. It's a way to distract myself too, obviously. Anything is better than being tried for murder.

The judge sits so we all sit. I rub my hands over my face as the judge says hello to everyone and nods to the jury, who have filed in when I wasn't paying attention. Then he gives a bit of an outline as to why we're all here. The eyes of the jury skip to me, then skip away, then come back. Like small sharp pebbles being thrown my way, grazing me as I try not to flinch.

I am innocent yet suddenly I have no clue what an innocent man looks like. My face feels twitchy and weird. I don't know what to do with my hands. I've never been one to welcome being the centre of attention and this is so warped that I am prickly with unease.

The judge finishes up and the state's prosecutor stands. I can't remember his name, but he's one of these self-assured, private-school-educated guys with floppy brown hair and a strong, clear voice. He has a nose that is made for looking down on people. He's tall, over six foot, and he casts a look in my direction down that long nose. I'm tempted to give him the finger, but I don't.

He turns to the jury.

'Good morning, ladies and gentlemen. I'm Peter Dundon and it's my pleasure to represent the state in this matter.' He smiles; some of them smile back. 'On March first, eighteen months ago, Marcus Dillon –' I jerk at the sound of my name, then because Melissa has said I mustn't do anything, I try to stare straight ahead, focusing on a patch of plaster on the wall, above the heads of the jury. It looks like there was a leak and it got discoloured. I tune back in as Peter Dundon describes what I'm supposed to have done, '– having stalked Mr Charles Hanratty for just over a year, made his way into Charles Hanratty's house and beat him with a blunt instrument and stabbed him. Not satisfied with that, he used the instrument to write the word "Cluck" with Mr Hanratty's blood.' He allows a pause to develop, so that the jury can absorb that.

It's shocking, I'll admit.

Then he continues, his eyes sweeping the room. 'He used a knife, cut Mr Hanratty's femoral artery and watched as he bled to death. It would have been a slow death, ladies and gentlemen. Then Mr Dillon broke a frame containing a photograph of Mr Hanratty's home place and threw it on the body. Not satisfied with that, he scattered disturbing cartoon images over the body. Finally done, he walked boldly down the driveway and to his car. This case is essentially about how Marcus Dillon could not control his anger at alleged injustices suffered at the hands of Charles Hanratty. It is about a man who fed his murderous anger by stalking, threatening, bullying and eventually murdering his victim. He will attempt to glorify his actions as those of a protector, he will attempt to gain your sympathy but we know you will see him for what he truly is: a man driven to seek revenge through killing an innocent man. We will ask for a guilty verdict on the charge of murder because, make no mistake, this was a premeditated act. In order to prove our case, we will call witnesses from the Garda Síochána to whom Mr Hanratty, in the last few months, complained about Mr Dillon's behaviour. We will call computer experts who have combed Mr Dillon's and Mr Hanratty's computer and phone records. We will call Mr Dillon's ex-employer who will testify as to the extent of Mr Dillon's anger towards Charles Hanratty during the time he lived in Applegate. We will also call on an eyewitness who observed a figure matching Mr Dillon's description fleeing the scene that night. Another eyewitness will place Mr Dillon's car a mere two hundred metres from the scene of the crime. Forensics will place Mr Dillon at the scene of the crime. Of course the defence will argue that the fingerprints could have been there before the attack but Marcus Dillon himself, in his statement to police, said he was never inside Charles Hanratty's house. Ladies and gentlemen, at the conclusion, we would ask you to find Marcus Dillon guilty of the murder of Charles Hanratty.'

He sits down, looking pretty pleased with himself.

Melissa stands up. She doesn't look nearly as imposing as Peter. She's tiny, like a bird. Her waist is the span of my hand. Her hair, long, straight, hangs down to her waist. And her braces. My God. They have a life of their own.

'Good morning,' she says and there is something about her that shines with sincerity, despite a slight lisp from the braces.

'I'm Melissa Curran and I'll be representing Marcus Dillon in this case. Charles Hanratty's murder was a terrible crime, there is no doubt about it, but my client did not do it. The prosecution said he has testimony from the guards indicating that Marcus Dillon was stalking my client. Marcus Dillon admits that himself. He regrets it deeply, but as you will see, during the course of the trial, he was a man determined to do good. He was not motivated by anger but by concern. And remember, a stalker is not a murderer, ladies and gentlemen. The prosecution has said that Marcus was seen fleeing from the house after the crime. It is true, he was outside the house, but he wasn't fleeing anywhere. The eyewitness was in her house across the road, over a hundred feet away. And yes, Marcus Dillon's fingerprints were found in Charles Hanratty's house, on two objects, ladies and gentlemen, one of which he gave to Mr Hanratty. So, in conclusion, I'd ask you to keep an open mind and listen carefully to all the evidence and return a not-guilty verdict.'

She nods to the jury and sits beside me.

'Keep calm,' she whispers again. 'We have a better than fighting chance.'

I try to look happy about that.

'You may call your first witness,' the judge says to Peter.

And we're off.

Sash

The guard, he can't be more than twenty-five, takes the stand. He's got a lot of files with him and my heart sinks.

Surely they can't all be reports from Hanratty on Marcus? But, yes, apparently they are.

'Mr Hanratty,' the guard says, once he has taken the oath and introduced himself, 'complained a total of fifty-six times against Mr Dillon's stalking.'

'Over what time period did Mr Hanratty make these complaints?'

'In the last three months of Mr Hanratty's life, from January to March 2012, he made fifty-six complaints.'

I inhale sharply, along with half the room. Dad raises his eyebrows at me. The prosecutor allows the information to sink in.

'Can you give us the nature of these complaints?' he goes on after a second or two. He's a cocky guy, bouncing around on his toes, his voice full of energy and a certain amount of innuendo. He reeks privilege. It drips from him like fat off cooking meat.

Marcus's solicitor stands up. 'I fail to see the relevance of this witness,' she says. 'My client has already admitted to stalking Mr Hanratty.'

'Judge,' the prosecutor argues, 'it is the sheer volume of complaints I wish to address. The inability of the defendant to see the seriousness of what he was doing.'

'I'll allow it.' The judge nods. 'But be brief.'

'Can you tell me what is in those files, very briefly?' the prosecutor asks.

'Complaints by Mr Hanratty of being persistently stalked by Mr Dillon.'

'And by stalking you mean ...?'

'Parking outside his house on Lime Tree Avenue in Dublin 6 for hours at night, following him when he went into the city centre, taking unauthorised pictures of him, emailing him, phoning him up and making threats.'

'What was the nature of these threats?'

'According to Mr Hanratty, Marcus Dillon would phone up saying things like,' the policeman flicks through some pages and eventually finds what he needs, '"I'm watching you every second of the day." "When you sleep, I'll be in your dreams." "You'll need more than your gun this time."'

'Threatening stuff.'

'He's leading the witness.' Marcus's tiny barrister pops up.

The judge nods. 'Don't do it again, counsel,' he warns.

'Apologies, Judge.'

'Strike one to Marcus,' Dad says to me in an undertone.

My dad has never been a fan of Marcus's. He'd assumed that just because his mother was an alcoholic that Marcus was bound to have issues. And I guess Marcus did, but nothing that was ever serious. It was only when I told my dad what had happened when Marcus and I were kids that he finally came around to admitting that he was wrong about Marcus. If anyone was trouble in those days, it was me. I had sought out danger like a heat-seeking missile and then, when I'd finally found it, I'd walked away, blocked it out and pretended that it hadn't happened. Marcus wasn't able to do that, just like he wasn't able to leave his mother drinking all night on her own in a pub in town, just like he faced her abuse when he dragged her out, just like he walked her home, got her to bed, stayed up and worried about her. He faced trouble and he dealt with it and maybe if I'd been the same, we wouldn't be here, in this court at a murder trial.

I tune back in.

'What sort of a state was Charles Hanratty in when he reported these incidents to you?'

'That's an opinion,' Marcus's barrister counters.

'As Mr Hanratty is not here to speak for himself, I think we need to ascertain the level of threat he felt from your client. I want to establish what was said, not to comment on the truth of it.'

'I'll allow it.' The judge nods.

Marcus's lawyer sits down, not looking too bothered.

'Again, what sort of a state was Mr Hanratty in when he reported these incidents?'

'I only took the later statements,' the guard says, 'so I'm not sure what he was like when he first noticed he was being stalked, but in the last few months he was definitely agitated.'

Good, I can't help thinking. Served him right.

'Agitated.' The prosecutor nods. 'Thank you.'

He sits down and Marcus's lawyer gets up. She thinks for a second and then asks, 'At any time, did Mr Hanratty actually state that he felt his life was in danger from my client?'

'No, but –'

'And did he ever say that my client threatened to kill him?'

'No, he never said that.'

'And is it true that the majority of stalkers never actually attack their victims?'

'Yes, that would be the case.'

'So what you have there is evidence of stalking but

nothing to say that my client ever made death threats towards Mr Hanratty?'

'That's correct.'

'Thanks.' Marcus's lawyer grins and sits down.

I like her.

Lana

When we moved to Applegate first, Dad took me to the orchard. Sash said she'd rather cut her toenails, which was weird because cutting toenails is not that exciting. Dad said she didn't mean it literally, she just meant that she really, really didn't want to go and see an orchard.

I went because I love apples and I thought that Dad seemed sad. Maybe he wasn't, it's hard to tell, but I went along anyway.

The orchard was about a mile up the road from our house, just at the turn for Applegate town.

When we got there, it was drizzling and the sun was fading behind big grey clouds. Dad and I climbed the stone wall that surrounded the orchard and stood on the fringes. There was a wall of apple trees in front of us that seemed to stretch for miles, on and on, up a hill, down a hill, on and on to the stream on the other side. The trees were small and twisted, their branches entwining with each other. Dad took my hand and together we walked into them. It was like entering gloom.

It was October so the apples were nearing their end and every step I took squashed overripe fruit and drops of juice splattered onto my new shoes. All I could smell was apples and damp leaves. It was like nothing existed in the whole world except the gloom, the smell and the sound of pattering rain on leaves. I thought my head would explode with all the smells and the sound and the strangeness. I took big breaths.

'Those trees need to be pruned,' Dad said. 'That way the apples will be bigger and better.'

I was afraid to speak in case my voice was swallowed up.

Dad kept going, straight through, on a path that had been worn by decades of walking. He told me how the orchard had come to be, how it gave free apples to everyone and what a kind gesture it had been by the mayor of Applegate.

'A fine gesture indeed,' someone said from behind. I jumped.

It was a small man, wearing a brown cap and a brown suit, with shiny shoes. He had a camera around his neck and he held out a hand. 'Charles Hanratty,' he said. 'Descendant of the first mayor.'

Dad shook his hand. 'I'm Kevin Donnelly, this is my daughter Lana.'

'The new sergeant.' Charles Hanratty tipped his cap and smiled. 'Pleasure. Nice to put a face to the name.'

'Do you live around here?'

'Just at the cottage on the corner there.' He pointed back the way we'd come. 'Top of your road.'

Dad nodded. 'We'll be seeing a lot of you so.'

'In a good way, I hope.' Charles laughed.

Dad laughed too.

I didn't because I wondered how he'd sneaked up on us so fast without us hearing him. He could have robbed us.

'Anything you need or want to know just call in,' Charles said. 'I'd be happy to help.'

'Thank you,' Dad said.

'I'll be on my way.' Charles dug his hand into his pocket and pulled out a fiver. 'Buy yourself some sweets,' he said to me, holding out his money.

'Not at all.' Dad waved him away.

'Call it a welcome gift,' Charles said, winking at me. 'Go on.'

'Just this once.' Dad smiled at me. 'What do you say?'

'Thank you.' I took the money though I didn't want it. Mammy had always told us not to take things from strangers and, though we knew his name, he was still a stranger.

'Make sure you buy Sash something out of it too,' my dad said to me. Then to Charles, 'That's my eldest girl.'

Charles smiled and tipped his cap. 'Be seeing ye.'

Dad and I watched him walk off.

I told myself that if he turned the bend in the road by the time I counted to forty, we'd be happy here.

It took forty-one.

It was close.

Marcus

When the court breaks for the day, everyone has learned that I'm a bit of a psycho. I watch as the jury file out, not able to look at any of them, in case something in my gaze or in the set of my face turns them against me. I have no idea if they stare in my direction.

'Well done.' Melissa pats me on the arm. 'You kept it cool. Tomorrow might be worse because they'll place your car at the scene and get that eyewitness out. But I think we're ready for them.'

She begins to pack her files away. Josh has already left on some errand. Despite her tiny frame, she is a powerhouse of energy. 'The good thing is,' she says, pushing the files into a box that barely contains then, 'and I know this is terrible, but you're nice-looking, Marcus. You have an innocent sort of face.'

'Fantastic.' I feel a bit hopeless. I think it's because, listening to that policeman and seeing the thickness of the file of complaints about me, I'd suddenly been confronted with how terrible I'd actually been. It was like looking at myself through someone else's eyes. And stupid as it may seem, I didn't want Sash to hear all that about me. Or any of my mates either. But it's too late now. It'll all be in the papers tomorrow. My life and mistakes to be digested over breakfast.

Melissa instructs me to follow her out. 'There are reporters out there, so ignore them. Let them take your picture and film you, but don't say anything.'

We pull on our jackets. I have no idea what the weather has done while we've been cooped up in here, but whether it's sunny or not, I'll still have my hood shielding my face.

'No,' Melissa says immediately, yanking it down. 'Don't try to hide. You're innocent, remember.'

'I know but—'

'It stays down.'

I feel a moment of panic, but there is no point in arguing with her. That was the first thing she said when we met. 'What I say, goes.' And I'd agreed.

I follow her out of the room.

We take the lift down to the ground floor. My mother and Alan are waiting for me.

'Are you OK?' My mother totters over in her too-high shoes and embraces me. She smells of flowers. I feel stifled by her concern, probably because I'd got so used to doing without it.

'I'm grand. Just sorry you had to hear all that.'

She takes my face in her hands and squishes it. 'Nothing you do will make me ashamed. That's what I'll be telling the jury when I take the stand.'

I wince. Melissa has convinced me that my mother getting up and testifying to my good character is a great move. I'm not so sure, but as she keeps telling me, she's the one who knows what she's doing. 'Thanks, Ma.'

Alan claps me on the back. 'Will we go?'

'Sure.'

They flank me as we prepare to leave. I wonder briefly where Sash has got to and if she had to brave the reporters too. A flash of guilt hits me. If it wasn't for me being so bloody stupid, she'd be happily married to Paddy now. Instead, they'd split up. Paddy had resigned from politics, moved out of Applegate and gone back to teaching. Sash had left Applegate too.

Melissa pauses to chat to the security guards on the way

out. They know each other well. After a bit of banter, in which one of the guards chortles at something Melissa says, she pushes open the door.

'Feeding time, you fucking vultures,' she whispers, and I grin.

Someone takes a picture.

Sash

Mona rings my dad to see how the first day went. I hear him talking to her as I crack a few eggs into a saucepan to scramble. I'm not hungry but I know I have to eat. I wonder how Lana is doing.

Dad has hired a self-contained apartment in the grounds of a luxury hotel for the two weeks of the trial. It's off season so it's not as expensive as it might have been and Dad made the decision to throw money at the situation so that at least we'd be somewhere nice while our world was being pulled apart.

It's a small place but it has everything we need for a luxury stay. The leisure centre at the hotel is also available to use but I'm too afraid to venture out. There was a time I loved being in the paper, standing alongside Paddy at some function or other, but now I hate it. I'll hate it more next week, I'm sure.

When I was engaged to Paddy, I was the darling of the media. We both were. Paddy, with his easy grin, his laugh, his total goodness, had wowed the press. He'd already wowed Applegate by the time he was a teenager, but the rest of the country had soon fallen under his spell when he'd decided to run for politics on a People First ticket. It was, ironically, a party he'd set up to help victims of crime. Imagine, then, the horror of your future wife having past ties with a man arrested for the 'Murder of the Decade'. That's what they were calling it in the papers.

I stir the eggs and drop in a dollop of butter and some milk, then switch on the hob. I get some bread from the press to make toast and think about how Paddy and I used to argue about whether doing the bread on one side or two was best.

Paddy. Paddy. Paddy. His name alone makes me feel like crying.

I remember the first time we spoke. I'd been new in Applegate. It was not easy moving there at fifteen years of age, having lost my mother six months previously, and though I didn't have a lot of friends in Dublin, those that I had were solid. I missed their company like my left arm. The secondary school in Applegate was so much smaller than the one I'd attended in Dublin. It was an old building with cracked ceilings and wooden floors polished to a deep shine. The place reeked of age with its thick walls and sash windows and the whistle of the wind in winter. I soon realised that in Applegate everyone knew everyone else and that their mothers knew all the other mothers. I hadn't got a mother to know anyone. And Dad wasn't a 'talking to other mothers' type unless he was arresting them for some misdemeanour.

In small schools, little differences make a big difference. And while I'd known Lana was different, so was I, though I'd never realised it until then. Aside from my mother leaving, which was devastating, my life up to that moment had been very happy. But when I walked into Applegate Post Primary on my first day, heads turned. I initially thought it was because I was with Lana, who was wearing an over-sized pair of headphones to block out most of the school noise, only it wasn't. From the coat I wore to the Doc Martens on my feet, every little thing I did was out of synch with the rest of the school. My interests too singled me out. No other girl in the school waited for the latest *Batman* comic to be released. I hoarded my comics the way other girls did make-up and clothes. I filed, labelled and catalogued them. I'd re-read the best ones, seeing what made them the best. I studied the stories and the way they were put together. I got to know why certain pictures worked for the storylines. Nothing gave me more pleasure than gazing for hours at the cover artwork. Art, back then, was my passion, the one thing I was actually good at.

In our local newsagent's in Dublin, John, the shop owner, used to keep the comics for me under the counter. If I didn't have enough money to buy a particular issue, he'd let me read it anyway, knowing that I'd be in to get it when I could. When I came to Applegate, the local newsagent seemed baffled that I wanted to order a *Batman* comic. Kids in Applegate never asked for *Batman*, he told me. Kids in Applegate had no taste, I said back. Then Marcus, only I didn't know it was Marcus, told me he'd order one in for me. He'd order me any comic I liked. It'd be no bother, he said, he read them too.

I'd never felt different until I came to Applegate, I guess because in my old school there'd been many kids weirder than me. In Applegate everyone was the same. I might have just remained a three-bit oddity but when Paddy Jones, the most desirable boy in school, chose to talk to me, I became a very high-profile weirdo indeed.

Paddy was in my year and hot property in a small village like Applegate. Tall, smart and the star player on the GAA football team, the whole school and local community loved him. Teachers gave him time off classes to go to training, girls queued up to do his homework for him, lads flocked around him when he spoke. Adults came up to him on the street to congratulate him on the 'fine goal' he'd scored in the local match. The whole town turned out to see him play as his dad strutted up and down the pitch, yelling out instructions to him. 'Attack first, ask questions later' was one of his sayings.

And on one of my first days in Applegate Post Primary, Paddy sat beside me and Lana in the canteen. He was with Margaret and Jennifer who, aside from Paddy, were the people to know. Being new, I had no idea of this, though even if I had it's likely I would have messed up anyway. Like I said, I seemed destined to go against the grain. Until then, none of the other kids had sat with me or attempted to talk to me. Maybe they were put off by Lana, maybe it wasn't cool to be friendly or maybe I was sending out bad signals, I don't know. I wasn't too bothered by it – a part of me wanted to be left alone because I wasn't yet ready to handle the 'why did you move here' conversation. I didn't want to be happy at that point either, I guess.

The whole table had been free and Paddy had chosen the seat right next to me. I flicked a glance at him and recognised him from photos which adorned the walls in the school. Paddy Jones holding trophies, winning debating competitions, young scientist. I was prepared to hate him.

'It's that guy from all the pictures,' Lana whispered to me as Paddy started signalling some other people to join us. She sounded agitated because it was a change from the normal run of things.

'People can sit where they like,' I said back to her. 'You just eat your lunch and say nothing.'

'OK.'

'Sit here, Madge,' Paddy called out as he patted a seat on the other side of him.

Madge came down and flicked the two of us a cursory glance. 'I wanted to join Dessie,' she said. 'I hate this table – it's in the shade.' Annoyance was peeling off her like dry skin, but she sat down anyway and began arranging her lunch on the tray in front of her. She was so precise, I saw, out of the corner of my eye. Even the act of eating her yogurt was accomplished with an elegance normally reserved for consuming a five-star meal. She was prettier than Jennifer, who had also joined us. Jennifer had a yogurt too but wasn't having much success in taking the lid off, probably because her fingernails were bitten to bits. She wore long, dangly parrot earrings that jangled every time she moved her head. They were a bit sad. She was tall, with big features and frizzy hair. Her face was caked in make-up.

'I hate this table too,' she said in a high-pitched cartoon voice, so at odds with her appearance that I had to bury my head in my comic so I wouldn't grin.

Lana's head shot up at the voice too but, because I'd told her not to say anything, she had to satisfy herself by staring at Jennifer. Lana has no clue that it's socially unacceptable to openly gawk at someone.

'Do you have a problem?' Jennifer asked Lana.

'Lana, eat your lunch,' I said. Then to Jennifer, I added, 'Sorry about that.'

Before she could respond, Paddy said, 'Sash, right?'

His eyes were brown and friendly. 'That's right.'

'I'm Paddy. I think I live up the road from you. Your family rent the McAdams' old house.' He bit into an apple and angled his body towards me.

His voice was light and pleasant and I warmed to it. 'I'm not sure who owns it. There's an orchard at the top of the road.'

'That's right. Your dad is the new sergeant?'

'Yes.' I was taken aback that he knew but I later learned that in Applegate people generally knew your business before you did.

'How do you like it here?' He took another bite of his apple and looked curiously at me. He seemed to genuinely want to know.

'How does she like Applegate?' Madge giggled. 'It's not exactly a happening town, Paddy.'

The other girl opposite giggled obligingly a second or so later.

'Applegate is a nice place,' Paddy said, then added, 'and who needs happening when you have me?'

The two girls laughed a lot more than this merited and

Paddy gave me an amused look. 'So?' he asked. 'How do you like our little village?'

'I haven't seen much of it,' I admitted. 'Me and Lana, that's my sister here, we just come to school and go home.'

'When you get to know it, you'll love it.'

He sounded so confident in the allure of his pokey little home place that I was charmed. I smiled and he smiled back.

'And what are you reading?' Madge asked, leaning across Paddy to get a better look at me. 'Is it a comic?'

'Yep.' I held it up.

'A *Batman* comic?' she said, sounding as if she was about to laugh. 'Really?'

'Really.' I imitated her tone and Paddy grinned.

'That's just for kids,' her sidekick chimed in.

'You ever read one?' I asked.

She looked at Madge and then back at me. Her earrings jangled. 'Eh, no – that's for boys.'

I reeled my irritation in. 'First off, comics have the best artwork and I like to study it.' I should have left it at that, but I added, 'And second, Batman is my favourite superhero.'

They looked stupefied.

'You have a favourite superhero?' Jennifer rolled her eyes. 'Seriously?'

'Yes. Kinda like the way you have a favourite band.'

'Eh, no, not kinda like that way at all.' Madge stood up abruptly. 'There's a seat free on Dessie's table now – are you coming, Paddy?'

'No, I want to find out why Batman is Sash's favourite superhero,' Paddy said, not taking his eyes from me.

Even I could sense the sudden tension that filled the small area around the table. Madge froze, tray in hand. Jennifer hesitated comically between standing and sitting.

Paddy smiled easily at them. 'Catch you later.'

'Suit yourself.' Madge tossed her magnificent mane of black hair and swung away, her friend trotting alongside her.

'Maybe you should go after them,' I said. 'That Madge girl seems annoyed.'

'Nah, I'd much rather find out why Batman is your favourite.'

I felt uncomfortable. I knew somehow that it was a bad idea to keep talking to him but I didn't quite know why. 'I guess because he's human and he has no special powers. He makes mistakes. I like that.'

'What else do you like?' He cupped his chin in his hand, and from the corner of my eye I saw the two girls glancing back and whispering. They did not look happy. He caught my gaze and waved over at them and they promptly turned away.

He repeated his question.

'Art, books, that sort of thing.'

'Sport?'

I shrugged. 'I like to run.'

'We have an athletics team. You should join it. I'll get Jenny to hook you up. She's the captain.'

'Jenny?'

'The girl you met just now?'

'With the voice?'

He chuckled, took another bite of his apple. 'Yep, with the voice.'

The idea of Jenny, with her big earrings, hooking me up didn't appeal but I said, 'Sure, great.'

He flashed me a smile and picked up his tray. 'Nice to meet you, Sash. And, eh …' he looked at Lana, 'Lana, is it?'

She shot him a suspicious look.

'Say "hi", Lana.'

'Hi.'

'Nice to meet you both.'

'Nice to meet you too.'

I saw him leave the canteen a little later with Madge. She put her hand on his arm and leaned her head close to him. He's mine, she seemed to be saying to anyone who was looking.

It soon became pretty clear that the only way to get along in school was by toeing the Margaret and Jennifer line. Apparently Margaret and Paddy had been going out from forever and Margaret guarded him the way a dog would a prize bone. Any girl getting too close soon found herself outside the magic circle. Unfortunately for me, Paddy seemed fascinated by the fact I read Batman stories. He made a point of finding me between classes and chatting to me about books and art. Occasionally, to be polite, I'd ask him about his match at the weekend or his training regime, but after a short, terse answer, he'd turn the subject back onto me again. His interest in me spiked the interest of the rest of the lads but alienated me from the girls. And every time Margaret passed by, Paddy would be standing beside me as I explained the mysteries of comic-book creation to him.

'Are you thinking about Paddy again?' Dad asks, coming into the kitchen, having finished his call.

He's become a lot more touchy-feely since he hooked up with Mona.

'Yep,' I say, 'but I'm fine. Get a couple of plates, will you?'

'Sure.' He gets the plates and makes a big deal of admiring the eggs I've cooked.

'It's just eggs.' But I can't help a smile.

I carry the plates to the table and we sit down. We eat in silence for a bit, until Dad breaks it by saying, 'It's only natural that you miss him.'

'Yeah.'

'He was a fine lad,' Dad goes on, his face reddening as he glances at me, then glances away.

'I know.'

'And he was going places.' He jabs the fork in my direction. 'I mean, he will still go places.'

'Yeah.'

'And such a sportsman. He's fantastic. A bit rough, mind you, but fantastic.'

'Yeah.'

'And a clever fellow.'

I half-grin. 'Dad, I appreciate all this, but telling me what I'm missing is not cheering me up.'

A pause. 'Oh, right,' he says. 'I get your point. Well, anyway, it's only natural to miss him.'

'I know.'

He smiles at me. 'Let's not say any more about it.'

I smile back. 'Thanks anyway.'

'No bother.'

Lana

I count up to one thousand that night in bed because it takes a long time, and by the time I get to a thousand I am still not asleep. I wish I was with Dad and Sash in Dublin now because after Mona talked to Dad on the phone earlier, I talked to Sash and whenever I talk to Sash I miss her over again. Also, Sash is doing something in Dublin that she doesn't really want to do and I know how that feels because Dad explained it to me. He said, 'Do you know when you don't want to do something and it scares you and you put your hands over your ears and rock?'

I said I did.

'That's how Sash feels about this trial only she won't rock or put her hands over her ears.'

I thought about that. I thought, so that's how I don't get people. Sash is scared but she makes out she's not and yet Dad gets that she is. I would just think she wasn't scared.

Anyway, I thought that I might like to go up to Sash right then. If she stands by me, I stand by her. That's our motto. But Sash said no, it was best I didn't come just yet. She said that telling everyone that I met her outside Charles Hanratty's house that night would be a bigger help. And that if I do that properly when the time comes in the trial that's all I need to do to make her feel better. I still can't sleep though.

I wonder if I'll be in the paper when I tell my story. I saw Marcus in the paper today. He looked mean. Also I saw him on the news when Mona was on the phone to Dad. He was running down some court steps smiling a bit. He wore a blue suit and a navy shirt and black shoes. And a navy tie. It was nice but a bit weird-looking too. Like him. Marcus looks weird. He is tall and skinny and has black curly hair and grey eyes and an unusual face. He hardly ever smiles. On the news they said he was stalking Charles Hanratty. Stalking means following him about but not in a nice way. They showed a picture of a policeman with a big file in his hand, looking important, coming down the steps too.

I think it'd be OK to be on TV.

Another thing that is OK was when Sash broke up with Paddy. I told Sash when she left him that it was fine because her and Paddy didn't match. 'You don't match up,' I said.

She wasn't pleased at all even though it was OK for me to say it because Sash had left him and wasn't going to be his girlfriend anymore or be in the Dáil or anything. 'That's not very nice,' she said. 'What do you mean?'

'I mean, you don't match.'

I couldn't explain more than that. I told Dad what I thought too but he loved Paddy. 'Paddy is a top man,' he said.

That didn't mean that he matched with Sash.

She was like a piece of blue sky and he was like a piece of blue sea and while they were both blue they were still different, see?

I could understand why he liked Sash but not the other way around.

I used to like Marcus with Sash even though he scared me. He scared me the day he came knocking hard on our door when our dad left one morning. I threw a knife at his head and nicked his face and he bled.

But we had a party and he bought me Jelly Babies and that is also a good memory to have.

But the row after wasn't.

Marcus never came back to our house after that.

I wonder is that what Sash is going to talk to the court about. Maybe I will say it for her.

I don't know why she's worried. All she has to do is take a seat and answer questions. That's easy.

DAY 2

Marcus

'Marcus Dillon – coming out of the Central Criminal Court yesterday.' A picture of me grinning at Melissa's joke adorns the front page of every newspaper in the country. Even upbeat Alan can't find anything positive to say in the wake of it.

'We know the truth,' my mother says, gripping my arm and giving me what I suppose is a look of solidarity.

'That's not enough to get me off,' I say drily before extracting myself from her grip. I leave the room and stand before the hall mirror, knotting my tie. I concentrate hard on it, so that I won't lose focus and start veering away into dangerous territory. While the trial is on, I am free. While the trial is on, I have a job. Tonight, I will come back and lock myself away in my studio and write another Slam Man story.

Slam Man is a character I created when I was a teenager back in Applegate. Then about ten years ago, when my mother was still drinking heavily and the debts were piling up and my cartooning was going badly, I resurrected him. I was stony broke for a year while I developed him and devised outline stories for him, and, finally, I managed to convince a comic-book publisher to meet me so I could pitch my concept. I learned later it was probably an arse-about-elbow way of doing things, but the character was so strong that they bought it. *Slam Man* comes out every month and while I was responsible for all the artwork and stories in the beginning, now it's a team effort. Two years ago, Slam Man was developed into a full-length film and sold a lot of merchandise. I am a very rich guy as a result.

Slam Man never fails to get justice. He's a superhero with a talent for wrestling and karate and kick-boxing. An ordinary guy, floundering, who just happens to have extraordinary talent. Most people think I'm a bit juvenile when I talk about him and maybe it's true. Maybe I never grew up. Maybe I don't want to. Growing up is overrated.

Tonight, I'll bury myself in his world instead of the one I'm now in. A bloody nightmare that I created in some twisted way.

'Are you ready?' Alan asks. He stands behind me and I see his reflection beside mine. He's not a guy I would ever have picked for my high-maintenance mother and yet they fit, like two pieces of a jigsaw. He's a comfy-slippers-and-corduroy man to her strictly non-casual look but they laugh at the same stuff, like the same awful music and believe all the crap they read in the trashy newspapers. I find I smile more when I'm with them and even though he knows all about my mother's alcohol-fuelled car-crash life in Applegate, I love that he doesn't give a toss. The woman he knows now is not the same woman I grew up with. He trusts her completely; I don't think I ever can. Even though she's off the drink nearly seven years now, I am always on edge with her. But it's nice to see her and Alan so completely in tune.

Once I got to know Sash properly, about four months after she moved to Applegate, we used to be like that. We'd even finish each other's sentences. We spent a lot of nights in the orchard, smoking weed, backs against the trees, telling each other stuff we would never have told anyone else. I knew her better than I knew myself, I used to think.

I remember the first time I saw her. She had come into the newsagent's where I worked and asked Peadar if he could order her some comics and if he stocked the *Batman* comic. I was doing something on the shop floor, packing shelves or pricing stuff, I don't remember, but when I heard her ask for the comic, I turned around to have a gawk.

I found myself staring at this exotic creature from the safety of the aisle. Everything about her was just that little bit different, from the way she wore her school uniform, with the cuffs of her jumper all ragged, to her short, spiky badass haircut. She wasn't stunning to look at but she had a way of moving that mesmerised me. She was leaning on the counter, wearing the secondary-school uniform and bleeding attitude. Her bag, multicoloured, dangled from one shoulder, a long, knitted scarf was wrapped around her neck and trailed past her knees. I wanted to draw her, just standing there in that pose, light filtering in through the badly washed window. I could see her as a cartoon. I was blown away. Another girl hovered alongside her, smaller, prettier but without Sash's presence.

Peadar, the old guy who I worked with, stood gaping at Sash for a full ten seconds before he answered her question. '*Batman?*' He rubbed his jaw. 'Kids hereabout don't read *Batman*. We've got *Spider-Man*.'

'They're not the same,' Sash said, her chin jutting out. 'Batman is a real guy. Spider-Man is a genetic abnormality.'

I think I fell for her right then.

Peadar nodded again. 'Right. Well, we've got *Spider-Man*.'

Sash heaved a big sigh.

'I'm sure the little boy won't mind,' Peadar said.

'What little boy?'

'The one who the comic is for.'

'Do I look like a boy to you?'

Peadar's mouth opened and closed like a fish. 'You'll have to make do with *Spider-Man*,' he said. 'That's all we have.'

'I can do it,' I interrupted, surprising even myself by speaking. As she turned her gaze on me, I thought that it was like Cyclops' from *X-Men* because I felt lasered. 'I order comics for myself, so I can add whatever ones you want to my order.'

'You'll do that?' Peadar folded his arms and raised his eyebrows and grinned suggestively. 'Good man yourself.' He turned to Sash as he thumbed to me, 'This fella here is being very obliging. I bless the day I hired him.'

I was mortified, but shrugged it off. I moved behind the

counter and, picking up a pen, I asked Sash her name. I think I stammered a bit.

She leaned across the counter and gave me her name, address and phone number. She wanted a comic a week and *Batman* was her favourite.

'Smooth,' Peadar teased after she'd left.

Of course, I knew I'd never have the courage to call her. But, I consoled myself, at least she'd come in every week to collect her comic.

And she did, though I used to think she barely noticed me. I was gangly, nerdy, I badly needed a haircut and I mumbled a lot when I talked. And that was on a good day. She was spiky and full of cool confidence. I used to watch her swagger down the main street when school got out, her bag slung across her body, her hair flying all over the place as the wind tossed it. Sometimes she'd spot me looking and wave, and that'd make my day, pathetic creature that I was. She was usually alone, except when her sister was with her, which was maybe twice a week. Sometimes Paddy Jones would run and catch her up. I knew that if Paddy Jones liked her, she was way out of my league. Still, the sight of her made me grin. Peadar would clip me on the back of the head and tell me to cop on and get back to work.

Sash

We meet Marcus on the way in to the courthouse. Yesterday, we'd managed to avoid him very successfully but today he rounds a corner just as Dad and I round the opposite one.

It's not that I don't want to talk to him – it's that there is such a chasm of unsaid stuff between us, it's impossible to bridge it.

It hurts me to even look at him.

He's with his mother and his stepdad. The guy that called the reporters 'fuckheads' and it went viral. Alan, I think his name is. Marcus's mother looks good. I only ever remember her as being drunk. I can still see her draped around Marcus as he attempted to hold her upright. I remember her berating him for dragging her out of the pub before loudly sobbing her sorrows into his neck as he patted her back and told her it would all be OK. She was bloated and dishevelled back then, the clothes she wore always verging on the tarty side. Now she looks healthy and, despite what's happening, she looks happy.

We stop in front of each other. I'm aware of the photographers. My dad nods a hello. His mother nods one back. No one says anything.

We turn to walk up the steps. I follow Dad. Marcus follows his mother and Alan.

We get through security without any hitches.

Out of the corner of my eye I see Marcus heading towards us as his mother and Alan look anxiously on.

Please, no, I think. But he comes to stand beside us. His mother and Alan, obviously worried, cross over too.

'Thanks for coming,' Marcus says, looking at me.

I don't know how to reply. He was questioned about the murder a week or so after it happened and, since then, I have spoken to him three times. The first two times, I told him not to involve me in anything he said in his defence and then, the third time, after he'd been formally charged, I contacted him to say that I was ready to help if needed. Turned out his solicitor thought I could help a lot.

'I know it's not easy,' he goes on.

I shrug, not trusting myself.

'How are you holding up?' Dad fills in the gap.

Now it's Marcus's turn to shrug.

'The papers assassinated him this morning,' his mother answers in his stead. 'Did you see it?' She sounds like she might cry.

'No.' My dad is apologetic.

She waves him away. 'It's just as well you didn't. They took a picture of him smiling and plastered it all over the front pages. I mean, is it wrong for him to smile?'

'Ma.' Marcus looks to Alan, who wraps an arm about his wife and brings her to a seat.

'She's more upset about it than me.' Marcus tries out a smile that fails.

We all look at our shoes.

'June Daly sends her regards,' my dad says after a bit. 'I was talking to Mona last night, that's my partner, and she said that June doesn't believe a word of it. She said Dessie will sort them out.'

Dessie was Marcus's best friend back in the day. Well, apart from me. He's testifying next week too.

Marcus tries another smile, fails, looks a bit upset. 'That's good to know.' He chews on his bottom lip and I have a sudden series of snapshots in my head of all the other times he did that. He sinks his hands into the pockets of his suit and bows his head.

'We'd, eh, better go.' I make to leave.

'Maybe when this is over we can talk, Sash, eh?' Grey eyes look up through the tangle of his hair which has fallen across his forehead.

What is there to say? But he's facing into a murder trial and I don't want to upset him so I nod. 'Maybe.'

'We'll go on up,' Dad says.

'Yeah. Bye.'

Dad steers me away, his hand on the small of my back. As we head towards the lift, out of earshot, he whispers, 'Do not talk to him if it'll upset you. You're testifying for him, that's enough.'

I hope it will be.

Marcus

Today it's the turn of the witnesses who'll place me at the scene. I was there, I'm not denying it, but they've got someone who says I went into the house and came out fifteen minutes later. That's bullshit.

The first witness is a woman that I think I recognise. She lives opposite Charles's and she's got this garden that's manicured to within an inch of its life and it's full of gnomes and garden seats and trees cut in triangles. She's always looking out her window.

She says her name is Angela something or other. She tells the jury that Charles had lived in the house opposite her for about five years and was always a very good neighbour. She hadn't known how rich he was until he was murdered, that's how modest a man he was, though she had to admit that she'd seen his picture in the paper now and again. Her voice sounds like the way my ma's used to when she was talking to the social workers years ago, sort of fake posh.

'Can you describe for the jury what you saw on the night in question?'

'I was in my front room,' Angela answers. 'It was around eight o'clock and I know this because I was going to watch my soap. I had a cup of tea in my hand and I just happened to glance out the window.'

'Can you tell us what you saw?'

'I saw a person outside Charles's gate, facing the house. I'd say he was about six foot or so and he was just sort of looking about, up and down. There was a bag on his shoulder. He was wearing a hood and black clothing. And it was the way he was sort of looking that caught my attention. Then he went up the driveway and I just assumed it was someone calling on Charles.'

'And then what did you do?'

'I watched my soap but at the break I went to draw the curtains and I saw a figure in black hurrying down the driveway.'

'And what exactly did you see?'

'The man's hood was down so I saw his face clearly.'

'And did you identify the defendant from an identity parade?'

'Yes.' Angela's voice shakes and she glances over at me.

Melissa has said to hold her gaze and so I do, but it's hard. I feel my stomach heave at her accusatory look.

'This was fifteen minutes later,' Peter goes on, 'you're certain?'

'Yes.'

'Thank you.'

Now Melissa gets up. She takes a few moments to shuffle a few papers before she glances at Angela and smiles. 'You saw Marcus clearly?'

'Yes.'

'You saw him going up the driveway and then down?'

'Yes, I already—'

'So, you saw his face clearly when he was going up the victim's driveway? Was he walking backwards?'

People laugh but when the judge speaks he's not happy with Melissa at all. She apologises with a smile.

'Did you see his face when he walked up the driveway?' she asks Angela.

'Obviously not.' Angela sounds annoyed. I wouldn't say too many people challenge her. Her husband is this tiny, stooped-over man who shuffles around the manicured garden with a miniature watering can in the shape of a boot. She shouts out instructions to him through the window.

'So you only saw Marcus's face clearly when he came down the driveway,' Melissa says.

'Yes.' Angela's answer is clipped.

'And to clarify, when he was going up?'

'No,' Angela says. 'Just his back.'

'You saw the back of someone and yet you can tell what they looked like?'

'If it was him coming down it had to be him going up.'

Melissa nods as if she's thinking about that. 'So, this person you saw walking up, what did they do exactly?'

Angela shrugs. 'Knocked on the door. Went in.'

'You saw that?'

'I saw them knock.'

'And fifteen minutes later this person left?'

'Yes.'

'You saw him come out the door and close it after him?'

'No, I just saw him walk down the driveway.'

'So you weren't watching all the time?'

Angela shrugs. 'No, I watched my soap, I already said.'

'That's right.' Melissa bangs her head as if she's forgotten. 'So, is it possible the first person you saw went inside and didn't come out and that Marcus—'

'I saw—'

Melissa holds up her hand. 'Just let me finish my question, please.'

Angela huffs.

'Is it possible the first person you saw, going up the driveway, went in and then Marcus called, didn't get an answer and left, and that's when you saw him?'

Angela makes a face. 'Two people in black?'

'Is it possible that they were two different people? You weren't standing there all the time – you said it yourself.'

'I know, but—'

'You said you turned away for fifteen minutes?'

'I know, but—'

'Is it possible they were two different people?'

Angela looks like she's struggling but, eventually, she says, 'I don't think so, but yes.'

'We deal in facts here, Angela,' Melissa says pleasantly. 'What you think doesn't matter. Is it possible they were two different people?'

'Yes,' Angela snaps.

'And this person, going down the driveway, that you say was Marcus, how did you spot him again?'

'The hood of his jacket was down.'

'His hood was down, even though he allegedly murdered someone?' Melissa makes a sceptical face.

'Yes, it was.'

'So this man,' she points to me, 'who had allegedly beaten up another man, never tried to disguise himself, casually strolled down the driveway and back up the road to his car. Tell me, did you notice any blood on his clothes?'

'I don't know. He was in black, it was dark.'

'It was dark,' Melissa repeats. 'And the weather?'

'Wet.' Angela goes red. 'I just meant that—'

'It was early March – the nights were still dark?'

'Yes.'

'So, would you agree that visibility was poor?'

'It wasn't the best.'

'Was visibility poor?'

'Yes, but—'

'And how far is it from your front window to Mr Hanratty's driveway?'

'I'm not sure.'

'It's forty-nine metres. Does that sound right?'

'Yes. I suppose.'

'That's over a hundred and fifty feet.'

'Yes.'

'And would you say that there are many people of my client's stature in Dublin?'

'Well, yes, but—'

'So, is it possible that on a dark night, with rain, at a distance of one hundred and fifty feet, you mistook the person going up the driveway for Marcus?'

'It was him.'

'I'm asking if it's possible you could have made a mistake.'

A long pause.

'Well?'

'Yes.'

'Thank you.'

Melissa keeps her face neutral as she sits down with me and the way she eyeballs me says I should do the same. Inside, though, I'm laughing.

The judge looks to Peter Dundon.

Peter gets up again. 'Angela, what stands just outside the gate of the victim's house?'

'A street light.'

'Was it on that night?'

'Yes.'

'Just for the record, do you wear glasses?'

'No, I have twenty-twenty vision. I had my eyes tested last week.'

'No more questions.'

Angela looks at the judge.

'You can step down now.'

She does, and scurries from the courtroom.

I think we won that round.

Lana

Mona goes to mass every single day. It's no bother when Dad and Sash are in the house as I can stay at home with them, but when it's just me and Mona, she makes me go with her. This morning, she made me go to light a candle for Sash and Marcus and the trial. I told her I could light a candle at home but she wouldn't listen. The church in Applegate is big but it was packed this morning because a funeral was on. Mona had us almost first in the church, even though we didn't know who died. The church was full to the brim and hot and sticky. I counted four hundred and forty-eight people all crammed in and that's not counting the sides. The priest was lucky, he had a seat up the top with only one other person, the woman who did the reading couldn't get her *r*s right so instead of saying 'a reading from' she said 'a weading from'. It was like a gardening programme. I was squashed in between Mona and a man with a smell. I don't like being beside people that I don't know but I just count instead of freaking out which was what I used to do when

I was younger. June Daly was in front of us and she turned around and smiled. Dessie was beside her. He's going to the trial too. Margaret Browne's mother was there – I can't remember her name, but she looks like Margaret, so I don't like her already. Margaret used to call me a 'half-wit' and Sash a 'quarter-wit'. Even I knew that wasn't nice. A man with a bald head was beside her but it wasn't her husband. Twenty people were wearing bright pink of the exact same shade which is unusual because there are infinite shades of pink, infinite shades of any colour depending on the colour mix. Sash told me that once when I asked her. Forty people had dyed red hair, four of them with the exact same shade. Sixty-two people were wearing skirts, including Mona who was wearing a black tight one and a black tight jacket and a white blouse. And they looked a bit small for her only Mona does not like it when I point things like that out. Thirty-five people, twenty-six of them men who wore black trousers. And—

Sorry, that's too much detail and no story once again.

The priest was talking about the dead person. Apparently he was a pretty nice man and as he talked about him, someone up the top of the church started to sniff real loud. Probably his wife. 'God help her,' says Mona, and she blessed herself.

I did not see why we had to be there. It should be a rule that you can't go to a funeral unless you know a person.

Mona had a husband who died. He was forty which is not that old to die. He had a heart attack and Mona says she never got over it. Then she met my dad and is in love with him now. Mona doesn't like when I say her life to people like this. She says it doesn't sum it up accurately, but those are the details.

After all the prayers and stuff and the coffin was gone out of the church and everyone was outside talking and four people were around the bereaved and others were making their way to the graveyard, Mona finally lit the candle we came to light and closed her eyes and said a prayer.

She looked very holy.

'Are you praying to be protected?' Brian Jones said, coming down from the top of the church to us and sort of hissing in Mona's ear. Mona jumped a bit, then she turned to him and said, 'I'm praying for Sash.'

Brian Jones stood back and looked at Mona with a smile. 'She'll need all the prayers she can get with all the lies she's telling.'

Brian is Paddy's dad. Paddy who used to go out with Sash. Brian doesn't believe Sash is telling the truth and a few weeks ago, when Sash came home for the weekend and we all went out to the pub for lunch, he said, real loud, that it was a disgrace making poor Charles Hanratty a scapegoat for Marcus and his murdering ways. Hanratty had helped put kids through school in Applegate, he said. He'd paid for the GAA sports grounds. He'd given college bursaries. Then he said, even louder, how Sash always put Marcus before his son Paddy and no wonder Paddy was walking about in a state. Then Sash poured a pint on him in the pub. Now no one talks to anyone anymore.

Anyway, back to this morning. Mona got up off her knees and took my hand as if I'm four. I shook her off. 'Come on, Lana, let's leave the bullies to their games.'

'You want to watch yourself,' Brian Jones said, 'something nasty might happen.'

Mona drew herself up. Oh-oh, I thought, Brian is in real trouble.

She marched back to him; her tight skirt looked like it would burst. She came up to the middle of his chest. 'If something nasty happens I'll know who to blame then, won't I?' she said.

Then she turned around and walked out of the church. I ran after her.

Mona walked as quick as she is able all the way away from the church, not even stopping to say hello to June Daly who is her best friend.

'June said hello,' I said.

'Did she?' Mona said. Then she stopped and closed her eyes and I could see she was shaking.

'Here.' I took off my coat and gave it to her. 'I'm not cold.'

She shook her head. 'Keep it, pet. Let's go.'

'What did Brian Jones mean about something nasty happening?'

'He meant nothing – he's just telling me to say my prayers.'

All I can think now is, oh God, not more prayers.

Sash

The court resumes after lunch and Dad and I both agreed over a coffee that Marcus's solicitor had nailed it so far. We sit in the same seat as before lunch and I stare around, wondering about all these people who turn up to see murder trials. How odd. It's like Marcus isn't even real to some of them; it's as if they think this trial is for their entertainment.

There are a lot of people here who were here yesterday. An eclectic mix of the retired and the young. The young are mainly female. There is a buzz in the room before the judge enters.

'You can tell this is going to be a great case,' the girl beside me says to her friend, 'it's all over the papers today.'

'And that murderer is so hot.'

'Jesus,' Dad whispers to me, 'are they for real?'

You'd never know that my dad spent thirty years in the police force as he still retains an innocence that police work hasn't touched. I like that the best about him.

The next witness called to the stand is a man who looks like a puff of wind would blow him over. He's old and he's wearing a suit that might have fitted him two decades ago. Even still, it bears a remarkable resemblance to Marcus's suit. I think the man notices it himself because, just as he gets into the witness box, he looks over at Marcus then down at himself.

'State your name and address for the court, please,' Peter says.

'I'm Walter Harte and I live in 24 Lime Tree Avenue.' His voice wobbles.

'Where is that in relation to the victim's home?'

'Two doors down,' Walter says. 'And may I say that Charles was always a lovely neighbour to me. I was shocked, shocked at what happened. If I ever wanted anything done in the house, he'd be able to get it done cheap for me because he had all these contacts in the hotel industry, you see.'

Peter smiles briefly, says, 'Let's focus on the details here, Walter, I know you're upset. So, let's go to the night of the murder. Can you tell the court what you saw?'

'I can.' Walter sits up real straight and stares at the jury. 'On Thursdays I go to my set-dancing class. Every Monday and Thursday for two hours it's on. Eight thirty to ten thirty.'

'And what did you see that night?'

'Well, I left my house at eight fifteen, it takes about ten minutes to walk to the class, you see, and that's on at eight thirty, so I have five minutes to relax myself before going in. It was a wet night and I was thinking of maybe driving over but that would mean I wouldn't get my walk in, so I decided to wrap up and brave the elements. It's good to get out every day.' Walter takes a noisy sip of water. 'Talking makes my voice a bit scratchy,' he says as he puts the glass down. 'Now, where was I?'

'You were walking to your set-dancing class?'

'That's right. Eight fifteen.' He leans forward towards the judge. 'I was walking up the road and I saw that laddo,' he nods at Marcus, 'coming out of Charles's house.'

'You identified Mr Dillon from an identity parade, is that correct?'

'That's right.' Walter nods. 'That was some horror show, let me tell you.'

'Maybe another time,' Peter quips and people laugh.

I don't.

'So, you saw the defendant that night and can you tell us what he was doing?'

'Walking,' Walter says. 'Walking down poor Charles's

driveway, bold as you like. Then he stood beside a fancy car that was parked two houses up from Charles's, four houses up from mine. I was walking towards him and next thing I see him sort of grab his head like this,' Walter holds his head in a despairing gesture, 'and I'm telling you, he looked rightly,' Walter looks up at the ceiling as if he's trying to find the words written there, 'shook or something.'

'That's the witness's opinion,' Melissa says.

The judge nods, says to Walter, 'Try to stick to the facts, Mr Harte, let them speak for themselves.'

Walter looks confused. 'Right,' he sounds a bit unsure, 'well, like I said, he had his head in his hands and so I thought it was a bit weird, you know.'

'And what did you do?'

'I asked him if he was OK, of course,' Walter says like it's obvious, 'and he jumped about a mile in the air.'

'And you are positive that this man was Marcus Dillon?'

'Yes. Sure after he jumped, didn't he turn around and I apologised for startling him and he just looked at me as if I had two heads.'

'What happened then?'

'Well, I didn't know what to do. He looked sort of, well, in shock, so I asked him again. And he sort of nodded and said that he was fine.'

'And what did you do then?'

'What could I do? I walked on but there was something about him which spooked me and so, after a bit, after I'd gone up the road a little ways, I turned back, ever so slow, and I saw him staring over at Charles's house and then he leaned on the bonnet of his car with his head in his hands.'

'Leaning on the bonnet of his car with his head in his hands,' Peter repeats. Then asks, 'Can you remember what he was wearing?'

'I can. I normally don't notice those sort of things. As my wife says, if she stepped out naked, I'd hardly notice her.'

People laugh. One person on the jury honks like a sea lion.

Peter doesn't look happy. 'What was the defendant wearing?'

'Head to toe in black. I noticed mainly because he had a big anorak all zipped up with a big fluffy hood, the kind my grandson has on his coat. He had these big shoes too, heavy boots.'

'I see. Was there any sign of the defendant or his car when you got back from your set-dancing?'

'No, he was gone.'

'Thank you.'

Marcus

I remember Walter. I remember him coming up to me that night. I didn't even see him – I was wondering if I'd done the right thing or not where Charles was concerned. Maybe I'd gone too far. Maybe I was losing my mind. But then I thought to myself, fuck it, it serves the old bastard right. Next thing, someone comes from behind and asks me loudly if I'm OK and I thought it was Hanratty and it scared me.

Even after all that time, he had the power to do that. Even though I stalked him, he scared me.

So, Walter is telling the truth, I did jump.

I watch, trying to stay detached, as Melissa gets up. She's upset about this morning's paper too – I think she blames herself over it, but it was me who grinned. Me that let myself be snapped. I've told Melissa to forget about it, mainly because I don't want it affecting the way she questions all these people. She's the best money could buy, my solicitor told me, and I had the money to buy it. Melissa has this way of twisting things, of making the truth not appear so simple, of making people say stuff they didn't even realise they said. Court is theatre, is what she told me. She said it didn't even matter if I was guilty, she'd find some way of making me look innocent. I wasn't too sure I liked that, but I figured, hey, I'm innocent so it should be no problem.

Melissa smiles at Walter. 'You like set-dancing?' she says.

'Yes.'

'And you go twice a week?'

'Yes.'

'Every week?'

'That's what I said.'

'Tell me, were there any other cars parked on your road that night?'

'Loads.'

'Loads.' Melissa nods. 'It's a busy road, isn't it?'

'It's quiet but people like to park on it.' Walter sounds a bit indignant. 'We're hoping to get some yellow lines painted on one side because sometimes it's damn near impossible to get up and down it with everyone parking there.'

'I'm sure it is.' Melissa nods sympathetically. 'Were there other people sitting in their cars that night?'

Walter thinks hard. 'I don't rightly remember.'

'Were there other people walking along the road?'

'I suppose.'

'Does a bus route go up your road?'

'Yes, a bus stops right outside my house which I'm not pleased about.'

'Busy road. Lots of people.'

'Yes.'

'And let's get this straight: you saw my client coming out of the victim's driveway?'

'Yes.'

'Did you see him come out of the house or just down the driveway?'

'Just out of the gate.'

'Was he rushing?'

'At my age, everyone appears to be rushing.'

People titter and Walter looks pleased. He's quite the comedian, I think. Now that he's relaxed, he seems to be enjoying his time in the box.

'I'll rephrase,' Melissa says. 'Did he appear to be in a hurry?'

'Not that I noticed.'

'And did he see you?'

'I don't think so. His back was to me when he went towards his car.'

'Good. And when you talked to him, did you notice if he had a bag of any sort?'

'A bag?'

'Yes, a previous witness testified that the person she saw walking up the driveway had a bag. Did Marcus have one?'

'Not that I noticed but then again I'm not observant.'

Bingo. Strike one to Melissa.

'You're not observant?' she says as she turns to the jury. 'And yet you want the court to believe that you spoke to my client that night? That he appeared to be in a distressed state? You want to place this man near a crime scene just because you say so? And you freely admit that you're not observant.'

Walter flinches but then sounds annoyed. 'I never forget a face.'

'Really?' Melissa folds her arms.

'Yes. And Angela confirmed it was him too.'

Melissa rolls her eyes as if Angela doesn't count. 'Angela said she saw someone at a distance of over a hundred and fifty feet, in the dark and rain. You're saying that you are unobservant. Isn't that the truth?' Melissa's voice has an edge to it that I like.

'You're twisting things.'

'I'm only repeating what has already been said.'

'I talked to Marcus Dillon. I know I did.'

'Marcus Dillon is six foot one, medium build, dark haired in dark clothes. Loads of people match that description, wouldn't you agree?'

'It was him I talked to.'

'I'm not asking you that, Mr Harte. I'm asking you if

you know many people that would fit the description of Marcus as being six foot one, medium build, wearing dark clothing?'

'I suppose, but it was—'

'Yes or no?'

'Yes.' Walter folds his arms.

'OK, now, let's say you're right and it was my client, did he appear to have any blood on his clothing?'

'I'm unobservant.'

Someone laughs.

'I think you might notice someone covered in blood,' Melissa says, smiling. 'It's not something people generally miss.'

There is a bigger roar of laughter.

Walter mops his forehead with a hankie, then takes a sip of water. 'He had his jacket zipped up.'

'Did his jacket extend all the way to his ankles?' Melissa asks pleasantly.

'No.'

'So, did he have blood on his shoes? His trousers? His jacket?'

'Not that I saw, but—'

A sudden bang makes people jump.

'Sorry, sorry.' Josh, the junior counsel, stands up and apologises. 'I just dropped this.' He holds up a huge file. 'Sorry, Judge.'

After a bit, when silence has resumed, Melissa turns to Walter. 'Are you OK? You look a little shaken.'

He looks a bit surprised at her sudden concern. 'I'm fine.'

'I just thought you got a fright.'

'I did,' he manages a smile, 'a loud noise like that, sure everyone got a fright.'

'Yes. A bit like you coming up behind someone who doesn't see you and asking loudly if they're OK, a bit like that, eh?'

Walter looks caught.

People glance at each other. A low murmuring starts up. I try not to grin. The girl is a genius. I glance at Josh, but he looks innocently ahead.

'Wouldn't you agree sudden shouts and noises can be startling when you're not expecting them?' Melissa says. She sounds really friendly to Walter now.

He doesn't look so friendly back. 'Yes,' he grinds out.

'That's all,' Melissa says, and with a swish of her ponytail she sits down beside me, flashing me a grin. I'm reminded unexpectedly of Sash. Everything these days reminds me of Sash, except the girl herself, who seems to have changed into someone else entirely. Looking at her now, as I do from the corner of my eye, as she sits up so straight, her mouth pressed into a line, her shoulders hunched, she is a million miles away from the girl who walked into the newsagent's that day full of spark, a million miles away from the girl who four months later was beaten up just outside the orchard. The girl who kicked and swore at her attackers, the girl that swung her schoolbag so hard it caught Jenny Ryan on the face and made her stagger, the girl that I waded in to save. The girl that invented the 'how to break into places' game.

But I guess I'm no longer the guy that went along with

everything she did either. Ever since that night, the one Sash is going to talk about, the one that I hope will exonerate me, the one Melissa is building my defence on, a little bit of me has eroded, piece by piece, like the light going out of the day, so that the only real part of me that is left is the piece people don't see. The darkness. The Marcus I was at seventeen is not a Marcus who would ever have spent his days trying to terrorise an old man, even if the old man deserved it.

I'd been a nice kid.

I am a terrible adult.

Sash

Court is over for the day and it's like coming up for air. I spent the day stealing glances at Marcus, searching for some clue as to his guilt or innocence. In my heart, I want to believe he's innocent because the guy I knew would never have committed a murder. But I don't know him anymore. It's been fifteen years since he snuck away from Applegate in the middle of the night without saying goodbye and he has changed beyond recognition. He's successful now; he has loads of money. He drives a cool car – I saw a picture of it in the paper. The suit and shirt he has on scream 'expensive'. He wears his wealth with unsmiling arrogance. The guy I used to know had nothing and didn't care. He wore tattered Converse and faded denims. His hair was never cut.

But we all changed.

I certainly did. In my head, there are three Sashes. Sash

number one was fun, I remember. When I think of her I see bright sunshine and brilliant green grass. I hear laughter like the trickle of a waterfall and I see four people in a white house with big windows. I hear echoes of songs and see the vivid colours of cartoons. There are no thoughts beyond play and life and dreaming and drawing.

When my mother left us, that's when the second Sash came. An angrier Sash, though terribly sad, who managed quite successfully to fake cool and edgy. Whenever I allow myself to remember my fifteen-year-old self, I see brooding days and nights spent creeping on silent feet through rotting apples. I hear the soft laughter of Marcus and smell the sweet scent of a joint. Our house wasn't cosy the way my mother had kept it, the windows stayed closed and music never played. Inside me, there was a black hole of loss that I couldn't navigate. I had no thoughts beyond life and death and finding out where it had gone so wrong. But there was fun too. Mainly with Marcus.

And then came the night they want me to talk about on the stand. That night made me what I am today. Since my last year of school, I've tried so hard to forget it. Like a snake shedding its skin, I left the first and second Sashes behind and moved on. I wiped my feet on the steps of childhood and stepped beyond Eden into the world. When Marcus and his mother left Applegate, though I was terribly hurt he hadn't said goodbye, I found that it was easier to put that night behind me. Armed with a determination to keep calm, to bury everything, I appear as a funny, quirky, charming best friend. Up until the news broke about Marcus being charged with murder, up until people knew I would be helping defend him, I was loved in Applegate. But I was loved because inside I am nothing. Inside I am scraped clean, ready to mould myself into whatever is required because that's the best. Inside I look out on the world to see how it ticks. For a long time, I had no thoughts beyond existing and surviving and moving on.

And for years, nothing shattered my calm. Failing art college didn't cause a ripple on the surface of my life. My drawings were crap and I was only surprised no one had noticed it sooner. When I was younger, I doodled cartoons, dreaming of creating my own superhero series one day. Lana had loved my drawings, she used to tell me I'd be famous, but after that night, I couldn't draw anymore. Not really. I didn't have the feeling for it. I didn't have the emotion. The edge. In college, through my drawings, they'd seen my fakery and failed me. I'd moved back to Applegate.

Dessie Daly, Marcus's friend from the pub, had taken pity on me and asked me to do some landscapes for the lounge. He really needed them, he'd said, and though I doubted that he did, I'd needed the money. I'd done a passable job. Competent landscapes expertly rendered, nice perspective, interesting angles. But there was no soul and no one seemed to care, which was a little depressing. After a while I picked up a job painting nails in the local beautician's because I had a steady hand. It was easy to have a steady hand when nothing ruffled my equilibrium. Bit by bit, I began, very tentatively, to experiment with the colours of varnish, to draw little pictures on people's nails. Paddy befriended me again, we started seeing each other, we bought a little cottage in Applegate together. He was persuaded to go up for election and I think I convinced myself I was happy.

Then one day, two and a half years ago, Marcus rang me. I'd nailed the memory of him shut in a box in my mind. I hadn't recognised the number and, thinking it was a client, I'd answered.

'Hello, Sash here.'

At first there was only silence on the line, then his voice, deep and cracked, just like I remembered, said, 'You sold your soul.'

My heart whumped. I tried to speak and nothing came out. I pretended not to know who it was. 'Who is this?'

'It's me,' he said. Then added, 'I saw your picture in the paper. With him.'

Sweat lined my palms, coated my forehead. 'What?' I managed to stumble out. My voice had lost its chirpiness. Images swamped me. Flashes of pictures, noise, horror, laughter all mixed together like some terrible collage. The whoosh and ebb of sounds, the squelch of apples, their scent rising up from the earth. Then, with a huge effort, I got out, 'You can't just call me out of the blue like this.' I lowered my voice. I turned away from my client – I think it was June Daly – and I walked into the small kitchen of the beauty salon. There, I clutched the rim of the sink with my free hand and took deep, silent breaths. My legs shook, my body trembled. I felt sick.

'I know it's years ago,' Marcus went on, 'but I saw your picture today in the paper at the hotel opening and …'

For some weird reason, a tear sneaked out. I felt it slide down my cheek.

'I take it you haven't told Paddy,' Marcus said.

I caught my breath. 'No. He's going up for election. He's hoping that Charles Hanratty will be his chief backer.'

'For fuck's sake. You need to tell him, Sash.'

'Tell him what?'

'Everything.'

I had to get myself together. Make it sound like I wasn't crying. 'Paddy needs Charles.'

'If he loves you, he needs you more.'

'No.'

'Don't cry.'

'I'm not. It's too late to save me now.'

He didn't say anything for a second after that.

'It's never too late.'

'It's finished, Marcus. No more.'

'It's not finished until he's finished. Tell Paddy, then we can—'

I felt a sudden spurt of anger. I cut him off. 'Don't ring me again.'

I hung up.

My phone asked if I wanted to save his number. I did because I wanted to never answer that number again.

I cried for an hour that night, with Paddy downstairs. My body shook with sobs, my head throbbed but by the next day, I was calm again.

Until Marcus was accused of murdering Charles Hanratty.

And now all my covering up and trying to plaster over

my reality has still led me to this point and I can't help feeling that if Marcus had murdered Hanratty, he'd done it for me.

Lana

Some people think I'm weird. Things like that are OK to wonder about in your head but saying it out loud, like for instance if you met me on a street and said it to my face, said, 'You're odd,' my Dad would get real mad at you and so would Sash. I probably might feel hurt but mainly I'd just think that you're rude and I'd probably say that to your face. Which would be rude.

It's all very confusing.

Anyway, I have some kind of Asperger's which is some kind of condition that isn't my fault. My dad says that a lot. 'It's not your fault, Lana,' he whispers whenever I scream or rock or flick my fingers. I only flick my fingers now and again, not like some other people who do it all the time. I don't even know I'm doing it and Sash has to tell me and then I stop because I like Sash and she looks after me and I want her to be happy with me. And she is mostly. The big time she did get mad at me, I think she has forgotten, but I remember everything. I have a video-camera brain, Dad jokes all the time. Only I'm not sure if it is a joke because it's not so funny as it used to be. The time she got maddest was when forty-four people in school told me things about Marcus Dillon's mother. Ten of them said she was a show; one of them said that she was in love with every man in town. One of them said that according to her mother, Charles Hanratty was fighting Marcus's mother off. Four of them said … maybe that's too much unnecessary information. The important thing for this story is that one person said that Marcus's mother would go out with a rabid dog. I looked up 'rabid dog' and was very surprised to see what one looked like and even more surprised to think that someone would like one enough to go out with it. So the next Tuesday, when Sash went to collect her magazines from Marcus, I asked him, 'Would your mother go out with a rabid dog?' Some people in the shop laughed. Marcus didn't answer my question. He just stood there. Sash pushed me out the door of the shop, real rough. 'Lana,' she said, 'are you trying to ruin my life?'

I didn't know what she meant so I said nothing.

Sash shoved her face in mine and I took a step back because she was too close.

'All you do is cause trouble for me,' she said. Then she said, 'You bitch.'

'That is not nice,' I said.

She grabbed my arm and dragged me along the street and I was crying and she was hurting me and no one came to help. Maybe they thought it was not their business. When we got to the road home and no one was about, she pushed me away from her and I fell.

'Serves you right,' she said.

I started to cry and I told her that I'd tell Dad. She said she'd just deny it. She said if I told Dad, she'd never talk to me again.

So I didn't tell Dad.

Another thing that annoys Sash about me is when I join in conversations that are private when I don't know.

Also I count things. All the time. And I rearrange things. I put things in order by size, shape, colour, style. Sometimes by all four. But mostly I count. That's something I can stop, Sash says. Counting is not really a part of Asperger's – it's just Lana-itis. Or Lana it is. That's a joke that Sash made. Isn't it funny?

When I counted all the time, they brought me to a person who tried to help me stop. It was important to figure out when it started and this person figured that it began when my mother left, when Sash told me to count as Mammy was leaving. It might be right because when this person asked me to describe how I felt when I counted, I said, 'Calm.' Counting blocks out all the noises and thoughts that swirl in my head.

I still remember how many steps it took me to get to school and what the difference was when my legs got longer. Not as many as you might think. I know how many steps get me to Sash's favourite apple tree in the orchard. The one with M and S carved in it. Marks and Spencer. I can remember how many boxes were on my best friend's duvet cover. I am great at remembering stuff like that. I cling to it, like as if it's important. I try to shake it out of my head but I can't.

I remember that night, the one they want me to talk about in court, how many steps it took me to reach the orchard and then how many it took to run across the road to Charles Hanratty's back field, which is a funny name for a field that comes out at a road. I wonder if I should say that in my statement.

Is that an important detail?

DAY 3

Marcus

I wake up as light filters into my studio.

I've basically slept on the sofa there because I spent so long drawing last night. It helped me not think about this trial for a while and, for the first time in months, I actually did get a couple of hours of shut eye.

I chose this apartment because of the light in this room. The rest of the place is bright too, being a south-west-facing penthouse in Malahide. It's all mod-cons and sleek machines and I love it. Lauren, a girl I went out with for about a year, the first girl to really get under my skin since Sash, used to tease me about them all. 'Do you actually know how to make a cup of coffee just using a kettle and instant?' she'd giggle.

She had a nice giggle, husky and sexy.

Our relationship had fallen apart about two months after I became fixated on Hanratty. There wasn't room in my head for her and him. I treated her badly, yet another casualty in the wreckage of the last few years. When I got arrested, she did make contact, but I didn't return her calls. It was better she stayed away. I miss her mainly, I think, because she really, really liked me. And aside from Dessie, no one had in such a long time.

My mother taps on the door.

'Come in,' I call.

She pauses in the doorway, slender as a reed, her hair gleaming in the light flowing in through the large window. Her eyes skip across me to my pictures. Finally, she points to the cartoon page I'd worked on last night. 'Is this yours?'

She's never seen one of my pages in the flesh before. She's avoided this room because I told her this is where I work. The art she is looking at is pretty good. Before last night, I'd almost finished it, just had to ink it in. I watch, bleary eyed, from the sofa as my mother crosses towards it and stares. 'You're so talented,' she says like she's surprised.

'Thanks.'

'Seriously, Marcus, you never said –' Her voice trails off as the rest of the room takes up her attention. My very best work hangs in frames on the wall. I'm not a show-off but I'm not a guy for hanging pretty pictures up either, so it's a cheap way to decorate the place. 'These are so,' she pauses, 'bright and fun.'

I think she means that I'm not. I'm dark and broody.

'Ta.' I flash a bit of a grin. I've never gone out of my way to show her anything I've done, and she's never asked. I don't know why really. Like, she's seen the Slam Man comics but I guess she never really looked at them as art before.

I watch as she walks around the studio admiring the work. She comes to a stop at the darkest picture on the wall. It's the only non-cartoon one in the place. 'That's a bit different to the rest,' she says.

'Yeah.' It's of a room, small, narrow and dark. Covered in pictures. Dark frames.

I'd painted it after I'd gone back to Applegate about seven years ago. A sneaky in-and-out visit. Hanratty had moved from Applegate to Dublin and his house had come up for sale. It was the big talking point in the town and Dessie had told me about it in a random phone conversation. It had suddenly seemed important to go visit the place, to finally confront the ghosts in my head. I'd gone to a viewing and just about managed to stomach seeing the front room. It had been cleared out, no furniture, just stacks of empty photo frames in cardboard boxes ready for moving. I'd looked through them but couldn't find what I remembered. And then the auctioneer had come in and asked me what I was doing. I didn't even know. I ran as fast as I could away from the place. I'd painted the picture on the wall that night and, while I hated it, it was good and I couldn't bear to throw it out. So I hung it up, just like any other piece.

'Alan,' my mother calls, 'come in here and look at what Marcus has done.'

'What?' Alan sounds alarmed. I hear him shuffling in from

the kitchen, slippers sliding on my white tiles. 'What?' He looks from her to me.

'This.' My mother flaps an arm in the direction of my comic-book pages. Her arm jangles with mountains of bracelets. 'Look.'

Alan looks. 'That's his job, Thelma. He draws comics.'

'But he's really good,' my mother says.

'Of course he is.' Alan sounds baffled. 'He invented Slam Man, who's only the best non-superhero ever.'

I love that this man knows what I do. I love that he just assumed I was good. I grin and it's real. 'Is there coffee going outside? I'm whacked.'

Alan slaps me on the back as I go by.

The paper is on the table; I'd insisted that we keep getting it because I don't want to be under any false illusions. I don't want to be thinking that Melissa is winning the case only for the papers to be hammering me without my being aware of it. Though, as Melissa says, they can't actually hammer me, that would be a miscarriage of justice, they just have to report the facts. But the facts can be skewed. The way they printed me grinning yesterday is a case in point.

Also, by knowing what's in the paper, I feel I have some control.

This morning there is just a piece about the trial on page two. It states what the witnesses said yesterday, who they were and what they saw. They rehash my life in Applegate. Again. All about how I left school early, how, out of the goodness of his heart, Charles Hanratty gave me a job in his newsagent's so that I could support my mother, who was drinking heavily. I don't know how they got this stuff. But it's balanced, I guess. It makes me and him look good. I skip over it all, reluctant to read anything that paints that man in a positive light. A little way down, there's a picture of Sash and her dad leaving the court. She's described as my childhood friend and there is speculation about whether she will be called as a witness.

On the next page there is news about a shooting down in Galway. It almost takes me by surprise. This trial has taken over my whole world, so that I've forgotten there is another world out there where other stuff is happening. I try to read about the shooting. Then I turn to a piece about a sick kid who needs treatment in the US and the parents are looking for funding. Poor kid.

Nothing quite goes in, though. My head is a mess.

Today, Melissa has warned me, will be the worst day. The expert witnesses are being called. People who will prove, apparently without a doubt, that I was in Charles Hanratty's house. That I killed him by stabbing him and hitting him with some kind of a pole. Today will be the day that Sash will look at me and wonder if I did turn into a monster.

Sash.

I have to stop thinking about her.

But I can't. I remember how I'd rescued her when she was being beaten up by Margaret Browne and her mates. I never quite got to the bottom of why. Not clearly anyway. I'd been on my way to work, taking the shortcut from my house through the orchard and on to the main road that led to the town. I'd almost reached the small wall that separated the orchard from the road when, still shadowed by the trees, I'd seen Sash pelting along, her school bag flying behind her. Suddenly she stopped, right in the middle of the road, and yelled out, 'Who's first?' She was swinging her bag, her face murderous, and I grinned a little, thinking that she was a bit small to be so ferocious.

Next thing, Margaret Browne, Jenny Ryan and two other girls that I didn't know arrived up. They were all puffing and panting, except for Jenny, who was pretty sporty.

'Well?' Sash said. 'Who's first?'

'Jenny,' Margaret Browne didn't even look at Jenny as she spoke, 'you get that bag off her.'

Jenny looked unprepared for that. In fact, I was surprised to see Jenny with Margaret. In primary school and for some of secondary, I'd been mates with her but once I finished school, she dumped me. She'd always been a soft kind of kid, but now she looked hard or something. I watched as she made a rush at Sash.

Sash swung her bag in an arc and caught Jenny on the side of the head.

Jenny staggered but remained upright.

Everyone, including me, went 'Ouch!'

Jenny, clutching her face, which was orange with make-up, looked to Margaret. Margaret, calling Jenny stupid, ran at Sash like some enraged pit-bull. Cleverer than Jenny, she dodged Sash's bag and ploughed right into her. Sash cartwheeled to the ground, her bag spilling books everywhere. Margaret sat on Sash's chest, yelling at Jenny to pin Sash's arms to the ground. The other two girls stood a little back, unsure of what to do.

'Get off me, you heifer,' Sash panted.

I don't know what Margaret was going to do, whether she was going to punch Sash or not, but I didn't wait to find out. I ran the rest of the way to the road, hopped over the wall and yelled at them to give it up.

They glared at me.

'You going to make us?' Jenny said in her high-pitched voice, that I used to think was cute. I'd had a crush on her one time because of that voice. 'You don't know what she's done.'

'I know four against one isn't fair, is what I know.'

'Get lost, weirdo loser,' Jenny sneered as the others laughed.

Hurt knifed me. 'Get off her,' I said, this time pretty angry.

'Yeah,' Sash said, her voice muffled and breathless. 'Get off. I've done nothing.'

'You're chasing Paddy and he's Margaret's,' one of the girls who was standing by said.

'Chasing him? He's not even running.'

Margaret gave a little scream of outrage and I choked back a laugh.

'Get that heifer off my arms,' Sash said then.

I can still hear Sash's howl as Jenny, with a viciousness I hadn't expected, stood up and stomped on her hand.

'Jesus!' Even Madge was appalled. 'Jenny!'

'For fuck's sake, Jenny,' I yelled at her.

'I'm not a heifer.' Jenny stared at us like she couldn't believe what she'd done before backing away and running off.

The others followed.

'If it's broken, I'll get my dad down to your houses,' Sash yelled after them.

I watched as she sat up, cradling her hand and wincing.

Now that it was just me and her, I was a bit tongue tied. 'Is it broken?' I ventured, hunkering down beside her.

She flexed her fingers. 'Nah.'

'You've made a bit of a mistake choosing your pals.' I tried out a joke.

To my relief, she managed a grin. 'And my superhero powers didn't work either, Marcus.'

I was pathetically thrilled that she recognised me from the shop. That she knew my name.

'It's good there's nothing broken so,' I said.

'Except my trust in human nature.' She was half-grinning. Slowly she stood up. 'Thanks.'

I stood up too. 'No problem. My own superhero powers did the trick,' I glanced about, 'all the baddies are gone.'

I know I sounded like a dork. But I *was* a dork.

She bent down to pick up her books. I gave her a hand. When we were done, she hoisted her schoolbag over her shoulder.

I was desperate to prolong our interaction. 'Are you OK to walk home?'

'I think so.' She turned to go.

'What was all that about anyway?'

'Nothing. They think I fancy Paddy Jones or something.'

'And do you?'

She gave me an odd look.

'Sorry. Not my business.' Fuck sake, I berated myself.

'His legs look good in a pair of shorts.'

I do not know how I smiled at that, but I did.

'You just look good anyway,' she said then.

'Sorry?' I know I flushed and stumbled and stammered. 'What? What did you say?'

'You heard.' She looked at me expectantly.

'Right, well,' I gulped, like the idiot I was, 'well, if you're in need of a friend, I make a good one.'

She smiled that smile at me and I felt myself being hooked like a fish on a line. 'I'll remember that.'

'I tend to hang about in the orchard around midnight. Maybe I'll see you some time.'

'The orchard at midnight? Is that a bit weird?'

I shrugged. 'Yeah. Probably.'

She laughed. I had made her laugh.

'I'll see you there tonight so,' she said.

I thought I'd heard wrong. I couldn't believe that this cool piece of Dublin would want to hang out with me.

But that night, after I'd brought my mother home from Daly's, after I'd reassured her that she was a great mother, after I'd laid her on her side so she wouldn't choke if she got sick, Sash was waiting for me under a tree outside my house. I walked her right to the middle of the orchard, pointed to the tree I normally sat at and told her, 'This is my patch.'

That night, it became our patch.

Sash

It's the turn of the expert witnesses today. That's what Peter Dundon calls the small man with the large glasses who slowly makes his way through the courtroom and up to the witness stand. He's dressed in a grey pinstriped suit and is wearing a bow tie. His hair is white and sparse and his face looks anxious to please. He reminds me in a weird way of Charles Hanratty. The thought makes me shiver.

'Can you state your name and occupation for the court?' Peter Dundon asks the man.

'Certainly, my name is David Long and I'm a forensic scientist working for the forensic-science lab in Dublin.'

'Can you tell the court what that involves, David?'

'I can.' David adjusts his glasses. 'I attend crime scenes and take evidence. It might be pictures of the scene itself, fluid samples, fingerprints, anything at all really that might help us determine how a crime unfolded and who did it. I bring these back to the lab for forensic analysis after which I write up a report which is submitted to the DPP. I also report on my findings in cases such as these.' He trots this out as if he's said it many times before, which he probably has.

'How much experience have you got as a forensic scientist?' Peter asks.

'Thirty years.'

'Great. Now, David, can you walk us through the crime scene for the benefit of the jury.'

The judge speaks up. 'These images are disturbing so anyone that wants to leave may do so now.'

No one moves. The girls who were beside me yesterday clutch each other as if they're about to watch a horror movie.

The lights go down and a photograph is projected onto a screen. At first, I don't quite know what it is and then, with revulsion, I see it is a picture of the crime scene. Charles Hanratty's body lies in a strange position amid a lot of blood and gore. It seems to have been taken in a kitchen, judging by the cream porcelain tiles on the floor.

'Gross,' the girl beside me murmurs.

'This is the way the body was discovered,' David says, his voice matter-of-fact. 'The victim was face-up, arms on his hips, feet twisted outwards. The body was arranged like this post mortem. This picture shows the blood splatter and from this,' he looks at the jury, 'we can determine pretty much how the victim was killed.'

'And how was the victim killed?'

'It appears that, upon opening his door, the victim was stabbed in the stomach and then pushed inside.'

Another picture is projected onto the screen. It shows an enlarged photo of Charles's belly.

'The blade was estimated to be about eight inches – we think a kitchen knife with a serrated edge. It was pulled out and, as the victim started to flee, he was hit in the back of the head with a heavy object.'

A photo of the back of Charles's head. His skull looks to be smashed in. I feel my stomach roll.

'From the evidence on the body,' David says, 'it appears that once the blow was struck, the victim staggered and stumbled into the kitchen upon which he was stabbed repeatedly with the knife in the chest and neck. You can see the stab wounds if we go back to the first picture again.'

The first picture is shown.

David goes on, 'Finally, it appears the perpetrator inflicted a wound to the femoral artery. That's an artery in the leg. I'm unsure whether the cut was deliberately angled but, basically, because it was angled, it meant that the cut remained open and allowed the victim to bleed to death.'

I shoot a look at Marcus. He's impassive, not looking at the pictures. Instead he's staring hard at the wall over the heads of the jury. It's like he's zoned out. I feel scared of him for the first time and yet scared for him too.

'Can you tell us anything else about the victim's wounds?'

'Yes,' David nods, 'judging from the angle of the blow, the perpetrator was between five foot eleven and six foot two. Taller by a few inches than Mr Hanratty. The perpetrator was strong, as Mr Hanratty was moved post mortem into this bizarre position. We think it's a chicken pose as there was a word, written in Mr Hanratty's blood, over the corpse. We feel it was done with the murder weapon, which we have not been able to trace as yet.'

On the screen the word 'Cluck' in blood appears.

'That's mental,' the girl whispers to her friend.

'Can you tell the court what else you discovered on examining the crime scene?' Peter says.

David nods. 'During an examination of a scene, like I said earlier, we dust for fingerprints, fibres, residue that can tie a suspect to a particular place, things like that. During the examination of this scene, we found prints that matched the suspect's on two items. One was on this envelope. It was found in the kitchen of the victim's house.'

The envelope is shown to the jury.

'Can you tell the court what was in that envelope?'

Up front, Marcus puts his head in his hands. It's the first sign of emotion from him. His barrister has a word with him and he tries to sit upright but can't seem to manage it. Instead, he watches with his hands covering his mouth, staring hopelessly up at the expert witness.

'This,' David says and then up on screen there are a number of comic-book pages depicting Slam Man vanquishing his nemesis, Jay Walker. All around me, people react with horror.

I don't understand why. It's just a magazine, one that Marcus has created. I'm admiring the technique Marcus has used, the way he draws his lines, the colours he chooses. Such a talent.

'Can we get a close-up of this part here?' Peter asks.

The image is magnified. Marcus winces.

Oh sweet Jesus, it's then I see it. Jay Walker is Charles Hanratty. His hair, his clothes, the hooked shape of his nose, the full, thick lips. He's being flung headlong into a mincer by Slam Man.

'Thank you,' Peter says.

He doesn't go so far as to say that Jay Walker is Charles Hanratty, but it's so clear.

'On what other items were the fingerprints of the accused found?'

'On the frame of a picture that had been thrown to the floor.'

'This is it.' Peter holds up an evidence bag containing a ripped picture followed by a bag with a broken frame.

I recognise both. They were given to Hanratty by the citizens of Applegate to celebrate the opening of his hotel extension.

Not a lot happens in Applegate so the unveiling of the extension was a big deal. Containing a spa and swimming pool, it meant employment and more tourists.

I hadn't been happy about it because I felt the spa would eat into Naomi's beauty business – where I worked – and that I'd be out of a job as a nail artist.

'Just apply to Charles for a job,' Dad had joked. 'I hear he's looking for people.'

I had to smile and say I'd think about it, but even hearing Hanratty's name had made my stomach turn. He'd been gone from Applegate three years at that stage and I finally felt that I could breathe.

Paddy, being the local councillor, had invited Charles, on behalf of the town, to a ceremony to celebrate the opening. Hanratty, to my horror, had agreed.

Paddy threw himself into organising the event. As a gift for Charles, to show the gratitude of the people of Applegate, he organised an official photographer and commissioned a picture of the town from the mountain top, which he had framed. He then purchased an extra frame for himself and paid the photographer to take a portrait of me and him, which he displayed in his constituency office. It was cringy but kind of cute.

The day following the ceremony, a picture appeared on

the back pages of a daily newspaper. It showed me, Paddy and Hanratty smiling fit to burst. It was after that that Marcus had rung me.

It was after that that Charles had offered to finance Paddy's political campaign.

That's what I remember about that picture and frame.

When I tune back in, the expert witness is yakking on about finding Marcus's fingerprints all over the frame.

They also found a hair on the victim that matched Marcus's DNA.

How did that happen?

'And is it true to say that there were a number of other fibres on the victim?' Peter asks.

'Yes, there were a number of fibres which we have since traced to a school that Mr Hanratty visited earlier that day.'

'Thank you. No more questions.'

Before Peter has sat down, Melissa is already up on her feet. She's like a rabbit, I think. A scary one with metal teeth.

'Can I ask you,' Melissa says to David, 'is there any way you can determine how long fingerprints have been on an object?'

'Not really, no,' David says. 'As yet we have no way of determining the decomposition of fingerprints over time.'

'So if, say, my client's fingerprints had been on that picture for a month, they could still show up fresh?'

'Yes.'

A pause as she thinks. 'And this hair you found that you say matches my client's DNA, there is no way of telling where that came from, is there?'

'It came from your client.'

Someone titters.

Melissa flushes. 'Apologies. I didn't make myself clear. There is no way of determining that it fell onto the victim directly from my client, is there?'

David thinks about this. 'You're saying the hair was deposited by a third-party source?'

'Yes. Is it possible?'

'Yes.'

'So, let's be clear. It is possible that the victim had a hair found on him that matches Marcus Dillon's DNA, without Marcus Dillon having to be at the scene?'

'It's possible.'

'No more questions, thank you.'

Marcus

Melissa is pissed off at me – I know by the way she thumps her case files back onto her trolley, by the way she ignores me when I go to help her out at the end of the day. I know why she's pissed off too but I pretend not to. She scares me, to be frank – it's why I was happy to employ her. I figured if she was on my side and she scared me, she'd certainly scare the other side.

'I think we should have a word,' she says to me when she's finished packing. 'You tell your mother and Alan to go on.'

'If it's about—'

'Not here,' she says, smiling at me so that no one looking on would know just how cross she was. 'We're going to take ourselves off somewhere private where we can be alone.'

'Isn't that a breach of your professional ethics?' I attempt a joke.

She turns away.

I heave a sigh and cross towards my mother. Alan is chatting away about Wales to the woman sitting beside him. He's recommending places that she should see when she visits. As I come towards them, the woman looks a little unsettled and then she suddenly peers harder at Alan. 'You're – you're –' She can't get the words out. Her face pales.

'I'm Marcus's stepdad,' Alan says, matter-of-factly, 'Alan.' He holds out his hand to the woman.

She shakes it with a weak smile, all the while eyeing me with some suspicion.

'Don't look at my son like that,' my mother snaps at her.

The woman titters uncertainly.

'Hey,' I say to her and she offers me a smile wide with fear. Dejected, I turn to my mother. 'Melissa wants to go over some stuff with me – you and Alan can go on.'

From the corner of my eye, I see the woman beat a hasty exit.

'Bye,' Alan calls after her.

She doesn't respond. I feel bad for him. For my mother. This will be our lives now. It'll be even worse if I get convicted. At least they both live in Wales – they can escape once this trial is over. I bless the day my mother met Alan. At the time I hadn't, though. I'd paid for her to treat herself because she was five years sober and she'd chosen to go to a fancy spa place in Wales. Just after she'd arrived, I got a phone call from her. 'I met the man I'm going to marry,' she said. 'He's here having a de-stress week.'

I could see my childhood repeating itself once again. Her falling for another waster of a man.

The following night she told me that she wasn't coming home, that she was hanging about Wales for a while to see how it went.

'For God's sake,' I'd fumed as anxiety for her clawed at my throat, 'you're not a bloody teenager.'

'And you are not my dad,' she'd said and hung up.

'—home?'

I realise my mother is asking me something. 'Sorry?'

'I asked, how will you get home?'

'Taxi.'

'You will not,' my mother says, 'we'll wait in the car for you.'

'It might be a while.' I glance up at Melissa, who's busy strapping all her folders onto her cart to bring back to her office.

'We'll grab a bite to eat.' Alan stands up. 'Text us when you're done. We're not letting you get a taxi.'

The last time I'd tried to get a taxi it had been a disaster. Every guy in the rank had recognised me and all of them had refused to take me anywhere. I'd been too shocked to be annoyed.

'OK, thanks.' I try not to show how relieved I am.

'I'll get a take-out for you and you can heat it up when you get back,' Alan says.

I have to swallow a lump in my throat at his kindness.

He holds out his arm to my mother, who takes it, and I watch as they leave.

I hear Melissa's high heels clicking up behind me.

The court has emptied and it's only the two of us. Without turning around, I say, 'Sorry. OK?'

'Not here,' she says again. 'We'll walk to the office.'

'Then let me help you with your cart at least?'

Melissa eyes me up. She puts a finger to her lips and tilts her head. Slowly she says, 'OK. It'll look good for the media. Client helps barrister carry evidence. Nice one. It'll humanise you after today's hammering.'

'That's not why I said I'd help.'

She doesn't respond. Instead, she allows me to pull the evidence trolley along as she strides ahead of me towards the lift.

It takes fifteen minutes to get to her workplace. They're a little down from the court, on the quays. Melissa's office is up high in the building.

She leads me down the corridor, pushing open the door to her office, and her assistant, Josh, looks up at us as we enter. He offers a bleak smile and says, 'Not a great day.'

'If we'd been more prepared, if Marcus had been honest with me, we might have had a better day,' Melissa fires out.

'I'm sorry, right?'

She doesn't look at me. 'Sit down.'

Josh winces at her tone. I'd say he's come in for his fair share of hammering over the years. He always seems to be in good form, though.

There is nowhere to sit. Melissa's office is a bit of a mess. She says that once a trial is over, she doesn't have time to get rid of the evidence and, as a result, large stacks of files are everywhere. It'd be a nice office too if it was cleaned up, a great studio. A huge window dominates the room, a panoramic view of the quays. I eventually sit down on a tower of boxes.

'Gives a whole new meaning to sitting on the evidence,' Josh chortles, then realising that Melissa is not in a joking mood, he asks, his voice pitched a shade too high, 'Coffee, anyone?'

'Yes, make it a strong one.' Melissa doesn't even look at him.

'I'm fine,' I say.

'No you're not.' Melissa is still standing and I wish I hadn't sat down because it makes me feel like a kid in playschool. 'You, Marcus, are so far from fine.'

'So, one coffee,' Josh says.

'I know I should have said something,' I say.

'I'll get that, so.' Josh leaves.

Melissa barely notices. She leans over me. 'Yes, you should have. Something like, Oh, by the way, the arch-villain I draw in my little comic-book stories looks exactly like the guy they're accusing me of murdering. Oh, and in my little stories, the arch-villain dies a gruesome death every month.' Then just as I open my mouth to answer, she spits out, 'What sort of an idiot are you?'

I snap a bit. Maybe it's the stress of the trial. Maybe I just want someone to be nice to me. I stand up and tower over her. 'I have a solicitor and you're my barrister – why didn't either of you bloody notice?'

'Do not put this back on me.'

'Will I tell you why I said nothing?' I stick my face right in hers. 'Will I?'

'Please do.' She makes a big gesture with her hand and does a mock bow. 'Go ahead.'

'I wanted to see if you'd notice.' I pause, then go on. 'I figured that if you did, I'd admit it, but that if you didn't see it, no one else would either.'

'You're a bloody fool. Peter Dundon is a smart guy. He wants you in prison. If there was even the tiniest, smallest similarity he would have made sure to point it out. But oh no, this was a fucking mirror image.'

'I'm back,' Josh announces, kicking the door open, holding two steaming mugs of coffee. He pauses and looks from Melissa to me. The air hums with hostility. Without another word, he leaves Melissa's coffee on her desk and thumbs in the direction of the corridor. 'I'll be just outside if you need me.'

'Go off home.' Melissa flaps her hand at him. She picks up her coffee. 'Thanks, Josh, I'll see you in the morning.'

'Sure. Bye, Marcus.' He hesitates in the doorway, as if he's gearing up to say something. Then in a rush says, 'I loved this month's edition of *Slam Man* by the way. It was so funny.'

It's so the wrong thing to say.

'Go home,' Melissa snaps.

Without another word, he's gone.

Melissa waits until his footsteps die away before taking a

few sips of coffee, all the while eyeballing me. I try to hold her gaze and can't. When I look back up, she has her eyes closed and is breathing in and out very slowly, like someone doing yoga. Finally, she looks levelly at me. 'I'm used to winning, Marcus.' Her voice is matter-of-fact. 'The only time I lose is when the defence are totally kick-ass. I never lose because my clients withhold information from me.'

'I should have told you. I just thought ...' I sink back down on the files and bury my head in my hands. I don't want to say it but I have to. 'I thought, if I had told you, it would only make me look more guilty. I guess I kidded myself that no one would notice because you hadn't.'

'I should have, I really should have.' She sits down behind her desk and kicks off her shoes. The big storm seems to have passed. I watch as she wriggles her toes and takes another sip of coffee. 'We need a way to explain it. We need a way for you to get up there and sound sympathetic and credible.'

'You're going to put me on the stand?' I'm not entirely surprised. The only one who can explain all the facts against me is me.

'It's your decision of course but that strip you posted to Charles Hanratty, it looks like a death threat, Marcus. That's the way the prosecution will play it.'

'It wasn't a death threat. It was –' I shake my head. 'His death in the comic strip was a metaphorical one.'

'Metaphorical?' Melissa shakes her head. 'As in?' She picks up a pink glittery pen. 'Start talking.'

'As in,' I swallow, 'I needed to do it to bury the past. To get rid of it.'

She thinks about this. Finally she nods. 'That's good.'

'It's also true,' I say.

'Of course,' she says, and I hope to fuck she believes it.

Sash

After tea, I pull on my T-shirt, shorts and runners and go for a jog. There is nothing like running for freeing up your mind. For keeping you sane. Only for the running, I would have cracked years ago. In Wicklow, where I live now, I run most days because there are so many nice routes I can take. When I visit Applegate, which is usually every second weekend to bring Lana out, I run up the hills to the ruins of the monastery and across into the next town and then I loop back into the village. I could run by the orchard too but I haven't done that in years. The smell of the apples always makes me sad.

This is the first time I've run since the trial started. I'm afraid to go out in public in case I'll be recognised. However, the hotel we're staying in has a five-kilometre loop that I can do. I studied the map Dad had got from reception and I'm pretty sure I know where I'm going. I'm hoping the short run will blow my terror away, at least temporarily. Say Marcus is guilty. Say I'm helping a murderer go free. But at the same time, if he did it, I understand. Maybe that makes me sound bad, but maybe I am a bad person.

I take off, far too fast as usual, up on my toes, running up the long hill towards the forest. I like running up hills. By the time I get to the top I'm panting and want to stop but the first ten minutes of any run is the worst. If you can push through that, you can keep going. That's kind of the way I think about this trial. When it's all over, I'll survey what's left of my life and make the best of it and keep going.

I take a right into the forest and dip my head, ignoring a fellow jogger as he passes me by.

I used to run a bit when I lived in Dublin as a kid and then, when I started in Applegate Post Primary, my PE teacher approached me after class one day.

'Have you ever done any running?' she asked as she fell into step beside me.

'A bit.' I shrugged. 'Just in PE, mainly, but I like it.'

'I've been looking at you. You're very fast. Some of the boys have trouble keeping up with you.' A pause. 'Would you mind if I timed you?'

'Timed me?'

'Just to see what you're at? I clock you in class and you're coming in at thirteen seconds for a hundred metres, which is not bad at all. We can do it now if you like – I'll write you a note for your next class.'

My next class was maths so I happily agreed to be timed. Plus, thinking about it, it was nice of her to take an interest in me. Ever since my mother had left, I kind of craved that. My dad was immersed in his job and I was left minding Lana a lot of the time, getting her ready in the mornings, walking with her to school, having lunch with her. I only got a break from Lana three times a week on the walk home from school, when she went for speech therapy. Lana was way more difficult back then and she could be hard work. I loved her but she swallowed up all my time and everyone's attention. It was nice to be noticed.

The PE teacher made me change back into my sports gear and meet her on the athletics pitch, which was just an uneven field with a track marked on it.

When I got there, she had placed a set of blocks on the ground beside the starting point. 'See that orange cone up there?' She pointed to a hundred metres up the track. 'That's where you'll finish. Do not slow down if you can help it – run through the line, OK?'

'Sure.'

'Now get into the blocks.' She explained to me how to use them but it was as if I already knew. My feet slotted into position. She called out 'marks, set and go' and I was off.

I felt a bit stupid running on my own but incredibly free. My feet barely tipped the ground as I whizzed towards the orange cone. It was only when I finished that the breathlessness hit me like a freight train in my chest.

I was so unfit. I started to laugh at the sensation.

The teacher jogged up, grinning at me. She held up her watch and showed me. Thirteen point three seconds. 'That's not bad.' She sounded delighted. 'With the right sports gear, some spikes and a bit of training, you could make a decent little sprinter. What do you say? Do you fancy joining our team?'

It was so nice to be wanted so I said, 'Yes.'

The first training session, I met the rest of the team. I knew no one on it, which was a relief. Even though the school was small, the years tended to keep to themselves. Most of the team was younger than I was. There were about six sprinters including me. I was busy asking them what it was like when I spotted Jennifer Ryan coming towards us.

At first I barely recognised her – she was out of her school uniform and instead wore a shocking pink Lycra vest that clung to her body, exposing her midriff, which was seriously ripped. The matching pink shorts were like bikini bottoms. Her body gleamed with oil or false tan or something and her hair was bunched up on her head.

I thought she looked ridiculous but the others greeted her like she was some kind of film star. I watched from the fringes as she smiled at everyone with a cool confidence that she lacked when she was with Margaret. She spotted me and froze.

'This is Sasha Donnelly – she's our newest sprinter,' Deirdre, our trainer, said to Jennifer. 'Sasha, this is Jenny – she's a thrower.'

She makes me want to throw, I thought, throw up, only I didn't say it. 'I know Jennifer,' I said.

'Hiya.' She wrong-footed me with a smile. 'Welcome to team Applegate.'

A little cheer went up as she said this and everyone laughed.

Jennifer's smile made me think that all her nastiness might be buried for a bit. As she went off to do whatever it was she did, I let myself relax and listen to what our trainer told us to do. We did a lot of warm-ups before the session began. I soon found out that I wasn't as brilliant as I thought I was. I kept getting pipped at the post every time we ran.

'You're doing great.' Deirdre took me aside at the end of

the session. 'Those other girls were nowhere near as good as you when they started off. You're building from a much stronger base.' Those girls were up and doing a warm-down jog while I could barely lift my legs from the track. I sat there for a bit, enjoying the pain and the achievement and the bit of banter I'd had with the other sprinters. No one had asked me anything about myself – it was all about the running, which I liked.

Finally, after their warm-down lap, the other sprinters flopped down beside me and started taking off their spikes.

Across the field Jennifer was with another coach. I watched her move away from him, all long legs and rippling muscles. She began to spin in such a graceful arc that I couldn't tear my eyes away. It was as if she floated for a second over the field, before a discus flew from her hand, hovering for a second before spinning high and true in the air, skimming across the grass and landing with a whump.

I heard her whoop and when she jogged back to her trainer they high-fived.

'She's a wonderful athlete,' Deirdre said, catching my gaze. 'We're hoping she'll win the schools' discus and javelin this year.'

'She is great.' I couldn't help it – it would have been churlish not to admit it.

Jennifer caught me looking and I tore my eyes away.

'You should try and do a little warm-down,' Deirdre advised, 'otherwise your legs will be in bits tomorrow.'

I hobbled to my feet, my legs sore already, and tried to jog a little around the track.

A few minutes later, Jennifer, looking every inch the perfect athlete, joined me. 'Trying to impress Paddy by getting all sporty, are you?' she said.

My heart sank. 'I'm not trying to impress anyone.'

'You should leave this team.'

'I won't be going anywhere,' I said.

'Paddy is Margaret's,' she said.

There was a desperation in her voice that made me pity her. I didn't reply, just upped my pace.

She kept up with me easily. 'You'd want to run a bit faster than that on the way home tonight,' she said.

That was when they attacked me. It was how I met Marcus. Properly.

By the time I get back from my jog, it's after eight. Dad is in the kitchen nursing a cup of coffee. He smiles at me as I come in. 'Good run?'

'OK.'

I pour myself a glass of water and join him at the table. 'Were you talking to Mona yet?' He rings her every night.

'I was.'

'Any news from Applegate?'

'A little.' His eyes meet mine and I know it's a bit more than a little. 'She had a call today, from Paddy. He was asking after you.'

I don't know how to feel about that.

'He was wondering,' Dad says carefully, glancing at me now and again, 'if you'd like him to go to the trial next week.

Here's his number, just in case you don't have it.' Dad pulls a piece of paper from his shirt pocket.

I don't touch it. I wonder why Paddy didn't ring me himself. But maybe he was wary of upsetting me. Scared of kicking it all off again. And we hadn't spoken in months, not since I left him.

I don't know if I want him at the trial or not. Does he feel he has to be there as an apology for what happened? Or does he think it'll help me?

'Mona got the feeling that he was struggling. She thought he just wanted to see you.'

I wouldn't mind seeing him too but, if I'm honest, the last year and a half without him has been a relief.

'I'll think about it.'

'Do.' Dad pats my hand. 'I was fond of Paddy. He would have done great things.'

'He would have been Charles Hanratty's lapdog,' I say back.

Dad doesn't respond to that but I know, sooner or later, if he'd lived, Hanratty would have asked something of Paddy and Paddy might have felt obliged to do it.

'Why did you never tell me what happened with Charles?' Dad asks suddenly. 'Don't you know I would have been on your side, I would have believed you.'

I swallow a lump in my throat. I wonder how things would have turned out if only I'd spoken up at the time. We wouldn't be here, that's for sure. 'I just –' I keep my voice as calm as I can, 'well, you were the sergeant in Applegate, Dad, and telling you about what happened that night would also have meant telling you that I was breaking into houses.'

'That wouldn't have mattered to me,' he says and he sounds heart-broken, 'you would have come first. I would have killed that man myself if I'd known what he'd done, sergeant or not. You would have come first.'

The trouble is I hadn't known that. The trouble is, since Lana was born with all her quirks and tics, she has always come first. Me and my world had never registered with my mother or my father, but to say that now would only crush him.

'You would have mattered more than anything,' he says again. Then with more force, 'You *do* matter more than anything.'

'Thank you.' I reach out and clasp his hand. He and Mona have been brilliant. If anything good has come out of all this, it's the realisation that I am really loved by him. I always thought I was a poor runner-up to my sister.

His eyes fill and he grasps my hand in both of his as if afraid to let me go.

Lana

Mona thinks I'm reading and I was for a bit. I was reading about apple trees because of the orchard in Applegate and I thought of Applegate and figured that it might be interesting. Interesting fact: apple trees need loads of attention to make sure they grow right. Aside from water and sun, you have to prune them because all the branches from the other apple trees will crowd one another and stop them from growing properly. The apples will be real small. I think that's what's happened to the apples in the orchard in Applegate. No one really takes care of them so the apples aren't so good anymore.

Another fact: there are five hundred apple trees in Applegate. The orchard is an acre big and it took me two hundred and twenty steps to walk across it when I was a kid. I took big steps too. I never really go near the orchard now, not since that night when Charles Hanratty almost chased me across it. And Sash hasn't really gone near it since the night she wants me to tell the court about.

It's not a big deal.

Nothing really bad happened that night, I don't think.

I have to tell the court about Sash always sneaking out to go on visits. That's what she called them, her visits. She'd wait until Dad was watching TV and I was asleep and then she'd put a pillow in her bed to make it look like she was still in it and, real soft, she'd slide open our bedroom window, climb out and then slide it closed after her. It wasn't dangerous because we lived in a bungalow. The first time, or maybe it wasn't, but the first time I noticed she was gone was one night after I'd had a bad dream. I hopped out of my bed and into hers because Sash would always wrap her arms around me and sing me back to sleep, and she wasn't in it. I sat in her bed and waited and waited for her to come home, getting more scared and more scared until I thought maybe I should tell Dad. And then she came back. And I was happy. And she said that I was never to tell Dad so I said I wouldn't but I didn't tell her that I would follow her either. And I did; from that night on, I went where she did. I was sneaky, walking on my tip-toes in my slippers, and she never saw me. In the beginning she went a lot to the orchard to meet Marcus. They would sit beside a tree, always the same one, and they would talk and he made Sash laugh a lot and she made him laugh and that's why I liked him a little bit. They smoked cigarettes too, ones that had a weird smell. I used to sniff real hard to see if I could inhale some of it too. After a bit, one night, Marcus kissed her. I never saw a kiss before except on TV and so I looked. After he stopped kissing her, Sash kissed him.

I suppose that made them boyfriend and girlfriend.

Then after more time went by and they kept kissing, they started to go places. Sash said later that she and Marcus were just visiting. They'd visit the backs of the shops on the main street, climbing up over walls. I hated that because I was too small to go over by myself and so normally when they started doing that, I would walk back home. It was a bit scary walking home in the dark all the way from town, but I stayed in the shadows so no one saw me. And I counted my steps so that nothing bad would happen.

And also it was funny how many people were out and about in the dark in Applegate at night. They never saw me because I hid but I saw them.

Anyway, after Sash and Marcus had visited most of the businesses, they started paying visits to people's houses. They were very popular. Sometimes, I think, they made a mistake about the house they were to visit because sometimes the alarm on the house would go off and they'd have to run;

other times, the people left the alarm off for them and they just went inside.

It made them happy – they laughed loads during that time. The night that I have to talk about is the one where they got invited to Charles Hanratty's house.

It was fifteen years and two months ago. It was summer. Sash didn't sneak out of our house until after one o'clock. I almost missed her, but it was the creak of the floorboard that woke me up. In the moonlight, out of the corner of my eye, I saw Sash climbing out the window and closing it real soft.

I waited for about ten minutes so she could get to the top of our driveway and onto the road before I followed.

When I got to the orchard, they almost caught me because, as I was going in, they were coming out. I hid real fast in the shadows of the roadway. In the country at night, it is pitch dark – you can almost touch it. And the stars glitter and the air smells fresh as clean washing.

That night was like that.

Sash and Marcus stood for a second opposite Charles Hanratty's house, her hand in his.

I used to hate people holding my hand.

They kissed and then, letting Sash's hand go, Marcus bent low and Sash copied him. I watched as they crept up Charles's driveway, keeping to the shadows. They were good at that. I could barely see them but after a little bit I saw one of them, I think it was Marcus, slowly lift up a window in the front of the house. I remember it was broken because I'd pointed it out to Sash three weeks and a day before that. 'Charles's window is broken,' I'd said.

The window gave a creak and I heard Sash giggle.

I wondered why they weren't going in the front door of Charles's house. Or the back door. Going in through a window did not seem like they had been invited. But maybe they just lost the keys.

Marcus tried the window again and this time I saw the window move upwards, slowly, not making a sound. When the window was most of the way open, Marcus hoisted himself up on the sill and slid on his belly through the window and into the room. A second later, Sash did the same.

And then it was quiet again.

I waited for a bit, I don't know how long because I didn't count, but after a while, I turned to go because waiting around was boring. I knew Sash would be back in an hour or so, that's how long visits normally took. I started back for home, keeping to the shadows of the trees in the orchard, just in case my dad spotted that Sash and I were missing.

I even jogged for a little bit until I ran out of breath.

One hundred and four steps later, and I was walking real slow so I was taking ages, I heard a sort of a shot. I froze. Then Marcus appeared like magic, pounding across a field at the back of Charles's house. He was running real fast, pulling Sash by the hand. And then, I saw him stop and I saw her stop and they stood looking at each other and Sash sat on the ground and Marcus went to put his arms around her but she put up her hands. That meant, No, I'm OK. Then Marcus left her and walked away from her and bent over. Then after a second, he turned back.

'Sash —' he said.

'Just go,' Sash said to him.

And then they saw me. I'd come out of the shadows to look.

First off Sash hopped up, then she saw it was me and she ran across the grass to me. She looked like she was tired; her face was puffy. Marcus followed her over. They both looked tired. But it was late in the night.

'What are you doing here?' Sash said to me, all smiles.

'Did you follow us?' Marcus joined her beside me.

'I just –' I didn't want to tell the truth. 'Just now. For a bit. Did you go into Charles's house?'

'Yes.' Sash laughed. 'He invited us. We danced, didn't we, Marcus?'

'Yeah.' Marcus nodded. He was fixing his shirt. 'We had a great time.'

Sash held her hand out to me and I took it. Her fingers felt all clammy. 'He had me dancing and everything.'

'That sounds fun.'

'Don't tell Daddy, though, OK? He'll get mad at Marcus – remember the last time? OK?' She peered into my face.

'Sash, I—' Marcus said.

'See you, Marcus.' Sash turned away from him and said to me, 'So, is it a deal? I'll tell you all about it if you promise not to tell Dad.'

'No way am I telling Dad.' I giggled. 'This is our secret, yours and mine and Marcus's.' I shot Marcus a big smile but he didn't smile back.

'Come on,' Sash said, looping her arm around my shoulder, 'let's get you home.' She turned to Marcus, 'I'll see you again.'

Sash didn't hear him leave because she was so busy cuddling me hard. Over her shoulder, I watched Marcus watching us and then, after a second, he turned away.

And Sash told me about the dancing and the laughing and the singing.

That's what I have to tell the court.

After that, though, Sash and Marcus never went out again, but after a bit, I started to. I missed the dark and the quiet and spying on people. It was good because there was no talking to people, just looking.

I would take four hundred and ten steps to the orchard and stand behind the apple tree to the left of Charles Hanratty's house. I wanted to see if there was any more dancing in his house because it sounded fun. Only there never was. Then one night, four weeks later and one day, when I was in the shadows, a person all in black came and stood opposite the house. I was behind the wall, near a tree, and they were just outside the wall. I couldn't see who it was, but it was spooky the way they stood real still, like a cat waiting on a mouse. I held my breath, hoping they wouldn't see me. Then I saw the person walk up Charles's driveway and throw a brick through Charles's window. There was a big crash. The person ran off.

I was going to run too only Charles came out of his house and looked up and down and then I think he saw me across the road. He started to come over towards me and he was shouting, 'Whoever you are, I'll kill you.'

Someone else came out of the house too. A lady. I don't know who it was.

I ran.

I'm glad he's dead because he was going to kill me. I never went out after that. And I never told anyone because I would be in trouble for sure.

DAY 4

Marcus

I am sick this morning. I dry retch into the toilet but nothing comes up. I'd known this day would come. All my computer files and phone records open for scrutiny. For a guy who guarded his privacy, it's a bloody nightmare. Melissa says nothing of any major relevance is going to come up except maybe some horrible notes and texts I wrote to Hanratty.

Those notes and texts were pretty bad.

And all those begging texts to Sash asking her to testify.

The morning they charged me, I'd known it was coming because I'd already been into the station a few times to 'help them with their enquiries', as they called it.

I retch again.

I sit on the cool bathroom tiles, resting my head against the wall.

I had never meant to manipulate Sash.

I hope she knows that.

'Are you OK?' my mother asks me as I join her and Alan for breakfast.

'Yeah.' I pour a coffee but I can't eat a thing.

Every morning Alan goes to the shop up the road, run by an Italian woman with a pile of kids. He buys us croissants and bread and eats most of them himself.

'You're losing weight.' My mother pokes me hard in the arm. 'Eat.'

I move away. In all my life she never worried about my weight, or hers. She ballooned up and down like a yo-yo.

There is a silence and I look up. My mother's finger is still poised in mid-air, a look of hurt on her face, and I feel bad. No one says anything as she lowers her arm. But I reach out and take a croissant.

'It's a very good likeness.' Alan breaks the quiet. He jabs at the page in the paper that shows a picture of my drawing alongside a picture of Charles Hanratty. There is no mistaking the resemblance.

'I think Jay Walker is better-looking,' my mother says.

I try out a smile for her. She smiles back.

Alan drives us to the court. He and my mother came over on the ferry from Wales so he brought his car. It's a beauty with cream leather seats and a shiny dashboard. It's a safe, dependable car, a bit like Alan. My car, which I rarely drive, is a show-off kind of thing. I bought it on impulse when the money from *Slam Man* started to roll in. I felt cool for about ten minutes; now I just feel ridiculous because driving around in a flash motor is just not me. I don't know what is me anymore, though; the only thing that keeps my brain quiet is drawing cartoons or heading out for long walks on the beach. I can't do that so much anymore because people look at me funny. One time, just after I was arrested and charged and a picture of me had appeared in the paper, I was standing by the surf and I was wearing a *Slam Man* T-shirt, because they're pretty cool. They're in bright colours and each one has a unique *Slam Man* comic strip.

This kid saw me and came up. He eyed my T-shirt and then eyed it up again. Before I knew it, he was standing right beside me. He must have been about six.

'I love *Slam Man*,' he said.

I turned to him. He was skinny and earnest and probably wore glasses. His face was freckled and his mouth was open in this massive grin showing two enormous front teeth. 'Me too,' I said.

'Which strip is that?' He pointed to my chest and I went down on my hunkers so he could see.

'It's the one where Jay Walker has invented this potion to kill off all the good in the air.'

'I loved that one.' The kid scanned the pictures eagerly, then pointed to the second from last. 'That made me laugh so much.' He laughed again, remembering.

A woman hurried up. Young, pretty, dragging a little girl in pigtails behind her. 'I'm sorry, is he bothering you?'

I stood and smiled. 'Nah, we're just shooting the breeze about *Slam Man*.'

'He loves that ridiculous thing.' She smiled up at me.

'See his T-shirt,' the boy said to her.

But her smile had frozen and she'd blindly reached for her son's hand. 'Come on, Jake, we've to meet Daddy in the coffee shop.'

'But his T-shirt!' Jake insisted.

'Looks like you're in a hurry,' I said to Jake, battling to keep my own grin. 'See you.'

'Bye,' he called out as the woman dragged him off.

'I love this song.' Alan breaks into my thoughts, tapping his fingers on the steering wheel. He always plays music in the car rather than a radio station, just in case they start talking about me and analysing the case. He has terrible taste in music. I told him that it'd be less painful to listen to them analysing my case and he'd laughed out loud.

'You give what you get ...' he warbles.

Out of the blue, I ask, 'Do either of you think I'm guilty?'

Alan almost swerves the car into a pole, earning a blast of a horn from some motorist coming towards us. 'No we don't,' he says as he rights the vehicle and waves an apology. He sounds annoyed. 'Now can you promise not to ask any more stupid questions while I'm driving?'

'Sorry,' I say.

I pretend not to see my mother pulling out a tissue and

patting her eyes as she blinks a little too rapidly. After a second, she turns around and looks at me sitting in the back. 'I always found Charles Hanratty a bit creepy,' she says. I hadn't known that. I feel she's just saying it to make me feel better. They still don't know the full story of what happened that night with Sash – they haven't asked and I've been grateful for that. I can never find the words or the right moment to tell them. To tell her. Maybe now … I open my mouth to begin. 'I'm glad you said that because—'

'And I'm not just saying it to make you feel better.' She jabs her bright red fingernail in my direction. 'There were so many things he did that people just overlooked because he was like a God in Applegate.'

'He still is,' I mutter.

'That's as may be, but we don't live in that pokey little town anymore, thank God.'

'What sort of things did he do?' Alan asks.

My mother thinks. 'Didn't he hike up the rent on the coffee shop one year and the poor man that owned it, Peter someone or other, was forced to close, and then he put his own friend in.'

'I suppose that's business, though,' Alan says.

'Business my foot.' My mother snorts. 'It was a huge hike.'

I'm surprised she can remember.

'Another time he stood by and let Brian Jones fire Lucy Ryan from the hotel.'

'Who was Lucy Ryan?' I ask.

'Lucy Ryan,' my mother repeats. Then at my blank look, adds, 'Jenny Ryan's mother?'

'Jenny Ryan's mother was fired from the hotel?' I didn't even know she'd worked in the hotel. Her family had run the local hardware shop until they moved away.

'Yes. Lucy worked in the hotel. Just to get out of the house, she used to say. She was a very nice woman. I was often on her shift.'

My mother had worked in Hanratty's Hotel for a few months until she got fired for not turning up.

'Do you not remember?' my mother asks. 'It was all over the local papers. A bracelet belonging to one of the guests was found in Lucy's coat pocket and Brian Jones, he was the manager at the time, he fired her. Still, he would have fired Christ himself if Charles Hanratty had asked him to.'

That was Applegate all over. Charles Hanratty either employed you, housed you or rented to you.

I have no memory of any of this, which is weird.

'And poor Lucy, she was as innocent as you are,' my mother says, tut-tutting. 'The rumour at the time was that Brian Jones had made a pass at her and she turned him down so he framed her.'

I think about that. I was never a fan of Paddy's dad, but I just couldn't see it. Brian Jones was way too up himself to bother making a pass at anyone. If anything, he'd have expected women to make passes at him. I don't have the energy to argue with my mother so I just pretend to agree.

'The Ryans left soon after,' my mother continues. 'Anyway,' she tosses her head, 'that's why I never liked Charles. He should have stuck up for Lucy – she'd worked for him for years. They got on well. Instead, he sided with his manager, brought us all in for a meeting and told us thieving wouldn't be tolerated.' My mother pauses. 'It's a regret I have that I never stuck up for her,' she says.

I know how that feels.

Taking my seat beside Melissa in court is always a relief because it means I've made it safely up the quays, dodged anyone who might recognise me and successfully passed by the swarms of reporters gathered on the steps. I'm convinced the court has been built in that particular place to make it easy for journalists to converge there. There is no escape from them. Melissa has instructed me to keep my head up as I pass them, to look them in the eye all the time. It'll make me look unafraid, she says. It'll make me look innocent. But whenever I see a picture of myself in the paper, and there have been a few over the past while, I feel as if I'm staring at a stranger. I look blank and cold, as if I'm hiding somewhere inside myself. Maybe other people don't see that. My mother keeps telling me how handsome I am, as if it's some kind of criminal photoshoot. Leaving in the evening is a nightmare too, especially if I've had a bad day and I know that what has just happened will be read over the breakfast tables of the nation in the morning. So, in contrast, sitting in the relative silence of an empty courtroom before the business of the day commences is like a mini oasis. The only one that acknowledges me is Melissa; everyone else, the guards, the other side, they all get busy preparing notes and shuffling papers and talking in low whispers to each other.

'How are you?' Melissa joins me, hauling in her evidence box, Josh following on behind.

'The prosecution should finish up today and then it's our turn. I am going to gut your life for them, Marcus, so be prepared.'

'I thought today is when they do that?'

'Nah, that's just your computer files and phone records.' A pause. 'You have told me everything, yeah?'

'Yeah. I just don't like …' I shrug.

'You don't like being exposed, I get it, but you did stalk a man and you're up on a murder charge, so tough.' She starts pulling out all her notes.

'Don't spare my feelings,' I say drily.

She ignores that and turns to Josh. 'Get us both a coffee, will you?'

'Sure thing, boss.'

Josh bounces off.

'He's so enthusiastic.' Melissa looks after him like you would a kid. 'He'll make a good senior counsel one day if he can keep his mouth shut.' A pause. 'He believes in you.'

I think that's her way of apologising.

Lana

Mona starts cooking stew first thing in the morning. She's doing it because Dad and Sash are coming home tomorrow from the trial. Stew always tastes better the next day, Mona says. Only her stew doesn't — it tastes just as bad. It's even thicker than it was on day one. I hate thick stew. Mona says that if it wasn't thick, you might as well call it soup. When we were kids and Dad made it, it was like soup and it was nice but Dad said not to say that to Mona.

I wander into the kitchen to get an apple because I like the scent of them. All along the road to the orchard, all you can smell in late summer is apples. Fresh, then not so fresh, then sort of sweet and rotten. I don't think anyone picks them now because they are not great apples anymore – they are too small now.

The doorbell rings. Mona jumps. I don't know if she's scared or excited. 'Wait,' she says to me as I go to answer it, 'just let me check who it is. I'm expecting June because we're going shopping but I just want to make sure it's her.'

She peers out the kitchen door and then sneaks into the hall. Then she opens the front door. It takes her five steps to walk the hall but only four for me: that's because she is small.

Happy voices at the door. It's June Daly.

'I'll be ready in about half an hour,' Mona says. 'I've just got some stew on.'

'No rush,' June Daly says, coming into the hall and giving Mona a hug. 'How are you? Have you recovered?'

I didn't know Mona was sick.

'I'm still a little shaken.' Mona leads the way into the kitchen. 'Come on in, I've just got the kettle on.'

'No you don't,' I say.

Both of them ignore me.

'Lana, get three cups and one packet of biscuits from the press, will you?'

When people say 'will you' it's not really a question, more an order. I put the biscuits on a plate and put the cups on coasters, just the way Mona does. It's a bit early for biscuits, I think.

'That Brian Jones has a right cheek.' June takes off her coat. She is round and fat like Mona but taller. 'He had a bit of a go at my Dessie yesterday too but Dessie told him to, well, you know yourself.'

Mona laughs.

'I should have done the same,' Mona fills the kettle and adds carrots to the stew, 'but he scared me a bit.'

'Coming up to you after mass, that was unforgiveable.'

'Yes.'

'But he's harmless. A bit worse since Mary died but all talk. I wouldn't mind him.' June takes a biscuit and pushes her feet out of her shoes.

'He's going about accusing Sash of lying.'

'Deep down he knows she's not. I bet he feels that he has to be loyal to Charles because Charles left him a load of money in his will.'

'Buying people even in death.'

'Yes. There was always something weird about Charles, I used to think, I just couldn't ever put my finger on it. Did I ever tell you about the time Dessie senior died and he arrived into the pub a week later wondering if we'd sell it to him?'

'He did not!' Mona says.

'He did. Dessie got fierce upset, threw him out. Told him never to darken the door again.' She pauses. 'I'll never forget, Charles turned around in the doorway and said he'd get the pub eventually.'

'The bloody nerve.'

'I sometimes think that's why he built the extension onto the hotel, to put us out of business.'

Mona sits back in her chair and fans herself. 'I must say, I never liked him either.'

That's funny. I always thought she liked Charles because the day Paddy presented him with the picture on the podium, Mona said that she was proud to know Charles.

'He did a lot of good too,' June says. "That's the problem. Sure when he died, didn't he gift all his business premises to anyone who was renting them.'

'I'd wonder at the motive of that.'

'Me too.'

The kettle clicks off and Mona hops up to switch it off. 'How does Dessie feel about testifying?'

'He's a bit nervous. He doesn't want to let Marcus down.'

Mona makes a huge pot of tea and when she is stirring it, she says, 'I just hope that Sash and Dessie have backed the right horse.'

Weird.

'Dessie's convinced that he has.'

'Sash too.'

They glance at me and start talking about the weather. It's boring so I leave, taking two biscuits with me. I'm looking forward to Sash and Dad coming home tomorrow because then we'll be a family again.

Marcus

By the time court begins, the place is full. Apparently there are queues on the steps outside to gain access to my trial now. Thanks to the media, this case is high profile. The fact that a guy who draws superhero cartoons apparently murdered a successful businessman seems to have attracted lurid headlines and morbid interest. I think the media sense that there is a lot more to come. I blame Melissa too. The media, she says, are sort of like starving people. Feed them the right food and they'll get to know you and be afraid to take the chance to go foraging elsewhere. So indirectly, somehow, I think she's dropped subtle hints that Charles Hanratty was not what he appeared to be. Everyone is waiting for this case to blow right open during the defence.

I hope she's right.

My mother and Alan are sucking Murray Mints. My mother, catching my eye, rattles the bag at me with a questioning look. I shake my head. The woman sitting beside her sees the exchange and studies her with a fascination, then looks at me before whispering to her companion. Then they both have a good gawk. I'm not sure if my mother even notices. I hope she doesn't. I'm glad my mother has Alan – she'd never have coped with this on her own. Sash's dad arrives and for one awful second I think that maybe Sash won't show up. But then I spot her, sliding into a seat beside him. I am grateful to her for showing up each day.

More and more people pile into the room until the bailiff is forced to shut the doors.

Ten minutes later my trial resumes.

Peter Dundon calls Colm Reilly to the stand. Colm is young, eager and earnest. I can see why Peter chose him to give evidence. He looks utterly believable.

Colm states his name and qualifications for the court.

'You've been examining the computer and phone records of the defendant and the victim?'

Colm nods. 'Yes we have. We seized the defendant's computer and phone records two weeks after the murder, on the fifteenth of March.'

Here it comes.

I feel like there's a train hurtling at speed towards me.

This awful madness of the stalker that had possessed me started when I'd seen a picture of Sash in the newspaper. It'd been over twelve years since I'd left Applegate and I'd tried my best to put that time out of my head, though the nightmares still plagued me. In them, I'm tied hand and foot and trying to run to save Sash, only I can't.

Maybe if I'd told her I was leaving Applegate at the time or promised to help her, the nightmares might not have been so real. But back then she wouldn't talk to me and so I'd snuck away in the middle of the night. I'd agonised over phoning her and didn't, over writing a note and couldn't. There were no words. There still are no words. I'd run and left her behind with a monster.

Still, I'd known, through conversations with Dessie, that Sash had hooked up with Paddy Jones. I'd been surprised.

I knew, way back, that Paddy had liked her but I always thought that Sash would go for someone a bit more … well, like me, I guess. But Sash was happy apparently so that helped ease my conscience a little.

And then, about three years ago, I saw a photo on the back page of the newspaper. A full-colour picture of Paddy, Sash and Charles Hanratty leering up at me. Even now, I could draw it if I had to. I blinked. Once. Twice. Looked again and felt my stomach heave. Sash was laughing, her head thrown back so that I could see the full length of her neck. Charles had his hand lightly about her waist and he too was smiling. Paddy was on her other side. The picture had been taken in Applegate and the caption read: 'Paddy Jones and Sash Donnelly sharing a joke with their good friend Charles Hanratty.'

It was as if someone tripped a switch in my head.

I dialled her number. I still had it after twelve years. There is something deeply unsatisfying about being angry while dialling on a smartphone. You have a ferocious need to punch buttons and there are none.

Sash answered, all chirpy and happy, without any of the sexy edginess that I remembered.

I can't really remember what I said but I knew what I wanted to say. I wanted to tell her that she'd sold her soul. That she'd brushed all that had happened under the carpet.

Maybe I had too but I could never have had that man near me.

She had sold us out, sold our souls and our young selves.

'Tell me,' I remember saying, 'did you ever tell Paddy about Charles?'

'And that is your business, why?'

'Because if you have and he's still friendly with that,' I couldn't think of an adequate way to describe Hanratty, so I settled for 'monster, then you have a serious problem.'

'You can't just ring me out of the blue.'

'I can when you're making a huge mistake. Have you told Paddy?'

'No.'

'You have to.'

'If this is about saving me, it's a little late, don't you think?'

I'm pretty sure that's what she said because I knew I couldn't speak for a few seconds; it was like I was winded. Anyway, I don't remember the whole conversation after that. I probably begged her a little more but she told me never to ring her again and then she hung up on me.

So I texted her. I said, 'You can't let that man back into your life.'

I got no reply.

I texted her again, saying, 'He will really kill you this time.'

She didn't reply.

A month later, there was another picture of the three of them. I texted her, *If you don't tell Paddy, I will.*

She didn't reply.

The next thing I heard was that Hanratty was backing Paddy in his political campaign and pictures of her and Paddy began to appear a little more regularly, usually on the society pages and once or twice in the politics section. They made a handsome couple. Paddy was like a cool, clean hero – I could see him in a billowing white cape and tight Lycra outfit, arms folded, fighting for justice. Sash was always his pretty sidekick, which disappointed me. There was a sort of generic cuteness about her now.

But I knew that, even if she wasn't like the Sash I remembered, I had to save her.

So, a while later, I went to Paddy's constituency office, where this ditzy kid had told me to take a seat before sitting down to paint her nails. After about twenty minutes, Paddy had arrived back from wherever he was, seen me and told the kid, I think her name was Janice, to take off. 'TY student, she's here for a week. It's been hell.' He'd grinned.

Then, after a bit of small talk where he asked me how I was and showed me naff pictures of him and Sash, I tried to tell him why I'd come. I blew it, though, because being back in Applegate made me jumpy. I got too intense too soon, my voice coming out all jumbled, echoing my frantic thoughts. Paddy thought I was mad: he told me to leave. I got worse and he lost it and threw me out, warning me to leave Sash alone and not to bother her with my ridiculous story.

So, after worrying about it and thinking about it for weeks, I decided to track Hanratty down myself. I wasn't sure why I wanted to. All I knew at the time was that I had to see him. For myself. For my sanity. For Sash.

Finding his address was easy – he was a well-known guy but not well-known enough to have to take precautions about his personal security. I kept an eye on the news pages, found out what functions he was attending and, one night, I stepped over the line and followed him home. I started to watch his house; I saw him come and go. And as my relationship with

Lauren fell apart, I saw him backslap friends, ply children with money, receive awards for his humanitarian work, open hospital units. I saw in the financial pages how his profits were soaring and, inside me, the silent rage of the unheard started to roar. He was happy and successful, people liked him and all the time he was a snake in Eden.

And so I became bolder and more daring and I got a sick satisfaction from seeing the way he'd startle whenever I showed up. I did nothing to him except intimidate him. I never laid a finger on him. Instead, I'd stand across a room and stare at him, my hands in my pockets, never taking my eyes from him. I'd follow him to his car.

Stalking him became my life.

I did it for a year.

And then he turned up dead.

And that's when I knew I'd wasted my time.

He was gone and, while some part of me was glad, the other part, the bit that still remained sane despite everything, mourned the gigantic waste of time. I should have just done something about him. I should have done it despite the odds. But I hadn't because it scared me. Because I needed Sash with me to do it.

The day they found his body, I had a text from Sash. '*Please say it wasn't you,*' she wrote.

I didn't reply.

And then, I got hauled into the police station to answer some questions they had. They made it seem like they were just asking me stuff to rule me out. I asked was I under arrest and they said no, but they'd appreciate it if I could go down to the station with them. I thought it would look good for me if I did. I'd been kind of expecting it. They seemed to believe me that I hadn't done anything. Yes, I'd been in the area. No, I had not gone into his house. They let me go. They found my fingerprints in his house. They hauled me in again.

I tried to explain the fingerprints. I couldn't do it without saying I was a liar.

I was seriously scared.

I talked to a solicitor, who talked to the police. It didn't look good. I was perceived as some kind of crazy. They found my connection to Applegate and Hanratty. They examined Hanratty's computer and found his letter to me, clever now, because it made him look like a scared old man. They also found massive documentation of evidence of my obsessive behaviour.

There was no one who understood. They wanted a motive. They asked me why I'd stalked the man and, without Sash to back me up, there was no point in telling them. And yet, by telling them my motive, they'd think I'd murdered him. I needed Sash to stand by me, to attest to the fact that murder was too good for him. I texted her, *I think they're going to pin this thing on me. I need you.*

She hadn't replied. I guess she was scared for how it all would affect her if I was charged.

And then one terrible night, I rang her. She didn't answer so I rang again and again all through the night. In the end, I guess she must have felt sorry for me, because she answered and agreed to meet me. I told her that I just needed someone to talk to, to be honest with, to help me clarify what the hell I could do.

I hoped that by seeing me she would remember and stand by me.

A week later, on a blustery day in Malahide, not too far from my apartment and miles away from Applegate, I met her. I was shit scared. I hadn't seen her in person for nearly thirteen years, though she'd never been out of my head. I worried about what to wear though I doubted she'd even care. In the end, I opted for the Marcus that I used to be. The one that might put her at ease. Scruffy jeans and a sweatshirt with Converse trainers. I shoved a packet of Jelly Babies into my pocket.

She was early. Even from a distance, I saw her. Like a magnet, my eyes were drawn to her. She wore a white furry jacket and high boots. Her hair was like I'd seen in the paper, long, straight and shiny, not short and choppy the way it had been when I knew her. In fact, she was a million miles away from the girl I'd known.

I dipped my head against the breeze and made my way towards her. With each step I grew more nervous.

I'd convinced myself a long time ago that I was done with her, that we were done with each other. Now that she was here, in my sphere, I was so far from done that I could hardly breathe.

When she finally lifted her eyes and spotted me, I stopped walking and we stared at each other for a moment. I realised in that second that, in all the world, I was the only one who knew this girl properly. She started to walk towards me then and I felt like a deer in lights.

She stood, facing me, and our shared past flashed in my mind's eye. I saw myself as I was back then, tall, gangly, nerdy and so bloody eager to please. I saw her, quirky, sparky, egging me to do stuff I would never have dreamed of. I saw us laughing and joking. I remembered her kisses, the way she'd slide her hand into my boxers and giggle when she heard me groan. I remembered the way I practised smoking in front of my bedroom mirror so that she'd think I was like James Dean. I remembered me carving out an M + S in script on our tree in the orchard. I saw it all in a spark of time and it got me right in the gut so that I was sad and happy and grief-stricken.

I wanted to touch her. I wanted to run as far away as I could.

'Hey,' I said instead.

'You've filled out,' she said. Her voice hadn't changed, that musical lilt lifting up even the tiniest word. Close up she looked tired and stressed, grey circles under her eyes, a frown line between her brows.

'All grown up.'

A pause. Then, 'You didn't do it, did you.'

It was a statement.

I blinked back sudden tears and shook my head. 'No.'

She reached for my arm and brushed it briefly. 'I knew it.'

'They haven't charged me yet but I think they will.'

'Fuck, Marcus. Why?'

I liked that she said 'fuck'; it was so at odds with her sleek exterior that I felt comforted.

'I was stupid. I did some stupid stuff.'

'Like what?'

'I stalked him. I mean, like crazy stalked him.'

'Why?'

And I shut down. If she had to pretend she didn't know, then I didn't want to go there. Instead I shrugged and asked her how things were.

'Good, you know …' Her voice trailed off, belying her words.

More silence. I had a sudden thought that words were too small for this. How do you broach thirteen years of the unsaid with small words? I jammed my fists into the pockets of my jeans. I tore my eyes from her face and stared at the ground.

'You look good,' she said then.

I hated that she was giving me a load of small talk. I met her gaze. 'I'm not, though. I'm sick worrying over this. I don't know what to do. They keep finding more and more stuff to pin on me. I –' I stopped abruptly and turned from her and started walking towards the seafront. She fell into step with me. For one brief, glorious moment, it almost felt like old times. Her steps in a rhythm with mine. The sea was the noise filling the silence.

'Do you still read comics?' The question popped out. I guess I was looking for common ground.

'Not so much now.'

I think I laughed. I wasn't surprised. That woman in the paper with Hanratty was not a comic-book reader.

'What did you say?' She sounded a little sharp. I was glad I'd rattled her cage.

'What?'

'Just now?'

'Nothing, just laughed.'

'Why did you laugh?'

'Because I guess once upon a time I never thought you'd give up Batman.'

'I grew up.'

She was angry, which was good. I glared back, not quite as cross.

This wasn't about Batman and we both knew it.

'I can't help you, you know,' she said then.

Her words devastated what little hope I might have had. With every passing day they were building a case against me. My solicitor had told me to be prepared. She'd also told me to find someone, anyone, who could vouch for my hostility towards Charles Hanratty. Someone who would understand it. Someone who wouldn't make me look bad in court. Who would say I was a decent guy. 'It's OK,' I managed, though it wasn't.

'It's just –' she started to explain, then stopped.

I held her gaze until she eventually looked away.

Without speaking, we walked on for another bit and, with each step, I felt weirdly that we were drawing each other back into our world. The way we used to walk for hours at night without speaking, the way I was always a half-step ahead, the sound of our feet.

I'd known that if I could bring back that shared camaraderie we'd had I might be able to convince her.

'Marcus,' she blurted out after a bit, maybe sensing my

intention, 'I can't do this, whatever this is. If you're innocent, they'll find you innocent. I can't be here.'

And I broke, hating myself. 'Unless you help me, I'm going down.'

She looked stricken.

'They have a really strong case, Sash. I need you.'

I watched as she gathered herself together before she shook her head. 'I have to go. I love Paddy and he needs me. He's not good since the murder. The man was his friend, sick as it sounds. I can't be involved with you and whatever trouble you're in. It'd destroy my dad and Lana if they knew what we did.'

'If they knew what *he* did,' I corrected bitterly.

Her shoulders slumped like I'd pulled the air from a balloon.

'Does Paddy love you?'

'Yes. Of course he does.'

'Then he'll stick by you.'

'It's not the right time. He's in bits.'

'I went to see him,' I said. 'Did he tell you that?'

I'd shocked her. 'When?'

'About a year ago. I tried to tell him about Hanratty but he didn't believe me.'

She laughed. 'Exactly. Who will believe us?' A pause. 'You had no right.'

I swallowed hard and said, without hope, 'I fucking need someone in my corner who can give me a bloody good reason for stalking Hanratty. That's what the solicitor says.'

'I can't,' she said.

It was so final.

Then maybe it was because of the expression on my face, but her voice grew more defensive. 'How will saying what happened to us help you? It'll only give you a bloody good motive for killing him.'

'What you say will explain why I stalked him, nothing else. If I wanted to kill him I'd have done it years ago.'

I thought she might cry. 'You should have let it go and you wouldn't be in this mess.'

'I have lived with the guilt of that night for years. I couldn't let it go.' I look at her pointedly. 'Or bury it.'

'At least I'm not up on a murder charge.'

I felt like she'd punched me. 'You know what,' I said, and my voice grew cold, 'when I saw you come prancing down the street with your high boots and your fancy white coat and your sunglasses in fucking spring, I thought, "That's not Sash." I was right. This,' I waved a hand at her, 'this isn't you.'

'It is me.'

'The Sash that I knew, she had spirit.'

'The Marcus that I knew didn't stalk people.'

We'd reached the bottom and yet I was desperate. 'I just need your help. Please.'

'Paddy −' Her voice trailed off.

I heaved a sigh, gave up.

There was a silence.

'You're still scared,' I said, 'aren't you?'

'No.' She was lying. 'My life has moved on.'

'Your life has been plastered over, you mean.'

'Fuck off!' Her voice was too loud and people stared. Then she turned away and I thought she might cry.

'Sorry,' I said, touching her sleeve.

She met my eyes.

'Don't cry,' I said again. I never wanted to make her cry. The lightest squeeze of her arm and I watched, guilt-ridden, as a tear dripped from her eye. I wondered then if I was always destined to feel guilty about Sash. 'I'm sorry.'

'So am I,' she said, and she sounded it. 'It's just ...'

'I know. Paddy.'

'If it wasn't for him, I'd stand by you in a heartbeat.'

'I know.'

'He's under so much pressure right now.'

I tried out a grin. 'I'm under a bit of pressure too.'

'You're innocent, you'll be fine.'

'Yeah, I guess I will.'

'I'm really sorry.'

I shrugged. I'd let her down once – maybe it was no more than I deserved. 'It's OK. If,' I paused, rephrased, 'when they arrest me, I'll tell them what he did to me, leave you out of it.' I jammed my hands into my jacket pocket and found the Jelly Babies. I pulled them out and offered her one.

I was rewarded with a smile.

'Do you still love the man ones?' I asked.

And she answered like I knew she would, 'Yep, because you get the extra little bit.'

I tipped a handful into her palm and when she looked up her eyes were shiny. I realised that we'd run out of things to say and it was kind of sad because, years ago, we were always happy in silence. Years ago, I knew what Sash was thinking – it was how we got so good at breaking into houses.

She thumbed in the general direction of the village. She looked relieved. 'I'd better go.'

I watched her leave.

Colm is still talking. Some of my texts to Sash and hers to me are read out. I have to admit they don't sound too great, especially when Sash asks if I killed him and I don't reply. Why hadn't I replied?

'I fail to see the relevance of this,' Melissa says.

She is overruled.

A catalogue of my all-nighter calls are read out.

'What do you deduce from this?' Peter finally asks.

'In my opinion, though Marcus Dillon hadn't been arrested, he knew he would be and was looking for someone to back his defence up. An alibi.'

'Thank you.'

I am humiliated.

Sash

When Melissa gets up to cross-examine, she asks, 'How many times does Marcus beg Sash to stand by him?'

'One hundred and five times in texts.'

'And when did these texts stop?'

'A week before he was arrested.'

'And how many times did Sash Donnelly reply to these texts?'

'About fifty.'

'And her replies were mostly negative?'

'Yes.'

'In any of her replies, does she ever accuse Marcus of trying to manipulate her?'

'No.'

'Does she ever accuse Marcus of asking her to lie for him?'

'No.'

'Can you read out again her text to him on the day she finally agreed to give a statement?'

'Yes.' The expert thumbs through pages and, finding what he wants, reads, 'I'll testify as to what happened to us.'

'And when was this?'

'The day after Marcus was arrested and his statement taken.'

'Thank you.'

Sash

I hadn't intended on testifying. Paddy had to come first. He was the real innocent in all this. But after I'd come back from meeting Marcus in Malahide I'd caught a glimpse of my face in the hall mirror and, for a second, I didn't recognise my reflection. Who was this person with the expressionless face gazing placidly back at me? Where had she come from? I moved closer to inspect myself, to try and see behind the eyes of this stranger. This person once wanted to travel and paint. This person never wanted to be a nail technician, never wanted to live right beside her dad in a small town.

And then I heard Marcus's voice, cracked and hoarse, asking me if Paddy loved me. And I had said yes. Paddy loves me. But, I wonder, was it me he loved? Or was it this invention I'd created to keep him happy? Could I spend my life as this blank page, ready to be erased and rewritten to suit the occasion? And though Paddy was a good man, I realised that, actually, I had sacrificed myself for him. I had become exactly what he wanted in a politician's wife. If he'd been a musician, I'd have become what he wanted for that.

I had lost myself somewhere along the way. The only person, I realised, who truly remembered me as I was was Marcus.

The realisation hit me with the force of a thunderstorm. It was as if I'd lived the last thirteen years in a vacuum, dry and airless, and now I was being rained on, soaked to the bone, left drenched and freezing, but finally able to breathe a bit.

Maybe it was because Hanratty was finally gone.

Could I continue to be this version of myself, I wondered. On and on forever? The thought gave me goosebumps.

But I held off. I held off because of Paddy, because of the expectation now loaded on his shoulders.

Hanratty's death had hit him hard but even as he reeled from it, even as the police interviewed him about his relationship with Hanratty, the pressure was building on him to win the election. In memory of Charles. The whole town got behind him. Each day, after work, more and more bunting urging people to vote for Paddy was hung up. Everyone I met on the streets greeted me, all asking after Paddy and telling me to make sure and let him know that he could count on their vote. Joking with me that I'd look good up in the Dáil, mixing with all the nobs. I'm sure my smiles were paper thin, but everyone saw what they wanted to.

Everywhere I looked there were pennants with pictures of Paddy in shop windows, hanging from lampposts. T-shirts with Paddy's face were sold in the local Euro Shop to raise money for his campaign. 'Vote for Our Own' was the slogan.

If Paddy pulled out, all this hope and excitement would vanish like perfume in the air.

I felt like a child who'd been led to a rollercoaster and now realised she couldn't ride it.

I couldn't eat or sleep. I made stupid mistakes at work. I lived on autopilot.

It came to a head about a week later, the day after Marcus texted me to say that he was going to be formally charged with Hanratty's murder. It was about a month before the election. I saw Marcus's message and I knew that my time had run out. I had to say something, but I didn't know what. I spent the day in a haze, one minute about to tell Paddy, the next pulling back. I knew that the minute I opened my mouth, I'd lob a hand grenade into Paddy's happy world and I hated myself for doing it.

'Are you OK?' he'd finally asked around tea-time as I was preparing dinner.

I was at the sink, my back to him. My shoulders tensed as I thought, here it comes.

'You've been washing that potato for the past ten minutes.' His voice was warm with laughter and the happiness in it cracked my heart.

I dropped the potato in the sink and water splashed out.

'Sash? Is there something wrong?'

I stared at the wilderness beyond the window. At our back garden, full of wild flowers and weeds. 'I don't know how to tell you,' I said.

He came up behind me and rested his chin on the top of my head, his arms encircling me. 'Just tell me.'

He wouldn't have said that if he'd known where it would lead.

I felt imprisoned in his embrace but it was easier too, because I didn't have to face him. I took a breath, my mind scrambling to find the right words. What came out was, 'I can't go through with this election stuff.'

He gave a soft laugh. 'I thought you liked being in the paper.'

I pulled free of him, knowing that I had to make him understand, and yet I couldn't say the words. My eyes locked with his, then skittered away. 'What I mean is I can't go through with this election stuff because Marcus is being charged with Hanratty's murder and I'm going to be a witness for him.'

A moment later he said, puzzled, 'I don't get you.'

I geared myself up to shatter his dreams. 'I'm going to say that Marcus didn't murder Charles Hanratty.'

'I'm lost. Marcus? Marcus who? Dillon?'

'Yes. He was stalking Hanratty and now they're saying he killed him. It'll be on the news later.'

I knew I wasn't making sense.

'And this has to do with you – what exactly?' Still confused. A little concerned.

I turned my back on him again; looking at him tangled me up. 'Marcus already tried to tell you,' I said, careful not to cry, 'only you wouldn't believe him.'

'Tell me what? That he tried to kill Hanratty?'

'No.' And again I was looking at him. 'He tried to tell you about Hanratty. He says he went to your office.'

For a second, nothing, then, 'He called last year. I threw him out. Sash, he was acting crazy.'

'He wasn't crazy.'

'He was saying that I had to keep you away from Charles. That Charles was evil. Honestly, I thought he was having a breakdown – the guy was mad.'

'He wasn't mad. Hanratty was *evil*.'

'For God's sake, Sash. You, you had dinner with Charles – you posed in photographs with him.'

'For you. Because he was your friend.'

'You invited him into our home.'

'He was your backer.' I couldn't even cry. The tears had been locked away years ago. I was looking at Paddy across an ocean.

'Exactly. So why would you say he was evil?'

Please, I mentally begged, don't make me say it.

'Because Marcus told you some stupid story, is that it?' Paddy sounded fed up. 'You always did listen to—'

'Because the man,' I swallowed, got my voice back under control, took a breath, 'assaulted me. Once. A long time

146

ago.' I closed my eyes, trying to shut down the images that were popping up in front of me. The silence from Paddy made me open them again.

Shock seemed to have pinned him in place. 'He assaulted you?' His voice was a whisper.

I nodded. 'I was just a kid. Marcus was there.'

The air seemed to grow thick all around us.

'And you never said.'

'I'm saying now.'

His eyes met mine and I saw what I'd always feared I'd see. He looked at me as if he didn't know me.

And he didn't.

I left then, told him not to follow me.

He found me hours later in the orchard. Sitting against the tree that Marcus and I used to meet at. The M + S was still there, carved beautifully into the trunk. I longed for Marcus right then because he knew and he got it. When Paddy walked up, I didn't hear him at first. I had my arms wrapped about my knees, my head buried into them. My stomach was scrabbling as if rats were running around inside it.

Paddy sat down beside me. He didn't attempt to touch me and he didn't put his arm around me. I was glad.

'I'm sorry,' he said.

I turned to look at him. He looked like he'd been crying – his eyes were puffy.

'I'm sorry too.'

'Don't you be sorry.' A pause. 'I should have at least asked you about what Marcus had said instead of dismissing it.'

I shrugged.

'Maybe I was afraid to know, I don't know.'

I said nothing.

'And,' he swallowed, 'I should have hugged you back there in the house but I was in shock.'

I moved nearer to him and hesitantly his arm snaked around my shoulder and he pulled me close.

We stayed like that for a while.

'Do you want to talk about it?' he asked.

'Just hold me.'

He pulled me closer.

After a bit, I said, in a whisper, 'Marcus didn't kill him, though.'

I felt Paddy tense beside me. 'How do you know that?'

'He swears he didn't do it and I believe him.'

Paddy said nothing.

'I have to testify in his defence.'

'And say what?'

'Say what happened to me. To us.'

He was silent for the longest time, then, 'You can't even tell me, Sash – how will you tell anyone else?'

'I'll get counselling or something, I don't know, but I have to –' I felt his eyes on me but I couldn't look at him. Finally, I blurted out. 'He raped me, OK? And, and he assaulted Marcus.' When I think of what happened to Marcus, my voice broke.

Paddy groaned a little.

More silence, both of us locked in our worlds.

After a bit, Paddy said, his voice soft, 'You telling that to a court might help convict him. It gives him motive.'

'Maybe,' I say, 'I don't know, but that's what he wants me to do and he needs someone in his corner and I,' I swallowed hard, 'I'm going to do it for him.'

'He shouldn't ask you to go through anything like that.'

'He's up on a murder charge.'

'You will not testify,' Paddy said, sounding desperate. 'No way, Sash.'

'Yes, I will,' I said. 'I will. And you can't stop me.'

His head dropped, his shoulders started to shake and I thought, Oh God, he's crying. He's crying, here in the orchard.

'Paddy—'

He waved me away, stood up and, turning his back on me, he placed his palms flat on a tree and bowed his head.

It struck me as weird that he was crying and I wasn't.

Finally, he said, 'It's all gone, isn't it?'

He meant our lives. The illusion we'd been living under.

'I can leave you,' I spoke the words I'd been rehearsing in my head. 'I'll leave and then when I testify it'll have nothing to do with you. You can go up for election.'

'Fuck the election, Sash.'

I loved him for that. I walked into his arms and he hugged me hard.

Another tech guy is talking, only now it's about a message that Hanratty emailed to Marcus through his website. Marcus deleted the message but the computer guys pieced it together. Or something. Or maybe they got it off Hanratty's computer.

I've lost track. After a lot of tech speak, the message is displayed for the jurors.

'Can you read it out for the court?' Peter asks.

The tech guy begins to read and I get the shivers. It's like a message from a dead man.

Dear Marcus,

I found this address through your website and I hope you read this all the way through. I'm sure you didn't expect to hear from me but I thought that maybe if I could apologise to you for whatever harm you think I've done, then we could put this nastiness behind us. I have always tried to live my life in the best way I can. I'm afraid that all I remember of you is when you smashed up my shop in Applegate. I know you had worries of your own at the time and that is why I never prosecuted you. I'm sure you've grown into a fine young man, you were always so good to your mother, everyone used to remark on it. I remember your mother from the hotel and I remember letting her go. That was a hard decision to make, but I am a businessman and sometimes hard decisions have to be made. As for your friend, Sash, I have met her in recent times and been charmed by her. She is the partner of the son of a very dear friend of mine. We have posed together for photographs. All I remember of her as a teenager is that I suspected she was the one behind a brick coming through my window one evening. It makes me smile now, the way she ran away, probably having been dared to do it. I might mention it to her the next time we are at a function together. I am sure we will laugh about it. I am an old man now, my memory is not as good as it once was but that is all I recall. Maybe if you make your allegations clearer, I might remember them better but you seem to be hedging the issue. I am almost seventy-five and this sort of harassment is not doing me any good. I am sure you are a good man who just needs some professional help. Maybe we could meet up and have a chat, figure out what to do about this. I sometimes wonder if you've mistaken me for someone else.

I am sad to say that if you do not desist from following me and posting notes through my letterbox, I will have no option but to report you to the police. I don't want to do this. Please, please, stop. You are frightening me.
Charles Hanratty.

Up at the top of the room, Marcus is shaking his head. He must sense me looking at him because he catches my eye. I nod. Hanratty, even from the grave, has set him up good. Hanratty was not scared or frightened. Of course he knew who Marcus was, the same way he knew who I was that day we'd posed for our first picture together. But whereas I'd played the game with him, Hanratty was setting Marcus up in case there would be any trouble. I feel like walking out but I can't – it'd be like abandoning Marcus. Marcus rises to leave, almost as if he's forgotten that he's the person in trouble. Melissa puts her hand on his arm and he sits back down.

'This message was received by Mr Dillon about a month before the murder. As you can see, Mr Dillon did not reply to it,' the tech guy says.

'That's because it's a fucking piece of shit,' Marcus calls out.

Everyone starts talking at once and I grin a bit.

Marcus turns and winks at me and something from years ago reasserts itself.

Marcus

I had to apologise to the judge for shouting out otherwise he would have put me in jail – that's what he said. I didn't want to say sorry because that was like saying I didn't mean what I said about the letter. So I said, 'I'm sorry if I offended anyone but that letter is a fucking piece of crap.' He gave me another chance and Melissa wrote on her notepad, 'Say sorry, you fucking piece of crap.' And that made me smile so I apologised very graciously. And received a wink from Melissa as a reward.

As we're going back into the courtroom after lunch, my mother points to a small bald man across the way. 'Is that Peadar?' Then adds, in case I've forgotten him, 'You know, Peadar from Applegate.'

'Yeah.' He's the last witness for the prosecution. I don't know how Peter Dundon and his team dug him up. Maybe Hanratty's letter helped them.

'Isn't that nice?' my mother goes on, smoothing down her skirt, getting ready to head over to him. 'I'll just go and say hello, thank him for supporting you.'

'He's going to testify against me,' I tell her in an undertone.

A beat. 'But,' she looks confused, 'you always got on so well with him.'

'Until I didn't.' It's an attempt at humour.

Peadar turns around and catches my eye. I think he looks a bit miserable.

'You should be ashamed of yourself,' my mother calls. 'My boy worked hard in your shop.'

'Ma, stop!'

'I will not. I cannot.' Her voice rises and people look. 'Is there no loyalty left? Charles Hanratty was a bad man and just because he had money you all think he was great.'

I suddenly feel like a kid again, back in Applegate, hauling my mother out of Daly's while everyone looked. Trying to stop her shouting out abuse at me and Dessie as we helped her home.

I walk away from her and into the court.

I reckon they've put Peadar up last because maybe what he says I did will stay in the minds of the jurors and give them a lasting impression of me.

Isn't it funny how sometimes all the lines in your life can suddenly converge and paint a picture of who you are?

There's nothing better for doing that than a trial.

All the little things I did in my life suddenly assume a huge significance. In wry moments, I wonder why I never volunteered to work in Africa or give generously to charity.

Charles Hanratty did both.

Peadar slides into the back of the courtroom and I feel a sudden grudging admiration for him. At least he hasn't hidden himself away in the victim support room. He's come alone too, without his daughter. That's got to be hard.

'The prosecution calls Peadar Smyth to the stand.'

There is a lot of shuffling as Peadar makes his way up the room. He has to push past quite a lot of people because they are jammed into the court like kids at a pop concert. My mother gives a loud sniff and Alan places a calming hand on her arm before fishing a large white hankie out of his pocket. She's crying, I notice, with shock. Why the hell is she crying? Alan wraps a hand about her shoulder, catches me looking and shakes his head as if suggesting that she'll be fine in a bit.

'Stop gawking at the court,' Melissa hisses to me. 'How many times? Look at the witness. Jesus.'

'My mother is crying.'

'She'll cry a lot harder if you're convicted.'

Heart of stone, but I do as she suggests. It's easier to look at Peadar than my mother anyway. Less upsetting.

Peadar is busy shifting about on the seat, adjusting his jacket and tie. He's not a man used to wearing suits. When we worked together, he wore a pair of brown trousers and a white shirt, rolled up to the elbows, every single day. He probably still does.

'State your name and address for the court,' Peter says.

'I'm Peadar Smyth.' Peadar's voice shakes with nerves and ridiculously I feel bad for him. 'I live in 42 Abberley Hall in Dublin.'

'And what is your relationship to the defendant?'

'Marcus Dillon used to work in a newsagent's I ran on behalf of Mr Hanratty. I managed it for Charles.' At the mention of Charles, Peadar's voice catches and I think, with something approaching wonder, that Peadar actually liked him.

I'd always thought it was because Hanratty was his boss, but obviously not.

Melissa had attempted to supress Peadar's testimony but the prosecution had argued that if she was going to call witnesses to attest to my good character then they were entitled to call someone who could attest to my volatility.

It was fair enough, unfortunately.

'And how long did you work there for?' Peter asks him.

'Close to twenty years. I gave it up when my wife died. I moved to Dublin then to be near my daughter.'

'And how long was Marcus Dillon working for you?'

'He started when he was sixteen. He left school, you see, and he needed a full-time job and so I asked Charles and Charles very kindly agreed. He worked for me for two years.'

'When you say "very kindly"?'

'Marcus Dillon's mother was an alcoholic. It was common knowledge that money was tight. Marcus needed to take a job to put food on the table for the both of them.'

I glance quickly at my mother. Peadar talking so casually about her failings makes me want to thump him. But her tears have stopped; Alan's tissue lies crumpled in her hand. She's looking straight at Peadar with her head held high and her chin up. Dignified. I get a lump in my throat so I turn away.

'How was Marcus as a worker?' Peter goes on.

'He was a good kid.' Peadar surprises me by looking directly at me. 'He was quiet, dedicated, did everything I asked. I was right fond of him, so I was.' Then he dips his head.

'And then what happened?'

'He became volatile, difficult to handle.'

'In what way?'

Peadar hesitates, then says, 'He grew very moody, he skipped work one or two days, he hit a boy that he saw his ex-girlfriend talking to, knocking him to the ground. I was the one who called the ambulance for him.'

'Was he provoked?'

'Not that I saw.'

'Anything else?'

'When I told him that Charles Hanratty had decided to let him go, he, eh,' again a quick glance at me, 'he destroyed the shop.'

'He destroyed the shop? How?'

'Broke the window, upended the till, poured minerals onto the floor, kicked a hole in the door, that kind of thing.'

'Did he say anything while he was destroying the shop?'

Peadar sighs. 'He did.'

'And what was that?'

'That one day he'd get Charles Hanratty back.'

Fuck.

'And did you, at any stage when you were working with him, suspect that he was capable of this?'

'Never.'

'He kept it well hidden?'

'That's leading,' Melissa says.

'I'll rephrase. Did you suspect that Marcus had a hidden side?'

'No. I was shocked. He always appeared like a nice quiet lad.'

'How did you feel when he left?'

'Relieved,' Peadar says, and I am ridiculously hurt. Then he adds, 'Frankly, I was a little scared of him by then.'

I bow my head. I can't look at him anymore.

Sash

It had been Paddy that Marcus had thumped that day. It was about a month after we'd broken into Hanratty's house and something weird had happened between Marcus and me as a result. I can't quite explain it, but it was like dry rot seeping into the cracks of our friendship. Whereas before we were solid, now I didn't want him near me. And he didn't get that. He kept calling up to me, he kept ringing me and every time I saw him he was a reminder of what we'd done, of what had happened. I was angry at him and I knew it was irrational. Nothing was his fault. I couldn't even bear to look at him. And yet, to tell him this would ruin things and so I kept silent and ruined it anyway.

Before that night, even when we were silent we were communicating. Now, even when we did talk, we danced around everything.

I started to avoid him rather than face the way he made me feel.

Instead, I began to hang around with Paddy, just happening to be about as he came out of his house on the way to school. He always had a slice of toast between his teeth. After a bit, he used to come out with three slices and hand one to me and one to Lana and we'd munch it on our way past Charles

Hanratty's house. In the evenings, instead of waiting for Marcus to finish up in the shop, I'd walk home with Paddy.

I did it so that I wouldn't have to walk past Charles Hanratty's house on my own.

I was so busy with all this self-preservation that it never occurred to me to wonder what Marcus was thinking about it all, but it must have bugged him because one Monday morning as Paddy and I walked past the shop, he stormed out of it and came after us. It was Peadar shouting for Marcus not to make a fool of himself that caused me and Paddy to turn around.

Marcus stood in front of us and I had never seen him look so furious. Fists clenched, his grey eyes narrowed, he said to me, 'You can't keep blanking me.'

Paddy grinned. 'It's a bit hard to blank you when you're standing in front of us.'

I shrieked as Marcus's fist flew out, catching Paddy under the chin, lifting him off his feet and sending him crashing to the ground. He hit the pavement with a crack.

'Christ, Marcus, look what you did.'

Marcus just stared at his hand as if he'd never seen it before.

Paddy made to sit up; he was chalk white.

Peadar hurried up and when he saw Paddy on the ground he hunkered down to him. 'Are you OK, son?'

I turned to Marcus. 'Are you all right?'

'Forget about him,' Peadar snapped at me, 'run in to the hotel and tell Brian his son is hurt and to get out here. And you,' he said to Marcus, 'get home.'

'I'm sorry,' Marcus said. 'Sorry, Paddy.'

Paddy, sitting up, waved him away.

Peadar ran into the shop to call an ambulance.

'Marcus?' I hated myself for driving him to this. 'Are you all right?'

He looked at me as if I'd just asked the most stupid thing ever. 'No,' he said. 'I am so far from it.'

Then he left.

I regret that I wasn't nicer to him. I regret that I wasn't braver. This court is painting Marcus as a bad boy: it was me who'd been the bad girl.

Marcus

If I ever get out of here, I'm going to create a cartoon for Melissa. She's like a mini superhero, in massively high heels, who flies in to save me when things look black. I wasn't sure how she could make me look good in front of the jury after they'd heard I'd put Paddy Jones in hospital and wrecked Hanratty's place. I can still remember the horror of knocking Paddy down, the fear that I'd killed him. And I wouldn't mind, but I liked Paddy.

Everyone did.

His dad had come roaring up the street and Peadar had to hold him back from planting me one. 'The lad's upset,' he kept saying. Then he told me to go. There'd been talk of a court case but it had been dropped. His auld lad had never even looked at me again.

Destroying the shop was different. I never regretted that. I needed to do it, if that makes sense. Hanratty, of course, played the magnanimous boss, letting me off, all the while laughing at me and at how powerless I really was.

Melissa is good at finding tiny details and making them much bigger. I like that. It just shows that you can use the facts to make a story stand out or not. And it just shows that even when you have the facts, it's not the story. I do that a lot when I write the comics.

'You say Marcus worked for you for two years?' Melissa asks Peadar.

'Yes.'

'Every day?'

'From nine to five Monday to Friday and a half day on Saturdays and bank holidays.'

'So, you felt you knew him well.'

'I did.'

'Did he talk about his mother?'

'Not in so many words, but we all knew.'

'Knew what exactly?'

'That she was an alcoholic.'

Poor Ma.

'Did you advise Marcus to get help for her, ask him how he was doing?'

'I didn't think it was my business.'

'Really? If you knew him so well?'

On the stand, Peadar goes red. 'I was his boss, we talked about the shop.'

'I see. So you didn't know him like, say, a good friend would.'

'No.'

'And yet you're here, telling us that he has this hidden side to his nature.'

'I never meant—'

Melissa consults her notes. '"Did you ever suspect Marcus had a hidden side?"' she reads. 'And your response was, "No, I was shocked, he seemed like a nice quiet lad."'

Peadar gives an audible gulp. 'I was shocked,' he states.

'Let's see if we can get to the root of this mysterious hidden side, shall we?' Melissa says pleasantly. 'Tell me about Marcus and his ex-girlfriend, Sash Donnelly.'

Peadar takes ages to answer. I reckon he thinks it's a trap and he's probably right.

'He liked her a lot,' Peadar says real slow. 'She used to come in to collects comics from us about once a week. Marcus was responsible for ordering them for her. Her favourite was *Superman* or something.'

'*Batman*,' I say, and people snigger. I ignore them. 'It was *Batman*.'

I see Sash smile. I don't think she knows she's doing it.

'That's right,' Peadar says. 'According to her, Batman was a real person with flaws and not a, I don't know –'

'A genetic anomaly,' I finish, real quiet. It's important to get it right.

'Who is giving testimony here?' the judge asks, though he sounds amused.

'A genetic anomaly,' Peadar agrees, and he smiles a bit. 'Anyway, she came in and ordered *Batman* and she was a right cheeky thing – her hair stuck out and she had these bright clothes and Marcus was stone mad about her. He always wanted to serve her, he'd keep her talking, he'd hang halfway out the window looking for her. I knew it'd end in tears. And that they'd be his.'

'So, Marcus was mad about her. Would you say he loved her?'

'Speculation,' Peter says in a bored voice.

'I'll rephrase. What would you say Marcus's feelings for Sash were?'

'I'd say, in his head, he loved her.'

I concentrate on looking straight ahead, as if it's all in the past.

'So Marcus was in love with Sash and it was over.' *Shut up, Melissa.*

'It appeared that way.'

'Did he talk to you about it?'

'No. But she never came into the shop anymore and she ignored him when she walked by.'

'Right. And in the meantime his mother was drinking. How do you know this? Did he tell you?'

'No.'

'So how do you know?'

'I liked a drink myself – in moderation, mind – and I would often be in the pub at night where his mother was drinking and at eleven Marcus would come in and haul her out.'

'Every night?'

'Every night I was there. She was very bad, quite aggressive.'

'I see. And did you ever mention this to him?'

'Like I said, it wasn't my business.'

'What age was Marcus during this time?'

'Almost eighteen.'

'Almost eighteen and he's lost his girlfriend that he was crazy about and he's responsible for his alcoholic mother and he doesn't ever talk about it to someone he spends most of his day with?'

Peadar shifts uncomfortably. 'No.'

'Was there any tension with Charles Hanratty at this time, between him and Marcus?'

'Not that I saw.'

'But you weren't that close to Marcus that he would tell you?'

'I don't know.'

'He didn't talk to you about personal things, did he?'

'No.'

'So you weren't close?'

'No. I suppose not.'

'So he would never tell you if there was friction between himself and Charles?'

'I can't see—'

'Why did Charles let him go?'

'He'd heard about the lad Marcus hit and he saw then that he'd taken a couple of days off.'

'No other reason?'

'Not that he told me.'

'Right. Getting back to his mother, how long was this situation with her going on?'

'Since he was a child.'

'A child.' Melissa pauses and lets it sink in. Then asks,

'Would you say that that is a lot of pressure for a young man?'

Peadar nods.

'Speak up, please.'

'Yes, I would.'

'So, is it possible that Marcus's sudden rage was not some hidden side but just pressure building inside a young man who couldn't handle it?'

'I suppose so, yes.'

'Tell me, did Marcus ever apologise for what happened in the shop?'

Peadar eyeballs me. 'Years later. He came to my wife's funeral and shook my hand. And we were square.'

'No more questions.'

I watch as Peadar gets down from the stand. Peter watches him too.

Melissa joins me back at the table. 'I think my esteemed colleague just scored a bit of an own goal, with my help of course.' A nudge. 'You can smile, Marcus. It's good.'

I hope it'll be good tomorrow. I'll be up on the stand.

I'm not going to think about it.

DAY 5

Marcus

I watch Melissa as she pulls out pens and folders and coloured sticky things. For such a ball-breaker, she's really kiddish about her stationery. In her office she has a diary with a pink horse on the cover. It makes me feel that she's a bit human.

I haven't been able to eat all morning and I'm wrecked because I couldn't sleep last night. My head feels panicked, my thoughts spinning in and out, not even making sense to me. Melissa has told me to speak slowly, to always be in control of what I'm saying, but I'm so on edge it'll be hard. All those faces staring up at me like I'm some kind of freak show.

Josh arrives in and he's carrying a cappuccino for me and one for Melissa. 'To wake you up,' he says to me. 'Betcha didn't sleep much last night.'

'Hardly at all.' I take a sip of coffee and my stomach rolls.

Josh twists the cap off his Coke and drinks deeply.

'Any plans for the weekend?' he asks.

I tell myself that we could be anywhere, talking about anything.

'Yeah,' I say, trying to embrace the subject, 'I'm hoping to meet up with Dessie, my mate from Applegate, after court finishes today.' It'll be great, just doing something normal.

'That's your character witness?'

'Yep. We'll probably go for a pint or something.'

'Have you a local?'

'I stick to Dublin. A quiet place called The Inn. Do you know it?'

'Great place,' Josh says. 'They have bands on there during the week and the manager is a headcase. We represented him on an assault charge last year – d'you remember, Melissa? He decked one of his customers for dealing in the pub?'

Melissa nods. 'Yes. One of life's gentlemen.'

I think she's being sarcastic. It's lost on Josh.

'He's a great man,' Josh agrees. 'Every time I go in now, I get a free pint. Best Guinness in town.'

'The Guinness is pretty good,' I say.

Josh sits on the edge of the desk and Melissa tells him that he better not sit on her notes.

'You going anywhere the weekend?' he asks her by way of reply.

'No, and even if I was, it's not your business.'

'Ouch!' Josh snorts.

The crowd trickles in. My mother and Alan arrive, having had a coffee in the coffee shop. They do it every morning for luck.

No, I don't get it either.

I rarely join them, preferring to hide away in here.

'Hello, Mel,' Alan says as they take their seats. 'You're doing a fantastic job—'

'Thanks,' she says.

'—walking in those high heels every day.'

Josh guffaws and Melissa grins.

'They keep me on my toes,' she answers back with a rare burst of humour.

Just before court starts, Melissa runs over how I should deal with being on the stand. 'It's good for you to go on it,' she says. 'you've made the right choice. Giving evidence makes you look innocent, but we don't want you on for too long in case you get time to fuck it up. Basically, you're there to refute all the evidence against you.'

'I can't refute the fingerprints on the photo frame,' I say.

'We'll fudge that,' she says back. I watch as she scrabbles through her notes and jots down questions. Then she glances up at me, pushing a strand of hair from her face. She looks impossibly young all of a sudden. When she smiles a bit her teeth show white.

'You got your braces off.' I grin. 'I've only just noticed.'

'I had them off yesterday,' she says.

'They look good.'

She dips her head. 'Just be brief with your answers when Peter asks the questions, OK? The shorter the better.'

'I know.' I take a risk and touch her arm. 'You've done good so far.'

'Not good enough,' she says vehemently. Then softer, 'I defend people, Marcus. I don't care if they're guilty or innocent: it's my job to get them off. And I win more than I lose. But what kills me is if I lose a case where I know the defendant is innocent. That stinks.'

'You know I'm innocent?' I feel like laughing for a crazy second.

'Yes.' She looks into my face. 'So get up there and give them hell.'

'Will do.'

'Atta boy.' She winks and turns back to her notes.

Sash

Marcus takes the oath and he looks so alone up there. I'll probably look the same when it's my turn. A sudden dart of panic grips me. I can't believe that I'll be doing this. I want to run away as far as I can.

'He looks good,' Dad says as Marcus states his name for the court.

I can't reply; my mouth is suddenly dry.

'Marcus,' Melissa begins, 'did you kill Charles Hanratty on the night of March first, eighteen months ago?'

'No,' Marcus says.

'Were you stalking him?'

'Yes.'

'Can you tell the court why?'

'Because I needed to keep an eye on him.' He flicks a glance in my direction and I lower my gaze. 'I didn't want what had happened to me and Sash to happen to anyone else. And I guess I was mad at him for what he had done to us.'

'In your initial statement to the guards, when they asked you why you had stalked Charles Hanratty, you told them that you had been a victim of assault at the hands of this man.'

A slow murmuring starts up in the court. Dad takes my hand and grips it.

'Yes,' Marcus says.

'Quiet, please,' the judge calls. 'Can you repeat your answer,' the judge asks Marcus when the noise has abated.

'I said, yes, the man assaulted me,' Marcus says.

'There was no mention of Sash being there.'

'She didn't want to get involved – you heard the texts – and I wanted to protect her, so I didn't mention her in my statement.'

'But later you changed your statement?'

'Yes, because Sash said she would testify and it meant that there were two of us saying the same thing about this man.'

'So, would you be protective of Sash?'

A pause and, once again, he catches my eye. Without looking away, he says, 'I failed to protect her once and I figured it had to be her decision to speak out.'

'OK. Can you describe to the court what you did do the night of the murder?'

'Sure. I worked until seven thirty. I'm a cartoonist and I had a commission and it needed to be filed by the next day.'

'Did you email this to your employer at seven thirty?'

'Yes. After that, I drove out to Charles Hanratty's house and parked up the road from it. At some time after eight, I got out of my car and went up Charles Hanratty's driveway. I rang his bell and, when there was no answer, I posted an envelope containing the images the court saw into his house, through the letterbox.'

'Did you hear any sounds from the house because we know that Charles Hanratty was murdered by someone around that time?'

'I didn't spend that long at the door. I just posted in the envelope.'

'How would you explain these cartoons being scattered over the victim's body?'

'I would say the killer did it. Why would I do it if I didn't want to be caught?'

'Then what happened?'

'I walked down the driveway back to my car. Then I met Charles's neighbour, who asked me if I was OK.'

'He stated that you had your head in your hands – why was this?'

'I knew that by posting in those cartoons, I had crossed a line. The minute I did it, I wanted to take it back, but I couldn't.'

'And then what?'

'I drove home. The first I knew of Charles Hanratty being murdered was on the radio the next day.'

'So you admit you stalked Mr Hanratty, your fingerprints

were on the envelope you posted in and that you were in the area the time he was murdered?'

'Yes.'

'Why did you ring his bell that night?'

'I wanted to scare him. He'd taken to jumping every time he saw me about.'

'Did you like scaring him?'

'Yes.' He looks ashamed but I get it. I wish I'd seen Hanratty scared.

'You admit you disliked Hanratty but that you didn't kill him.'

'I hated Hanratty but I didn't kill him.'

'No further questions.'

Melissa sits down and Marcus braces himself for the cross.

Marcus

This is where I'll sink or swim. I know it like I know the best cover-art editions of *Batman*. Peter walks towards me all shiny-toothed and sharp-suited. I feel as if I'm poised on the edge of a cliff. One tiny push and he'll make me fall over. It's going to be hard to brace myself against it. I wonder if many innocent men have sat in the witness box and mentally pleaded with twelve strangers to see the truth of their claims.

'Lets us rewind, Marcus,' Peter says conversationally. 'You say you stalked Charles Hanratty to stop him doing to others what he allegedly did to you and your girlfriend Sash one night fifteen years ago?'

'Yes.'

'He assaulted you both?'

'Yes.'

'Your statement is a bit vague on the details of this alleged assault.'

'Is that a question?' Melissa asks.

'Why is your statement so vague on the details of this assault?'

I stare at a point over his head. 'Because I was ashamed of it.'

'Ashamed you were assaulted?'

'Yes.'

'And not just vague because nothing happened?'

'It happened.' My voice catches.

'And this was a serious assault?'

'Yes.'

'Would you say very serious?'

'It was bad.'

'It made you angry.'

'Yes.'

'But you never told anyone.'

'No.'

'Even though it was bad.'

'Yes.'

'And so you say you stalked him.'

'Yes.'

'Because you wanted to protect Sash?'

'Yes.'

'But you never reported this man when you could have.'

'Sash didn't want to.'

'Did you always do what Sash said?'

'Pretty much.' I had adored her.

'Because you loved her?'

'Probably.' I die a bit inside.

'And yet when you rang her up asking her to tell her partner about Charles Hanratty, and she told you to leave her alone, you refused.'

'That was years later.'

'I see. But years later you still wanted to protect her.'

'Yes.'

'There was no mention of Sash in your statement to the police when you were arrested, was there?'

'No, I already—'

'Oh yes, you were waiting for her to come around to the idea of testifying.'

'Yes.'

'So you lied in your first statement?'

'It wasn't a lie.'

'You omitted the full truth – is that what you're saying?'

'Yes.'

'To protect Sash?'

'Yes.'

'At your own expense?'

'Yes.'

'You omitted the truth, which meant you had no witness to your statement, in order to protect a girl you hadn't seen in years.'

'Yes.'

'Tell me, what was your real grudge against Charles Hanratty? One that's not quite so dramatic?'

Wrong-footed, I flinch. 'Sorry?'

'It's not about an alleged assault, is it?'

I realise, in horror, that he's trying to make out I'm lying about everything. Melissa had thought he'd turn my defence against me and use it to prove I had murdered Hanratty, which might have meant a manslaughter charge, but he wants me on murder. He's trying to negate what Sash might say by ruining it now.

I feel a chill creep up my spine.

'You told the police Charles Hanratty had assaulted you and that was why you stalked him, isn't that right?'

'Yes.'

'Did Charles Hanratty fire your mother from her job in the hotel?'

'There is no relevance to that question,' Melissa snaps.

'There will be,' Peter promises. He turns to me. 'Well, did Charles Hanratty fire your mother from her hotel job?'

'Yes.'

'And he fired you?'

'Yes.'

'So, is it not more accurate to say that Charles Hanratty fired both you and your mother from jobs in the same week and that's why you stalked and murdered him.'

'No. That's ridiculous.'

'Did he not fire you from jobs?'

'He did, but—'

'Did you not tell your employer that you'd get him one day?'

'I did, but—'

'Did you destroy his shop?'

I feel defeat coming over me like a cloak. 'Yes, I did.'

'And after the loss of your income and your mother's income, you both lost your house?'

'Yes.'

'And you both had to leave town and go live in a council house in Dublin, isn't that right?'

'Yes.'

'And did that make you angry?'

'Yes.'

'So you stalked Charles Hanratty.'

'No.'

'You didn't stalk him?'

'I did, but—'

'You drew cartoons with Charles Hanratty's face, did you not?'

'Yes, but—'

'And Slam Man, the character you invented, killed this character each episode, did he not?'

'Yes, but—'

'And you gave these pictures to Charles Hanratty?'

'Yes. And I said that I regretted it.'

'But you agree you drew him being murdered?'

'A drawing is a different thing.'

'Did you ever wish he was dead?'

'No. Being dead was too good for him. I wanted to bring him to justice.'

'You had fifteen years to bring him to justice if you're telling the truth.'

'I know.'

'During that fifteen years, you never made an attempt to report this incident?'

'No.'

'Tell anyone?'

'No.'

'No,' he repeats flatly. 'But you admit that you stalked him.'

'Yes.'

'Did you send him abusive texts?'

'Yes.'

'Did you send him unsolicited emails?'

'Yes.'

'You admit that you harassed him?'

'Yes.'

'To keep an eye on him?'

'Yes.'

'How is this keeping an eye on him?'

'It – well …' I shrug, heaving a sigh, 'it got out of control.'

And by the time I realise what I've said, it's too late. I'm not sure there would have been any other way to answer that question though.

'You lost control?'

'I didn't murder him.'

'But you just said your stalking got out of control.'

'Yes.'

He lets a pause develop and I hang my head.

'You also said in your statement that you were never in Charles Hanratty's house.'

'I said that, yes.'

'And yet your fingerprints were found on a photograph frame there.'

'Yes.'

'So, you were never in the house and yet your fingerprints were. A hair was also found with your DNA.'

'Is this a question?' Melissa asks.

'No more questions,' Peter says.

He walks away from me and I feel hollowed out.

The judge asks Melissa if she'd like to redirect.

'Marcus, for the benefit of the jury, can you tell them again why you first contacted Sash after not seeing her in years.'

'I contacted her to tell her to get Charles Hanratty out of her life because she was being forced to be in his company and I told her to tell Paddy, her partner.'

'And this was before Charles was murdered and you needed an alibi?'

'Over a year beforehand.'

'Thank you.'

The judge tells me that I can step down now.

I know I've made a mess of it.

The judge asks for a break for the weekend and Melissa and Peter agree.

I feel sick.

WEEKEND

Sash

Applegate. I want to duck down in the car as Dad drives up
the main street. I shouldn't have come back while the trial
was going on. Since people found out I was giving evidence
against Hanratty, coming home at the weekends has been a
stress. Some people are openly rude to me; others just ignore
me. It's always a relief to head back to my tiny apartment in
Wicklow town on a Sunday evening. I don't know how Dad
stays in Applegate now, what with all that's happened, but
he's stubborn, like me. He says why should he move when
he isn't the one in the wrong. And because of this, I feel I
have to acknowledge his courage in some way, so here I am,
sitting up straight in the car and back for the weekend.

As I gaze out the window, I think that Applegate will probably stay the same for centuries to come. Its main street will be small and narrow, its shops kind of quirky with their old-style interiors, the hotel will continue to dominate the left-hand side of the main street and attract visitors. I hope the people will change. I hope they won't ransom their souls to another rich businessman.

As he drives down the street, my dad waves at a few people. They go to wave back, then realise who it is and stare right through him. He pretends not to notice so I say nothing either. Once I take the stand, things will get worse for him and Mona. No one believes me here. Or maybe they are afraid to, because what does it say about them at the end of the day? That in their tiny town, they had a snake like Hanratty who didn't even need to force them to take a bite of the poisoned apple. They did it willingly. To them, Charles Hanratty was a saint. And in some ways he was. He did give jobs, he did keep people from having to leave their families in search of work, he did offer cheap housing when people couldn't pay. But it came at a price. Even now, with their blindness, they are paying it.

When dad drives by the orchard, I ask him to let me out.

'For old times' sake.' I haven't walked the orchard in a long time.

'You sure you're OK?'

'I'm not going to hang myself from a tree.'

'That's not—' He stops, because we both know that is exactly what he was thinking. 'Good,' he says instead.

I hop out and wave him off, then stand right on the edge

of the orchard and stare across the road at Hanratty's house. This is where we stood that night. Me and Marcus, hand in hand. I think of Marcus today, stepping off the stand. I'd wanted to run up and embrace him, tell him thanks for looking out for me. Instead, he'd walked straight out of the courtroom. I'd seen him a little while later, with his mother and Alan in a coffee shop downtown. The three of them had looked shell-shocked. He'd blown things a bit by admitting the stalking had got out of control.

I remember us as we were that night, impossibly young. Marcus's smile slowly spreading across his face before we both turned to stare at the house.

It has changed so much since then. It was sold and done up some years ago. The new owner rents it out to summer visitors. All through the years, it was the house I remembered most clearly. Sometimes, I think I'd like to go back into it, to see those rooms again. In my mind, they have taken on nightmare qualities, and maybe by seeing them, they'll lose their power to haunt me.

Without further thought, I dash across the road and up the driveway.

The window we slithered through is new. It's a cream sash Weatherglaze. The pebbledash walls have been sprayed cream to match the windows and, despite the garden being a little overgrown, someone has planted flowers. From the outside at least, it's bright and cheerful and a million miles away from the cottage we broke into.

I knock on the door, preparing to invent some excuse if someone answers, but no one does. It's empty. Steeling myself, I peer in the downstairs window. With the glare from the late summer sun, it's hard to see properly, but from what I can make out, the whole downstairs has been opened up. All the walls have been knocked so the room is now one big kitchen diner. Through an open doorway, I see that the dark wooden hall stairs has been replaced with a lighter one. Curious now, feeling braver, I pick my way around the back.

There is a floor-to-ceiling sliding door in the kitchen which leads out to where I'm now standing, a grey paved patio. There are some chairs and tables covered over by a canopy. Weeds are pushing up through the slabs, but the grass looks as if it has been cut in the last couple of weeks. I look in the kitchen window and inhale sharply at the change. Instead of dirty cream presses and a chipped Formica worktop, it's all been replaced with a state-of-the art oak kitchen.

It's hard to believe that anything awful happened to me here.

It's like it happened in another life.

Maybe one day I'll be able to walk the rooms.

'Hello?'

The male voice makes me jump. Whirling around, I come face to face with the local auctioneer, Tommy. 'Hiya.' I grin at him.

He shows no sign of recognition. 'You're trespassing on private property,' he says haughtily. 'Now if you don't mind, I've a client to show around this place.' He moves to allow me to pass.

Tommy was a year behind me in school. He was on the athletics team. We used to sneak vodka into the sports drinks. I'd liked him.

'It's me, Sash? You can cut the scary act.'

'I know who you are,' he says, and the way he says it makes me flinch.

'If that's how it's to be,' I say, 'you can show *me* around this cottage as well.'

'I wouldn't have thought this was somewhere you'd want to see, unless of course the rumours are wrong.'

I keep my voice even. 'I want to see it.'

'You'll have to make a booking.'

'I'm making a booking now.'

'What is the hold up?' a woman with an American accent calls out. 'Can I see this place or not?'

'Of course, Miss Kennedy.' Tommy drags a pile of keys from his pocket. 'You,' he says to me, 'go.' I watch him scurry around to the front of the house before I follow.

'Hi,' I say to the American, who's standing impatiently in front of the door, glancing at her watch, 'would you mind if I gate-crashed your tour? I'd like to see this house too.'

'Sure, honey, no problem.'

'I said you have to make an appointment.' Tommy doesn't look at me as he inserts the key in the lock.

'She's my daughter,' the American woman says. 'Let's get going.'

I laugh, though it hurts.

Tommy's face hardens, but he says nothing as he pushes open the door. The American woman enters and Tommy follows her, leaving me on the doorstep. I see her open the door to the living room.

And I'm back there. The dark room, the pictures, the smell of dirt. The hall lengthens and narrows and lengthens. I hear Marcus and me laughing, laughing and dancing and kissing.

And I run.

I thought I could do it, but I can't.

The orchard is cool, the way it always is. No light really gets in under the thick branches, which twist and entwine. The quiet calms me, the smell, so familiar, soothes me.

I'm in the centre, beside our tree where our carved initials still remain. I touch the rough bark, wanting so hard to peel back time and step inside and return to that day fifteen years ago and make it right. Me and Marcus, we belonged together. I trace our initials, remembering his soft laughter as he did it. The extravagant 'M' and the sexy 'S'. I'd given out to him for doing it, but Marcus had said that the tree would be fine, save for a scar to say we were there.

I slide into a sitting position. The apples on the ground beside me are tiny marbles. Not like the generous ones that grew when we were young.

I wonder if this place needs to be replanted, given some new trees to replace the ones that have been here for a century. Or maybe it's just a case of judicious pruning.

I pick up an apple and study it. It's mean and shrivelled. Wiping it on my sweatshirt, I bite into it, but it's too bitter and I throw it away. Are all the apples like that now, I wonder?

Has Marcus ever come back here?

I cross right through the orchard to the other side, near the stream, where Marcus lived. It's been done up too. Has he ever wanted to have a look at what has become of his old house? Though it wasn't his – it was owned by Hanratty, like everything else in this place. I don't go too close because it's obviously lived in. Some children's toys are scattered about the garden. The front door is wide open and, as I watch, a woman and a child come out. The woman raises her hand in a wave, obviously not knowing who I am, and I wave back.

Maybe in time, I think, new people will come to Applegate and change the way people see things.

Marcus

I'm outside The Inn, waiting on Dessie to show up. I've left my ma and Alan brooding in a coffee shop and headed straight here. I'm going to get wasted. I'm going to forget about my shit life just for one night. I'm still wearing my suit but if it gets wrecked, I don't care. I've got a pile of cash in the bank so buying a suit is no problem. A pile of cash and limited freedom.

It's nice to be out, to feel part of life again, but I only hope no one glances at me too hard. I pull a packet of cigarettes from the side pocket of my jacket and stare at them. I'd given up smoking three years ago but in the last month some of the old cravings started creeping up on me. I'd bought the cigarettes yesterday but didn't buy a lighter, in the hope that it would stop me. No chance. I ask a girl in the doorway for a light. She asks me for a cigarette and we smoke away in contented silence for a bit.

'You from Dublin?' she asks.

'Mostly. Living here fifteen years now.'

'You sound like you're from the country.'

'So do you.'

She tells me she's from Cavan and that I shouldn't make jokes about mean Cavan people because the only ones who find those funny are Dublin people. Most Cavan people are not mean. I assure her that I have no prejudice one way or the other.

She's glad about that.

I wouldn't like to see her if she wasn't.

Finished smoking, she flicks the cigarette onto the ground and grinds it out. 'Would you have another one for later?' she asks.

I pop open the packet and she takes two. 'One for luck,' she says before disappearing inside.

I grin and take a last drag on my cigarette, enjoying the smoke filling up my lungs. It's like yoga only with toxins.

'Are you back smoking again?' Dessie hollers from down the street. People jump.

I laugh and we do a back-slapping thing and he catches me in a headlock and I try to trip him up and we're good.

It's nice to feel normal.

The inside of the pub is dark and half-empty. It's why I always liked it. The seats are tattered and the wood has been marked from years of heavy use and neglect. I suppose it's a rough enough place, but I was always drawn to hard edges.

Bert, the barman, greets me like an old friend.

'Haven't seen you here in a while,' he says as he pulls two pints of Guinness for us.

'I've been busy.'

'How's the murder trial going?' he asks.

Dessie splutters out a laugh and my face flames red.

'You know about that?'

'The whole country knows about that,' Bert says. 'So what's the story? Have they let you out?'

'It's still going on and—'

'Objection!' he shouts out, then chortles with laughter.

'How much?' I ignore him and thumb to the drinks.

'Overruled.'

I lay my cash on the bar.

'No.' Bert pushes it back at me. 'In all seriousness, no charge. On the house. Just, you know, the best of luck with all that murder stuff.'

It's always the people you don't expect.

I have to bite my lip and swallow hard. 'Ta.'

We take our drinks down to an alcove and sit together in silence for a bit, just enjoying the stout. It really is the best in Dublin.

'How is it going?' Dessie asks me after a while. 'Is this Melissa one the hotshot that you thought?'

'She seems to be doing well. She's a bit scary, though. Thanks for doing this for me.'

'You did a lot for me.'

We clink glasses and sit for another while, not talking.

'It went a bit shit today, though,' I say.

'I heard it on the radio,' Dessie admits.

I laugh, only I'm not really laughing.

'How's your ma coping?'

I think about yesterday and how rough it must have been for her to hear Peadar talking about her like that. She'd been a good mother when she was on the wagon. I'd loved, as a kid, when she'd take me out of school so we could go on picnics. Looking back, I reckon she sensed that sooner or later she'd lose me to social services again and she wanted to spend as much time with me as possible. And in the end, she'd given up the drink because of me. I still cringe at the memory. I'd broken down one night and told her that I couldn't do it anymore. Apparently, me crying had been her rock bottom.

'She's doing better than I thought,' I finally answer Dessie's question. Then add, 'It's weird, though – when I left her this evening, she told me to stay safe and I got annoyed.' At his look, I explain, 'I still can't take her seriously trying to be my mother after years of neglect.'

Dessie laughs a bit.

Then I tell him about the other day when she admired my drawings and he laughs louder. It's probably because I do a great take-off of her.

'Still,' he says, 'at least she's trying.'

'Very trying,' I mutter.

He grins, then says, 'Don't be so cold.'

'Ahh, I'm not really. It's just, people going all mushy on me creeps me out.'

Dessie nods. 'Yeah, I heard that.'

I look at him. I get the feeling he's itching to say something. 'What?'

'That's exactly what Lauren said about you.'

'Nooo,' I groan. 'Just don't. Don't go there.'

Dessie and Lauren had got on like a house on fire. I think he was more disappointed when it was over than I was.

'What happened between yez?' Dessie asks.

'I'm sure she told you, you two being so cosy and all.'

'She messaged me on Facebook at the time,' Dessie said casually. 'She said that you were an asshole, so it wasn't exactly full of detail.'

'I *was* an asshole.'

'What did you do?'

'I just stopped talking to her. I stopped taking her calls.'

Dessie sits back and regards me. 'That's shitty.'

'I know, so can we just leave it.' I'd done it because I knew I was doomed. I knew stalking Hanratty was wrong and I did not need her to talk me out of it. So instead, I dumped her.

'If you weren't interested—'

'I was, but,' I drink some more, 'I wasn't, OK.'

'Sash is a long time ago,' Dessie says. 'Jesus, you were a kid and—'

'It wasn't about Sash,' I say quickly. He looks sceptical so I add, 'It was a mess, I was a mess. I was stalking Hanratty at the time.'

He dips his head. I know the thoughts of me doing stuff like that makes him uncomfortable.

'What about you?' I change the subject. 'Is Mammy June still the only woman in your life?'

'Lauren Facebooked me this week. She wondered if you'd like her at the trial.' He holds his hands up in a gesture of surrender. 'I said I'd ask.'

I heave out a sigh. 'That was nice.'

'She *is* nice.'

I know that. She'd been better than I deserved. I'm not sure I want her at the trial. I haven't seen her since we broke up, though when I was charged with the murder, she texted me to say she was there if I needed her, but I never replied. How could I have? Instead, I sent a card on her birthday this year. I'd done it just to let her know that she'd mattered to me. That I was sorry. Dessie is looking at me, expecting an answer. 'Tell her it'd be good to see her,' I say, not totally convinced.

'Will do.'

More silence, but with Dessie that's grand. Our friendship is more about silence than anything else.

'Have you seen Sash?' Dessie asks.

'Nah, not really. Have you?'

'My ma talks to Mona, Sash's stepmother-to-be or whatever.' Dessie makes a face. 'She says Sash is holding up well.'

'Good.' How did I get into this horror show, I wonder bleakly.

'It must be weird being on trial,' Dessie says after a bit.

'Nah, it's not weird at all. I'm fucking loving it.'

He snorts out a laugh.

'It *is* weird,' I concede. 'Like my whole life is up there for everyone to pick over. And they choose the bits that suit their side of the story.'

Dessie nods. 'It must be extra horrific for you seeing as you are the most reclusive person in the whole fucking world.'

'You know everyone in the whole fucking world?'

'Yeah, as a matter of fact.'

I laugh a bit. Then stop. Then drink some more great Guinness. 'I didn't do it,' I tell him, like I've told him before. 'I don't know who did, but it wasn't me.'

'I know that.' He sounds like he does.

'And how's things for you in Applegate?' At his look, I add, 'Testifying in my defence.'

He shrugs. 'You know Applegate – it's Hanratty's town.'

His answer tells me everything I need to know about how good of a mate he is. 'Fuck,' I say.

Dessie nods. Then asks, 'Do you fancy getting totally pissed?'

Lana

Dad said he would be home with Sash by nine o'clock at the latest, but it's eight thirty, which is thirty minutes earlier than he said he would be. When Mona hears his car pulling up in the driveway, she pulls off her apron and fixes her hair. She doesn't need to bother because it'll just be awful anyway. It's a mixture of blonde and grey and it looks like wire. I haven't ever touched it. It sticks out all over the place too. Mona says she wants to go grey and that's why her hair is a mess. Maybe it's true.

My mother's hair was brown and shiny and sort of curly. I felt it one time and I curled my fingers in it and I liked it so much I wanted it and tried to pull it from her head and she screamed and I got scared and then I couldn't let it go at all. And anyway, I never touched people's hair again but I wouldn't want to touch Mona's. If wives were cars, Mona would not be a good replacement for my mother because she would not match the space my mother left. My mother looked like me, my dad says. I'm small and dark and have a very white face with brown eyes. Marcus told Sash once that I gave him the creeps. I wasn't supposed to hear but I did. I'm not sure if my mother gave anyone the creeps – maybe she did too. Anyway, Mona is not small or dark. She is big and round and wears dresses that look like she made them herself. But the thing about her is that she laughs and that whenever she sees Dad or me or Sash, she opens her arms wide and there is loads of space inside them, because she is a very big woman who probably weighs about as much as four apple trees and their roots.

'There you are,' she says as Dad gets out of the car. Then her muddy-colour eyes crease up in a smile and all the lines on her face appear. Mona is quite ugly really but it's not something you notice. You can only see it when you look at the details instead of the whole picture. 'Where's Sash?'

'Gone off looking at apple trees.' Dad shrugs. 'I didn't ask.'

I can't believe that she'd want to look at apple trees and not come home. That's rude.

'How's my girl?' Dad says to me and I allow him to hug me.

Mona's hugs are nicer than Dad's. I don't like his hugs so

much – they feel too close. Like he wants me to hug him back. I don't do that.

When Dad lets me go, Mona asks, 'And what has she to look at in an orchard?'

We all follow Mona into the house.

'She can look at the trees,' I say. 'She can see if they have proper drainage and sunlight, which those trees don't because of the way they need pruning. She can look—'

'Are you starving?' Mona talks over me, which is rude.

'That's rude to talk over someone.'

Then she pretends that she hasn't heard me. She does that a lot. Instead she moves to the cooker where the horrible stew she cooked yesterday is. She has made loads of it.

'I only want a bit of your stew because I don't like it.'

'You're having something to eat, whether you like it or not.'

'Not,' I say.

'Lana,' Dad warns. 'Mona has cooked you dinner so it's nice to make an attempt at it.'

'Is it?'

'Yes.'

'OK.'

'Good girl. Now go upstairs and wash your hands.'

I always wash my hands. Three times before dinner. Then I dry them really well. And I always wash them in the bathroom.

I know that when I am gone they will want to talk about the case because they always do when I leave the room. I'm part of the case so I don't know why the big secret. When

Mona and Dad have finished talking about the case, they will switch on the TV and they will watch quiz shows.

I am going to Daly's with Sash tonight. I haven't been out in three weeks and six days and only then with Mona and Dad. That's not cool.

I wash my hands and am at the fifth step from the top, which is the ninth step from the bottom, when I think that Mona and my dad are not talking about the case because if they were their voices would be loud and not sort of whispering so that I can't hear. When people don't want you to hear something, it generally means that it's something you should hear.

Very quiet, because I'm good at that, I go up on my toes and creep down the stairs. I put my ear to the door, like they do in movies, but it doesn't make it easier to hear. They are whispering really low, but Dad says, 'I'm not sure if it'll do any good, it might just make her more determined.'

'She's your daughter,' Mona says, and I hear her pouring her horrible stew into bowls. 'You know her better than I do – I'm just telling you what she said.' She stops then.

Is this about me?

'I'll say it to her,' says Dad.

'Lana!' Mona calls. 'Dinner.'

I push open the door and they look at me. Too late I realise that they knew I wasn't upstairs.

'Did you hear what we said?' Dad asks.

'Yes.' I watch as Mona puts the bowl of stew in front of me. 'Eat up,' she says. 'It's brown so you'll like it. See, a real dark brown.'

It's also a bit thick, which I don't like. I poke at it with my spoon. 'What daughter were you talking about?' I hope it's me.

'Sash. Now eat up.'

It's always Sash. 'What about her? Who said something about her?'

'Nobody. Eat up.'

'How can nobody say something?' Then I ask, 'Is that a lie?'

'When Sash comes in we'll tell her and you'll know then.'

'This is too dark a brown.'

Mona pours milk on top of it and swirls it about. 'Now.'

It looks OK. It's not even thick. I taste some and it's milky.

I do my best to eat it anyway.

Sash comes back, sadly for her, in time to get some stew. If she had left it ten minutes later, Dad would have eaten it all because he was taking a ladleful approximately every three hundred seconds and he took four ladles and there were about two ladles left and then Mona took one. Luckily, Sash only has to eat one ladle.

Mona hugs her and makes her sit down and puts a bowl in front of her.

'Thanks, Mona.' Sash smiles. 'Any news from here?'

'No,' Mona says.

'Yes,' I say.

'Not now, not for the table,' Dad says, real quick.

'You told me you'd tell her when she came in.'

'I know, but—'

'What's this?' Sash helps herself to stew.

'Stew,' I say. 'It's rotten.'

'Thank you, Miss.' Mona is annoyed because she called me Miss.

'I mean, what's this news?' Sash says. She has no problem eating the stew.

Dad looks at Mona, who looks at Dad. I think they've forgotten.

'Something about if they tell you it'll make you more determined but that you're Dad's daughter.'

'Quite the listener,' Mona says. I think she's impressed.

Sash looks at Dad. 'Spill.'

Dad shoots me a cross look and I think, too late, I've made some kind of mistake again. I'm much better when it's just me and one other person, not when it's a crowd. There's too many people to concentrate on then. 'Mona was saying that the feeling in the town is quite high with this case going on.'

'Tell me about it,' Sash says, spooning stew into her mouth like she likes it, then scraping the bowl to lick up the end bits. 'Tommy Foster was a right little shit when I ran into him.'

'Yes, and Mona was talking to June Daly and June was saying it might be best to keep a low profile for a bit.'

'Ehh,' Sash screws up her face, which means she's thinking, 'no,' she says.

I'm not sure what a low profile is. Something to do with tyres.

'She just thought,' Mona says, leaning across the table to Sash, 'that for your own sake—'

'I'm going out,' Sash says. 'That's final.'

We do go out. Dad and Mona come too, which is not good. I thought it would just be me and Sash and that we could sit in the pub with all the people who know us. When we get there, it's two minutes and seven seconds past ten and it's busy. People turn to look at us as we walk in. Music is playing. I see Brian Jones up at the bar and he's talking to Margaret Browne and her husband, I forget his name, and Josie Millar from the sweet shop and the horrible woman who runs the newsagent's now and Naomi who Sash worked for in the nail bar in Applegate but who let Sash go because business was down. I like Naomi. I haven't seen her in ages and she always used to pluck my eyebrows for me for free and, though it hurt, she used to tell me that it would improve my face, because eyebrows are like the frame on a picture only not square. She hasn't offered to pluck them in ages – maybe if we sit beside her she will.

'Hi, Naomi,' I call to her. She's sitting with the new girl who works in the salon now. Business picked up real quick after Sash left for Wicklow, Mona told me. It was just bad timing.

Naomi looks over at me and smiles.

'Here looks like a good spot.' Dad finds a seat ages away from everyone.

'I want to sit here.' Sash picks a seat near everyone else, which would be my choice too.

'Here, Sash,' Dad says.

'No,' Sash says, and she's being really cross with Dad now. She hadn't wanted him and Mona to come either. Like, who goes out with their parent and their parent's new partner when they are our age?

'Folks,' June bustles down to us as we sit where Sash wants, 'can I get you drinks?' She's in a really good mood because she's smiling loads.

'Sash didn't want to do the low-profile thing,' I say.

'I can see that.' June grins bigger. Then her face changes. 'How are you holding up, pet?' She asks Sash this.

'I'm OK.' A sigh. 'Look, June, I appreciate your concern earlier but I have to do this.'

'I know.' She nods. In an undertone, she adds, 'Dessie went up today for Marcus.'

'Has all this affected business?' Sash asks.

'Some.' June smiles a bit.

Probably because Dessie isn't there to pour the pints.

'But,' June adds, 'we're the best pub in town and, at the end of the day, people don't want to travel too far for their pint.'

'It's busy enough tonight all the same,' Dad says, looking about.

'The music brings them in,' June answers. 'Now, what can I get you?'

'A peg for her big mouth.' Margaret Browne, surprise, has come over to our table on her way out of the pub.

Sash claps. 'Hilarious,' she says.

'Now, ladies,' June says.

'Making a show of the town.' Margaret's voice is real loud and high – it hurts my ears.

'I think you manage that all by yourself,' Sash says back. 'Those tan lines on your leg look a bit patchy. Like you've started to moult.'

I laugh because it's funny. And true.

'Shut up, you, you weirdo,' Margaret says to me.

That is very rude. First to say 'shut up' and then to call me a weirdo.

'That is rude,' I say.

'Now, Madge,' her husband says. 'Let's just leave it.'

'Listen to your husband, Madge,' Sash says with a big smiley face.

'You were always a cow,' Madge says as her husband heaves a big sigh. 'No wonder Paddy saw sense and left you.'

The music stops and, all of a sudden, it's like everyone is looking over at us. I feel X-ray eyes staring, like prickles on my skin.

'Mooo,' Sash says. Her voice is all happy. 'He left you too, don't you remember?'

Someone laughs at that. I think it's Mona.

June holds up her hand. 'Girls, can you cool it please?'

'Paddy called Sash this week, if you must know,' Mona chimes in. 'I'll bet he never called you when he dumped you.'

'I'll not have my son's name dragged into this,' Brian Jones calls from his seat at the bar. 'You keep your mouth shut,' he says to Mona.

'And you won't talk to my partner like that.' My dad stands up and suddenly the room seems to hum and buzz.

Brian Jones hops off his bar seat and crosses right over to our table. He looks like Paddy, only fatter with a red face. He's huge. And Paddy always smiled; Brian Jones is not smiling. I don't know what is happening. He pokes Dad in the chest.

'Stop now,' June says.

'Come on out, Lana, pet,' Mona says to me.

I can't move.

'Charles Hanratty was a good friend of my family,' I hear Brian say, even though I have my hands over my ears. 'He employed me and he was good to my son. Your daughter abandoned my son to go making up stories to save that troublemaker.'

'I never abandoned your son!' Beside me I feel Sash stand up. 'And I'm not lying. You're making up a story about Hanratty because you can't face the truth.'

'Spare me, you little cow.'

'Charles Hanratty bought you,' Sash yells. She looks at them all. 'He bought this whole town.'

'How can you let these people in here?' I hear Tommy, the guy who works in the estate agent's, ask June. 'I'm leaving.'

'Your choice,' June says.

'"These people"?' Sash whirls on him. 'We won the schools' athletics together, Tommy. Remember, you cheered me on when I had to run the four hundred because someone pulled out. I was half dead on the line and you picked me up and hugged me.'

'Yeah, and I remember how Charles Hanratty paid for my mother to get surgery when we had no health insurance.'

That was nice of him, I think.

'It's the truth that matters,' Sash says, 'not what anyone did.'

The buzzing in my head is hurting my ears.

'The truth?' Brian Jones shouts and it's like he's right beside me. 'You weren't very truthful to my son, were you?'

'Stop shouting at my daughter,' Dad says.

'Leading him on and all the time, from what I hear, you were just a tramp.'

I hear a crash and lots of noise and shouting and someone pulling me and I can't move. I can't move.

Head is humming. Ears drumming. I start to count.

Marcus

It's eleven at night. We're totally pissed. Dessie is telling a joke that makes no sense and I'm laughing anyway. I don't get drunk too often – I can't seem to enjoy it – but tonight, I needed the release of it. And it's good to laugh.

We're walking up Harcourt Street in search of a taxi but no one will take us, probably because Dessie is staggering all over the road and I'm dragging him back and we're falling about the place.

Dessie is meant to be staying in my place but I don't know if we'll ever get a cab. 'Maybe we'll book a room somewhere?' I say.

'Come here, come here.' Dessie wraps an arm about my neck. 'I love you, like, you know, a brother. But sexually, it's not my thing. No offence.'

And he's off laughing again.

A gang of lads and girls walk by. One of the girls notices Dessie and grins at me. I roll my eyes and grin back.

And her face whitens. Her mouth opens and she gives a small squeal.

Oh shit.

I try to hustle Dessie into hurrying up.

'What's wrong?' I hear one of the lads ask the girl.

'That guy, the tall one, he's that murderer.' She whispers it, but I'm pretty sensitive to the word 'murderer' being whispered in my vicinity. I push an oblivious Dessie onwards.

'What? That fella there?'

Now Dessie hears them. 'Fhat wella where?' he asks.

'You might want to run,' I say to him.

Dessie sways a little on his feet.

'Oi! You! Turn around,' the fella says.

I should run but something in me resents the way he's talking to me. So I turn.

The guy looks. 'Nah, it's not him.'

'It is,' the girl says. 'I know his eyes. He has,' she lowers her voice, but I can still hear her, 'weird eyes. Let's go.'

'Are you that murderer fella?' the guy asks. He's small, about five eight, and just the sort of guy who's itching for a fight.

'What murderer fella?'

'The one in the paper, the one that killed that businessman and then stabbed him all over the place and then ran out into his car and drove off, that fella.'

'He's not,' Dessie says, 'a murderer.'

'I'm not,' I say, then add, 'but I am the guy in the paper. Have you lot got a problem with that?'

'No,' the girl says. 'It's fine.'

'I've a problem with that,' the fella says. 'You shouldn't be out on the streets. I hope they lock you up for a long time. I hope they throw away the key.'

'I hope you grow,' I say back, and Dessie snorts out a laugh.

And then they are on us. Six lads against me and Dessie.

It doesn't last long because it's Harcourt Street and the police station is just across from us and I manage to gasp out a 'Here's the cops' and they scatter like leaves in the wind.

My lip and face hurt and Dessie has been kicked in the leg and hit in the face but he's so drunk he can't even feel it.

'Sorry,' I say.

'No, I get it.' Dessie nods. 'You're innocent. Fuck them.'

And we keep walking.

WEEK 2: DAY 6

Marcus

She's top of the queue to get in. I spot her red-brown hair almost immediately.

'There's Lauren,' Dessie says. He shouts, 'Hey, Lauren, come in with us.' He makes it sound like we're heading to a party.

Lauren turns and I'd forgotten how beautiful she is. Her skin is that flawless creamy white, her eyes the golden brown of new pennies. She's dressed in black with a cream sort of cape thing.

'Who's that?' My mother sounds impressed.

Lauren crosses to us and gawks. 'Jesus, what happened you two?'

Dessie and I currently look like we did ten rounds with Ali when he was at the top of his game. My eye is swollen almost shut and the bruise surrounding it is big enough to have its own sun. Dessie seems to have broken his nose and he's also limping.

'We sort of fell against people's fists,' Dessie says.

Lauren gives a bit of a shocked laugh.

'Poor you.' She reaches out to touch my eye and I flinch away, just because it'll hurt. I think Lauren gets embarrassed.

'It hurts like hell,' I explain. Then add, 'It's good to see you.'

'Yeah. You too.' But she's still embarrassed. And now so am I.

'Hi, I'm Thelma.' My mother has run out of patience. She holds out her hand. 'Marcus's mother, and this is Alan, Marcus's stepdad.'

'I'm Lauren. I'm a friend of Marcus and Dessie's.'

'It's lovely to meet you. Where did you meet Marcus or was it Dessie you got to know first?'

'Ma!'

She flaps me away and takes charge of Lauren as she walks with her to the court. I can almost see her thinking, 'Now this would be a nice girl for Marcus.' Too late, Ma, I want to say.

Some journalist spots my face and snaps a picture. I do what Melissa advises and hold my head up.

'Melissa, Dessie is here.'

Melissa, who has been bent over her case notes, hands

splayed, ass out, glances up. A pause. She straightens and stares from me to Dessie and back again. 'What happened?' Her voice has that low quality that's kind of scary.

'Some lads went for us in town. They recognised me, you see, and—'

'Come,' she cuts me off, her voice low and even. She strides ahead of us, out of the courtroom and into another one that's currently empty. When she turns to us again, there is no mistaking her quiet for anything but fury. Hands on hips, she says, 'I got you bail while this trial was going on. Do you know what that means?'

'It means he's free until the end of the trial,' Dessie volunteers.

'It means,' Melissa eyeballs Dessie and then me, 'that the judge believed you were not a danger to society. He was happy that you would be bound by the law. All this looks good for your case. For you. Now look at the state of you.'

'They came at us – what could I do?' I say.

'Run.'

'We couldn't even walk,' Dessie says. Then he starts to laugh. 'We were in bits.'

I elbow him to shut up.

'Sorry,' he tries to look contrite, 'I know this is dead serious and all.'

It reminds me of when we used to get into trouble at school. My mouth twitches too but one look at Melissa and I cringe.

'Sorry,' I mumble. 'If it's any consolation, we didn't hit them back. I told Dessie not to.'

Melissa perks up a little. 'That might work for us.' She throws Dessie a disgusted look and marches out.

'I'm glad she's on our side,' Dessie says.

I'm glad Dessie's on mine.

Dessie takes the stand and swears the oath. 'Can you state your name and address for the jury?' Melissa asks.

'Dessie Daly. I live on the Main Street in Applegate. I run the pub with my ma.'

'Would you please describe your relationship to my client?'

'He's my best mate.'

'For how long?'

'We got along in school, then drifted apart a bit, but we grew close again later on.'

'Describe how you grew close.'

Dessie grins over at me. 'I was in the same year at school for ages with Marcus, until he dropped out to take the job in the newsagent's. I was mad jealous of him because I hated school. When I was about sixteen, same as him, I started work in the pub with my ma because my auld fella had died. And every night at eleven Marcus would appear at the door to take his mother home.'

'Why?'

Dessie flicks a look at my ma. 'She just had a problem, that's what my ma always said. She drank a bit. Anyway, one night she was really bad, shouting and swearing, and she hit Marcus in the face and then she started crying. A few people helped him out with her, including me. By the time we got her outside, she wasn't as bad but I offered to help Marcus take her home anyway. He told me no.'

My language had been stronger than that, I remember.

'But I helped anyway – it was sad, you know, and the fact that she drank in our pub made me feel bad even though we sold her watered-down drink sometimes.'

Some people laugh. My mother bows her head.

'And then what happened?'

'Well, we got to Marcus's place –'

'I fail to see the relevance of this testimony.' Peter stands up. 'Do we need the whole story?'

'I'm getting to the good bit,' Dessie says.

'The reason for the story will become clear soon,' Melissa says.

'I'll allow it, but hurry up,' the judge warns.

'Cut to the chase, Dessie,' Melissa says.

'Right. In the kitchen of the house there was all these pictures – you know, his cartoon stuff – and while he was putting his ma to bed, I was looking at the pictures. I was impressed, like seriously, they were great. Anyway, he told me he needed some art supplies and that he was saving up for them but I had some to spare from school and I gave them to him, just pencils and paints and stuff. He told me that he'd pay me back and I said no and eventually we agreed that if his cartoon made any money, he'd pay me ten per cent. Turned out what he was doing right then was an early version of *Slam Man*.'

'And did he keep his promise?'

'Yeah. I mean, I forgot all about it. Him and his ma moved

away after he lost the newsagent's job and we kept in contact
a bit but not much. Then one day in the post I get a check
for twenty grand. Like, what? So then I find out it's from
Marcus and he tells me that it's the first of many. And it was.
He's made me a rich guy.'

We grin at each other.

'You're hardly just friends with him because he sends you
money?'

'No, but it's a great basis for it, isn't it?'

People laugh but Melissa is not one bit happy. 'Why are
you friends with him?' She sounds a little icy.

'He's sound.' Dessie's voice grows all weird and I am
mortified. 'He's done other stuff too, good stuff that I know
if I mentioned it, he'd kill me. But mainly, he's sound. You
knew that way back anyway from how he treated his ma.'

'Can we just rewind,' Melissa says. 'Marcus would not
actually kill you if you mentioned the good things he's done,
would he?'

'Shit. No.' Dessie winces. 'Sorry. But he would not be
pleased.'

Sash is grinning at the slip-up, same as me. Her eye looks
bruised. And her dad, holy shit. He has a bandage on his head.

Lauren is beside my mother and she's grinning up at Dessie
too. That's Dessie all over, he makes things lighter.

'On a final note,' Melissa says, 'it would be remiss of me
not to mention your face, Dessie. And the state of my client,
which I'm sure the newspapers will have a field day with.
Can you tell us what happened to cause these injuries?'

Peter Dundon doesn't know whether to object or not.

'Some lads went for Marcus when we were out drinking in town on Friday night. They recognised him from the paper, words were exchanged and they jumped us.'

'Thank you. And these lads, were they injured?'

'No, because Marcus told me not to hit them, so I didn't.'

'Thank you. Your counsel.' She turns to Peter.

Sash

My face does not look too bad compared to Marcus's. I have a swollen eye, caused hy Margaret Browne sticking her finger into it. I'm still not sure if it was an accident. And I certainly look better than Dessie, whose nose is so swollen his whole face looks misshapen.

Dessie is a pretty chilled-out guy. He's almost sprawled across the witness box. If June could see him she'd tell him to sit up straight. But he manages to do it without looking disrespectful.

'You say you're Marcus's best friend, yes?' Peter asks. His voice is ice cold.

I feel a flutter of anxiety thinking of what he'll ask me.

'Yep.'

'You know him very well, since when?'

'On and off through the years. We've become tight in the last seven or so years.'

'Since he sent you the cheques?'

'I guess.'

'He bought your friendship.'

'No. I just thought he was decent to remember his promise,

I liked that. I liked him for it. Plus with the cheques coming from him, we have contact with each other more.'

'So, how often would you talk?'

'No idea. We're not, you know, girls.'

'Not girls? What do you mean by that?'

'We don't chat on a regular basis. Or, like, arrange to chat. It's informal. Maybe once every two weeks.'

'And how often would you meet up?'

'Whenever I'm in Dublin.'

'Which is?'

'Four, five times a year.'

'Never in Applegate?'

Dessie hesitates. 'Some. Not much.'

'So, roughly, you chat twice, maybe three times a month and meet up every few months.'

'Yes. Then, like, there's Facebook and Instagram and stuff.'

'So, a lot of contact.'

'Yeah.'

'And what do you talk about when you chat and meet up?'

Dessie makes a face. 'Everything. Sport, girls, whatever.'

'So, when he was stalking Charles Hanratty, he must have told you.'

Bang. I can almost hear the trap closing.

'No, but—'

'When he was hauled in for questioning, surely he said something?'

Dessie glances at Marcus, says, 'He told Sash.'

'But you're his best friend?'

'Maybe he was ashamed.'

'He told you this?'

'No, but—'

'So, he didn't tell you anything about this double life he was leading?'

'No.' Dessie looks sullenly at him.

'And when you found out about all this, what did you think?'

'Judge, it is irrelevant what the witness thought.'

'I wish to make a point, Judge. It will become clear soon.'

'I'll allow it, but be brief.'

Peter looks at Dessie. 'How did you feel when you found out?'

'Shocked. Surprised.'

'Surprised because he was secretive or surprised because he was up on a murder charge?'

The sparkle has gone from Dessie now. He opens his mouth to speak, then closes it.

'Well?' Peter asks. 'Surprised because he was secretive or because he did what he did?'

'I wasn't surprised he was secretive,' Dessie says eventually. 'That's just Marc.'

'So, would you say that he's good at leading this, for want of a better word, double life?'

Dessie looks wretched.

'Well?' Peter presses.

'I guess. Yeah.'

'Thank you.'

Dessie looks a little shell-shocked. As if he's somehow let Marcus down.

But what he doesn't realise is that anyone, given the right circumstances, can lead a double life.

'You can step down now, Mr Daly,' the judge says.

'Right.' Dessie looks over at Marcus. 'Sorry.'

Marcus mouths, 'It's grand,' and watches as Dessie walks out.

Lana

I send Dad a text. *Take your tablet now.* He has to take a painkiller every four hours for his head. I told him that I would text him to remind him because I'm good at timetables and remembering.

I lie on my bed, texting and also staring out the window at the grass and the flowers.

The fight in the pub, where my dad hurt his head, lasted four hundred and ten seconds. I counted out loud, real fast, so I wouldn't have to listen to it. After a bit, outside the door, I heard the police siren and the policeman came in and I heard him say, 'Sarge?' because that is what they called Dad in the station.

Dad was very embarrassed, I heard him say that, and then Brian Jones asked him what he was embarrassed about, the fight or his daughter, and then Sash threw something at Brian Jones and more fighting started.

Then it stopped when the policeman asked who would like to spend the night in the police station and said that if they didn't stop he would book them all and they'd have a record. I would have liked to spend the night in the police station – at least with police all around you're safe. I tried to say it but my words got all mixed up. That happens me sometimes when I get stressed. I try to talk and the words won't come out.

I am still not able to talk too much but at least I am able to send Dad texts telling him when to take his tablets.

After the fight, Mona hauled me up and out into the air. I just kept counting in my head.

Then Dad and Sash followed us and the policeman came out and told Dad that it's better for us if we lie low for a while. 'I'm sorry, Sarge, but there it is,' he said. And he did look sorry because his mouth was turned down and that's always a sign. Then he said, 'You should get that head stitched.'

'I will,' Dad said. Then he said, 'And we'll stay out of town.'

Sash said real loud, 'I am sick of this piddling little town.'

'Stop it,' Dad said to her, real sharp, and she jumped and glared at him.

Then she glared at me. 'Stop counting,' she said. I was at seven hundred and five by then.

Then she shook me and said, 'Stop that counting. Stop it.' But I didn't.

Maybe I was counting out loud, I don't know. Then I think Sash was going to yell at me again and Dad, still in his cross voice, told her to stop.

'You've done enough damage,' he said to her, and Sash got upset and ran down the road.

Mona ran after her but Mona is not a good runner and she had to stop after forty steps.

Then Dad asked if he could put his arm around me and I nodded and he did. His big arm came around my shoulder. We walked towards Mona, who was panting hard and clutching her chest.

'Why was everyone horrible?' I asked him.

He thought about this for a long time. Then he said, 'You know this trial that Sash is going to and that you will be going to?'

I said yes.

'Well, some people think that Sash is telling lies, that Charles Hanratty was a good man. They're angry at Sash.'

'Sash wouldn't tell lies.' Then I think that maybe she would. She told lies about visiting houses. And about Marcus coming to our house that day when I threw a knife at him.

'They think she's doing it to help Marcus out. But we know she's honest.'

'Yes.' I think she only lies to help Marcus out.

Then Dad cuddled me and some blood dripped onto my clothes.

My phone buzzes and it's Dad with a thumbs-up and a smiley.

Marcus

After I get out of court, I find Dessie and Lauren sitting together on one of the benches. I cross to them and Lauren looks up. 'He's a bit upset about how today went,' Lauren says in her ultra-husky voice, which is pretty damn sexy. I met her, if 'met' is the word, when she answered a phone call I made to a company about having my car insured. I managed to dazzle her with the bit of charm I had. She jokes that she became interested in me when I told her what kind of car I drove.

When I listed my occupation as a cartoonist, she says she was smitten.

Lauren is great: she's just not for me.

I sit beside Dessie on the bench. 'You did good.' I wonder how to make him feel better, then say, 'Honest, Des, it's that guy's job to pull you apart. He wants me to be a secretive shit so he traps you into saying it.'

Both of them look at me. Then look away.

We sit in silence until Dessie says, without looking at me, 'You are, though. And he was right: you told me nothing about what was going on.'

I don't quite know what to say to that. It's not the sort of thing you can tell someone anyway. It had never crossed my mind to say over a pint, 'Oh yeah, by the way, I'm stalking Charles Hanratty.'

I knew it was bonkers, I knew he'd think I was bonkers and I didn't want that. The stalking made sense to me but I wasn't so far gone that I'd think he'd be happy with it.

'What would be the point?' I end up saying.

'You were stalking a guy like someone crazy.' He looks at me. 'You must have known it was crazy.'

'Which was why I didn't tell you.' My voice is flat.

'What else are you not telling me?'

At first I think I've heard wrong, but it's the way Lauren flinches that makes me think he's actually said what he said. 'I don't believe you just asked me that.'

Dessie meets my gaze square on. 'What else are you not telling me?'

'Fuck you.' I stand up and walk off.

My mother and Alan are waiting downstairs. They've booked dinner in a restaurant in Malahide, a place that knows me.

'Is Dessie not coming?' my mother asks. 'We've booked for him too.' She loves Dessie, everyone does. 'Lauren can come too,' she offers. Then adds, 'She said you went out with her for about a year ...'

'Neither of them are coming, Ma, so can we just get a move on?'

'Don't speak to her like that,' Alan says.

It's the first time he's ever been short with me and I roll my eyes.

'I mean it,' he said. 'She's my wife.'

'Yeah, and you're not my dad.'

'She is your mother. A bit of respect.'

'She is my mother and, in case you haven't been listening over the past week, she has let me down time and again so I think I can talk to her any way I like.'

Even as the words are tumbling out like hailstones, I'm thinking, 'No, no, don't,' but my tongue is running away with me.

I'm hurt at Dessie and I need to lash out and she's always been an easy target.

'If she'd been around like she should have been,' I continue, 'I wouldn't have been out breaking into places every bloody night.'

'Marcus!' Melissa's voice cuts like a whip through the tension. She totters towards us on her high heels, Josh following along with the evidence trolley. 'If this is some kind of a domestic, do not row in full view of the vultures outside the window. In fact, don't row full stop. Your mother is on the stand tomorrow, so she needs someone to care about her tonight.'

Her gaze is like ice. Then she pauses and takes a second and suddenly she looks a bit human again. 'Can I just say, people are often mistaken into thinking that the defence is the easy part of the trial for them. It's usually not. The prosecution will force answers from us that we didn't think we'd have to give or even say. People question themselves, it's only natural. That friend of yours, annoying though he is, did good today despite everything.' Then she is gone in a waft of some awful, but probably expensive, scent.

'We're leaving now,' Alan says, and he doesn't sound too friendly. 'Are you coming?'

I hear Lauren's voice behind me and I know she's with Dessie. I can't face him after what he asked. 'Sure.'

'Dessie,' Alan calls over, 'do you and Lauren want to come for a bite to eat, our treat?'

'Nah, Lauren and I said we'd grab a drink somewhere before I head back,' Dessie says.

'You can come with us if you like, Marcus,' Lauren says.

I glance at Dessie and shake my head. 'I don't think so.'

I turn to go.

'I had to ask,' Dessie calls after me.

'No you didn't.' Then I am gone.

Sash

Dad is not talking to me. Ever since the weekend, he has answered me in monosyllables, not looking at me, not even bothering to discuss the trial today.

Right now, we're stuck in traffic on the N7 on the way back to the hotel. The radio is playing some sort of classical music which I know neither of us can stand. I reach out to turn it off.

'Leave it,' he barks.

'But you don't even—'

'I said, leave it.'

I heave a sigh and turn to the window. Rain is snaking down the glass and it looks like being a miserable evening. Dad turns on the wipers. *Swish. Swish. Swish. Swish.*

Outside, people are putting up umbrellas or holding bags over their heads to cope with the sudden squall. The sky closes over a moody grey. Life is going on for everyone else and I'm always taken by surprise each day when I leave the court to see that the world is still there, time is still passing, while my life seems temporarily suspended.

'I did it to make something happen,' I finally blurt out.

He's thinking of ignoring me again, but finally says, 'What?' It's an exasperated 'what', not even mildly curious.

'I went to Daly's just to make something happen.'

Dad continues to stare out the window, inching the car along bit by bit. Then he says, 'You put us all in danger.'

'That's a bit over the top.'

'They hate you in Applegate,' Dad says baldly, and I flinch.

They hate me?

'Mona got an apple thrown at her last week from a car when she was making her way into town, did you know that?'

'No,' I say meekly. Poor Mona.

'And Brian Jones had a go at her in the church, of all places.'

'I'm so sorry.'

'They send her notes telling her to get out of town. It's explosive, Sash.'

I feel tears fill my eyes. I'd known it wouldn't go down well, even as a teenager – that was what held me back from saying anything, that and my doubt. If everyone else thought so highly of Hanratty, maybe I was wrong about him. 'What am I supposed to do, Dad? I have to help Marcus.'

'Do you, though? Do you really, Sash?' His voice is thick with emotion. 'Haven't you been through enough without this as well?'

'It's the right thing to do.' And there it is. The pure, unvarnished truth. Telling the court about that night is the right thing for Marcus and for me. Maybe it will make him look even more guilty, but both of us want it, the chance to tell people what that man was like, to set ourselves free. Perverse as it is, this murder might just release us.

I'm not sure Dad is convinced, but he nods anyway. 'OK then,' he says slowly. A slight shake in his voice. 'It will break my heart if that prosecutor tears you apart, but if you feel you have to –'

'I do. I'll be fine.'

'Then just remember,' he turns and smiles at me a little bleakly, 'even by doing it, you can't change the world. Or Applegate.'

I look out the window again. 'I just want to change my life,' I eventually admit. 'I want to have some power over it. And yes, I am scared in case no one believes me but I have to do it.'

'You only need twelve people to believe you in court. And outside of that, me, Mona and Lana believe you too, so who cares?'

He's right. 'Yeah.' He turns his face to the windscreen and smiles a little.

'I'm sorry about dragging you to Daly's and scaring Lana and all of it.'

'I know.'

'And I just want you to talk to me again.'

'Was I not talking to you?'

I smile. He smiles. We're good.

Lana

June Daly calls over. She drives up in her big jeep, the tyres crunching on the gravel, then there is a bang where she crashes into the kerb beside the flower bed. She never sees it, especially as the jeep is so high. She is not a good driver at all. One time she drove into her garage at the wrong angle and then wasn't able to get her car back out. The more she tried the worse it got and, in the end, no one would chance it so they had to take down the garage bit by bit.

June didn't care. She is like Dessie, just likes to laugh.

She isn't laughing when she comes in the door, though. I come down the stairs because I like to talk to her.

'Hello, Lana,' she says, 'how's things?'

I know she means how am I and not how are things. Once I didn't get that and I would tell people that I didn't know how things were because I didn't know what things they meant and they used to laugh at that and I didn't know why they were laughing and then they used to think I was weird. But anyway, I say to June, 'I am fine.'

'Come into the kitchen,' Mona says. 'I've the kettle on.'

Mona always says this to people and normally she doesn't have the kettle on. Normally she has the TV on with the quiz shows. I follow June into the kitchen and I see that Mona really does have the kettle on because it's just boiling. She lowers the volume on the TV and makes a pot of tea while June sits down. I sit down too.

'I'm sorry about Saturday night,' Mona says to June after she has laid the cups down on coasters. 'There was no talking to Sash.'

'Don't keep apologising,' June says. She pours milk into a cup. 'It wasn't just your fault. Or Sash's. You should be allowed to have a drink in peace. Brian Jones is like a bull in a china shop.'

'I probably made things worse,' Mona admits, 'throwing it in about Paddy calling Sash when I know fine well Paddy hasn't talked to him in a good while.'

'Margaret says that they haven't spoken since Paddy left Applegate.'

'Shocking.' Mona shakes her head. 'They were always so close.'

Junes nods. 'You just never know,' she says, and Mona agrees.

You just never know what? I'm trying to figure that out as Mona carries the teapot to the table. It's huge and her hand wobbles with the weight of it. She puts it down with a thump and takes out some biscuits from the press that they are not normally in. She hides biscuits so I won't eat them all. She told me I was very sneaky once and I said that I knew that. These biscuits have nuts and chocolate in them. They are a light brown. I like brown. I take two when Mona puts them on the plate and she says, 'That's enough now.'

I only ever have two at a time.

'We won't be in the pub again,' Mona says, 'not until things quieten down. Kevin has sworn he'll have a word with Sash, though how he will when he's refusing to talk to her, I don't know.'

'Aw, don't take it out on Sash. She's been through the mill.'

I was never through the mill – it doesn't sound like a place I'd really want to go.

'What happened afterwards?' Mona takes two biscuits for herself. I watch her and she glares at me. I bet she'll take two more.

'Not much. Naomi was very upset. I had to drive her home – she was shaking like a leaf.'

Mona snorts. 'That one only thinks of herself.'

'I think she feels bad about letting Sash go that time but her business was plummeting.'

'Sash thought she was her friend.'

June nods but says nothing about that; instead she changes the subject completely. When I do that, people think it's rude. 'Dessie rang from the court earlier. He was a bit upset. He felt he'd let Marcus down. The prosecutor hammered him, apparently.'

'Will he hammer me?' I ask. No one said anything about hammering.

'Hammered as in asked him questions he found hard to answer,' June explains.

'Like maths?'

'Definitely no maths,' Mona says. 'You'll be fine. You just stick to the facts and keep saying them.'

I'm good at facts. Facts are my thing.

Then Mona says, 'We try not to mention the floorshow in front of some of the cast.' And she nods at me.

That is so weird.

Mona is weird.

Their conversations are weird.

I think about Sash at the weekend. She had said sorry the day after the fight at ten o'clock in the morning. She crawled into my bed and wrapped her arms around me and whispered in my ear, 'I'm sorry for shouting at you.'

I said that that was OK because that is what you do when someone apologises. Holding a grudge only hurts you, that's what Dad says.

'I'm just stressed, Lana,' she said. 'It's horrible not being liked here.'

Then I said to Sash, 'It's OK.' Then I thought of something

and I asked, 'Do you remember when Jennifer said that Paddy's mother was fucking Hanratty?'

Beside me Sash flinched. 'Jesus, Lana—'

'That's what she said. Do you remember?'

'I remember.'

'That's who you're like. Jennifer Ryan, shouting out bad stuff about Hanratty in the street only you'll do it in court. No one liked her that time either.'

Sash was quiet for a few minutes, then she nodded. 'That makes a lot of sense,' she said to me. 'Only I'll be telling the truth and she was lying.'

The story, in case you're wondering, is this. I was walking home from school with Sash, and Paddy was with us. It was fifteen years and two months ago. We were passing the newsagent's and Sash wasn't going in for her usual comic and I was tugging at her sleeve for her to go in and she said, real cross, 'Just leave it, Lana.' So I stopped tugging her sleeve and she started talking to Paddy again. Paddy did try to include me but he sort of talked to me real slow like I was stupid so I never talked back. Next thing, a Granny Smith apple hit Paddy on the head and bounced onto the ground. It was a waste of food. We all turned around and Jennifer Ryan was standing there. Then she threw another Granny Smith at him. It hit his nose. She was a good shot.

Paddy grabbed his face and Sash said to Jennifer, 'What is your problem?'

I said, 'You are meant to eat apples.'

Then Margaret Browne, the girl who smelled of flowers and hairspray, ran down the street and she said, 'Jenny, what are you doing?' Then she said to Paddy, 'What are you doing with her?' Meaning Sash, not me, I think.

Before Paddy could say that he was walking home from school with us, which was obvious, Jennifer said, 'I'm hitting him with apples – what does it look like?'

Then Paddy told Jennifer to cool it, that they were friends, that there was nothing he could have done, that he tried his best to talk to his dad.

'Your fucking dad,' she said real loud, and people looked over. 'He's just a yes-man for Hanratty.'

'He is not, he tried his best,' Paddy said.

'He didn't try hard enough. My mother is not a thief and he fired her.'

'I'm sorry about that,' Paddy said.

'What are you apologising to her for?' Sash said to Paddy. 'Her mother probably *is* a thief.'

'You bitch.' Jennifer shrieked so loud, I felt it in my stomach and it made me feel sick. She threw an apple at Sash, but quick as a lick, I reached out and hit it away.

Anyway, if I write all the conversation down, that will be too much information. In the end, Jennifer yelled out, 'Rumour has it that your mother and Hanratty are fucking each other. That's why your dad has the job he has.'

Then Margaret said that she was not going to be Jennifer's friend anymore. And Sash walked off and left Paddy standing with Margaret on the street. And I ran to catch up with Sash, who caught a stomach bug because she was sick a bit down the road.

Anyway, the point of the story is that after Jennifer said

that, no one liked her anymore. Just like they don't like Sash.

Sash

Like I said before, telling my dad had been the hardest part. As I said the words, 'Charles Hanratty raped me,' it was as if I reached out and ripped apart the pages of his life. Everything afterwards was changed and shifted.

For a second he seemed stunned, as if shell-shocked. Then he looked at me and I had to repeat myself. And I watched him crumple, as if the air was being slowly sucked out of him. He folded over on himself, caught his head in his hands and he sobbed. I was afraid he'd never stop. He reached blindly for me and pulled me into an embrace and cried and asked me why I'd never said anything. 'Because it was Hanratty,' I answered.

And he knew what I meant.

And once the secret was out, it needed more and more air. I couldn't rebuild only some of my life – I had to keep going. Paddy's dad, Brian, was next on the list. Paddy was making arrangements to pull out of the election but he had to tell his dad first.

'We've a bit of news for you,' Paddy said on the phone to him. 'Come over for dinner tomorrow.' Then, 'No, not that. No, not that either. No … no … look, Dad, it's bad news, OK.' Then he'd slammed the phone onto the table and walked out of the house.

Of course Brian arrived over twenty minutes later, looking freaked, a massive bunch of sunflowers that he'd taken from his garden with him. 'For you,' he said to me as he kissed my cheek. 'Where's Paddy?'

Before I could answer, Paddy came in. 'What are you doing here?' he said to Brian.

'That's lovely.' Brian made an attempt at a laugh. When Paddy didn't smile back, he said, 'You told me you had bad news – how could I wait until dinner tomorrow to find out? What's going on?' He looked from me to Paddy.

I carried the flowers to the sink, knowing that Paddy wanted to be the one to tell him.

'Is someone sick?' Brian asked into the silence. He lived in fear of people being sick. His own wife had died after a supposed stomach bug. 'Sash?'

'I'm fine.' I chopped the stalks off the flowers. 'No one is sick.'

'Good.' He sounded relieved. 'That's good.'

More silence. Then Paddy said quietly, 'Dad, I'm thinking of pulling out of the election.'

At the sink, my hands stilled. *Thinking?*

'Will you get a grip!' Brian laughed at that. He shouted across the kitchen to me, 'Has he lost his nerve?'

'No,' I said, my back to him. 'And if you want to blame someone for his decision, blame me.'

'We're having some issues about running,' Paddy said quickly, and his voice shook.

'What issues?' At Paddy's lack of response, he said, 'Will one of you tell me what's going on?'

'We've other stuff to worry about,' Paddy said.

'Like what?' He sounded a little frustrated.

'For starters, Marcus Dillon has been arrested for Charles Hanratty's murder.'

'I know that,' Brian snorted. 'He was a weird lad but sure with his mother so bad, he was never going to turn out right.'

'Sash keeps in contact with Marcus,' Paddy said hastily.

'You'd want to stop that.' Brian directed this to me. 'That will not look good come election time.' A pause. 'Is that why you're pulling out? There's no need—'

'No,' Paddy cut across him. 'That's not why. It's because—' He stalled.

'Because what?' Brian gave a chuckle. 'For Jaysus' sake, you're worse than a politician for information.'

'Marcus says he's innocent and Sash is, well, she's testifying in Marcus's defence,' Paddy gabbled out.

'Why?'

'Because she believes Marcus is innocent.'

This was not what we'd said we'd say. 'It's not so much that,' I said, deciding to cut short Paddy's meandering explanation. 'It's more what I'm going to say about Hanratty in defence of Marcus that's the problem.' I turned around and faced them, my back against the sink.

Paddy threw me a look that I couldn't quite fathom but, when I saw it, the ground under my feet shifted a little.

'What are you going to say?' Brian asked.

I gathered myself, stared Brian in the eyes and said, with as much composure as I could, 'I'm going to say that he was a – a rapist.'

Boom. I could almost hear the impact the words made.

Afterwards, there was silence. Paddy's head was bent; Brian rocked a little.

'Jesus Christ,' Brian said after a bit. 'That's shocking.'

'Isn't it?' I said.

'Sash,' Paddy said quietly, lifting his gaze from the table, 'please.'

'Please?' I looked at him, suddenly annoyed. 'What do you mean, "please"?'

'I mean—'

'Why on earth would you say a thing like that?' Brian's voice was a mix of shock and outrage. 'You can't blacken a man's name like that.'

'I say it because it's true.' He hardly thought I was making it up.

'I can't—'

'What? Believe it? Well, do.'

'Is she for real?' He directed that at Paddy.

'I am,' I answered for Paddy, afraid suddenly that he would back down or say something to negate what I was telling Brian. He looked like he would. He wasn't standing up for me the way he should have been.

'She is,' Paddy said after me, though without any passion. 'And, Dad, if I go up for election now, using the sympathy of Hanratty's death, it'll make me a hypocrite.' He got up from the table then, distancing himself from me, I realised with a little hollow thump of my heart.

'You hardly believe her.' Brian followed his son across the room.

'I'm not making it up.'

'I wouldn't put it past you.' Brian turned, pale-faced, towards me. 'You and that Marcus lad were always thick as thieves. He had a violent streak, put Paddy in hospital for two days or have you forgotten that?'

'That doesn't mean he's a murderer.'

'Maybe not, but slandering a good man is no way to behave. You can't condone this, Paddy.'

'He believes me.'

If he had backed me up right then, stood beside me, strong, we might have had a chance, but he didn't. All he said was, 'I'm not going up for election.'

'You can't let her do this,' Brian said.

'I can do what I want,' I said.

'It's more than what *you* want.' Brian whirled on me. He thumbed at his son. 'What about him? What about what he wants?'

'What do you want, Paddy?' I asked him.

'This town will implode.' Brian got there before Paddy could answer. 'Think about the future of the hotel, the tourism.'

'Think about an innocent man in jail.'

'I will not let my son ruin his life over you.'

At that, Paddy said, 'Just go, Dad.'

Brian looked at me, then at Paddy and then back to me again. He seemed about to say something, but in the end he just left, slamming the front door after him.

I crossed back to the sink; Paddy sank down into a chair.

The silence built until I could stand it no more. 'Thanks for your support,' I snapped.

'It's not that easy to shatter my dad's dreams, you know,' he said, with a lot more anger than I was expecting. 'I have to let a whole town down, Sash, and it's hard, OK?'

Hurt sliced me in half. 'I thought this was what you wanted. I thought you were happy for me to testify.'

'Happy?' He barked out a laugh. 'Telling everyone how you broke into houses. Standing up for Marcus like you always did. No, Sash, I am not happy. I'm drowning here.'

'But it's the right thing.'

'If he's innocent.'

'He is.'

We glared at each other before he finally said, 'I hope so.'

'I know so.'

We turned away from each other. I wanted to leave the room but nothing was finished.

'I just wanted to be elected,' Paddy said softly into the space between us. 'And I can't be. Even if you don't testify, I can't do it, it's gone. And, yes, I'm angry about it. And maybe I'm petty, but with testifying, it's like you've chosen Marcus over me.'

'I've chosen the truth.'

'Good for you.' He sounded bitter. On a sigh, he added, 'I believe you, Sash, I do, but I don't believe you have to testify.'

We were in a small kitchen but it might as well have been a whole continent, so far away from him did I feel. 'I'm testifying for me as well as Marcus: that's what you don't get.'

'And you don't get how doing it will destroy this town. If

231

I pull out of the election and you don't testify, no one will ever know the truth about that man. But testifying …' He shook his head. 'It'll split the place asunder.'

'So, I just leave Marcus looking like a liar on the stand?'

'If he's innocent, he'll be OK.'

'He might not be.'

Silence.

'Do you think I'm doing the right thing?'

His expression told me more than anything he could have said.

'You'll eventually hate me, won't you, if I do this?'

'No.'

He sounded like he meant it, but he would, I realised. If he thought that my sticking up for Marcus was misguided and that by doing it I was trampling on his dreams, he would hate me.

For both our sakes, I had to cut him free.

He tried to put up a fight but I told him I was ending it. For us both. Maybe I should have resented him for not understanding but, in a way, how could he have understood? His voice had always been heard – there was no way he could have comprehended the depth of my desperation.

He never did go up for election. I'd ruined it for him.

He teaches in Dublin now.

I haven't seen him since.

DAY 7

Marcus

'Are you sure you can handle this?' I ask my mother as she comes out of the bathroom, having been sick.

'I will be fine,' she says. Her eyes flick to my hair – she seems about to say something, then stops herself.

'What?'

'Nothing.' She walks past me into the kitchen and pours herself a cup of ginger tea. She's gone big into health stuff. My presses are filled with nuts and seeds and different types of herbal teas and biscuits that look like, quite frankly, pieces of vomit.

I can't wait until they go home, but that won't happen until the end of the trial. It's part of my bail conditions.

I gear myself up. 'About yesterday—'

She holds up a hand. 'Let's just leave it, OK? We need to think about today.'

She is utterly composed, which is surprising, as I'd grown up with this semi-hysterical woman. All my life she'd fallen to pieces at the smallest thing, unable even to go into a post office on her own to pay rent in case they'd ask her something she didn't know. But somewhere between then and now, she'd grown up. Maybe it was Alan or the AA but she seems a lot more together than before. And yet, I still can't trust it. My whole life with this woman had been one big drama, as she careened from one tragedy to the next, crying over lost boyfriends, asking me what did I think went wrong, what did I think she did wrong. I'd tell her that she did nothing wrong, that she was perfect, and she'd say, 'But you're a man, you must know.' I was probably eight at the time.

Alan arrives in and, placing a hand on the small of my mother's back, he bends over and kisses her cheek. She leans into him.

They are a perfect unit.

I never thought I would envy my mother her life, but right now, I do.

At ten thirty, she takes the stand. Melissa has warned her that it might get rough during the cross-examination, but my mother said that Melissa didn't know the meaning of rough. I think Melissa was pretty impressed with that.

I watch my mother sit down and smile at the judge.

Surprisingly, he smiles back. She is a good-looking woman, I guess. And I keep forgetting that she is only forty-eight. She swears her oath. She states her name and her relationship to me. Her voice is clear and strong and so not like the needy woman I know.

'I was a single mother,' she says, without any self-pity. 'I had Marcus at sixteen and left home to live with my boyfriend. It fell apart, as most of my relationships tended to in those days. After it did, I was alone and unhappy and unable to cope with motherhood, so I started to drink. And I couldn't stop. From about the age of three to fourteen Marcus was in and out of foster homes.'

She says it very matter-of-factly. It's like she's learned it off, or practised it so that she can actually say it.

'And when Marcus was with you, what sort of a relationship did you have with him?'

My mother takes a while to answer. She stops and starts and sips some water. 'When he was small,' she says, 'he loved me, he was always delighted to see me after his holiday. That's what he thought the foster homes were. When he was with me, we'd go on picnics, go to the zoo, things like that. But I'd always meet someone, get dumped, start drinking again and it would end with Marcus being taken away. My life back then was as predictable as the sun coming up.' She gives a self-deprecating smile which wobbles a bit. 'He went missing from a foster home when he was fourteen. For three days I didn't know where he was. I was frantic but he came back to me and he told the social workers that he was never leaving again.'

I remember that. It'd taken me two days to find my way to Applegate and on the third day I stayed in the orchard, eating apples. Finally, hunger drove me home. All I'd ever wanted as a kid was to be with my ma because when she wasn't drunk, she was good fun. Just a kid herself, I guess. And I hated going into foster care where they had rules and looked after you. I was way too independent by then for any of that.

'And did he leave again?'

'They tried to take him but he kept running off. In the end they left him and just checked up on us from time to time.'

'So, in effect, your son became your carer?'

'Yes,' my mother says, and her voice wobbles a bit. She takes a breath. 'The bigger he grew, the better he got at it. He made it easy for me to drink. I knew he was always going to be there. Marcus is dependable. And everything you've heard about me in this court is true. He did carry me home most nights from the pub. He tucked me in. He bought painkillers and antacids. He washed my clothes and dried my tears. He was a brilliant son.' Her eyes get shiny.

'Take your time,' Melissa says.

'If you need a break,' the judge says.

'I'm fine. He was a brilliant son,' she says again, and she looks at me.

I dip my head. Not that brilliant ...

'Did Marcus ever get frustrated with you?'

'Sure wouldn't anyone? When I was sober, he used to sit me down and ask me why I couldn't stop. He'd tell me all the damage I was doing to myself. He'd have printouts and

I'd promise to do better and never mean it. Sometimes he'd shout at me, but Marcus is not a guy that can do intimidation that well.'

'Did he ever get violent with you?'

'No.' She talks to the jury. 'I got violent with him. I used to hit him and throw stuff at him. He never once retaliated. Marcus is the gentlest guy you could meet. That whole stalker stuff, I don't know,' she flaps a hand, 'but he's not a killer.'

'How would you describe your relationship with your son now?'

'Terrible.'

My head shoots up. Is that how she sees it? Really?

'Terrible,' she says looking at me. 'And I blame myself, fair and square.'

There is a bit of a stir in the court. Melissa waits for it to die down before continuing. 'Why so?'

'Do you really have to ask? The boy grew up and got sense. I was a terrible mother but, somehow, I raised a great son and I pinch myself every day wondering how that happened.'

For fuck's sake, Ma. I glare at her. No one needs to hear this.

'Let's be clear, Mrs Epson, you didn't have to testify today, did you?'

'No, but I wanted to because he has done so much for me and I want to give back by telling the truth about what kind of a man he is.'

'Thank you.'

My mother wipes away a hasty tear.

'I think we'll take a break,' the judge says, and I want to hug him. For me and for her.

As Melissa crosses to my mother, I make for the door.

Sash

Marcus passes by me, and he looks pretty upset. I don't blame him. It's awful for him to have to hear all this stuff, though his mother looks great and sounds great. I thought she'd crumple like cheap wood in the rain, but she's impressive.

I can remember one night when Marcus stood outside Daly's waiting to collect his mother and I was with him. I hadn't known him that long and he'd been quite evasive about his home life. While I had spewed forth about my dad dragging me and Lana to Applegate, Marcus had listened to me and said very little. Then one night, he'd kind of smirked and said, 'You don't know you're born.'

'What?'

'Your dad cares about you. You go home and you know what to expect. That's not a bad deal.'

I was pretty annoyed. I think he was too, only in a quieter way.

'And you go home and don't know what to expect, is that it?'

His eyes regarded me as if wondering something. Then he said, 'Haven't you heard? My mother is the –' He paused and looked a bit sad. 'She drinks,' he finished off. 'Every night at eleven, I pick her up from the pub. I put her to bed and I come and meet you.'

Then he got up and walked off.

The following night, I was there. Waiting with him. When he'd seen me coming up the street towards him, he'd looked a bit shocked and a bit pleased. 'I'm here to help,' I said.

It was a Saturday; my dad thought I was out with school pals. It wasn't exactly a massive lie.

He said nothing, just nodded, and we waited.

'If she doesn't come out, I go and get her,' he explained, after a bit. 'Once the hotel clock chimes, in I go. She knows this, mostly accepts it.'

At eleven, it sounded and we waited. Thelma didn't appear.

Marcus shot me a rueful grin, rolled up his sleeves and said, 'Here I go.'

I watched him stride across the street, only to see him emerge a couple of seconds later with this wild creature on the end of his arm. Her fists were flailing all over the place and he was holding her firmly so she wouldn't fall and she kept calling him a bastard.

'I am a bastard,' he said mildly, 'unless you can point me in the direction of my father.'

That garnered a bit of a laugh from her and she calmed.

'You make me laugh, Marcus.'

'I aim to please. Mother, this is my friend Sash. Sash, I'd like you to meet my mother.'

I approached with caution. 'Hello,' I said. I knew that woman, but I'd never associated her with Marcus. He was tall and dark and nerdy; she was small and attractive, though her skirt and top were both too short and tight. She wore this awful tatty fake-fur jacket and her face was covered in orange make-up.

'Marcus has a friend,' she said. 'Good for him.'

I winced and saw Marcus's eyes grow cold at my reaction. Maybe I looked as horrified as I felt. 'Yes, it is,' I said. 'Marcus is nice.'

'I like her.' His mother poked him in the chest. 'Keep her.'

Marcus hoisted her up a bit. 'Come on, let's get back before you fall asleep.' He looked at me. 'I won't be able to carry her then.'

'Can I help?'

'You can talk as we go.'

So I did, tripping along beside him, telling him about my running and how I was now coming second last instead of last and making him laugh.

An apple butt whizzed past my ear as someone yelled over at us. It was Margaret and Jennifer sitting on the windowsill outside the hardware shop that Jennifer's dad ran. They were all dressed up, as if they were heading out somewhere.

'Did your mammy fall asleep because Sash is so boring?' Margaret Browne called across, as Jennifer giggled. There was something desperate in the sound of it. She was a different person on the athletics track. More confident, more in control. When she was with Margaret, it was almost as if she was running fast to keep still.

'No, she's got her eyes closed because she saw you and didn't want to look,' I shouted back.

Marcus chortled. 'Good one, Sash.' We high-fived.

Jennifer took a swig from a vodka bottle and handed it

to Margaret. 'You should see Sash in athletics,' she said. 'It's pathetic, her trying to catch up with everyone.'

'You should see you in athletics,' I flashed back. 'It's pathetic, you trying to get in with everyone.'

That struck home. In fact, I think it hit her harder than it should have because she flinched.

'Are you going to let her away with that?' Margaret gave Jennifer a shove. 'The cheek.' At Jennifer's lack of response, she tossed out, 'Maybe Sash is right and you *are* pathetic.'

'You are a cow, Margaret Brown.' Marcus surprised me by shouting across the road. 'You think you're something special because your dad has this big farm and you're loaded. You're a fool hanging around with her, Jenny, you really are.'

Jenny, I thought. He called her Jenny.

'And you're a fool to hang around with that weirdo,' Margaret retaliated.

'She's not a weirdo. She reads *Batman*.'

I almost choked on a laugh. Marcus grinned at me and we walked on.

'Freaks,' Margaret called after us.

'So, what's with calling Jennifer "Jenny"?' I asked Marcus after we'd settled his mother and were sitting under the tree in the orchard.

'I always called her Jenny. I used to hang around with her until she dumped me.'

'No way.'

'Yep. She even liked comics.'

'Did she get a personality transplant?'

'She was nice,' he said again, and I was a bit taken aback at his defence of her. Then he shrugged. 'I dunno, she changed when her dad got the hardware shop. I think it went to her head.'

I made a face. 'That's a bit pathetic.'

Marcus shrugged. 'Well, she changed right at that time,' he says grinning, 'and I'm not a shrink so I'm only going on the facts.'

I poked him with my toe and he caught my foot and didn't seem to know what to do with it, so he let it go. 'Maybe your taste in friends just improved,' I said.

'My taste definitely improved,' he agreed, then he smiled, sort of slow.

He had a great smile, mostly because it was unexpected.

I leaned over and kissed him.

I hadn't planned to, but the whole 'Jenny' thing kind of shook me up and I wanted him to know that I really liked him.

Lana

If Marcus's mother doesn't go on too long, I am up in court tomorrow morning or else the afternoon. Mona is fussing around, telling me that I should dress appropriately. A nice pair of trousers, she says to me, and a blouse. I don't have any blouses, I tell her. I don't go out to work.

Mona offers to lend me one of hers. It's white and frilly and way too big. I tell her so and she is a little annoyed with that. She tells me that maybe we'll have to go out shopping for one.

I don't like shopping. I don't like new clothes because they have a funny smell and feel scratchy. Mona says it's my imagination but Dad lets me wash them three times before I wear them. That's because three is a lucky number only Mona thinks that's all nonsense.

Three persons in the one God, I say, what's all that about. And she doesn't know what to say to that because she goes to mass and she can't say it's nonsense now.

I tell her I will get a blouse if it's white and if she will wash it three times.

She says alright then, fine. She says she hopes I'm as good in court as I am at giving back answers to her.

She starts up the car and off we go. As we near Applegate, I ask Mona would she mind if I ducked down just in case anyone will fight again.

'We're in the car,' Mona says, 'no one will fight, but if it makes you feel happier, do.'

I go right down so the seatbelt hurts my shoulder. Underneath is very different to up on top. I can see all the dirt on the floor of the car, bits of gravel and pebbles and muck. Also a lot of dust. Also a sweet that Mona must have dropped. I try not to tip off any of it. 'It's dirty here,' I say.

'Excuse me, Your Highness,' Mona says.

I say nothing. I close my eyes and I count. It takes sixty-two seconds for Mona to say, 'OK, you can pop up now.'

I count to three three times and then up I get.

We are on the road out of town, hurtling along in Mona's car. Mona has her own car because she is an independent woman, she told me once. Women did not have to have men drive them around. Or they didn't just have to have one car in a family. My mother couldn't drive. But she could teach me songs and how to count. She made me eat lumpy food too. I didn't want lumpy food – I only ate mushed bananas – but one day she sat me down and wouldn't give me bananas. She made me chips. They scared me because they were not brown, they were shaped and golden. It would be like eating pieces of the sun or a door handle.

Now I eat them.

It takes three thousand and seventy seconds to get to Lynhall, which is the big town near Applegate. It's not as pretty as Applegate but it has more shops. I counted them once. It has ninety-five shops.

Forty-two are for clothes so we might be a long time.

We find a white blouse in the very first shop. It is fine, it has buttons and a soft collar because I don't like stiff ones like I had to wear to school. Stiff collars are not good for thinking. Mona says that it is a boy's shirt. I said how did she know and she said that the buttons were on the other side and so they were. That is amazing. I would not have been able to cope with a shirt whose buttons were on the wrong way. So then we get one exactly the same for a girl. It only costs five euro and Mona says that is good value. Mona says am I happy with it and I say yes.

The woman in the shop thinks I'm stupid. Some people do. She hunkers down to my level because she is a tall woman and she puts her hands on her knees and looks into my face and her breath smells of coffee. She speaks real slow. 'Is this for a special occasion?'

'Yes. I have to go to court to talk about a man who might have murdered another man.'

The woman looks as if I smell.

'Not your average occasion,' Mona says, sort of laughing. Then she pays for the shirt and we are free.

'You're a gas ticket,' Mona says as we leave. 'I never know what you'll come out with.' And she laughs and says, 'Wait till I tell Kevin.'

I don't know what she is on about. She brings me for a coffee and a cake. Mona always likes coffee and a cake to celebrate her shopping. If Dad goes shopping, he will never celebrate.

Over the cake, she says to me, 'Just remember, talk real clear so that everyone can hear you because by doing that you're helping Sash too. Your story makes her story true.'

I know that. I'm like a witness to Sash's story – that's what the solicitor Melissa said when I met her.

She is some cool lady. She wears cool shoes and has red lipstick and long swishy hair and cool braces that are big hunks of metal in her mouth.

'The man, he's called a prosecutor, he might sound cross with you, but that's just pretend. He has to sound that way.'

'Why?'

'It's just his job.'

I take a bite of my bun. I've seen the courtroom because, before the trial started, Melissa got someone to show me and Sash around it. It is twenty-five of my steps by twenty steps so it is sort of medium sized. There is a place for everyone to sit and I will sit in a room before they call me to sit in the witness box. That is what it is. There will be a crowd but not a pushing crowd so that will be OK. Also, they ruled that I am OK to testify.

When we get back, I have to pack. Mona has given me a list of things to bring. 'You're only going for a day,' she says, 'so you won't need to pack loads.'

Mona is making me pack for myself. She thinks it will make me independent. I don't want to be like her and drive a car. She has given me a list to make it easier.

I have never gone on a holiday even for a night before. The only place I ever was was at home with Mammy and then in Applegate without Mammy. This will be scary but we are going to get up at eight in the morning, the same as normal, and be at the court for ten. Then I will testify and then we will have lunch at twelve, same as normal. Then I might have to testify again, then we will be home in the apartment for tea. Then I will sleep with Sash in her room. I don't mind a new room if Sash is there.

Mona is watching *The Chase* when I go down to query the list.

'What?'

'Is the apartment warm?'

'What apartment? Alien!'

Mona does that, shouts out answers to quizzes when she is talking to you. It doesn't bother us anymore.

'Dad and Sash's apartment.'

'Sphere! I suppose. It's probably the same as here. Why?'

'Then I don't need those pyjamas you put down for me.'

I show her the list and she looks, then looks away. 'I'll take lighter ones. The ones you put down are my winter pyjamas when the temperature drops to below four.'

During this she has yelled out: mushroom, Cajun, taco, hedgehog and lice. 'Fine,' she says.

I go back upstairs to finish packing.

Marcus

As Peter Dundon crosses to my mother, I dig my fingers into my palms. I hope he goes easy on her.

She still looks very composed. Out of the corner of my eye, I see Alan give her a thumbs-up, then he turns and says something to Lauren, who smiles. I was surprised to see Lauren back today after the way I'd behaved yesterday. She'd arrived at lunchtime, having taken a half day from work.

'Me and Dessie, we know you're innocent,' she said. 'Call him.'

But I can't. Maybe in a while when this whole thing is not so raw.

Peter stands in front of my mother. 'Hello, Thelma. You had Marcus when you were sixteen, is that right?'

'Yes.'

'And the relationship with his dad broke down so you started to drink.'

'Yes, I already—'

'And you've been drinking for years, is that right?'

'On and off.'

'More on than off?'

'In recent years, no, but earlier on, I'd have to say, yes.'

'Would you say that all those years of heavy drinking took their toll?'

'In what way?'

'On your health?'

'I suppose.'

'How?'

'The witness isn't a medical professional,' Melissa says.

'Sorry, I'll rephrase.' Peter smiles at Melissa but she doesn't smile back. He refocuses on my mother. 'During the time you were drinking, would you have suffered from blackouts?'

'Some.'

'Would this mean that your memory was impaired for a time?'

'That's what blackout means.'

'Did you have them during the times your son brought you home from the pub?'

'Yes.'

'So, it's true to say that if your son did get aggressive with you during this time, you might not remember it?'

'My son never got aggressive with me.'

'If you had blackouts and memory loss, how would you know?'

'Because Marcus wouldn't do that. And if he had, I'd know because I'm his mother.'

Melissa pushes a note towards me. A smiley with the words 'She's doing great.'

I feel a little tightness in my chest, looking at my mother. It's as if she's a child taking her first steps away from me. I'm terrified she'll fall.

'After you remarried, did you see Marcus often?'

'Not really.'

'But you can tell if he's done something that he shouldn't?'

My mother stares at Peter. She grinds out, 'I can tell when he's upset or guilty, which he would be if he'd done something wrong.'

'Is stalking wrong, Mrs Epson?'

'Yes.'

'Did you see Marcus at any stage in the last six months of his stalking of Charles Hanratty?'

My mother darts a panicked look at Melissa. She knows where this is going. 'I – I'm not sure—'

Her eyes flick to me. I nod to her. I don't want her to lie.

'Well?' Peter presses.

'I saw him once.'

'And did you notice anything different about him? Was he guilty?'

My mother closes her eyes.

'I didn't see him for too long. It was a flying visit.'

'So you need a certain amount of time, do you?'

'That's harassment,' Melissa warns.

'Judge, it was a question. The witness said that—'

'I am aware of what she said,' the judge said. 'Let's bin the sarcasm. Ask the question in a different way.'

'Did you notice any guilt about your son when you met him briefly in the last six months?'

Peter gets right in her face. I bite my lip.

'No,' my mother says. Then adds, 'But I do know when my son has done wrong.'

'I'm asking you if you can always tell when your son is hiding something.'

Her head bows and she closes her eyes. It's ages before she whispers, 'Obviously not.'

'Can you repeat that?' Peter says.

'I think we heard,' the judge says.

'Moving on. In your evidence you've said a couple of times that you were a terrible mother. Do you wish you'd done better?'

'What Mrs Epson wishes has no bearing on the evidence.' Melissa sounds annoyed.

'Judge,' Peter sounds annoyed too, 'I believe Mrs Epson's wishes have a great bearing on her testimony.'

'I'll allow it, for now.'

'Thank you, Judge.' Peter repeats the question. 'Do you wish you'd been a better mother?'

She eyeballs him. 'Every day. Every second.'

'In what way?'

'In every way.' Her voice shakes. 'In all the ways that matter.'

'Like maybe being a witness for his defence in a court case?'

It's like he's slapped her – her head whips back. 'No, not like that.'

'Are you sure it's not some misplaced guilt that has you here?'

'No.' She looks to me; her eyes fill up. 'Marcus is a good man.'

'He stalked an old man, he sent him threatening post, he's up on a charge of murder – are you really sure about that?'

'Stop.' A silent tear falls.

'You piece of shit!' I'm on my feet. 'Just leave her.'

'The defendant will sit down,' orders the judge.

'I will when he leaves her alone.'

'The defendant will sit down or I will hold him in contempt.'

'Marcus, sit down.' My mother dabs her eyes. 'I'm fine.'

'He made you cry.' I turn to Peter. 'You had no right to make her cry.'

'Sit down. I'll hold you in contempt.'

'I didn't make her cry,' Peter says.

'Piece of shit.'

'Marcus,' Melissa hisses, 'he's trying to provoke you. Sit.'

'I'm not sitting.'

'Then I'll hold you in contempt,' the judge says. 'One night in custody, that'll sort you out. Any more of this and I'll revoke bail.'

Melissa sinks her head in her hands.

My mother turns to Peter Dundon. 'Happy now?' she says.

'I would be if you answered the question. Are you here because of some misplaced guilt?'

'I am here,' she says, and her voice shakes and I want to wrap my arms about her and hug her, only I won't, 'because I believe my son is innocent.'

'But you are his mother, are you not?'

'And proud to be so.' She looks over at me. Melissa has dragged me down to sit. 'Proud to be so.'

'Your mother is fucking brilliant,' Melissa says in awe.

I guess she is.

'You, on the other hand, are stupid.'

I guess I am.

Sash

At the end of the day Marcus is led off by a couple of policemen. They allow him to say goodbye to his mother and his stepdad. A woman kisses him on the cheek, resting her hand lightly on his shoulder, a beautiful-looking woman with red hair and porcelain skin. I wonder who she is.

The two girls who have sat beside me and Dad for the past few days speculate on it too. 'That's a bit disappointing,' the blonde one remarks. 'He's, like, the best-looking criminal to come up in ages.'

They're driving me mad with their remarks. Every day they talk about motive and murder weapons and fingerprints and then they start discussing how hot Marcus is. They're giving him a nine out of ten – he loses a mark because he's a bit skinny.

'He's not a criminal.' I interrupt their discussion on how thin is too thin.

They look at me in surprise.

'Course he is.' That's the blonde one again. She does most of the talking. She always has a packet of sweets handy too for the boring bits. She needs them for her stomach otherwise it'll start rumbling, which is embarrassing. Between eleven and twelve each day, she chomps and sucks and chews. She looks at me now as if I'm bonkers. 'Sure wasn't he stalking the guy? I don't know what trial you're listening to, but if they have that sort of evidence, they normally go down.'

I feel a chill creep up my spine. 'You go to a lot of trials, do you?'

'That's what me and Heather use our holidays for.'

Heather nods.

'We take two weeks twice a year and just come in. It's free and it's always nice to be at a case from the start.'

'Right.'

'I'm dying to meet this Sash one they keep talking about. I'd say she'll give evidence. Apparently she was dating some hotshot but I never heard of her.' The blonde one looks at me. 'Did you?'

'I think I did.' I pick up my bag. Beside me, Dad has started to grin. 'See you tomorrow.'

'Yeah. Bye. I'm Shirley, by the way. This is Heather.'

'Yeah, I'm Heather, hiya.' Heather speaks for the first time.

I shake hands with them. 'I'm Sash.'

It was beautiful.

Dad is still chortling away as we go down in the lift to the foyer. 'Apparently she's dating some hotshot but I never heard of her.' He takes Shirley off surprisingly well and I giggle.

'Wait until I tell Mona about it,' he says. 'She'll enjoy that.'

Dad met Mona when he enrolled for a course called Dealing Successfully with the Asperger's Adult. Mona had been the facilitator. They'd hit it off when Dad realised that he'd been doing a lot of things wrong over the years. I could have told him that. He's way too soft with Lana – he could never deny her anything. He'd kept her a child and now, with Mona's guidance, Lana is finally becoming a little more independent. In the past couple of years she has blossomed, though I think she resents Mona and her bossy ways sometimes. It's like water off a duck's back to Mona, though.

'When are you going to tie that knot?' I ask. The question pops out, the way the most important things I have to say generally do.

Dad looks startled. His grin dies and he stares at me. The lift doors slide open and he makes no move to get out. Instead he closes the door and presses the button to make the lift go up again. 'What?' he asks.

'Dad, you were meant to get out down there.'

'What did you say?'

'I only asked when you and Mona were going to tie the knot. It's a bit embarrassing having my old man living in sin when I can't even get a fella.'

'You'll get someone,' he says with a smile. Then he asks, 'You wouldn't mind?'

'Mind what? If I got someone else?'

'If I asked her to marry me.'

'It's not my business.' I probably would mind a little bit. It's like saying any hope of my mother coming home is gone and though I know this and though I'd be a right eejit to think she was ever going to come back after more than a decade and a half away, there is something about finally closing it down that hurts.

'It *is* your business. She'll be your stepmother. And I

know, despite that cavalier attitude,' he pauses and looks at me gently, 'that you still miss your own mother.'

His perception floors me. My gaze skitters to a point over his head. Feelings that I've half-buried rush to the surface.

The lift pings as it reaches the top. The door slides open and one person gets in.

We have to can the conversation then. I'm glad because I don't know how to react. Him saying that makes me acknowledge it, I suppose. The person gets out on the second floor and Dad presses the lift to go back up.

'I don't miss her.' Even as I say it my voice catches.

'You've always missed her,' Dad says, 'even more so than Lana. You used to follow her around like a chicken after a hen, copying her, saying what she said, wanting to be like her. How could you not miss that?'

The memories crash in and I hadn't thought that they would have the power to hurt me after all this time but blades don't become less sharp when they're not used. I ache in the pit of my stomach when I think of my small self, chattering away to her, watching her as she baked, mimicking her stirring bowls of cake mixture, helping her paint our kitchen. She had endless patience, especially when I fought with Lana over something. Her leaving had been the greatest single tragedy of my life. I could never talk about it – I still can't. A tear slips out of my eye and Dad presses the button to stop the lift. It judders to a halt. Down below, people exclaim over it.

'Are you OK, pet?'

'I'm fine.'

Dad looks upwards. I think he might cry too. 'I always think that when she left, you stopped trusting people. You let no one in. You became hard to manage. You fought all your battles alone.'

He's right. I'd even pushed Marcus away when together we might have done something, and then he wouldn't be in this mess now.

'I'm sorry, Dad.'

'No.' He touches my shoulder, rubs it and then finally pulls me into an embrace. 'I'm sorry. I should have tried harder to win her back instead of agreeing to the divorce.'

'She was never coming back.'

He heaves a sigh. 'No, maybe not.' Then adds, 'I should have tried to talk to you about it, to talk to Lana about it instead of bringing you both to somewhere new so we could all start over. I just – I hadn't a clue.'

We stay like that for a bit, ignoring the calls from outside for us to press the button to get the lift going. Finally, Dad pushes me away, his hands firmly on my shoulders. 'I'm not going to marry anyone without my daughters being OK with it,' he says. 'I love Mona, but you, me and Lana, we're a little team now.'

'If Mona makes you happy, you should marry her.'

He looks at me. 'Then maybe I'll see.'

I smile, and he hugs me briefly again before pressing the button for the lift to descend.

Someone cheers.

Dad loops his arm about my shoulder and pulls me to him.

We walk out into the chaos of reporters.

Marcus

The good thing about being in custody is that I don't have to push past the reporters on the steps. The police drive their van up around the back and I'm bundled into it. Some members of the public see me being hauled away in handcuffs and I'm sure they think that I'm some kind of a dangerous criminal. I try to keep my head up, but the plain fact is that I don't want to be seen like this.

After court ended, my mother hugged me. I tried to hug her back – I've always had a thing about hugging her. It was like hugging smoke: you didn't quite know how long it would last and it was always a bit toxic. I know she senses my stiffness when we're physically close and I know that it hurts her. I can't help it. It doesn't mean that I don't care about her and I never thought it meant that we had a terrible relationship.

Dysfunctional, maybe.

'You did great,' I told her. 'I was proud of you.'

And like the woman I remember of old, she dissolved in tears.

I couldn't take that. I stared at her, frozen. Alan saved me by ignoring my mother and clapping me on the back. 'She'll be fine, she's glad she did good – aren't you, Thelma?'

'Yes.' Teary eyed, she looked at me.

'Now, you get on,' Alan said, like I had a pressing appointment.

Lauren followed me across the room, where I was handcuffed.

She went up on her toes and kissed my face. 'You take care.'

The policeman pulled me away and I was frogmarched out.

I'm in a small cell with another guy. He's up on trial in a week for robbing cars. He's small and undernourished with a thin face splattered with freckles. He's dead jittery and twitchy and he keeps taking off his jumper and pulling it back on.

'You are a murderer and you're out on bail,' he says, gawking at me, 'and all I did was rob a bloody car and I'm banged up in here until my trial.'

I shrug.

'Did you ever murder someone before?' he asks.

'I didn't murder anyone ever,' I tell him.

He rolls his eyes and gives a snort and paces. 'You're saying you never done a murder before this one.'

'Yes.' Then I add, 'I didn't do this one either.'

'This is my twentieth time up for robbing cars,' he says, 'so maybe that's why they kept me in this kip.'

He yells out 'in this kip' at the top of his voice and I wince.

'Does that offend you?' He swaggers up to me, skinny hips protruding from dirty tracksuit bottoms.

'Yeah, it does. I want to get some sleep,' I say.

He doesn't seem to know what to do with that. So he does nothing. I reckon it's because he thinks I'm guilty and, for tonight, I can live with that.

Lana

June Daly calls to wish me luck in the trial and tells me that she knows I'll do great. I don't know how she knows that. Maybe she is psychic. All I have to do is tell the truth, Mona keeps saying. Nobody will blame me for anything if I'm just honest. Honesty is the best policy. If you're honest you have no need to remember, she said.

I had to think about the last one for a long time. Four hours and three minutes and twenty seconds to be exact. I didn't want to ask her what it meant because then she would think I'm not improving. And I finally figured out that it means that the truth is the truth is the facts. It means that I'm not making up anything.

That's good advice and I filed it away so I could say it to someone else one day.

I am lying in bed now and I think that this time tomorrow I'll be lying in a different one. That's scary. It might be cold. It might smell weird. I have packed my own duvet for it so that some of the smell is familiar.

This will be a new experience for me and I have to learn to embrace new experiences: that way I will grow.

DAY 8

Marcus

I got the best night's sleep in ages. The thing about prison is that the rules are the rules. Lights out is lights out and everyone has to be quiet. No messing. And it's so quiet. I'm obviously on a civilised wing. I wasn't attacked or beaten in the shower. I had a nice breakfast, more than I'd have had at home. Then I was taken to court in the van so that meant that I didn't need to worry about traffic or getting there on time.

It was actually quite relaxing.

When we arrive at the court, the journalists snap me getting out of the van as I'm walked in through a back entrance where Melissa is waiting for me.

'Are you ready to purge your contempt?' she says.

'And good morning to you too,' I say wryly.

'Marcus, I don't have time for your sense of humour. To purge or not?'

I actually have to think about this. If I hang about in prison, I won't have to face my mother just yet. I won't have to endure the accusing stares of my neighbours on the rare occasions that I venture out of my apartment. On the other hand, Jerry, my charming cellmate, didn't look like the most predictable sort of chap.

'Yeah,' I say. 'Fine.'

'Good.'

I'm led into court in handcuffs, which is a bit humiliating. The place is filling up as I come in. My mother and Alan are up front. There's no sign yet of Lauren. They look relieved to see me in one piece. I'm not allowed talk to them, but I throw over a cheery smile.

I spot Sash. This morning, instead of her dad, she is accompanied by a big, broad, motherly-type woman who is looking around her with great interest.

Lana isn't with them; they've probably brought her to the victim support room. I'm a bit nervous about her testimony. It could go either way. Melissa said she was prepared to take the chance. It's the only way of backing up my and Sash's story of that night and, though it's flawed, Lana's perception of things will be explained to the jury.

It all depends on the questions Peter Dundon asks her.

'This is what you say.' Melissa hands me a card. 'Learn it, say it and don't fuck it up. You do another freak out and, I swear, I'll put someone else on your case.'

'It was my ma,' I say to her. 'Wouldn't you do the same if it was your ma?'

'If I'd known who she was, maybe,' Melissa says matter-of-factly.

'Shit. Sorry.' I'm immediately contrite.

'Fooled you,' she says cockily. Then, 'Look, Marcus, your loyalty is commendable and, in fact, the papers seemed to love it, but it's not good to have the judge pissed off. Alright?'

'The papers loved it?' I hadn't seen a paper this morning.

'They did seem to find it quite ...' She frowns, thinking.

'Moving,' Josh says, coming up behind us. He grins at me. 'I have the latest *Slam Man* – would you sign it for me?'

'Josh!' Melissa hisses.

'Chill,' I tell her. I take a pen from the desk as Josh produces the magazine, which he has cleverly hidden in a file. I do my best to sign the front cover with a flourish. It's difficult while wearing handcuffs.

'I have two,' he says in an undertone, as Melissa turns away. 'Would you do another one? I can sell it on eBay.'

'Quick.' I grin.

He produces another file with a hidden magazine and I scribble my name on it too.

'You are legend,' he says, grinning. We bump fists as he sits down.

The judge enters, greets everyone and looks to Melissa.

'Judge, before we begin, if I may, my client would like to purge his contempt.'

'Good.' He doesn't sound impressed. 'Well, let's hear it then.'

I stand up, look him in the eye and say with as much sincerity as I can what Melissa has prepared for me.

It takes a few seconds before he nods. 'I don't want any more outbursts. If it happens again, I'll revoke bail, is that understood?'

'Absolutely, Judge,' I say.

'Then let's get going. Who's up first?' He looks to Melissa.

'Judge, I'd like to call Dr Derek Stephens to the stand.'

A tall guy carrying a sheaf of papers makes his way up the room and takes the oath. He cites his qualifications, all of which sound pretty impressive.

'For the purposes of the next witness, I'd like Dr Stephens to explain to the court about Asperger's syndrome,' Melissa says. She nods to the doctor. 'If you would, please.'

Dr Stephens begins, 'Well, in layman's terms, Asperger's syndrome is similar to autism, though people with Asperger's function a lot better than those who are autistic.'

'And their social skills?' Melissa asks.

'They tend to have difficulty processing social signals. In other words, they can have problems understanding body language and interpreting facial expressions. It's like a language they haven't learned. They tend not to be able to process irony, sarcasm or wit. Because of this they accept many things they are told at face value, so for instance if someone was being sarcastic and said, 'Isn't it a lovely day,' when it was raining outside, a person with Asperger's might not recognise this for the sarcasm that it is. Instead they might think that the person means it and maybe wonder at their sanity.'

There is a titter in the courtroom.

'So, for instance, if someone pretended to be happy but they were miserable, would a person with Asperger's be likely to recognise that?'

'No, most likely not, though they can be taught to.'

'Anything else we should know about this condition?'

'People with Asperger's tend not to have empathy. This does not mean they are unfeeling: they are just unable to walk in anyone else's shoes. Their world is who they are. As a result, their speech can sound quite monotonous. It might appear they are being evasive when they are not. Coupled with the fact that they don't tend to make eye contact, this can be a problem for them in social situations.'

'I see. But they are reliable witnesses in court?'

'As reliable as anyone else.'

'Thank you.'

Melissa steps down and Peter stands up.

'One question, doctor, if I may. Do people with Asperger's lie?'

The doctor considers this. 'Generally, they like facts, they like detail, it would be hard for them to be creative.'

'So they tend to tell the truth?'

'As they see it, yes.'

'Thank you.'

'You may step down, doctor.'

The doctor steps down and Melissa calls Lana in.

A door at the side opens and Lana walks out accompanied by her dad. She has grown into an incredibly beautiful young woman. She's a better-looking version of Sash. But even as she takes her seat, you know there is something a little different about her.

I bite my lip, praying that this doesn't backfire.

Sash

Lana is dressed in a long black skirt, because she has a thing about keeping her knees covered, and a white school shirt. Her shoes are the black flat ones she always wears.

'She insisted on that shirt,' Mona whispers to me. 'She wouldn't look at anything else.'

'It's grand.'

She looks so vulnerable as she sits into the seat and stares up at the judge and, though she had been prepared for this by Melissa, it's still new to her. I hope she won't have a meltdown. But in a funny way, I think she's been looking forward to it too.

In a clear voice, she states her name and address for the jury.

'And what is your relationship to the defendant?'

'Nothing.'

'How do you know him?'

'I don't.'

Someone titters.

'How did you come to know his face?'

'He is a friend of Sash, my sister.'

'Now?'

'Not now.'

'When?'

'This could take all day,' Mona says, sounding amused.

'She knew him fifteen years ago. Maybe,' Lana thinks, 'maybe fifteen years and seven months ago. She used to sneak out at night and meet him in the orchard or in the town.'

'And how do you know this?'

'Because I used to sneak out and follow her.'

'And what did Sash and Marcus do on these nights out?'

Shirley and Heather are gawking across at me. Then they nudge someone else and point me out. The someone else is agog. I let on I don't see them.

Lana is in the middle of one of her famously long answers: '... they talked some and sometimes they would sit down and then maybe Marcus would smoke and then Sash would have some and then one time Marcus would tell a joke and Sash might not find it funny and—'

'That's great. What did they do the night of July fifteenth that year?'

I'd given Melissa the date. It wasn't one I'd forget.

'It was hot so Sash just wore her shorts out and a T-shirt and a hoodie. She met Marcus in the orchard like usual and then I don't know what they did from the beginning because I was five hundred seconds behind them but when I caught up they were going across the road to Mr Charles Hanratty's house.'

The atmosphere in the courtroom changes. You can feel it, like the tension at the start of a world-class sprint. Like a pack of hunting dogs getting a scent, they are up on their toes, senses alert. Something big is coming.

'What did they do then?'

Lana describes how we broke in and the aftermath. I feel nauseous listening to her version of it even though I've heard it before. It's like I'm outside myself looking on and I want to shout, 'No, don't go in there. If you do, your life will change forever, please don't go in.' But in the story I always do and my life does change.

Lana

I tell the story as best I can. I think I remember everything. Mostly I remember the counting and the numbers and Melissa doesn't seem to mind when I say them even though I try to stop myself.

In the end she asks me, 'And Sash said that she was happy and she danced.'

'Yes.'

'And did she look happy?'

I like Melissa's shoes. They are red and pointy and have a red sole so I know they are expensive. I would be scared to wear shoes like that on my feet but they are nice to look at.

'Lana, did she look happy?'

'I like your shoes.'

People laugh. Why?

'Did Sash look happy to you when she came out of the house?'

I shrug. 'She said she was happy.'

'But you didn't observe how she looked?'

'She was normal, like her hair was the same and her eyes—'

'Her expression?'

I show a smile.

'What was her expression like?'

'Like this.' Again I smile.

'One word to describe her expression.'

'A smile.'

'Good. Afterwards, did Sash ever tell you that she'd lied to you that night?'

'No.'

'Would there be an occasion where Sash might lie to you?'

I think about this. 'Maybe.'

'Why would she lie?'

'Sometimes Sash says there are white lies to make people feel good. So you never say that someone is fat, you just say nothing. Or maybe you say that they must like their food. Things like that.'

'Any other times?'

I think about when Sash would lie. Then I remember. 'She lies when we fight so Dad won't find out and also to protect me.' It's the right answer because Melissa gives a smile and that means that she is happy.

'So your sister would lie to protect you?'

'Yes. The time my mother left, she didn't tell me that she left because she was tired of being our mother until I was a lot older. She said it was to protect me.'

'Thank you. I've got no more questions. Mr Dundon will talk to you now.'

'He's the mean one?'

People laugh again. I wish I could get the joke just once in a while.

Peter Dundon comes over. He's got a big hook nose and big lips and bulging eyes. His hair is floppy. He says, 'I'll try not to be mean.' His voice is posh.

'That would be great. Thank you.'

He bows his head and I think that maybe he's nice. I don't know what Sash was going on about.

'So, Lana, let's go through this again. You followed your sister and saw her and Marcus enter Charles Hanratty's house through the window?'

'Yes.'

'And then you left and after a bit they ran towards you over a field?'

'Yes.'

'What did they look like?'

'Like themselves.'

People laugh again.

Peter thinks. I think.

'So, no different to normal?'

'No. A bit tired. Sash had puffy eyes. Their clothes were a bit messy.'

Peter nods.

There is a long silence.

Marcus

The silence goes on and on. Melissa and I can barely breathe. She has been clever putting Lana up before Sash because Peter needs to ask his questions a certain way. He doesn't want to scare Lana and get the jury offside and yet he needs to discredit her, because our story rests on the fact that she had been there that night too, even if Sash had lied to her and she'd taken it at face value. It's a fine balance. Melissa chews on her pen as she looks at Peter looking at Lana.

She is growing uncomfortable under the scrutiny.

Peter seems to be thinking things out. And then it's like the sun bursting through a cloud and I think, Oh fuck, oh fuck, oh fuck. He's going to go for it. He thinks he has something.

'You say Sash would lie to protect you?'

'Yes.'

'Did she need to protect you that night?'

'No.'

'So she genuinely appeared happy?'

'She was smiling.'

'OK, I understand. Has she ever, to your knowledge, lied to protect anyone else?'

Melissa hisses out through her teeth. 'What a fucking good question,' she says.

If Lana says 'no', Peter has done no damage to his case. If she says 'yes', he has inflicted a bit of damage to ours.

And when Lana answers, she shoots our case down in a hail of information.

'She lied to protect Marcus once.'

Oh shit. The event, half-forgotten, comes back in technicolour as she recounts it.

It was no big deal but it was still Sash going to bat for me. And in this courtroom, its significance takes on monstrous proportions.

It was a week before Hanratty, sometime in early July.

The weather was great. Sash and I were rocking it. The only crap part was that I had to work during the day and Sash spent her days minding Lana and wasn't allowed out because apparently you couldn't predict how Lana would react to a new environment.

Sash was bored and lonely and I decided to surprise her with a visit.

Just before eight in the morning, I rang into work sick. Then, holding a bottle of vodka and a couple of joints, I hid behind a large shrub on Sash's driveway. I sat there for two hours until her auld fella drove off to work in the squad car. I didn't see him, just heard him call out a 'goodbye' and a warning for Sash not to leave Lana on her own, then the slam of a front door followed quickly by the slam of a car door and the sound of an engine taking off and fading away in the distance. I waited a second or two, dusted myself down and walked up to the front door and rang the bell.

It was a few minutes before it was answered and it was Lana who opened the door. I guess she must have been about twelve or so, tall for her age but pale, with eyes too big for her face. As she looked at me, her eyes grew even larger, but she didn't say anything, which was a bit unnerving.

'Will you get Sash for me?'

She shook her head. 'No. You don't belong here. You belong in the shop.'

'Please, just tell her Marcus is here.'

She made to close the door and I put my foot in it. 'Just get Sash.'

Probably I scared her, but she ran off, leaving the door

open. I took a chance and walked in. 'Sash!' I yelled. 'It's Marcus!'

Lana was in the kitchen because I saw her at the table through the open door. I crossed towards her and she fired a knife straight at me. She was a decent shot.

'Jesus!' I stepped out of the way and it clattered to the floor.

'Hey!' Sash said from behind and I turned and saw her, still in her PJs, her hair tousled from sleep. I remember thinking that they were not the sort of pyjamas I'd have imagined Sash in – not that I went about imagining her in pyjamas or anything. Her pyjamas were pink, with a bunny and love hearts on them. Maybe, it occurred to me in a blast of pain, this isn't the girl I always thought she was. This girl is different here, in this place. I felt a bit awkward then.

Sash folded her arms and took in the vodka bottle. A grin. 'Jesus, Marcus, you shouldn't be here.'

A spoon hit me on the side of the head. 'Fuck sake.' I rubbed the space where it had landed. 'Can you tell her to stop that?'

'Lana, pet, go upstairs and get dressed. I'm OK here. This is Marcus.'

Lana, still looking at me suspiciously, stood up and sidled by us. She gave me the creeps with those eyes and her silence.

'And if Dad asks did anyone call, we say no, right, because he doesn't like Marcus.'

'Your dad doesn't like me?'

Sash shrugged. 'My dad knows your mother from the station.'

'Oh, right, I'm the drunk's kid.'

She looked upset. 'I'm sorry.'

I understood, though. 'Not a word, Lana,' I said to her, and instead of going upstairs she went and sat in the corner of the room and observed us.

I held up the vodka and the joints. 'I thought, seeing as you're so bored and I hate my job, that we could have a party.'

'You don't hate your job and, anyway, I've to look after Lana.'

'Do you like parties, Lana?'

She nodded.

'Good.' I threw her a packet of Jelly Babies.

Sash laughed. 'They're our favourite, aren't they, Lans?'

Lana was already digging into the bag. I dangled another packet in front of Sash. 'I got one for you too.'

She made a grab for it and I wouldn't let go until she gave me a kiss.

'I like the man ones best,' she said, her eyes laughing, 'because you always get the extra bit.'

I thought this was hilarious. She laughed at me laughing. 'Grab us a couple of glasses to go with the extra bits,' I said.

'It's ten in the morning, Marcus.' She giggled.

'Great, we've the whole day.'

She took two glasses from the press and put them on the table. I lit a joint and poured us each a vodka. She put on the radio.

'You look sexy when you smoke,' she said, as she took a sip of her drink.

'Yeah?'

'The way it dangles over your bottom lip, I like that.'

'Cool.' I felt my insides fizz.

The fizz was dampened by the sound of the kitchen door opening. What with the noise of the radio, we hadn't heard Sash's dad come back. The shock of seeing him standing in full uniform in the doorway made me grab the joint from my mouth and curl it into my palm. The pain was excruciating but I didn't make a sound. I still have the faint scars.

'What the hell is going on?' Red-faced and furious, he advanced into the kitchen, took in the vodka and sniffed. 'Have you got drugs in here? Have you?' It was directed at me.

'It's my fault,' Sash babbled, 'I invited him over. I got the vodka and the, the smokes and—'

'Get out,' Sash's dad roared at me. Lana started howling.

'Don't shout at him,' Sash said to her dad. 'It was my fault.'

Her dad advanced on us. I made to leave but Sash put her hand on my arm. 'Marcus, stop,' she said. 'Report me, Dad. Go on. I dare you. If you say it was Marcus, I'll just say it was me.'

'Get out,' he said to me again. He caught me by the collar, marched me right through the house and flung me out the front door.

Sash yelled at me to run.

Sash

As Lana finishes off her story, I want to weep. How can something I did fifteen years ago suddenly come back to haunt me like this? It barely meant anything. Most kids would do the same if they could. I knew there was no way my dad would cite me for drugs but that he'd have no hesitation in reporting Marcus. I couldn't let him away with that.

As Peter Dundon sits down the judge looks questioningly at Melissa, who waves him away.

'You may step down,' the judge says.

'Thank you.' Lana smiles brightly down at us and I'm forced to smile back.

I stare up at Marcus and he looks gutted.

Marcus

'Melissa says she can pick it up on Sash,' I tell Alan and my mother as we drive back to the apartment that night.

Neither of them reply; I don't think there is much to say. It was a pretty bruising testimony.

Then my mother bursts out with, 'I hope she does. It was all her decision to put that girl on the stand – she knew it could have gone either way.'

'It was my decision too, Ma. We need someone to back up Sash's story. Otherwise they'll say we made it up or something. And at least we've still got that.'

'He's already proved the girl will lie for you.'

'That was fifteen years ago. We've moved on since then. She owes me nothing now.'

More silence.

Finally, we arrive back at my place and Alan drives into the underground car park. We head to the lift in silence and arrive into the apartment in silence. When Alan asks what I'd like for dinner, I tell him to just order for him and my mother. I can't face food. Instead I head into my studio and sit on the red sofa which runs along one wall. My drawings, bright and happy, full of twists and jokes, leer at me from the walls. How far is that from my life right now? I wonder if I'll ever think of another joke. And yet, the drawing keeps me sane.

My mother knocks on the door. 'Can I come in?'

'Sure.'

I watch, slightly irritated, as she skirts around the edges of the room, afraid to touch anything. Finally she joins me on the sofa, sitting right down the far end. She angles her body towards me. Softly, she says, 'Thank you for standing up for me yesterday. It meant a lot.'

Bleakly I look at her. 'You're my mother – it's practically my job.'

She stares down at her hands, which she has folded in her lap. Then back up at me. 'It's not your job, I want you to know that. You are free of me, Marcus.' Then, seeing something in my expression, she says, more firmly, 'I mean it. No more minding me.'

'Until the next time,' I quip.

I see I've hurt her. It was only a joke. Sort of.

Her lip quivers, but showing the same composure she did yesterday in court, she says, 'I don't know what it'll take to make you understand, but you are my son. I love you. I've treated you terribly and I'm sorry.'

Her words wash over me. She's said sorry so many times now, I just don't believe it. Each time, in the past, when I allowed myself to hope, it was dashed on the rocks of some drink or other. Even now, though she's years sober, I can't find it in me to just let go and trust completely.

So I say instead, 'We had some pretty cool picnics, though.'

A small, faint glimmer in her eyes. 'You remember those?'

'Do you?'

She flinches. 'Yes. Of course I do. We went all the way to Galway one day, remember?'

'And we couldn't get home.'

'I'd forgotten we had to get home. I just wanted us to escape somewhere nice.'

'It *was* nice.' Now my voice cracks a tiny bit. I say, trying to be cool about it and failing, 'It wasn't all bad.'

Her gaze locks with mine. This time, I hold it.

'Thank you,' she says.

She waits, I'm not sure what for, before she stands and leaves, closing the door behind her.

Lana

The apartment doesn't smell like our house in Applegate. It smells of wood and polish and Windolene and washing-up liquid. It doesn't smell of people and home. I don't know how I will sleep in it. I say that to Dad.

'You close your eyes the same as normal,' Dad says. 'We're all here too.'

'If I close my eyes and open them I won't see the crack on the ceiling or the chip in the door or look into the hall with the peeling wallpaper. I will miss the spider web that hangs from the left-hand corner of—'

'You make Applegate sound so attractive,' Mona says. Then, 'When you open your eyes you will see Sash because she will be with you. And you can smell her and talk to her.'

I look at Sash. She has been real quiet since the court. I thought I did good. I answered all the questions. I told the truth, like Mona said.

'Have you a pain?' I ask Sash then.

'What?'

'You're quiet so I think maybe you have a pain or you feel sick. If you feel sick or have a pain, maybe it's better you don't sleep in my bed or in my room because there's no point in two of us being sick and—'

'I'm fine,' she says, a bit loud.

'Sash,' Dad says.

Then there is more silence.

'She's feeling nervous about tomorrow,' Dad says to me. 'Sometimes people are quiet for that reason too.'

That's OK then. Once she's not sick, she can sleep with me. Then I think of something nice to say to her. People like it when you do that. 'It's OK,' I say, 'Peter is not scary and all you have to do is tell the truth.'

'Fuck off,' Sash says.

That's rude and ungrateful but nobody says anything to her.

DAY 9

Marcus

Today is the day that'll bring the whole case home. Sash will be on the stand, probably for a while. I am sick for her, sick for myself and burning with shame – I'll never get rid of that. But we're telling the truth, so I only hope it'll shine through.

There are two letters for me on the worktop – they must have been there last night only I didn't notice them. One has been forwarded from the court and the other is from my employers in the UK.

I tear open the UK letter first, hoping it's a cheque, though it's unlikely, as they normally pay me electronically.

It's a letter.

Dear Marcus,

On behalf of Comic Lines, I'm letting you know that we will not be commissioning any further Slam Man comics as of January next year. The general feeling here is that the story lines have run their course. While we know this will be a shock to you, we would welcome any ideas you may have for further superheroes. Ideas to be submitted by 31 October. Please note that other cartoonists have been approached to submit ideas too. An email to this effect will be sent to you shortly. Thanks for all your hard work, enthusiasm and brilliance and can't wait to hear from you.

All the best,

The Comic Lines team.

This is accompanied by a drawing of a big thumb with a smiley face.

I fold the letter up and put it in the pocket of my shirt. If I think too much about it, I'll probably do something stupid like cry. I'd been wondering if this would happen. I thought maybe news of an Irish court case wouldn't make it across the pond, but it obviously has.

I feel sorry for Slam Man.

They must be running scared to can him, though. It has been their biggest success in decades. But I suppose if people have had the same reaction to it as the woman on the beach, sales of the comic have fallen.

I still feel betrayed.

'Ready?' Alan asks.

'Sure.'

'Thelma,' he calls. 'We're ready to go now.'

My mother joins us and I unlock the door. Too late I realise that I've forgotten to open the other letter. I figure it'll keep till later, when we get back.

Sash

I thought I'd be composed, I thought I'd feel sort of detached and together, but I don't. I'm actually shaking as Dad and I walk up the steps of the court. The only consolation is that today might not be too bad, as I'll just be telling my story, though the only person to ever hear it in full, up to now, has been my counsellor. It's awful exposing myself to the court, especially a hostile one, because, who am I kidding, Lana's testimony has done a lot of damage. And the tragedy is, she's thrilled with herself.

Still, Melissa says she will take me slowly through my story and try to patch up any holes she sees on the way. I can call for a break whenever I like. I hope I won't have to.

The journalists know who I am now. They take my picture as I go in.

'Sash!' The voice, completely unexpected, catches me unawares. I spin around and there he is. My throat constricts and tears spring to my eyes.

Paddy, looking a bit wretched, stands a little down the street.

'I'll go on in,' Dad says, and I barely hear him.

Paddy and I stare at each other for a bit before I walk towards him. He's wearing a jacket that looks a little big on him. Dark blue trousers that need a bit of an iron. His shoes are dull. His hair has been buzzed close to his head. But his eyes are the same; the small smile he gives me is the same. The snappers take more photos. We face each other. 'I thought, well, I rang Mona last week,' he flounders.

'I know, I didn't …' Now I flounder.

'I just, well, I wanted to see if you wanted me to come today. For support.'

I can't speak for the lump in my throat.

'I know it's a little late and I know I should have done better for you, but I just wondered …' His voice trails off.

I look into his warm brown eyes, which appear tired right now. Him, turning up here, touches me something rotten. 'Would you?' My voice shakes.

'I'd be honoured.'

'Thank you.'

He walks beside me up the steps.

Marcus

Sash comes in and Paddy is with her. I probably should have expected that. He's that kind of guy, always appears on time to do the right thing. I haven't seen him since he threw me out of his office. I'd called him a coward, I'd told him he was scared of facing the truth but he hadn't been. He really did think I was mad. I probably was a bit. Unhinged, maybe. Right now, I admire his courage. From what I know of the citizens of Applegate and their feelings towards Charles Hanratty, they won't like the fact that their ex-golden-boy is supporting someone who, in one day, will hopefully destroy that man's reputation forever. I watch as he solicitously lets Sash's dad into the seat, then sits in himself, leaving Sash to sit on the outside. She looks at him and he looks at her, then I see him take her hand and squeeze it.

My heart squeezes a bit just looking.

I'm glad he's here for Sash. When they split, I wondered what had happened. I even wondered if he believed her or not. I think I would have knocked him flat again if he hadn't believed her story after she finally admitted it. He didn't know me, but he knew what Sash was like. She'd never lie about a thing like that.

Paddy catches my eye and, after a second in which he studies me, he nods.

I nod back.

Melissa arrives in. She sits down and heaves a sigh. Then, without acknowledging me, she starts pulling files from her trolley.

'Are you OK?' I ask.

She turns briefly. 'No. I'm kicking myself for yesterday.'

'What Lana said proves nothing.'

She gives me a look as if to say I'm being naive, then asks, 'And how are you doing?'

'Aside from being told I just lost my job, I'm doing great.'

'No?' Her face falls and she groans. 'I'm sorry.'

'It's not totally unexpected.' I try to be upbeat. It deflects from what's coming with Sash's testimony. 'If I get out of this alive, losing my job will be a minor thing.'

'That's true,' she agrees. 'And if you don't, you won't need a job: the state will put you up.'

'Not funny.'

'Sorry.' A small grin before she beckons Josh over. 'Check through these files, will you? We've a big day today.'

'Sure thing, boss.' Josh picks up a folder and begins scanning through it.

'Buy *Slam Man* at the end of January,' I tell him. 'I'll sign it for you and you'll make a killing.'

He looks at me questioningly.

'Unless you don't agree with insider trading?'

Melissa raps me with a file. 'Don't corrupt my staff,' she says.

Josh suddenly smiles, then frowns, then perches on the edge of the desk. 'Aw, shit, you lost your job?'

'Yep, but, you know, I mightn't have been able to do it from prison.'

'That's hard, man.' Josh shakes his head at the unfairness of it. 'And you aren't going to prison. Is he, Melissa?'

'Not if we can help it.'

Our attention is caught by a mild scuffle in the front row. I cringe when I see that my mother has kept a seat for Lauren. She's put her black jacket on it and is telling people that it's reserved. Some woman is tutting loudly and then her companion whispers to her and she looks at my mother and looks at me and backs off.

The advantage of being up on a murder charge.

Lauren arrives in a couple of minutes later and makes her way to the front. She must be taking days off work for this and, while it's nice of her, I'm not comfortable with her doing it. As she squeezes past people, she flashes a smile at me then turns to my mother for a chat.

I wonder how much she'll like me by the end of the day. By the time court finishes, everyone will know what Sash and I have spent fifteen years keeping secret and I'm not sure I'll be able to hold my head up for the cameras.

At ten thirty, the room filled to bursting, the day gets underway.

'I call Sash Donnelly to the stand.'

Sash gets up and her dad kisses her cheek. Paddy gives her hand a squeeze, as if unsure of what he should do. As she approaches the stand, Sash's dad puts his head in his hands.

Sash is wearing jeans, which surprises me. I guess she just wants to feel like herself. Her hair curls and she doesn't have the polish she had when she was with Paddy – she looks more like I remember. It's like she's slowly finding herself again. She glances over at me and I smile at her. She smiles back. We're in this together, I want to say, but I can't.

And I can't protect her or I'll be back in jail.

The sense of powerlessness is terrible. My fate is in her hands and in the hands of the twelve people opposite me.

Please believe her, I beg.

As Sash sits and takes the oath, her voice shakes a little. The silence in the room is like the way the orchard used to be after dark. The artists start to sketch, glancing up and down at their pages.

They will never capture her spirit, I think.

Sash

I am going to vomit – my legs had shaken so much as I made my way up the room with everyone looking at me. Everyone in the place is craning forward, expecting the big reveal. Unlike the way it was when I was with Paddy, I don't live in fear of letting these people down. They will get their story; they will have something to gossip about with their friends over tea. The papers will have a field day this evening.

Melissa smiles at me reassuringly – she is like my boat in an ocean of dangerous currents.

'I'm going to take you right back to when you moved to Applegate first,' Melissa says. 'Can you tell us about it?'

As I talk, I remember. My words weave their way into the air of the courtroom, conjuring up pictures. My first glimpse of Applegate had been on a wet, soggy autumn day in a car with the windows fogged up and a radio talk-show host bleating on about the dangers of escalators. Lana was beside me in the back of the car, playing with her doll. She was a strange kid, mostly happy, albeit in her own way, though the loss of our mother had changed her, just like it changed me. In front, my dad was pretending to listen to the radio, while all the time glancing at his rear-view mirror to see how I was.

I wore a scowl all the way from Dublin. My facial muscles were aching, my heart was breaking but I didn't cry. I had said goodbye to my two best friends earlier that morning and they'd given me some presents – photographs of the three of us along with some music vouchers and a year's supply of the *Spider-Man* comic to be delivered to my door. At my new address.

They'd promised to keep in touch.

'Applegate,' my dad said.

I hadn't replied. Lana sat up straighter and wiped her window and peered out. The windscreen wipers swished back and forth and I could see that we were passing through a small main street with some huddled-up shopfronts on one side and what looked like a hulking hotel on the other. A massive church dominated the skyline, its cross puncturing the air like a fist. The streets were deserted. It was as if we were passing through a ghost town.

'That's the police station,' Dad said in a big cheery voice. 'That's where I'll be working from, Lana.'

She nodded and went back to her doll.

Dad handed me some directions. 'Read these out, will you, so I can find our new house.'

'I'd rather go back to our old one.'

'We can't. Now read them out.'

'I hate you for bringing us here. I will never forgive you for this.'

'Don't fight.' Lana put a hand on my arm. 'Don't fight.'

I looked at Dad and he looked at me, daring me to upset my sister when she'd been through so much. Nothing about upsetting me.

'Keep driving through the village,' I read from the paper, before snorting, 'village? Half a village more like.'

Dad ignored the jibe and kept driving.

'Two miles on you will see an orchard on your left. This is

where the town gets its name. Opposite this, there is a house. Take the turn by this house.'

Dad followed my directions. 'Now what?'

'You will pass two houses on your right. The third shack is yours.'

'Shack?' He crooked his eyebrows.

'Sorry, house,' I ground out.

I think he smiled but it could just as easily have been a grimace.

We pulled up outside a bungalow, a house Dad had agreed to rent before making any commitment to staying in Applegate.

There were cakes in tins on the porch, all wrapped up and sheltered from the rain. Cards welcoming the new sergeant. One from Charles Hanratty.

'I think we'll like it here,' Dad said.

I found it creepy.

I then talk about moving school and the way I was different to everyone else in Applegate because I read comics.

'Why did you read them?' Melissa asks.

'It was an escape. I was unhappy. Things in comics always worked out. The superhero always won.'

'And you were picked on because of this?'

I tell how I was bullied, how the only people in school who talked to me were Paddy Jones and his mates and the guys on the athletics team.

'How did that make you feel?'

'Angry,' I say, without hesitation.

'Can you tell the court how you met Marcus?'

I tell them about being beaten up by Margaret Browne and Jenifer Ryan. My dad, who has never heard this before, looks appalled. Paddy pales; he was seeing Margaret back then, before he got up the courage to break it off with her in sixth year. 'Marcus rescued me,' I say. 'We joked that he was a superhero.'

Across the courtroom, Marcus's smile illuminates his face.

'How did the friendship develop?'

'He asked me to meet him in the orchard at night and I did.'

'That seems a foolish thing to do? Risky?'

'I didn't care about risky – I was angry. All I wanted was a friend. And the riskier the better. It helped numb the pain of my mother going. Numb the pain of being an outsider.'

I heave and take a shaky drink of water. It's cold when it hits the back of my throat.

'Would you like a break?' Melissa asks.

'No, I'll keep going.'

'Was Marcus a risky friend?'

I smile a bit. 'I think I was the risky one.'

Marcus

For a long time I couldn't believe my luck, that Sash Donnelly would hang out with me. Paddy Jones used to come into the shop and slag me over her. Looking back, I reckon Paddy was trying to find out exactly what our story was because he definitely fancied Sash himself though he was probably too terrified of Margaret to break up with her. Everyone loved Margaret and Paddy together. They were like the golden couple. Sports star and supermodel. Paddy liked to make people happy, and if being with Margaret made people happy, that's what he would do.

Sash and me mostly hung out at the orchard. In the beginning that had been fun but then she started on at me to break into places and I knew that if I didn't she wouldn't want me anymore. So I did. I was addicted to her.

Sash

'You were the risky one, how so?'

'Marcus and I were dangerous together – I knew it as soon as we'd begun to be friendly. He'd taken to walking me home from school when he was free. I hadn't wanted him to as I thought it made me look weak in front of Margaret, but he'd insisted. Margaret and her pals left me alone after that. After a few weeks, without even talking about it, we went to the orchard after school and sat on the grass, eating apples and chatting.' I stop, arrested by the memory. Every time I eat an apple now, I think of those days.

'Sash?' Melissa prompts.

'Sorry. Yes. Well, Marcus and me, we had far too much in common. Our love of comic books, the things we laughed at that no one else got. The fascination we had with *Star Wars* and *Star Trek* and *Batman*. We liked computer gaming and I'd go to his house sometimes and play. He rarely came to mine. We ate the same foods; we wore the same type of clothes. We finished each other's sentences, knew what each other wanted. We met at night in the orchard. It was as if we were creating our own little world that no one else could enter: in it we were protected, invincible. We could do anything, be anyone. That's what I thought anyway,' I say, my words trailing off as I remember.

Melissa asks softly, 'And then what happened?'

'After a bit, the edge wore off for me. I needed a bigger thrill. I invented this game, just for a laugh at the start, where we would wander into the shops in town and case them out. I mean, it started as fun, each of us throwing in an idea of how we'd rob a particular place. Very few people in Applegate had an alarm in those days and we figured that even those that had never actually believed they'd be robbed. I'd witnessed alarms going off and then resetting after half an hour. If you set an alarm off enough times, the owner would be convinced there was something wrong with it and leave it off the next time. It was all a matter of watching and waiting, we believed. And thinking about all the ways we could break into places was actually fun. At the start. But then I thought, what's the point of just thinking about it? And there were two places I really wanted to get into. And one of them was the hardware shop owned by Jennifer Ryan's dad. Marcus had noticed that there was no alarm there, so I said that all we'd have to do was force the back door and avoid the dog.'

'So you suggested it first?' Melissa says.

'Yes.'

'And remember you are under oath: you're not saying this to protect Marcus?'

'I'm telling the truth. I wanted to break into the hardware

store because I guess I thought I'd get one over on Jennifer Ryan. And I'd like to clarify something from yesterday?'

Melissa nods – she looks pleased with me. 'What would you like to clarify?'

'I did lie to save Marcus that time in my house. Who wouldn't have? We were kids, I fancied him like mad. I'm an adult now, we've gone our separate ways, we're not enmeshed the way we used to be.'

'Thank you. So, back to your testimony. You suggested that the two of you would rob a shop?'

'Yes.'

Marcus

I would have agreed to anything. I never thought to wonder why she wanted to target the hardware shop – I was happy to let her lead. I was wild, but not in Sash's way. I just had this streak of independence running through me. I never expected anything I did to be monitored, I did what I felt like, when I felt like it, and when you're almost eighteen, you do a lot of crazy stuff without actually thinking it's crazy. Sash, on the other hand, was a loose cannon, suddenly unleashed on the world. She knew what was normal and chose to do the opposite.

'Were you planning on destroying the shop?' Melissa asks.

'No, it wasn't about robbing the places or damaging them; it was just about getting inside them because we could,' Sash says.

292

I was shitting myself that first time. My job was to distract Tony, Jenny's dad, by asking him some stupid question about something I didn't really want at the far end of the shop. Sash was to take his keys and get them copied in the shoe repair shop up the road. We'd already seen the back door, so we knew roughly what keys she'd need. It shouldn't take too long. Out of the corner of my eye, I watched as Sash ducked behind the shop counter and lifted them. Then, as bold as brass, she sauntered out of the shop. I almost laughed. I kept Tony busy by asking him about the various merits of door locks and asking how Jenny was. He liked talking about Jenny. A few customers wandered in and Tony excused himself to talk to them. I watched as they took his attention and I knew that my time had run out. There was no possible way for me to stay in the place without looking suspicious. I was on my way out when Sash arrived back in. She saw me and rolled her eyes at how hopeless I was. I watched in awe as she swaggered back up the shop and, leaning over the counter, dropped the keys on the floor. Then she waited to be served and when Tony crossed to her she asked him if they were his keys on the floor.

Then she bought a screw from him for ten pence.

With a wink at me, that set my heart racing, she was out of there.

Sash

'The fact that step one of the plan had been so easy almost frightened us, I think. So we waited a little while, neither of us suggesting using the key, until one day: I'd asked Marcus to meet me in the orchard that night.

'He knew why without asking. That was the way we were. It's hard to explain now. Anyway, we agreed on one o'clock because Lana would be asleep and Marcus's mother would be out cold. At one, I climbed out my bedroom window and ran up the road to meet him. He was waiting at the tree we sat at during the day and, without a word, he started to walk in the direction of town. Both of us were probably nervous because I don't remember us talking on that walk. Those times are like photographs in my head now. It was wet, I remember. My heart was hammering. The main street was deserted.

'Just before the laneway that led to the back of the shops, we stopped. Marcus looked at me and I looked at him and nodded. He gave me a thumbs-up. We ran down the laneway and around to the back of the buildings. We counted along the walls until we came to the hardware store. I remember I almost laughed and he did too and then he laced his fingers together, making a step, and I put my foot into it and climbed onto the wall that ran around the yard. Marcus climbed up beside me. Then we let ourselves down on the other side.'

'And then what happened?'

'The yard was small; boxes and rubbish bins stood against one corner of it. The dog, who was in a kennel, growled at us and I sort of yelped and stepped back but Marcus stayed where he was and then the dog made a dart for Marcus's leg before he jerked to a stop. There was a chain on his neck that confined him to not more than three feet from the kennel.

'We laughed again, then Marcus took out some ham and

threw it at the dog who sniffed at it before eating it. I was pretty impressed that he'd thought of that.' I stop suddenly, a lump in my throat.

'Are you OK?' the judge asks.

I take a sip of water and nod.

I'd forgotten how we used to laugh.

'So, you're in the yard and the dog is happy,' Melissa says. 'Then what?'

I take a deep breath, 'Then, I put the key into the back door, wiggled it around a bit before we heard a *click*. The head rush was thrilling.'

'And what did you do then?' Melissa asks.

'Nothing much really. There wasn't much to do unless we fancied wrecking the shop, which neither of us did. Marcus found a kettle and made us a cup of tea, which we drank with our backs to the wall, hidden behind the counter. We smoked a bit of dope and it was nice. Calm. We kissed. It was a bit spooky, though, because the shelves threw these massive shadows onto the walls from the streetlight outside.

'Opposite where we sat, there was a shelf and, when I'd finished my tea, I crawled across and had a look. It was a dumping ground for things. I remember bits of scrawled-on paper, leaky pens, stuff like that, but right at the back, there was a photograph. I had to rub it clean but it was a picture of a girl, about five or six, in a swimming suit. Her hair had these sausage ringlets and her tummy stuck out and she was beaming. When I turned the picture over, it said "Jenny, aged 5". I told Marcus that I was taking it so that I could stick it on the school noticeboard.

'That was the start of me taking my souvenirs from the places we broke into.'

Melissa holds up a tattered box that I'd brought with me from Applegate. I haven't looked inside it since before we broke into Hanratty's. I can't even remember what I put in there. Seeing it now hurts.

'I'd like this to go in as evidence of the truth of the witness's claims. There are items in this box that can only come from the places she and Marcus broke into.' Melissa turns back to me. 'Aside from what's in this box, did you ever rob anything?'

'No.'

Melissa starts to take out various items from the box. They are sealed in plastic envelopes.

'Each of these items has been identified by its owner and each one of them has signed a statement to that effect. This establishes without a doubt that Marcus and Sash did indeed break into places.'

As she holds the objects up, my memory sharpens. She won't need the stories behind them but they were things I thought significant at the time.

Marcus

I never knew Sash took stuff. She must have slipped things into her pockets as we were leaving. I wonder why she did that. The stuff she took from the businesses isn't too interesting – a nut, a bolt, a sweet, a saucer. But from the houses, the objects are a lot more personal. There are photographs, tiny ornaments, fridge magnets, lots of bits and pieces.

Breaking into places was cool, I have to admit. For a guy who, up until then, had led a pretty boring life, I was suddenly doing exciting stuff with a girl I was crazy for. It would have been better if we didn't do it but I never got up the nerve to say that to her. To me, it felt wrong a lot of the time, especially when we started doing the houses. It was like peering into people's souls without permission. Sash didn't care. The first house we broke into was June Daly's. Sash had taken Dessie Daly's keys at lunch in school and I got them copied and returned to her by the end of class. Sash said that she'd leave the keys in a place where they'd be handed in so Dessie would get them back. We both liked Dessie, that's why.

I knew what Dessie's was like anyway, but Sash had this need to see if they were as happy as they appeared. They were. The rooms were covered in family photographs, all over the walls and perched on top of dressers and shelves. In them everyone was smiling. June even had a mat on the floor that said 'Welcome to our home'. In my ma's it would have been 'be careful you don't slip on the dirt'.

I remember telling Sash this and she had to choke back her laughter. June Daly's house smelled of soup and warm dinners. And clean clothes. Sash sat on the sofa for about an hour just soaking up the atmosphere in that house as I paced uneasily up and down, feeling bad about being there.

The second place we entered was Margaret Brown's. Sash really wanted to go here. She scared me a bit she wanted it so much. I think she was annoyed because it was surprisingly cosy too. There were photos of Margaret and her parents beaming from the walls, doing things together like a family should. In some of the pictures, there was a boy of about eight. But in the more recent photos, he had disappeared.

'Did he run away?' Sash asked. 'I wouldn't blame him if he did.'

'He died,' I told her.

She peered more closely at the picture but said nothing.

We managed to get into eight houses and each one told us things about the people living in them. Sometimes people were out, sometimes they were sleeping upstairs. Paddy Jones's house had plaques all over the place. There were medals mounted on a board. Shelves were devoted to trophies all aligned in order of size. It wasn't only Paddy winning stuff in this family – his dad's GAA trophies were all over the house too. Pictures of Paddy being handed prizes were framed on the walls.

'Like a shrine,' Sash breathed. It was pretty intimidating.

There were photos of Brian Jones holding the Sam Maguire. In one picture he was drinking from it; in another, baby Paddy was sitting in it; while in another, he was holding it aloft as people cheered. In the middle of all this, there was a picture of Paddy's mother holding him as a baby. I remember thinking how much she seemed to love him in that picture and I wondered if my mother had ever looked at me like that. I didn't expect the sharp knife-like stab of jealousy for Paddy's life that ripped through me. We broke into Jenny's house, which was big and clean and airy. I'd been in there before but Sash hadn't. She looked at everything with disdain, as if she resented it. It was a beautiful house, cosy and welcoming. Jenny's kitchen stretched for miles. I saw Sash scrape the wooden countertop with a piece of stone but I pretended not to.

Some houses were dark and dirty. Some had everything all neat and precise. In almost all of them, there were pictures of mothers and their children. I liked that.

We grew even closer during that time. We made a pact that, whatever happened, we'd have each other's backs.

I wish we'd never made that pact because I never forgave myself for what happened when we broke into Hanratty's.

Sash

'Now, Sash, can you take us back to the night of July fifteenth, just over fifteen years ago?' Melissa asks.

I have to gather myself before I speak. I do not want to break down. This is too important. I have to tell this in as clear a way as I can. I want to do justice to what I went through. To what we both went through. I want them to see Marcus as the driven man he is.

'It was a hot night. The summer had been good. I can't remember what I wore exactly but I remember the heat. It had built through the day and the ground was still giving it out after dark. I climbed out the window and met Marcus at our tree. It was about one o'clock. It had been my idea to break into Hanratty's. Marcus hadn't wanted to.'

'Why Mr Hanratty's house in particular?'

'Because I was curious. This man was the richest guy in the place and yet he lived in a tiny house. No one ever went into it – he seemed to meet everyone at the hotel. And also there was a broken window frame so I figured we'd get in easy.'

'How do you know no one ever went into it?'

'I passed it every day going to and from school, and I never saw anyone there. During the day, he was in Applegate a lot. I was just nosy, I guess. I thought he'd have interesting things in his house, having all that money.'

'OK. So what happened?'

'That night, when I met Marcus, he just said, "Hanratty", and I could feel the excitement because this time we had no key.' I look at Melissa, look at them all, just so they're in no doubt. 'It was a break-in, I'm not making excuses. It was wrong.'

'Describe what you both did.'

'We stood looking at the house for a bit, you know, getting up the nerve. It was always scary: that was part of the thrill. Then, without saying anything, Marcus just went for it. He ducked down and so did I and we crept into the shadow of the wall. The place was in darkness. Nothing stirred. So we crept up to his gate and crawled up his driveway. There is no way we could have been seen – we kept to the shadows. We got to underneath the window ...' My voice falters; this is the part where I want the story to have changed, but it's always the same. If I could step back in time and change it, I would. Sometimes it's a physical ache, how much I want to do that.

Melissa pushes the glass of water towards me and, taking it in both hands, I gulp some water down. I keep hold of the glass, like a raft. Someone coughs.

I glance at Marcus and he looks sort of detached. I know he's as scared as I am.

We've never told anyone the full story. We've never wanted to. We've never even talked about it with each other. Instead, we've held it in our hearts and it's poisoned our lives.

'Anyway,' I go on and make my voice steady, 'the window made a noise and we hesitated. We waited to see if anyone would come but no one ever does the first time they hear a noise, do they? They tend to wait and see if it happens again. So we waited, for just a few minutes, and then Marcus tried again and this time,' I wince, 'well, the window sort of popped up and Marcus managed to open it.' I can see it in my head. 'He slid in first and then I did and, oh God –' My voice breaks, and I'm back there for a split second. My fingers grow white on the glass; I take deep breaths. I have to get through this, I tell myself. I have to get through it. I need to get this over with today.

'What?' Melissa makes her voice a whisper.

I'm sure everyone in the place is hanging on my words. The court is utterly still. All those faces looking up at me. I fix my gaze on Marcus and talk to him.

'The room was full of pictures. Framed. Of kids. In the orchard. Walking. Or with their parents. Or just close-ups of their faces. We stood up in the room and it was as if it screamed at us.' I stare at her. 'Faces everywhere, from every wall, all over the fireplace, piled up on the floor. Years and years of faces. Mostly young children.'

'Can you describe a typical picture?'

'A face. Sometimes just a torso. The faces smiling. Nothing,' I pause, 'pornographic but just really weird.'

'And then what?'

'We sort of stood in the room, just, I dunno, a bit freaked. Maybe we gasped or made some noise, I don't know. Then, it's not that clear, but Marcus turned around and he said, real low, "Run," and I didn't know what he meant and the next thing he grabbed my hand and pulled me into the hall but it was too late.' I swallow hard.

'Why?'

'Because he must have been in the kitchen all along and he came into the room with a gun.'

'He?'

I choke saying his name. Since it happened, I've never been able to say his full name. 'Charles Hanratty,' I mutter.

'What did you do?'

'I blubbered a bit.'

Melissa smiles briefly. Asks gently, 'And what happened?'

I hesitate, afraid to go there. I have never gone there yet, not fully. 'I told him that we were sorry, that we'd only done it for a laugh.'

'Did Marcus do anything?'

'Just held my hand tighter. And I talked and talked. And then in the end, when I stopped, Hanratty,' I hiccup on a sob, 'he asked me why I wasn't laughing.' I have to rein my voice in at the memory. 'He said,' I swallow and choke back tears, 'he said, "You broke in for the laugh, so laugh."'

Marcus flinches, but holds my gaze.

'And?' Melissa gently probes.

'We laughed. He hit Marcus with the butt of the gun for not laughing enough.'

'What did he do then?'

'He took pictures of us.' My voice flattens out suddenly. It's too hard to stay emotional.

'And then?'

'He got us to take our shoes off and dance. If we slowed down he told us to put out our feet and he burnt them with the butt of a cigarette.'

'Did you at any time protest?'

'Marcus tried but Hanratty hit me then. And then, then he made us kiss and he filmed us.'

The court is silent. Marcus's grief-stricken gaze reflects my own.

'Did he appear to be angry at all?'

'No, it was like he was detached, studying us. As if we were insects. It would have been better if he'd been angry. I was crying and he didn't even react. Then,' I take my time, damp down my anguish and say, 'he made me tie Marcus up and he, he did things to me while Marcus watched.' I can't elaborate. I can't remember anyway. I think I've spent so long putting distance between me and that memory that the sharp edges blur.

A tear drips onto my hand and I realise, to my surprise, that I am crying. Silent tears. I wipe my face with my thumb.

Marcus

I feel like I did all those years ago. She's there and I'm here and I can't do anything.

Aw, fuck it. I stand up and cross over to her. She lifts her head and our gazes lock.

The judge orders me to sit.

Sash says, 'It's OK. I'm OK.'

She'd said that that night too, when he'd eventually got her to untie me and I'd made a lunge for him and he'd pointed the gun at me. He'd put it to my head and said, 'I own this place. I own you, Mr Dillon. Who'd blame a poor man for shooting a burglar?'

Sash had put herself between us. 'He's not going to say anything. Me neither.'

'Good, because around here no one will believe you.'

Sash was right: it was like we were insects to him.

We ran and he fired off a shot.

The next day he told everyone someone had been prowling about his lands.

'You will sit down,' the judge says.

'You're OK?' I ask her.

'Are you?' she says.

And I nod and turn to go back. Her perfume assails me – it's the one she always wore. The smell carries with it echoes of good times, yet now sadness washes through. I want to hold her – she's the only one who truly understands what it was like. And yet, it's driven us apart. Both of us coped in different ways: I hated myself for letting it happen while she blanked it. And I think a part of her hated me too.

'Can you go on?' Melissa asks Sash. 'I've only a couple more questions.'

'Yes.'

'What did that night do to your friendship?'

'It destroyed it.'

I bow my head.

'I know we were wild, but it was innocent and that innocence was gone. The world looked different – we were separated from everyone else but from each other too. We were both humiliated.'

There's a world of sadness in the words.

'Did you ever hear from Marcus again?'

'He tried to talk to me but there was nothing to say. There was a huge chasm. And then one day, he saw me with Paddy Jones and he hit him. And the next time we talked was years later, after he'd left Applegate when he rang me after seeing me in the paper with … with,' I struggle on the name, 'Hanratty.'

'What did he say to you?'

'That I should tell Paddy – he was my boyfriend at the time – about Hanratty. He said if I didn't then Hanratty would be in my life and did I want that?'

'So how long before he was arrested for murder did he want you to tell your boyfriend this story?'

'About a year before. He wasn't looking for a witness then.'

'OK. Thank you.'

'I think we'll take a recess until tomorrow,' the judge says.

Sash looks relieved. She can barely stand up to get out of

the witness box. A man in the front row helps her down and then I see her father put his arm about her and walk her from court. Paddy Jones gets up and follows them out.

In the front row my mother is crying openly and Alan is staring at me, looking upset.

I guess I should have warned them.

I can't meet his eyes.

The shame is too awful.

Sash

Paddy comes back with us to the apartment. My dad, after hugging me again, says that he will walk up to the hotel and grab some dinner. I think he does it to leave Paddy and me on our own.

'I'll bring you some dinner back, will I?' he asks me.

'I'm fine.'

'You have to eat. Paddy?'

'Yeah, thanks, Kevin. I'll have whatever you're having.'

'Grand.' Dad nods and is gone with a bang of the front door. I hear him outside, greeting whoever is renting the place beside us.

Paddy and I are in the sitting room. I'm on the sofa with my feet up; Paddy is in a chair opposite. We are drinking whiskeys.

'That was tough today,' he says.

'Yeah.' And yet, while I am utterly drained, I also feel light, as if I've somehow unburdened myself. It's as if I'd put down some horrible weight I hadn't even known I was dragging around with me. In that moment of clarity, I think, let the press do what it likes, let Peter ask me all the questions he likes, never again will I lift up that burden.

I feel oddly liberated.

I surprise Paddy with a grin. 'Thanks for coming today.'

'Of course I was coming,' he says and his voice catches. 'I just wasn't sure if you'd want me.'

It was only when I'd seen him standing on the street that I'd realised how much I needed him there. Just to validate my story. To say, I know you're doing the right thing. I believe you.

'I know I let you down. I just … I suppose I was scared of the Applegate fallout.'

I take a sip of whiskey.

'I should have been more scared of losing you.'

'Forget it.'

He smiles bleakly.

'How's things with you?' I ask, because, from his appearance, they don't look so good.

'Not too bad.' A wry smile. 'At least until tomorrow when I appear alongside you in the paper. There'll be no going back to Applegate for me then.'

'You're the golden son – they might forgive you in time.'

'I don't want forgiveness. I'm glad –' he pauses, 'I'm glad I'm out of there.'

More silence. He can't be too glad, I think. Applegate meant so much more to him than it did to me. He was so loved. I love that he has lied like that.

'What?' He returns my smile.

'Nothing,' I say.

'What will your dad do?' he asks after a pause. 'Will he and Mona stay?'

'I hope not.' I tell him about the trouble in the pub last weekend and he curses his father.

'He's not a bad man,' he says, sounding dejected. 'He's just angry that he's lost everything.'

'You should make up with him.'

'Nah.'

'It's hard to lose a parent like that.'

'It was harder to lose you.' His voice is soft, as if he's afraid to awaken all that drove us apart.

'You're here now.'

He looks sad. 'I couldn't stand up to him. To Applegate. I knew you were right but I just ... I didn't want the hassle.'

'You didn't go for election in the end, though. You told your dad you were pulling out.'

'Only after letting you down in front of him first.' He's bitter.

'It takes courage to stand up to Applegate.' I half-smile. 'It's taken me fifteen years.' I reach out my hand and he clasps it. We look at each other. 'Don't beat yourself up over it, you're a good man.'

A smile. He squeezes my hand, drops it, and pours us both some more drink.

'Do you think he deserved to die?' Paddy looks at me.

What a weird question. 'I don't know. I wish, sometimes, that I'd just spoken out. Done something about it. Helped protect others maybe. There must have been others. I'll never have that chance now.'

He swirls his drink around; the ice clinks. I watch him, his head bent, staring into it. He's a million miles away from the guy who wowed Applegate two years ago. Maybe, I think with a chill, he was putting on a show for me too. Then, out of the blue, he says, 'I never knew Madge and Jenny picked on you like that in school.'

I roll my eyes. 'They were awful. Margaret, I think, was terrified that I'd steal you away from her and poor deluded Jennifer was like her lapdog.'

'Margaret was right to be terrified. I fancied you right from the off.'

I feel a pang, thinking of that kid who'd come bouncing into the seat beside me all those years ago. Hope and niceness had shone out of him – that's why he was so popular. Paddy never had an agenda. He was the polar opposite to Marcus's moodiness.

'It got better when Jennifer and her family left town,' I say. 'Maybe Margaret wasn't as brave without her or something.'

'Madge wasn't talking to Jenny by then,' Paddy says. 'No one was. I often feel bad about it.'

'Your dad firing her mother was nothing to do with you.'

He shrugs.

'And anyway maybe her mother did take that bracelet or whatever it was she was accused of.'

Paddy makes a face. 'I dunno. Dad swore he found it in her pocket but Lucy Ryan was a nice person.'

I say nothing.

'And Jenny was alright too.'

I remember now why I'd loved this man. 'How can you say

that after she told everyone that your mother and Hanratty had been together? Jesus, Paddy.'

'She was upset, she wanted to lash out. It was horrible but, you know, no one believed it. She shot herself in the foot.'

She certainly had. A spectacular own goal.

'I wonder what's she doing now?' I'd thought of Jennifer on and off over the years. If Marcus had liked her, I kept wondering why I hadn't. It was probably the only thing we disagreed on.

'I dunno. I think she's a PE teacher in Dublin somewhere.'

Silence falls between us. Paddy sits back in the chair and I lie back on the sofa. I must fall asleep because the next thing I know, Dad is coming in and the light has crept from the room. I'm covered with a blanket and Paddy has gone, leaving a note. 'I'll see you tomorrow. Phone me if you change your mind and don't want me there.' And his phone number.

Dad sees the note too and smiles. 'A great lad,' he says.

I wish he hadn't left it so late though.

Marcus

We have no words to say on the journey home from court. I know they're shocked, struggling, unable to think of anything to say that might be of value. All my life, I've lived with the guilt of sitting in that chair, tied hand and foot, unable to do anything. All my life, I've lived with the 'what if I'd taken action sooner' or 'what if I'd just stood up for us' but I hadn't. And it's no use telling me that I'd done all I could or that there was nothing I could have done: it doesn't wash. I let Sash down. The only thing I could do afterwards was see that Sash was alright by asking Dessie for updates and later on by keeping an eye on Hanratty – which has worked out wonderfully.

We enter the apartment. My mother is last in and she closes the door.

'Marcus,' she says, 'I—'

I hold up my hand, not facing her. 'Don't.'

'You should have—'

'Please.' I go to walk away.

She grabs my arm. I go to shake her off, she staggers and stumbles and, appalled, I go to catch her but Alan gets there first. 'Sorry,' I say.

'Sit down,' Alan says to me, his arm around her. 'Now.'

All five foot seven of him looks up into my face.

Despite everything, I'm amused. 'No.'

'You can't keep this up. This silence, this moodiness. Sooner or later, you're going to have to face it. Face everything you're blanking out. It might be a good idea to start now.' It's all delivered in his beautiful Welsh accent, rolling up and down like soft hills.

Trouble is, there is a wall inside of me and I can't pass that. I can't cry. I just feel nothing. It's easier that way.

'I should have told you both what was coming,' I say instead, 'but it was too hard, OK? I'm sorry.'

My words fall like rain on dry earth. My mother looks relieved. 'Don't be,' she says, 'no one likes to talk of things they feel somehow ashamed of. You're afraid that, if you let it into the light, you'll be seen differently.'

I stare at her. All those AA meetings have turned her into a shrink.

'I know what it's like,' she goes on, as I cringe inside. 'I could never go back to Applegate because I'd be afraid how people would look at me now. They'll always see the alcoholic, never the person I am.'

That's how I still look at her, I think.

'But Marcus,' she says, 'I will always see you. My son. Not the boy who was hurt by that … that bastard.' Tears spark her eyes. 'I will never see you as any less than the great guy you are.'

I should nod, thank her and go on my way but she has aimed her words well. They find their way into the armour that surrounds me, finding a space where the chinks don't quite meet. A little way from the heart maybe but enough to pierce me. I open my mouth to say 'thanks' but nothing comes out. I take a deep breath and just nod. I stare at these two people who have given up their life in Wales to come over and be with me. These people who have put up with my moodiness and sullenness and ungratefulness. It has not been an easy ride. Poor Alan has only been married to my mother for about two years and in those years his life has been overtaken by this case.

'That's all your mother wants to say, isn't that right, Thelma?'

She nods.

I shoot a look at both of them. 'And I … I'm grateful but I can't go there with you.'

They don't stop me from leaving this time. I pick up the

letter I hadn't opened that morning and take it with me out of the kitchen, tearing open the flap of the envelope on the way.

You fucking scum bastard I hope you die in prison I hope they throw away the key

I burn it.

DAY 10

Marcus

Sash is walking up the steps of the court just as I reach them. Her head is bent against the media onslaught. Paddy accompanies her. He's got his arm around her shoulder and is protecting her against the worst of it. My mother and Alan follow in my wake. I am heartsick. Everyone knows what a useless idiot I am now.

I walk through security and the guard gives me a nod. He's a nice enough guy. It's funny how you get to know people after a while.

Sash must sense me behind her because she turns around. 'I –' she stutters, 'I – well, I thought you were my dad – he's gone off to park the car.'

She's five feet away and a million miles. I can't bear it. 'Thanks for yesterday,' I stumble out.

She moves away from Paddy and comes towards me. I don't know what she's going to do. I stand there, ready to take anything.

It's like we're in a dream. Her gaze is hypnotic. She comes to just under my chin. Slowly she reaches up and runs the back of her hand down my face. I lean in to her touch. 'You take care,' she says, and then her hand is gone.

I watch her re-join Paddy, who gives me a curt nod and follows her into the court.

Sash

After today, I will be free: that's the way I look at it. No matter what happens on the stand, I will be able to walk out of this court and know that I've told my story and I never have to go back. I don't know what the newspapers are reporting, though from the way people are looking at me in this place, they all know who I am now. I say it to Paddy as we squeeze into our usual spot.

'A couple of years ago, you were all over the papers too,' he says, 'when you were with me. Next year it'll be someone else.'

He's right.

Someone tips me on the back. It's Heather. She and Shirley are sitting behind us today. Shirley is fanning herself with a newspaper.

'I am so sorry about what happened you,' Heather says,

'but you look great in the paper today. You're so photogenic. Isn't she, Shirley?'

'They got you at just the right angle coming out of court.'

'That's good to know.' I smile politely.

'But, still, we're terrible sorry, aren't we, Shirley?'

'It was shocking,' Shirley says, nodding vigorously. 'That Hanratty looks like a right sleaze – we said that from the beginning. I wouldn't blame Marcus for killing him. I'd kill him myself if he wasn't already dead.'

'Thanks.'

'Good to know,' Paddy chimes in, with a bit of a grin.

Marcus, accompanied by Melissa, passes by and both girls turn to stare at him.

'You just don't know what goes on in people's lives,' Heather says, almost swooning.

'Tell you what, though,' Shirley grins, 'I wouldn't mind tying him to a chair and having my way with him.'

They both giggle and Paddy looks at me in disbelief.

'Life goes on,' I say wryly, and he catches my hand.

Marcus

Sash walks to the stand. After today she is free. She looks more relaxed than she did yesterday, which is kind of weird. I thought she'd be all over the place, but I guess by saying out loud what had happened to her, she has somehow got rid of it. I hope so anyhow.

Peter approaches her. 'May I call you Sash?' he asks.

'Sure.' She smiles at him.

'Can I briefly run through your story from yesterday?'

'Sure.'

'You moved to Applegate at fifteen and you were unhappy?'

'Yes.'

'You were bullied and Marcus saved you and befriended you?'

'We befriended each other.'

'You met in the orchard and decided to break into businesses and houses?'

'Yes.'

'And it was your idea?'

'Yes.'

'And Marcus went along with it?'

'Yes.'

'Did he ever question it?'

'He said once that he thought it was wrong.'

'But it didn't stop him?'

'No.'

'Because he liked being with you?'

'That's an opinion,' Melissa says.

'It is,' the judge agrees.

I did, though. I loved being with her.

'Despite Marcus thinking it was wrong, he continued to accompany you?' Peter goes on.

'Yes.'

'So, he was easily led?'

'No.'

'Do you know what easily led means?'

'Yes.'

'What does it mean?'

'If someone does something under the influence of another person.'

'Based on your own explanation, was Marcus easily led by you?'

'I think—'

'Answer the question, please. Was he easily led by you?'

'Yes.'

Hell and back, I think.

Peter nods and moves on. 'One night you break into your neighbour's house and he comes at you with a gun?'

'Yes.' Her voice catches a bit.

'And you allege that he humiliated both you and Mr Dillon?'

'Yes.'

'And your sister backs this story up by saying she met you both that night and that you were running across the fields in a bit of a dishevelled state?'

'Yes.'

'And what did you tell her?'

'I told her that we had been happy and had been dancing.'

'Why?'

'To spare her knowing the truth.'

'Which was that Charles Hanratty had assaulted both you and Mr Dillon?'

'Yes.'

'And did you ever tell her the truth?'

'No.'

'Did you ever tell anyone that you had been assaulted?'

'No.'

'No one at all?'

'Not until I decided to testify.'

'And in the months leading up to his death, you say you had contact with Mr Hanratty fairly regularly?'

'Yes. He sponsored my ex-partner's political campaign.'

'Was that hard for you?'

Sash swallows and even from where I am sitting I can see her eyes fill. 'Very.'

'And you didn't confront him with what he had done?'

She shakes her head.

'Answer, please.'

'No, I didn't.'

'This man assaulted you and your friend, whom you loved, and yet you kept silent?'

'Yes.'

'But you posed in pictures with him?'

'Yes.'

'Did it upset you?'

'I suppose it did.'

'In what way?'

'I dreaded meeting him. I was sick at the thought of it.'

'And you say that when Marcus saw you in the paper with Mr Hanratty, he begged you to tell your partner about what had happened in your past?'

'He did.'

'Did he say why?'

'Because it would destroy me if I didn't.'

'And you refused?'

'Yes, I did.'

'And what was his reaction to that?'

Sash looks reluctant to answer. I know I'd gone a bit mad, though I can't remember exactly what I'd said.

'Well?' Peter pushes.

'He was not happy.' Sash is hedging – even I can see it.

'How could you tell?' He's onto a scent like a dog.

'His voice.'

'Did he say anything to indicate he wasn't happy?'

Sash fires an apologetic look at me. 'Yes, but I'm not sure if I remember it exactly.'

'What was it?'

'It sounds worse out of context. Marcus would never—'

'Let the court be the judge of that.'

'I said that it was over. That part of my life. That it was finished. And Marcus, well, he said, it's not finished until he's finished.'

'By "he", he meant Hanratty?'

'I think so, yes.'

There is a murmuring through the courtroom. I rub my hand over my face and despair at how some ill-chosen words have come back to haunt me. I'm sure I'd meant 'finished' as in testified against. I'd always thought that, given enough time, Sash would take him to court. I'd always planned to back her up.

'You say your sister met you and Marcus that night, the night you were both assaulted.'

'Yes.'

'Your sister says that your clothes were dishevelled and you were both smiling.'

'Pretending to smile.'

'Tell me, did you and Marcus ever have sex during your break-ins.'

I watch the embarrassment flicker over Sash's face. 'Just once.'

It had been a week before that. In Jenny Ryan's gazebo at the bottom of her garden. I'd pulled her in and ...

'That night that you allege you were both assaulted, you were both having sex, weren't you?'

'No.' Sash swallows and her voice wobbles. 'I was raped that night.'

'Is it possible you looked like you'd been having sex?'

'I don't know.'

'This assault never happened, did it?'

'Yes, it did.'

Someone hands Peter a note and he reads it, then looks at Sash.

'Moving on, you talked during your testimony of taking souvenirs from places you broke into.'

'Yes.'

'Is there a souvenir from Charles Hanratty's?'

'No, of course not.'

'Because he caught you and ran you off?'

'No.'

'You said he caught you.'

'Yes.'

'You said he ran you off.'

'I thought you meant—'

'There is no souvenir from Charles Hanratty's because he caught you and ran you off.'

'Yes.'

'And the souvenir from the hardware store? That's in the evidence box, is it?'

Sash pales. 'No.'

'No? Why?'

'Like I said, I used it in school.'

'How?'

Oh fuckety-fuck. Sweat beads my forehead.

'I pinned it up on the noticeboard in school.' Sash's voice wobbles.

'Why?'

'I was only a kid. I was angry.'

'Why did you pin this photograph up in school?'

'To get back at Jennifer.' Sash's voice is low.

'This was the girl who was bullying you?'

'Yes.'

'What happened when you pinned this photograph up?'

'People laughed.'

'So you got revenge on the girl who was bullying you?'

'Yes, I suppose I did.'

'You have no problem taking revenge, then?'

'Not in—'

'Did you or did you not get revenge?'

'Yes.'

He smiles. 'No more questions.'

Sash

And suddenly it is over. This thing that has hung over me for two years is over and I'm oddly relieved and horribly upset.

I take a final look at Marcus as I step down and I feel somehow as if I'm abandoning him.

WEEKEND

Sash

Way before, when I was a kid and we lived at home, on Sunday mornings my father would fish. He'd take his rod and his waders and his box of bait and pack the car up. Most Sundays, I'd go with him. My mother would pack egg and onion sandwiches, our favourite, along with some apples and chocolate and Dad and I would head off for the day. Most times we ended up in Kilkenny, down by the River Nore. We'd find a spot far enough away from other anglers and set up camp. It was never about catching the fish – it was about sitting side by side on a riverbank and passing the day. He'd talk about work in a fun way, tell me about the people he caught, the things they'd say to get out of trouble. The advice my dad gave them was to keep their noses clean. It was only later I realised that this advice was aimed at me. I'd chat to him about school, about my friends, tell him what was happening in the world of Batman. Dad liked Batman too, but not as much as I did. And then after a bit we'd lapse into silence, but a silence where everything was said. A raise of an eyebrow would be: keep still, there's something sniffing about the line. A flash of a smile would be: get me different bait, there's a good girl. A grimace meant: the moment is lost, the fish is gone.

In Applegate, the moments were lost. Each Sunday when he wasn't down at the station, he'd pack up his rod and his waders, the same as always. Only things had changed: now there was no one to make our lunch, no one to remember to boil the eggs the night before so they wouldn't be too hot to use on buttered bread in the morning. There was no one to wave us off, no one to tell us to be careful, and each Sunday it punched me afresh.

In Applegate, Lana went with him and I'm not sure if it was because she wanted to or she sensed his disappointment in me. Lana was funny like that: she could say the most tactless things, cause endless trouble for everyone with her tantrums, and yet she could sense changes in emotional temperatures in nanoseconds.

Dad thought I was punishing him by not going, that it was my way of saying to him that he should never have brought us to Applegate, that he was the one who drove our mother away, but it wasn't. It was my way of saying that everything had changed and that new routines had to be found. If our old life had to die, then I wanted no reminders of it.

So each Sunday, when Dad and Lana were going fishing, I stayed in bed, my fingers plugged into my ears so I wouldn't hear them. When they left, I'd stay in bed for a while before grabbing some breakfast and spending the day watching TV. Numbing my brain, never thinking about anything.

It became a habit after a while, numbing my thoughts.

Today, Dad knocks on my bedroom door, wakes me and Lana up and asks if any of us would like to fish. He hasn't done it in years and his fisherman's clothes look a bit grimy and dated. Lana and me, tousle-haired, look blearily at him.

'Mona's coming too,' he says. 'She's packed us all lunch – what do you think?'

His face is hopeful, eager.

'I love it.' Lana hops out of bed.

I love it too. It's like, I think, coming home.

Marcus

Tomorrow the barristers each give their summing-up, then the judge will make his speech and by the end of next week I'll know if I'm considered guilty or innocent. I can't quite get my head around it. It can't come quick enough; it can't come slow enough.

The papers today are full of the case. They report Sash's testimony word for word. Radio shows devote themselves to analysing the evidence. The TV plays footage of the day the body was discovered and rehash the facts again and again.

Reporters have camped themselves in Applegate and are

interviewing people on the street. Familiar voices haunt the airwaves until my mother turns it off.

'I need to hear it,' I tell her.

'No, you don't. You need to put on a cap and get out into the fresh air.'

'What? Find some friends to play with?'

She smiles. The sunlight falls through the kitchen window and shows up the lines around her mouth and eyes. She has aged in the last couple of years. Maybe I have too.

'Lauren said to give her a ring,' my mother says, as if she's just remembered and not been trying to think of a way to tell me all day. 'She says if you do, she'll pick you up and bring you out to somewhere you won't be recognised. And, you know –' She stops abruptly, suddenly arrested by what she was about to blurt out.

I finish the sentence for her. 'And it might be my last chance for a while, right?'

'Yes.' She sighs. 'Let's hope not, but still …'

I think it might make her happy if I call Lauren, so I say, 'Fine.'

'I pinned her number to the fridge.'

'I have it on my phone.' I shake it under her nose and she smiles.

She looks good when she smiles.

Lauren pulls up outside my apartment twenty minutes later. She drives a bright green Ford Fiesta. 'No way will anyone notice me in this.' I grin as I hop in beside her.

'It's less noticeable than your flashy heap of junk,' she teases.

'A Porsche is not a heap of junk,' I say back, feigning horror. 'Don't you know anything, woman?'

'I know you seem in better form.'

I'd been a bit down on Friday after Sash's cross-examination. But I'd decided that if this was to be my last weekend, then I wasn't going to fuck it up for everyone by brooding. 'Your car makes me smile.'

'Then get out and keep looking at it.'

'And miss out on this place you're bringing me to? No chance. Where are we going?'

'Look at me and guess.'

She's as pretty as ever. She's wearing skin-tight black trousers and a skin-tight black top. She looks great. 'No clue.'

'This trial has scrambled your brain. Look in the box on the back seat.'

I turn around and see a large brown cardboard box. I open the lid. Inside are what look like costumes. I pick one up. Spider-Man. I grin slowly. 'Comic Con?'

'Yeah, I thought you might like it and you'll have a mask on so no one will recognise you.'

I laugh but it's bittersweet.

Two years ago, I'd been a guest at Comic Con. Fans had queued up to talk to me. I'd signed all their magazines and artwork. Still, I can't blame them for not asking me this year.

'I thought we could go as a pair,' Lauren says. 'I'm Catwoman and you'll be Spider-Man.'

I haven't the heart to tell her that Catwoman would go with Batman. 'Sounds great.'

'No,' she says, 'it sounds awful. It sounds like my worst nightmare, but hey, you've never grown up and I like you.'

I probably should say I like her too, but she might take it up wrong. 'You legend,' I say instead. If she is disappointed, she doesn't show it.

My costume is a bit small. As I pull on the all-in-one suit, I begin to fear for my manhood. 'Jaysus.'

Lauren snorts back a laugh as I join her at her car. We've got changed in a pub near the Dublin convention centre.

'You'll be like Spider-eunuch!' She giggles.

'The only thing that fits me right is the mask.' I pull it over my head.

'That's the only thing that has to fit you right,' she says, adjusting it. She looks doubtfully at me. 'Do you think you can survive a day in that suit?'

'I'm bringing my clothes in a bag, just in case.'

She laughs. She looks sensational. The cat ears and half mask only add to her sexiness.

'You ready, partner?' she asks.

She links her arm in mine and we walk together up the street, ignoring a group of teenagers who insist on yelling out that she has a 'nice arse' and I've got a 'mighty pair of balls'.

Comic Con is bursting with enough madness and geekdom to create another race. Everyone is in some sort of costume. If I stood back and analysed it, I wouldn't for one second understand it. I am a thirty-two-year-old man and I like comics and cartoons and costumes and superheroes. I know it seems a bit sad but it makes me incredibly happy.

As we enter, we are assaulted by a wall of sound. Music pounds out of speakers and people call to each other over the noise. Stands selling all things geek are everywhere.

Within the first ten minutes, three Batmen have made shapes at Lauren.

'All the people dressed as Batman are weird,' she declares, wrinkling up her nose.

'Yeah,' I say, grinning. I wonder how long it'll take her to cop on.

I gravitate towards the comics section, where crowds are poring over vintage covers and artwork. Lauren stands beside me as I riffle through the plastic folders containing rare editions. I inhale sharply as I unearth an original *Detective Comics* with Batman on the cover. 'Class.'

Lauren peers over my shoulder. 'Does that magazine cost a grand?' she asks.

'And worth every cent.' I inspect it. It's mint.

'You're going to buy that?' She looks at me in disbelief.

'It's an investment.' I catch the attention of the seller and he crosses to me.

'That's a good deal you've got there,' he says, nodding.

'Have you any more like this?' I ask.

He frowns. 'A lot of them are gone – you could check that pile there if you like.' He indicates a rack containing a few hundred magazines.

Lauren throws me an anguished look.

'Ten minutes,' I promise.

'Go on.' She rolls her eyes. 'I'm going to look around. No rush, text me when you're done.'

Of course, I lose track of time. I get into conversation with just about everyone who stands beside me and then the seller gets involved and soon we've a heated discussion going about whether *The Dark Knight Returns* issue one cover art is better than the *Batman* issue two-fifty-one cover art. Most think *The Dark Knight Returns* is better.

Three hours later, I realise that Lauren has texted me twice wondering where I am.

I text back that I'm just finishing up with the magazines.

She texts, 'What!!!'

I tell her I'll meet her at the door. She's probably bored stupid.

Next year, if I'm free, I'll bring along some new characters and try to get an editor interested. Now that I've had *Slam Man* it'll be hard to go back to pencilling and inking someone else's stuff, but I might have to for a bit to keep some money coming in.

'Hey, Spidey, how's it going?' A Green Goblin greets me and I move into classic Spider-Man pose. Fucking hell, I'm in agony.

Green Goblin high-fives me and moves on.

Lauren is at the door. She's being chatted up by Captain Picard and she doesn't look too happy about it. 'So, what's your favourite *Star Trek*, then?' he asks as he unsuccessfully affects a casual air by trying to lean back while simultaneously crossing his arms.

He ends up staggering into me.

'I hope you haven't been drinking on the bridge,' I joke.

He eyes me up. 'Tea. Earl Grey. Hot,' he says, and I laugh.

Lauren rolls her eyes, mystified.

'You ready to head, Catwoman?'

'I've been ready for the last two hours and fifty-five minutes.' But she's smiling.

I loop an arm about her shoulder and she loops an arm about my waist and we leave.

'That was the best day I've had in ages,' I say to her. 'Thanks.'

'It's good to see you happy,' she says, and I think that this girl really does care about me and I feel shit that I can't give it back. 'Are we good?' she asks.

I don't know what to say that won't hurt her. I stop walking and face her.

'I take it that hesitation doesn't bode well.' She laughs before I can answer. Her face flushes a bit.

'I could be in custody by the end of the week. I could go down for years. It's not fair on anyone.'

'Maybe I'm naive, but what we had, I miss it. I can wait for you.'

'I've enough guilt to deal with without making someone wait.'

I'm not sure I love her enough either but I don't say that.

'Guilt?' Her eyes search my face. 'What have you to be guilty about?'

'Nice arse,' a young fella walking with his friends calls out.

'That's not a good way to talk about your mates' faces,' Lauren shouts back and they chortle. She turns back to me. 'Well? Why are you guilty?'

I should have kept my mouth shut. 'Let's forget it, it's been the best day, let's not do this.'

'You couldn't have saved Sash, you know.'

Am I that obvious? 'Yeah, well …'

'You still have feelings for her, don't you?'

I think about that and end up saying, 'I don't know. What we had, we were kids, it just ended so weird that I can't get past it or something.' I reach out to her but she flinches. 'I want your friendship. I'm too …' I think, 'too messed up for anything else.' The problem is no one else gets me. No one else fills that space that Sash left. The old Sash would have loved Comic Con.

Lauren's answer is to lay her head against my chest. I cautiously embrace her. I rest my chin on the top of her head.

'Are we good?' I ask.

She nods.

Lana

Fishing is calm and quiet and us all being together. The facts are: Dad, Sash, me and Mona. We look like a family but we're not and yet we are.

We don't catch any fish but we eat all Mona's sandwiches, which are very nice and they have beef in them which is brown and nice. She says that next time she will make me eat ham. I don't like pink meat.

Mona is bossy.

Then, and this is the weird part, Dad takes out some buns that he had bought especially. My dad never buys buns so it was a big surprise. There is a blue one, a yellow one, a pink one and a brown one. The blue is like the bright blue of the sea in a foreign country, the yellow is like rapeseed and the pink is Barbie colour. The brown one, which is like soil, is mine so I take that. Then Sash reaches for the yellow one but Dad says, 'That is Mona's because yellow is Mona's favourite colour.' Mona says, 'Let Sash have it if she wants it.' Mona says that she likes to wear yellow, not eat it. Sash goes to take the yellow one again and Dad says, 'No, the yellow one is Mona's and Mona should have it.' Mona looks cross now and she takes the pink one instead and says to Sash, 'Your dad is being ridiculous – have the yellow one if you want.'

'I bought the blue one for Sash,' Dad says.

'Fine,' Sash says, real snotty, and she takes the blue one.

Then there was only the yellow one left.

'Aren't you having one yourself?' Mona asks my dad.

Mona's bun is nearly gone.

'No, I'm fine,' Dad says.

Three bites and Mona's pink bun is gone.

Mine will take seven probably.

Mona eats like a horse.

'Would you like the yellow one now?' Dad asks Mona.

'What do you think I am,' Mona says then, sounding cross, 'a garbage compactor?'

Then Sash finishes her bun and says, 'I'll eat the last one if you like.'

'For God's sake,' says Dad, and he takes the yellow bun and sticks his finger in the icing, messing it up.

Mona asks him if he has gone mad.

Dad finds a ring in the bun.

A sparkly ring.

And Mona gives a big shriek and jumps on top of Dad and knocks him over and the ring falls out of his hand and we all have to look for it.

It takes one thousand and four seconds to find it but Mona gives my dad a big kiss in front of us.

And then she says why did he ask her now, in the middle of this horrible time, and Dad says that's exactly why he asked her.

And we all agree that it's the best thing ever.

Marcus

Lauren drops me off home with a *bip* of her car horn. I ask her in but she won't come and I'm a bit relieved. I'm not sure where we stand with each other now. I get the feeling that today was about seeing where she stood with me. And now she knows.

I feel bad for both of us.

I press the code for my building and share the lift with a man from the floor below me.

'You're that guy that's up for murder, aren't you?' he says, which, under the circumstances, is quite brave of him, seeing as we're both in a lift.

'I'm innocent,' I say. It's like a mantra for me.

'I've been following the case in the papers and, to be honest, you're not looking too innocent.'

'How nice to have your expert opinion.' I know I sound sarcastic but, really, what can you say to a guy who tells you that?

'There's no need for that tone,' he goes on, and he reminds me unexpectedly of Sash's dad. Sort of grave and serious. 'I said the papers are making you look guilty but journalists are a shower of wankers. I think you're innocent – I mean, why would a man like yourself, living in a lovely place like this, swap it for a jail cell? It makes no sense.'

'So, if I show the jury my apartment, they'll know I couldn't possibly have murdered anyone?'

He chortles a bit at that. 'It's worth a try.' The lift pings and he gets out. 'Good luck now.'

'Ta.' I press the button to get to the top floor.

'I'm back,' I call, as I push open my apartment door.

'In here,' my mother shouts from the kitchen. There's something in her tone, a nervous sort of twittering sound. I'm immediately apprehensive. I wonder if she's been drinking, but, nah, Alan would never let her.

I take a deep breath, knowing I have to let it go, this anxiety I have for her.

I push open the kitchen door, a manufactured smile on my face, only to find Dessie sitting at the kitchen table. He looks a little apprehensive and I feel guilty about that.

'Hiya,' he says.

'Hey.'

'I'll leave you two.' My mother beats a hasty exit. 'Alan

and I are going out for dinner. Did you have a nice time today, Marcus?'

'Great, yeah.'

'Alan!' she calls. 'Now.'

He clatters out from the dining room and they virtually sprint out the door.

'I think they're afraid you'll hit me,' Dessie says with a grin.

'I wouldn't hit you,' I say back, not smiling, just feeling so glad to see him.

'I'm sorry, man.'

'Yeah, yeah.' I nod. 'I know. Me too.'

He stands up, awkward, not knowing what to do now.

He holds out a hand.

I lean in and shake it.

He pulls me into a thumping embrace.

WEEK 3: DAY 11

Marcus

The atmosphere in court this morning is like breathing in toxic fumes. Maybe it's because the case is nearing its end. With every person that comes through the door and takes a seat, I sense some sort of expectation: I feel like a gladiator about to face the lions. I sit alongside Melissa. I spot Sash, her dad, Paddy, my mother, Alan and Lauren. A group of people sidle into the back of the room and my chest tightens. An Applegate brigade. Brian Jones and Margaret Browne among some others. They shoot looks at me and I return them as brazenly as I can. A woman with short blonde hair, sitting in the middle of the room, catches my eye because she offers me a shaky smile. Who is she? It takes a few moments before

I recognise Jenny Ryan. I smile back and she nods. She looks thinner, older. I'm glad she's here. It gives me hope that not everyone wants me behind bars.

It's a surreal thing, my past and present together in this room where my fate will be decided.

I look at the jurors for the first time as Peter gathers up some notes to make his closing statement. I guess I'd been avoiding their gaze the whole trial, not wanting to make eye contact, not wanting to see their gaze flick away from me, not wanting to second guess what it meant. There are nine women and three men. Of the women, half of them appear to be in their fifties while the others are younger. They all look pretty serious, as if they're going to give this verdict their best shot. That's kind of reassuring. The three guys are younger. One of them is a heavy metal fan, judging by his long hair and his T-shirt which advises us to 'Rock on'. I wonder if they know how much I'm depending on them. The way I feel right now, I'd bloody bribe them if I could.

The hush in the room deepens as Peter takes the floor. 'Ladies and gentlemen,' he begins, 'you've now heard two weeks of testimony. It is up to you to make sense of all that you've heard and to give a just verdict. Marcus Dillon, by his own admission, stalked and terrorised an old man. We presented you with evidence that showed the extent of his stalking.'

He goes into a lengthy summary of this evidence and I cringe all over again, hardly believing that it was me. I was possessed, I think. 'Make no mistake,' Peter says eventually, 'this stalking was vicious and cruel. By his own admission, it got out of control. Yet again, by his own admission,

Marcus Dillon was in the area the night Mr Hanratty was murdered. That fact is not in dispute, ladies and gentlemen. What is in dispute is whether Marcus Dillon had motive and the necessary rage to carry out such a brutal crime. The prosecution believes he did. The evidence of stalking, the emailing, the texting, all show a man with cruel intent.'

He goes on to my *Slam Man* cartoons and the horrible deaths Slam Man subjected Jay Walker to. Slow, cruel deaths. He reads again rejection emails from the magazine which said that, though 'entertaining', the deaths were in fact 'too graphic' for the comic. Peter Dundon manages to make it look like those deaths were my sick fantasies. Maybe they were and I was too blind to see it.

Pictures of Charles Hanratty's body are projected onto the screen for the courtroom.

I can't look at them again, and even though Melissa pokes me, I don't raise my head.

'These pictures clearly show that Charles Hanratty was viciously beaten with a blunt instrument and then stabbed. You heard how he bled slowly to death from a severed artery. This would have been a painful way to die. Marcus Dillon had researched ways to die for his comic-book creations: he knew how to make it happen. Marcus Dillon then scattered the comic-book images over the body of Mr Hanratty and wrote 'Cluck' in blood over his head. He then took a picture that was awarded to Mr Hanratty to celebrate the opening of the Hanratty Hotel extension in Applegate and smashed it over the dead body. A symbolic killing, ladies and gentlemen. Artistic in its way.'

He shows a full, graphic picture of the whole crime scene apparently. I don't look.

'And that's where Marcus Dillon made his fatal mistake,' Peter says. 'His fingerprints were all over that picture frame. It is these fingerprints that are the vital piece of evidence in this case because Mr Dillon, in his statement to police over the course of the investigation, said categorically that he had never set foot in Mr Hanratty's house. He lied, ladies and gentlemen. This was a crime of rage. You heard yourselves how Mr Dillon admitted to hating Mr Hanratty. If you believe the defendant's testimony, he and his teenage girlfriend were subjected to a brutal assault by Mr Hanratty and this, he wants us to believe, led to his stalking behaviour. Marcus Dillon made no mention of Sash in his initial statement to the police. Instead, he alleged that he alone had been abused by this man. But he pestered Sash Donnelly to back up his story, to make it look good. And Sash, by her own admission and her sister's admission, has lied to protect Marcus in the past. Lana Donnelly admits she saw her sister on the night in question but that her sister seemed happy, her sister was laughing and she talked about dancing. You heard the defence's expert witness – people with Asperger's find it hard to lie – so we can believe Lana's statement more than anyone else's.

'What really happened is that Marcus Dillon was fired by Mr Hanratty for not turning up to work. He wrecked his employer's shop and swore that he would 'get' him one day. He was due to be evicted from his house by Mr Hanratty for non-payment of rent. His mother lost her job in Mr Hanratty's hotel. It was these circumstances and these alone that made Marcus Dillon stalk and eventually kill Charles Hanratty.

'No assaults ever occurred, ladies and gentlemen. That was yet another lie in the statement, a vile attempt to blacken a good man. No complaints regarding Charles Hanratty have ever been received by anyone. Mr Hanratty was a model citizen of Applegate and a generous benefactor. And even if an assault had occurred, wouldn't that be yet more motive for this most brutal of killings? The defence is playing this card in the hope that the defendant, rather than being charged with murder, will be charged with manslaughter. Or better yet, be found innocent of any involvement whatsoever. But this was murder, ladies and gentlemen. Premeditated murder with cruel intent. He did not commit this crime to keep Sash Donnelly safe – he hadn't seen her in twelve years. He had no need to keep her safe, as no assault occurred. He committed this crime because his rage at what had happened in Applegate got too much for him. Marcus Dillon has been proven to have issues with his temper. Marcus Dillon is guilty, ladies and gentlemen. Thank you.'

He sits down. It's taken almost two hours and my head is spinning. I would convict me.

The judge orders a recess until after lunch.

Sash

We don't venture out of the courts building at all. Instead, we sit in the coffee shop in silence. There isn't anything to say. Peter Dundon totally threw out our story.

I'd been expecting it but I feel a mixture of anger and despair that he should treat us this way. Does he not understand how bloody hard it was for me to go up and say those things?

'It's his job,' Dad says, before he goes off to phone Mona with an update.

What a horrible job, I think.

Paddy and I sit opposite each other, nursing cups of coffee. He flashes me a downbeat smile when he sees me looking. I don't think he knows what to say to me.

'Does your school mind you getting off classes?' I ask, feeling a bit sorry for him. I spoon some more sugar into my coffee. I seem to have developed a bit of a sugar craving since the trial started.

'I told them I'd need time off and they got a substitute in.'

'I'm glad you're here.'

'I'm glad I'm here.'

Over his shoulder, I see a blonde-haired woman looking uncertainly in our direction. It's a second before I place her and when I do, I groan. 'Shit.'

Paddy looks at me, catches my gaze and turns around. His face tells me that he's recognised her too.

'Sash?' Jennifer calls out, in her distinctive, high-pitched cartoon whine. I catch my breath. 'Paddy?' she says. Then, hastily, 'I haven't come to cause trouble.'

Paddy looks nervously at me and I nod.

'Join us.' Paddy stands up and beckons her over.

I remember the last time I'd seen her, that day on the street, shouting at Paddy. She hadn't come back to school after that. It has a surreal quality now, like the flickering images of an old movie. The months after the assault are like that, the life half-lived.

As Jennifer arrives over, I take her in. She's wearing colourful trainers, blue tracksuit bottoms and a bright-pink sports jacket. She looks … I try to think and the only word that comes is 'well'. She has more lines on her face than I have – they make it appear that she has spent fifteen years frowning while trying to figure life out. She looks as if she's done her best to take care of herself, like you would a car that's running on empty.

'Hi.' Jennifer smiles at us a little nervously. Then blurts out, 'I, well, I've been following the trial and I wanted to come and offer support. I just came for the morning, I've to head back now.' She turns to me. Sounding a little emotional, she says, 'I'm really sorry for what he did to you.'

It's weird, but coming from her, my childhood tormentor, it means a lot. 'Thanks.'

'And poor Marcus,' she goes on, 'as if he'd ever murder anyone. He's not that type.'

'Is there a type?' Paddy asks, then, at a look from me, amends, 'It was just a question. I'm not saying …' I want to thump him. 'Can I get you a coffee?' he asks Jennifer instead.

'And you,' she says, rushing on, staring at Paddy. 'I've always felt bad about how things ended. I have no excuse, I was just really, really upset and—'

'Forget it,' Paddy cuts across her. He offers her a smile. 'Coffee?'

'No, it's fine. I'm rushing. I just wanted you all to know that I'm thinking of you.'

'You've time for a coffee,' I say, feeling a little sorry for her for some reason.

'No, I really have to go.'

'Please?'

She hesitates, then slowly sits down. 'OK. Thanks.'

Paddy heads to the counter. I wrap my hands about my coffee mug, searching for something to ask.

Instead she says, 'I read your evidence in the paper over the weekend. I, I just want to say that I am sorry for the bullying and,' a pause, 'everything.'

'It's OK.'

Silence. She swallows hard.

And I think, it really is OK. It's funny how a heartfelt apology can change your view of a person. So I add, 'I should never have put that picture of you on the school notice board.'

'I deserved it.'

'Still ...' my voice trails off.

'Thank you.'

She sounds emotional. My brain scrambles for a subject that's safe. I settle for, 'Did you have far to come?'

'No, just, well, I work in Tallaght, so I hopped on a Luas.' She's nervous, I think in surprise. I suppose it must have been hard for her to come and face us all.

'You're still into sports?' I indicate her tracksuit.

'Yeah, I teach it and I run strength and conditioning classes at night.'

'Sounds ... ouch!'

She smiles. 'I always liked that stuff.' She pulls a tube of sugar from a dish in the centre of the table and plays with it, folding it up and rolling it.

'Do you compete in discus anymore?'

'Nah. Too busy really.'

More silence.

'How is Marcus?' she asks eventually, and I feel it's him she's really here to see.

'He's OK. I haven't talked to him much.'

'I always liked him,' she says, and she sounds sad about that. 'He was another person I was horrible to.'

'He got over it.'

She smiles a bit. 'I hear Applegate is totally divided.'

'Yep. Though there are a lot more on Hanratty's side.'

'I was glad to get out of there.' Her voice is surprisingly bitter.

More silence falls between us. I wonder where Paddy is so he can rescue me from this. I should have gone to get the coffee.

Across the room, I see Thelma and her husband, with Marcus following behind.

'You need a coffee,' Thelma's voice floats across the foyer. 'Come on.'

'No, I don't, Ma. I'm grand.'

'Here's Marcus now.' As Jennifer turns, I add, 'You should go over and say hello.'

Jennifer half rises, then sits down. 'They seem to be having a bit of a domestic.'

'You need to keep your strength up,' Thelma insists. 'Get a table and Alan and I will bring it down.'

Marcus looks mortified and I grin because he's been on trial for the last couple of weeks and this is what he's embarrassed about.

Marcus spots me and offers a glum grin before doing a double take when he sees Jennifer.

She raises her hand.

Marcus says something to his mother before crossing to us. 'I thought it was you in court.' Marcus smiles down on Jennifer and I can see that he's forgotten how unbearable she was. 'Long time no see.'

'I came to offer support.' She stands up. She sounds like she might cry. 'I won't be staying, I've got work in a while.'

'I appreciate that.'

I watch as they embrace, his arms around her waist as she hugs his neck. I wonder if he still smells of lemon.

Marcus

Jenny hugs me. It's weird, the last time we met, she'd been such a cow to Sash, but they seem to have made up and I'm glad. She'd been nice before she started hanging about with Margaret.

'It's lovely to see you.' She lets me go. 'Anyone with half a brain will know you're innocent.'

She looks good. She reminds me of a more anxious version of the kid I knew when we were hanging around together.

My mother, holding two cups of take-out coffee, minces over in her too-high heels. 'Jenny Ryan,' she exclaims. 'It's been a long time.'

'Thelma?' Jenny looks to me for confirmation. 'Wow, you look amazing!'

'Oh, now.' My mother blushes, thrilled, and flaps her hand. Coffee slops out onto the floor. She hastily hands me the cup. 'Take that, Marcus. Drink it all up.'

Jesus.

'You look so great,' Jenny says again, like she can't believe it.

'Doesn't she?' I say, and the smile my mother gives me could power America for a week.

She likes me to say stuff like that, I realise. It's kind of touching that my opinion matters so much to her.

'I'm living proof that anyone can bounce back.' My mother grins. 'Alan calls me ping-pong.'

'Or pong for short,' Alan says, joining us, carrying two enormous cakes.

My mother laughs and he laughs and they look into each other's eyes and it's all very embarrassing. 'How's your ma?' I ask then, just to divert attention from my mother.

It takes a second before Jenny says quietly, 'She died. Almost nineteen months ago now. Suddenly.'

Shit.

We all chime in with how sorry we are and Jenny thanks us. I think she might cry. My mother gives her arm a squeeze. 'Lucy was lovely,' she says. 'She was so good to me when I was working in that awful hotel. She'd cover for me if I was a bit drunk, which was basically all the time.'

Jenny smiles at my mother's self-deprecation.

'I couldn't work there once they accused her of stealing,'

my mother goes on. 'The cheek of them. She was the best person in that place.'

Jenny nods, not able to speak.

I like my mother's retelling of the truth. Once Lucy had gone, my mother had probably been turfed out for being drunk on the job.

'A true lady,' my mother says.

Jenny dips her head. She is going to cry and I mentally beg my mother to shut up. Instead, she wraps an arm about Jenny's shoulder and cuddles her.

'Sorry if I upset you,' she says.

Paddy comes back with more coffee. He looks uncertainly at Jenny and my mother before proffering Jenny a cup. 'Would you like this?' he asks.

'Thanks.' She takes it in both hands, holding it like a life raft.

'Jenny's mother passed away,' my mother fills Paddy in.

'There he is,' someone shouts across the foyer. 'Murderer.'

At first, I'm hoping the comment is not aimed at me, but when Sash whispers, 'Shit' under her breath, I realise that of course it is.

It's the posse from Applegate. I don't know them all, or maybe I just don't recognise them after all this time, but Brian Jones is unmistakable, as are Margaret Browne and her dad. There is another man with them, so I guess he's Margaret's husband or something. A couple of the lads that I went to school with are there too, as are a few people who rented shops from Hanratty. Brian Jones leads the charge.

They stop about three feet away. Ten of them to six of us.

Out of the corner of my eye, I spot some onlookers moving away nervously.

Paddy pushes himself in front of me and faces his dad. 'Don't start,' he says in a low voice.

Brian Jones seems taken aback. 'Paddy, what are you at?' His voice wobbles.

'I'm supporting Sash,' Paddy says. He looks at everyone. 'She's telling the truth, lads. And you know it, Dad.'

'I do not.' Brian shakes his head. 'Sash has always stuck up for that fella.' He jabs a finger in my direction. 'You used to say it yourself. You think it's any different now, you're kidding yourself. It's a yarn they've made up to justify killing an innocent man.'

The scary thing is he actually sounds like he believes it.

'It's not made up.' Sash joins Paddy at the front.

'No, it's not,' I say evenly. 'And if Hanratty hadn't employed half of you and bought the other half, you'd see it.'

'How?' Margaret says. 'I knew that man, my dad worked for him and he paid him well. He never went near me. But then again, I never broke into his house.'

Someone laughs.

'Think, Paddy,' Brian goes on, 'Applegate and Charles Hanratty have been good to you. They put money into you, paid for the third year of college for you, and now you go and side with the people who want to ruin our town.'

'I'm siding with the people who are telling the truth.' Paddy puts his arm around Sash's shoulder.

'I'm telling the truth,' Brian says. 'You're making a mistake.'

'You wouldn't know the truth if it hit you.' It's Jenny. She's pulled herself out of my mother's arms and is advancing on Brian. I don't think he knows who she is. 'You fired my mother on Hanratty's say-so. You knew she was no thief.' Her voice shakes – I'm not sure if it's rage or terror.

'I have no idea who you are.' Brian dismisses her with a look.

'Jennifer Ryan,' Jenny says. 'You accused my mother of stealing.'

Brian gawks at her. 'She did. She had jewellery in her pocket. What could I do?'

'You could have asked the right questions.'

'You think I like firing my neighbours? It was terrible. But I know what I saw that day and it was a brooch in your mother's pocket.'

'Yes,' my mother chimes in, 'but you knew Lucy Ryan too.'

'Says the local drunk,' Brian snaps.

I catch him by the scruff of the shirt. My mother screams and Jenny tries to pull me off. I'm shaking Brian Jones and he's roaring at me to let go. Someone somewhere screams.

In the end, Sash's father, who has arrived back, stands between us. He holds up his hands and looks me in the eyes. 'Put him down, son,' he says. 'This won't help you. This is what he wants.'

And I know he's right and I curse my sensitivity about my mother and I let Brian Jones go, just as security are rushing up.

Brian Jones yells something after me. My mother yells

something at him. Sash's dad attempts to calm everyone down.

Jennifer runs out.

I just want this to be over.

Sash

Paddy tries to lead me away, but I can't go. I will not let Marcus be baited by Paddy's dad. I see him now for what he is: a bully. He's bossed Paddy all his life to be the best and the most brilliant – well, he won't scare me off. I wrench myself away and watch as Marcus stumbles off, looking sickened.

My dad is trying to placate everyone as security arrives. Jennifer seems to have disappeared. Margaret Browne is gone too. Brian Jones is trying to bluster his way out of it.

'Come on.' Paddy tries to pull me away but instinct makes me follow Marcus.

'Leave him,' Paddy calls, but I can't.

I go after him as he pushes open the door of an empty courtroom. He heads towards the jury box and takes a seat. I watch for a second in silence before joining him. We sit side by side; I can hear him breathe. He does smell of lemon.

We say nothing for ages and just when I think we're going to spend the whole time like that, he says softly, 'I'm trying to figure out what they see.'

I bump his shoulder. 'I don't know about you but when I was in the witness box, they saw the best-looking face ever.'

He manages a grin.

We lapse back into silence.

After a bit, I say, 'You were right to stick up for your mother.'

'Thanks.' Then, so soft I barely hear, he says, 'I'm scared, Sash. I am so bloody scared.'

He turns and his eyes meet mine.

Without a word, we hug each other. Tight.

Marcus

Melissa gets up. She has no notes, which is kind of brave of her. She has told me to be prepared for what she is going to say. I've told her to say what she likes once it gets me off.

'Ladies and gentlemen,' she begins, with a sweet smile, 'I know your brains are probably fried having listened to the prosecution earlier. Doesn't he present a compelling case?'

To my horror a couple of the jurors nod.

Melissa smiles. 'It's a pity it's not true, though. I'm going to tell you why it's not accurate, why it's based on flawed evidence. I promise I won't take long but I still ask you to try and concentrate on what I have to say for the next few moments.' She takes a breath and announces, 'Marcus Dillon is guilty.'

My head shoots up.

Some people gasp.

She has them hanging on her words now as she continues, 'He is guilty only of what he has already admitted to. He was a cruel and vicious stalker showing no mercy to a frail old man. He was fiery and sometimes violent. He was abused by Mr Hanratty when a teenager, he saw his girlfriend assaulted by this man, so, yes, he had a grudge and a motive to stalk and terrify Mr Hanratty. But killers are a different breed of person. Marcus Dillon is not a killer. He has stood on the stand and admitted to this court something that he has been hiding all his life: that he failed to protect the girl he loved. This, ladies and gentlemen, is why his stalking got out of control.

'If my client wanted to murder Mr Hanratty, he had fifteen years in which to do it. Instead, he forged a very successful career for himself. He found a good life. He tried to forget about the terrible wrong that was done to him. He tried to forget it because of the shame he felt for failing to protect the girl he loved. Marcus Dillon did not want to use this as his defence, but he had to because it was the truth. Yes, he fudged his initial statement to the police, but he wanted to keep his friend out of it. It was misguided but consistent with what we know of this man. He protects those he cares about. We have heard testimony of how he remembered promises made long ago to his friend. We have heard from a number of witnesses of his care for his mother. It is not so hard to believe, then, that he stalked Mr Hanratty to protect Sash.

'Ask yourself, if my client had murdered Mr Hanratty, would he have then calmly walked down Mr Hanratty's driveway? Would he have conversed with Mr Hanratty's neighbour? Would there not have been blood on his clothes? Even the most impulsive murderers attempt to sneak away from a crime scene, not boldly march down a driveway lit by a streetlight without shielding their faces. Would he not have been conspicuous by his bloody clothing? Would he have used his own cartoons as part of the crime scene? Indeed, if Marcus Dillon is a murderer, he is the most incompetent one in the history of the state.'

Someone titters.

'The prosecution have failed to provide a murder weapon. They have failed to positively identify Marcus Dillon going into Mr Hanratty's house that night. They have failed to find any evidence that my client murdered this man except fingerprints.' She pauses and takes a step nearer the jury. Lowering her voice, as if it's just them and her in the courtroom, she says, 'If Marcus was a murderer and was pleading not guilty, he would not hesitate to lie on the stand. He would say that he had been in Charles Hanratty's house and that he touched that picture some time ago. It would make his defence easier because, remember, there is no time limit on fingerprints. Instead, Marcus has stated that he was never inside that house, though there is no doubt he handled that picture frame at some point. Only he can't remember when. Can we remember everything we ever touched? Everything we ever saw? It is this fact, the fact that Marcus admits he doesn't know where the fingerprints come from, that mark him out as truthful. Marcus Dillon is not a murderer. I would urge, in the interests of justice, a not-guilty verdict. Thank you.'

There is a murmuring as she sits back down. 'Chin up,' she says, 'I think the judge is going to urge the jury to consider manslaughter.'

It's as if she's punched me. 'I didn't kill him.'

'I know,' she says, 'and hopefully they'll see that, but if not ...' She lets her voice drain away.

And I think to myself, even she has given up.

Sash

Marcus covers his face with his hands as the judge starts to speak to the jury. Most of what he says goes over my head – there has been so much talk today and the court has been so full and oppressive that I can feel a headache starting behind my eyes.

'There are three options,' the judge says eventually. 'If you believe that the prosecution has proved its case beyond reasonable doubt, you can find Marcus Dillon guilty of murder. However, in light of the evidence presented, I would accept a lesser charge of manslaughter if you believe, without a doubt, that Marcus Dillon and his girlfriend were subjected to an assault by Mr Hanratty when Mr Dillon was seventeen and that the murder was therefore a result of impotent rage and not premeditated. Finally, if you feel that the prosecution has not proved beyond reasonable doubt that Marcus Dillon killed Mr Hanratty, then you must find him innocent. By beyond reasonable doubt, I mean that no other logical explanation can be derived from the facts except that the defendant committed the crime. I would prefer a verdict on which you all agree. However, if you can't agree on a verdict after two days, I will accept a majority ten to two verdict.'

He then discharges the jury and I watch them file out.

None of them looks at Marcus. I wonder what that means.

Marcus

I'm listening to music in Melissa's office, my feet up on her desk, my eyes closed. The sun is warm through the window and it heats my face and bare arms.

Josh bursts into the room, the door slamming off the wall. I jump up, my iPhone clattering to the floor. I must have drifted off, which is kind of weird, as I thought I'd be all over the place.

'You scared the life out of me.' I grin, picking up my phone.

Josh just looks wretched and doesn't even grin or apologise. Instead, he says, 'They're back.'

I glance at my phone. 'After an hour?'

'Yep.'

'What does that mean?'

'I guess it means that whatever decision they've reached, it's pretty unanimous.'

My heart whumps. 'Where's Melissa?' I wrap my headphones around my phone and put it in my pocket. I have to stay calm, I tell myself. At least I'll know one way or the other pretty soon. And yet, my legs shake a bit and my throat is dry. I unroll my shirt sleeves, button the cuffs and shrug on my jacket.

'On her way. She said to go nowhere until she gets here.'

I nod.

Josh holds out a hand. 'You deserve to get off,' he says.

We shake. He thumps my shoulder. I know he can't think of what else to say.

We stand in uneasy silence until Josh says, 'Melissa would make a great cartoon character, wouldn't she?'

I grin. 'I've already done a few roughs.'

Josh chortles. 'Any chance I could see them?' Then he stops and remembers that by tonight I could be behind bars.

'If I get out,' I answer, 'I'll drop by one day and you can see them. If not ...' I turn to stare out the window. I don't need to look like a wuss in front of him. But if I can't draw –

'They'll let you draw in prison,' he says. 'One fella we defended once, he was as guilty as sin but great with his hands. He carved Melissa a stone statue before he went in. He still does it in there, apparently.'

The sun is sliding down the sky a little, the rays lengthening. I watch commuters heading home from the city, chatting, laughing, and I wonder if they realise how bloody lucky they are just to know that tomorrow they'll wake up in their own beds, with the freedom to do what they like guaranteed.

Melissa bursts through the door, startling us, her hair mussed by her dash from wherever she has been.

'I wasn't expecting it this soon,' she says, as she hastily gathers her briefcase and slicks on some lipstick. She pulls a brush from her bag and expertly twists her hair into a ponytail. A flash of a smile at me. 'If it goes against us, we'll appeal,' she says.

I can't even think of that.

'I've called your mother,' Melissa says. 'She's on her way to the court with Alan and your girlfriend.'

'Lauren isn't my girlfriend.'

She ignores that. 'Is there anyone else you want me to ring?'

'Sash?'

'OK.' She looks up Sash's number and calls her. I only hear Melissa's end of the conversation.

'She's on her way back now. She's about ten minutes away.'

'OK.'

A lull. We all want to say stuff. No one can.

'Let's go,' Melissa says.

Twenty minutes later, I'm back in the courtroom, flanked by Melissa and Josh and my solicitor. My mother is up at the front with Alan. He is holding her hand in his, really tight. Sash is with her dad and Paddy. All the Applegate people are down the back and as one they seem to shift on their feet as I arrive in.

The tension in the air is a dangerous mix of apprehension and excitement, tinged with the possibility of violence. I feel apart from everything, as if I'm watching from a long way away, through a tunnel. Sounds are muted, the light is filtered and the odours of sweat and heat barely register. There is nothing left for me to do. All the nerves came from having some control, but now it's out of my hands.

I watch the jury file in, one by one. As they do, a palpable shift takes place, like everyone in the room suddenly leans forward. Edges of their seat. Waiting.

Melissa has said that if the jury looks in my direction, it's a good sign. I watch them. None of them glances our way. A sort of slow dread starts making its way through my body. Seeping in through the numbness. I damp it down, stare ahead.

The judge enters. We stand.

'Can the foreman of the jury hand the verdict to the registrar, please?'

I watch as a tall, gangly woman walks across the room and hands the registrar a slip of paper. I will her to look at me. She keeps her neck bent. Her shoes clatter on the wooden floor. She takes her seat back in the jury box.

'Will the defendant please rise.'

I do, my hands by my sides, soaking in the silence, telling myself that I will take whatever happens like a man.

'I hope they hammer you,' someone shouts out.

People roar.

I flinch, biting my lip hard.

'I will have silence in court,' the judge orders, his voice cutting through the room like a whip. 'Can we ensure complete silence, please?'

The man who shouted is led out. Silence descends.

'How does the jury find the defendant on the charge of murder?' the judge asks.

In slow motion, the foreman of the jury opens her mouth.

I swallow hard.

'The jury finds the defendant guilty of murder,' she says.

I know now why people don't react when the sentence is read out. It's the shock. It's like witnessing an accident, only the accident is the car crash of your life.

It's all I can do to stay standing. Melissa says something, I don't know what.

I stare dazed at the jury and none of them looks at me.

Vaguely I register that people are cheering.

I glance towards my mother and she has her head buried in Alan's chest. He catches me looking and shakes his head, closing his eyes. Lauren looks shell-shocked.

'He's innocent!' The anguished shout hurls itself up the room. 'You stupid people, he's innocent!' Sash is standing on her seat, shouting as Paddy tries to pull her down. She shakes him off. 'I told the truth.'

'I will have order!' The judge hammers his desk.

'Putting an innocent man behind bars is not order,' Sash yells.

The judge tells her to leave. She stares up at me.

I can't even react.

It stops her short. I hold her gaze and it's as if she suddenly realises what she's doing. She steps down from the seat and allows Paddy to lead her out. They have to push their way past the Applegate people, who can't contain their glee. I watch Paddy eyeball his father, who says something, and Paddy shakes his head and walks past him.

Then the judge says, 'The defendant will be taken into custody to be sentenced on Monday week.'

Two policemen come towards me, but before they arrive,

my mother pushes her way through the crowd and hugs me. I wrap my arms about her, knowing that it'll be a long time before I do it again. Her hair brushes my chin; I close my eyes.

It feels good to be hugged by her. I wonder why I never let myself know it before.

TWO MONTHS LATER

Sash

I've had to go back to counselling since the trial. I stopped it six months ago, finally believing that I was strong enough to go on by myself. The last day of counselling, I was a bit terrified, afraid of negotiating this new life on my own. And it did feel like a new life, a life no longer lived in the shade of what had happened, a life no longer dictated by secrets. But scared as I was, I was excited too.

And now, here I am back in front of Abby, my counsellor. I feel I've failed somehow.

'I was expecting you,' she surprises me by saying, with a bit of a grin. 'You held off long enough.'

'I tried. I didn't want to give in.'

She squints at me. 'Give in to what?'

'Failure.'

'You never failed,' she says.

'I have. I've been a complete mess for eight weeks.' A tear starts up in the corner of my eye and rolls down the side of my cheek. I take a deep breath. I've never cried in front of her. I never cry much, full stop. 'I haven't slept. I haven't eaten.'

'How did you fail?' Abby asks. She hands me a box of tissues and I take one and ball it up in my fist.

'They didn't believe me.' The words hiccup out. I sound like I'm five. 'They said he committed murder and they didn't believe me.' I dab my eyes.

'You stood up in a courtroom and you told everyone what had happened. You didn't break down.'

'And it did no good. They said I lied.' Oh God, this is terrible. Tears are streaking down my face. I'll never be able to go outside after this. My make-up is not this tough.

'No one said you lied. I know it feels that way. The person they didn't believe was Marcus.'

'His story was tied to mine.'

'You were not on trial.'

'I just feel,' I heave a shaky sigh and will myself to stop my stupid tears, 'violated. As if I cut myself open and no one noticed.'

'Your dad noticed, I bet. And Lana. And Mona. And all your other friends. I'll bet they were good to you.'

They had been. Even my boss in the salon had given me two more weeks off work with pay.

'They believe you.' Abby pushes her hair behind her ear and leans towards me. If I saw her in the street, I'd never have thought she was a counsellor. She wears a lot of short skirts and tight blouses and long dangly earrings. She talks in a thick Dublin accent. But there is something solid about her, like a mother, I think. I'd liked her immediately. 'And you did the right thing, testifying. That's all you can do.'

'Not being believed was what held me back all those years ago,' I tell her. 'And I was right. No one does believe it.'

'So, not being believed was your greatest fear?'

'Yes.' I dab my eyes.

'And yet,' Abby makes a gesture towards me, 'here you are, still going on.'

'Just about.'

'Just about is good.'

I blow my nose. Take another tissue. Her understanding is making me sniffle harder.

'Can I tell you something?' She eyeballs me.

'I guess.'

'Even if you felt they had believed you, a few days after the trial, after that elation had worn off, you'd still feel the way you feel inside right now.'

She pulls back and lets the words settle around me.

I think about that. Maybe I would have. How would twelve complete strangers believing me really make me feel better inside? Inside where it matters. Inside where I am. And I think, the only one who can make me feel better is me. But how do I do that? How do I make myself feel better?

'You have a choice,' Abby says, like she heard my thoughts.

'You can feel bad because the trial didn't go the way you thought, or you can feel bloody proud of yourself for still being here after that setback. You can choose, believe it or not.'

And it's so simple, what she's saying, and yet so bloody hard. And so bloody right. I can choose. And only a fool would choose not to feel proud of themselves.

More tears snake their way down my cheeks. 'Thanks.'

'You are going to be fine,' Abby says. 'I know you are.'

I like that she thinks it.

Marcus

My cellmate, Louis, a small guy with slicked-back hair, murdered his wife. He thought she was having an affair with a neighbour. It turns out that she wasn't but, as he says himself, 'the damage was done'. He hadn't meant to kill her, he told me on the first night I spent in the cell, it just sort of happened, like a flash of red coming over his brain, so that when it cleared, he barely remembered what had happened. Was it like that for me, he asked.

I told him I didn't do anything, but he doesn't believe me. None of them do.

It's probably just as well because it gives me a certain tough-guy persona which helps navigate the tricky waters of trying to stay afloat in this cesspool.

When I get back to the cell, after recreation, there is an envelope on my bed. 'Marcus Dillon' is scrawled across it in Sash's beautiful handwriting. Opening it, I pull out the latest edition of *Slam Man* and *Spider-Man*. She's the only one who remembers to send me these. My mother keeps trying to smuggle in sweets and, no matter how many times they tell her that she can't bring food in to a prisoner, she insists on doing it. It's her rebellion against my sentence, I think. She sends me money too and then pesters me to make sure I got it. She's convinced that, given half a chance, the prison officers would run off with it. I have to laugh at that. Lauren visits and she just brings herself, which is nice. I wish she wouldn't come and waste her time on me, but she says she's not wasting her time. I wonder will she still be visiting years from now? I shiver at the thought of all those years in here.

I lie back on the hard bunk and open *Slam Man*. It's one I did before I got fired. It's pretty cool despite the fact that they've changed Jay Walker's name to Tim Terrible, which is pretty terrible. Anyway, in this issue, he gets knocked down by a car and I grin as I read it. I did the story and the pencilling and inking. It looks good.

Louis comes in, back from his woodwork class. He spots the *Spider-Man* on my bed. 'Is that the latest issue?'

'Yeah, knock yourself out.'

He climbs onto his bunk, my comic in his hand, and the two of us spend a peaceful thirty minutes reading. Then we swap over. In a weird way, it's like being a kid again, reading under the apple trees in the orchard. I don't know if I was put with Louis deliberately, but both of us are comic-book geeks.

After a bit, his skinny legs dangle over my bunk and he hops down, tossing me the *Slam Man*. 'Your girlfriend is legend,' he says. 'No one ever thinks to bring them in for me.'

I don't bother telling him that Sash isn't my girlfriend. I've told him before and he's just chosen to ignore it. He's like that – he believes what he wants to believe. 'She's into them too. She's probably read them before she gives them to me.'

'She's a keeper. My wife, the one I killed by accident, she hated seeing me read them. She said it made me look like a big kid. I had to read them in secret.'

It's hard to know how to respond to that, so I say instead, 'I'm hoping to get my stuff in here so I can draw. You wouldn't mind, would you?'

He looks like I just asked him to share in my Lotto winnings. 'That'd be cool. I can give you ideas for *Slam Man*.'

'He's been fired as of next year. I'm doing a new character now: "Don't Diss Meliss". She's like an anti-hero. Saves all the baddies and makes them good.'

Louis doesn't look convinced. 'A woman?'

'Yes. Like Wonder Woman.'

He shrugs. 'I kinda prefer Slam Man. When I tell my mates that I'm sharing a cell with you, they're dead impressed.'

'Yeah, well, I got dumped from my job. No one wants to work with a murderer.'

'I thought you weren't a murderer.' He gives a grin.

'I'm not, but what does the truth matter?'

'It doesn't,' Louis thumps me on the back, 'what matters is what people see and think. Get used to it, buddy.'

And there's something in the way he says it that makes me wonder about him.

Sash

The prison is pretty busy today, with people queueing up outside to get in. I'm sandwiched between a teenage girl with a screaming baby and an older woman who is holding a tray of cupcakes.

'They'll never let you bring them in, love,' a woman behind her says. 'They'll think you're trying to smuggle in drugs.'

The woman with the cakes looks devastated. 'I thought it'd cheer him up,' she says. Her voice is posh. 'He loves a cupcake. I thought he could share them with his friends.'

'It'd cheer him up if there was drugs in it alrigh',' someone cackles, and everyone laughs.

The woman manages a little smile too. She holds out the tray. 'Would anyone like one?' she says. 'I made them this morning.'

She takes the cover off and a few women gasp as if they've never seen anything quite so lovely. Some of the cakes are decorated with blue and white stripes, some are pink with a brown button in the middle, some are dark brown, but it's only when you look at it the right way, you see that together they all make a prisoner. 'I thought it might give him a laugh,' she explains.

After a bit of 'oohing' and 'ahhing' from the people in the queue, she passes them around. She hunkers down and hands one to the screaming tot in front of me.

'He hates coming here,' his young mother explains, taking a cake herself. 'But his daddy likes to see him. If I don't bring him, he'll be almost a teenager by the time his da gets out.'

'Terrible,' the woman says, patting the young girl on the shoulder. 'It's important for a little boy to see his daddy.' Then she turns to me. 'Last one?'

'You've had none.'

'I ate plenty when I was making them. Go on.' She pushes the tray towards me.

'Thank you.'

We must look like a funny bunch, standing outside prison gates, munching on cupcakes in the dreary morning.

'First time here?' I ask the woman.

'Yes. How could you tell?' She waves the cake tray in the air and gives a bit of a laugh. 'I'm seeing my grandson. Such an idiot. He was always easily led. Committed a robbery and got caught. You?'

'Second time. I'm visiting a friend.' At her questioning look, I add, 'Murder.'

She shudders, then apologises. 'I'm sorry, but murder is, well, it's the worst, isn't it?' Then she does a double take. I hate double takes. 'You're the girl from the Charles Hanratty trial?'

'Yes.' I dip my head. Then think, what am I ashamed of? I did nothing. I look up again.

Her gaze softens as she stares at me. 'I was so sorry for you, reading about your evidence. How horrible.'

She even sounds like she believes me. The bun lodges in my throat and I have to swallow hard to get it down.

'OK, line up now, please,' a guard shouts, breaking off the conversation.

One by one we are searched, our coats are taken and I follow the others into the visitors' room. I take a vacant seat. Some prisoners are already there, including the woman's grandson. She shakes her head at him when she sees him and he gives a glower in return.

Marcus arrives about a minute later. He stands in the doorway, scanning the room, and I raise my hand. A slow grin crosses his face as he makes his way over.

'You've blue all over your mouth,' he says, as he sits opposite.

I smile now too and wipe my face with the back of my hand. 'I had a cake on the way in.'

'Life on the outside is good then, yeah?' Another grin.

I love his smiles, I think suddenly. They're rare and yet, of everything that has changed, they have remained the same.

'Thanks for the *Slam Man*s.'

'No problem.'

'I've something for you.'

'Yeah?'

'There's a box in my apartment with your name on it.'

'What is it?'

He taps his nose. 'You'll see. You'll like it, I think.'

I know better than to ask any more.

He tells me that his mother has his mobile phone now so if I ring it she'll give me his address. She's leaving next Sunday for Wales and is just packing up his apartment for him, so I should pick the box up before then. His eyes turn serious and he says softly, 'I'm sorry if you ever felt I let you down. I did try to pull free.'

It's the first time he's mentioned the past. It tugs at me. 'I know.'

'So why did you blank me afterwards?'

I stare up at the ceiling, wondering if I can get the words out without choking up. 'I couldn't bear for you to look at me.'

'Sash.' There's a world of devastation in the way he says my name.

'What he did,' I stop, start over. 'It just ruined what we had. I loved you, Marcus.'

'I know.'

More silence.

'I liked you a bit too.' He cracks a tiny smile. 'Just about this much.' He makes a small space with his fingers.

I laugh, I always do at his shit jokes. Most people would call them dorky.

'So, how's everyone?' he asks, changing the subject. I know we'll come back to the more serious stuff another day. And I want to, that's the thing now.

'All good,' I say, before remarking, 'You've lost weight.'

'It's a bit shit in here.'

'It *is* prison.'

We convulse laughing at that.

'It's hard to get used to,' he says, 'the tiny bit of light in the cell, the space. It's like –' he tries to think, 'being in prison.'

More laughter.

'Though it's not all bad – I've had propositions from at least three women wanting a relationship with me.'

'Feck off.'

'Yeah, what's not to like?' He winks at me and my heart hops suddenly.

My lack of reply and whatever expression I have makes his smile fade and his eyes grow serious. We stare at each other a little too long.

'Have you seen Jennifer since?' I ask after a bit. I haven't been able to get her out of my mind. She hadn't appeared since that day in the courthouse and, for some stupid reason, I just want to make it up with her properly. It was brave of her to come, I think.

'Yeah.' Marcus surprises me. 'She's asked to visit next week, so I said OK.' He pauses, then asks, 'I wonder how many more people like us there are out there?'

'We won't ever know – it's too late now.'

'It's never too late. He's dead but we're not.'

'For someone in prison, you're very positive.'

'It's not called The Joy for nothing.'

We crack up.

Marcus

Jenny visits Saturday morning. I spot her easily because she looks so terrified. Her shoulders are hunched up about her ears and her eyes are trained on the table in front of her.

'Hiya.' I sit opposite her.

'Hi.' She smiles nervously and her eyes dart around a bit.

'I've been here almost ten weeks and haven't seen a fight yet.' I offer her a smile.

To my horror, her eyes fill with tears. 'Stop,' she says. She swipes her hands over her face. 'Don't make a joke of it. It must be terrible in here.'

'It's not great but it's survivable.' I hope that's true.

'Is it?'

'Yeah.'

'Good.'

I can't reach over and touch her because you're not allowed to touch people – if you do, the visit will be cut short, and it's nice to get out of the cell and talk to people who live outside. As a tear plops onto the table with a tiny splash, I say softly, 'Don't. Don't let people see you do that. Don't get upset.'

'Sorry, I'm not much of a visitor.' She scrubs her face with a tissue. 'I guess, I'm just not prepared for this place. Can you appeal?'

'Maybe. Without new evidence it's difficult.'

'But why didn't they believe Sash? And what he did—'

'They thought I planned it, the jury. I was the one on trial, not Hanratty. So my solicitor says.'

'But, but that's not right.' Her voice pitches even higher than normal. She looks devastated. 'Everything he did ...'

'He's dead. It's too late. We should have told our story earlier.' Despite what I'd said to Sash, not coming forward will be the one big regret of my life. I like that Jenny believes us, though.

'What will you do?'

I heave a sigh. 'Make tables in the prison workshop or something.'

'It's not funny.'

'I know that.' Sash would have laughed, I think with a pang.

'We were good friends, weren't we?' she says suddenly.

'What?'

She lifts her eyes to mine. 'Back then, when we were kids. We got on.'

'Yeah.'

'And I ruined it. I'm sorry about that.'

'It's in the past. You had bad taste.'

I'm rewarded with a shaky smile. 'You've always been so ...' she thinks, 'nice, Marcus.'

'Nice? Come on, you can do better than that.'

'Fun?'

'I'll take that.'

Another smile. 'Don't lose hope, OK?'

'I'll try not to.'

A really long silence before she says, 'I won't be coming in again, Marcus.' At my look, she says, 'Please don't think badly of me. I just ... can't come in here.'

I feel a stab of disappointment because I like visitors – everyone in prison lives for them – but I can't let her see that. And to be honest, I hadn't expected her to visit in the first place; we're not friends now. 'I'd never think badly of you. I like that you came now.'

She dips her head. Her hair falls across her face. I have a sudden urge to reach out and touch it. I lift my hand before remembering and I pull back. 'We were friends a long time ago. You owe me nothing.'

'I owed you a visit and an apology,' she says, 'but I need to move on.'

'Yeah. And coming to the trial was brave.'

She gives me a look that I can't fathom. Like as if she's trying to puzzle something out. 'I wish we'd stayed friends,' is all she says before standing up and adding, 'I have to go.'

'Sure.'

'Goodbye, Marcus.'

She can't leave quick enough.

'The Marcus charm didn't work too well there,' Louis calls over to me.

A few people laugh.

I give him the fingers and let the screw escort me back to my cell.

Sash

Paddy drives me out to Marcus's apartment on Saturday. I'm hopeless at locating places I haven't been to before. I read out the Google Maps directions to Paddy and he finds it relatively easily. We drive through a large archway and past a huge green area with a fountain. Marcus lives in the block at the very back.

'His cartoons must have been doing well,' Paddy remarks, pulling into a space marked 'visitor'.

'*Slam Man* was the biggest-grossing comic-book character last year,' I say. I can't help it, I feel quite proud of Marcus for taking on the big guys. 'Which is amazing considering he was up against *Batman* and *Spider-Man*.'

Paddy rolls his eyes in amusement. 'Go on in and collect your surprise,' he says. 'I'll hang on here.'

'Don't you want to come in with me?' I'm not that keen on meeting Marcus's mother alone.

Paddy shakes his head and looks a bit angsty. 'I'm afraid she'll start crying or something – I wouldn't like that.'

'Some sensitive politician you would have been.'

The minute I say it, I know I shouldn't have. Less than two years on, his election hopes being dashed is still raw for him and it takes a second before he smiles.

'I don't know why I said that.' I wince.

'It's OK.' He shrugs. He doesn't sound convincing.

'I'm sorry.'

'Don't be. I just feel ashamed of myself when I remember.'

I know that, sooner or later, we're going to have to have a heart to heart on what we want, on where we might be going, but not now, I'm not really ready. I don't know what I want. 'I'll go get that box,' is all I say as I hop out of the car.

Marcus's mother hugs me when she opens the door.

'It's just great to see you,' she says with emotion, as she holds me at arm's length and studies my face. 'You were so brave on that stand. It can't have been easy.'

It hurts that she gets it so completely. 'It wasn't, and it was worse because they didn't believe me.'

'Don't think like that,' she says. 'It was more that the evidence against Marcus was so bad. His conviction was nothing to do with you. His solicitor says,' she swallows hard and looks away briefly, 'that they went for murder because they believe he planned it.'

'Idiots.'

She nods before letting me go. 'Come into the kitchen, have a coffee.'

I'm about to tell her that I won't, that Paddy is waiting outside, but somehow I think that might hurt her and so I follow her up a tiled hall, with stark white walls. There are boxes everywhere but despite the fact that everything is packed away, it's impossible not to see what a beautiful place it is. Airy and bright, white floor tiles reflecting sunlight. Thelma leads me into the kitchen, which is sleek and minimalist and looks as if it's never been used. A huge window dominates the far wall.

'Coffee OK?' Thelma asks.

I spot a large coffee machine on the countertop and think, *yum*. 'Great.'

Thelma flaps a hand at the coffee machine. 'I'm afraid it'll just be instant. Marcus has these ridiculous gadgets all over his house, but I haven't a clue how to work them.'

My heart sinks but my smile stays firmly in place. So much for a good cup of coffee. Thelma fills two massive mugs with boiling water from what looks like a tap, saying, 'This is one thing that's great. Boiling water all the time.' Then she spoons a generous amount of instant coffee into the water and hands me a mug.

'Sit. I'll grab some milk.'

I sit down at a glossy table and she pulls a jug of milk from the American fridge and hands it to me.

'Thanks.'

'Biscuit?'

'No, thanks. Have you sugar?'

'I don't, sorry.'

'It's fine, I'll be grand. I take a sip and it's rotten. I smile. 'Lovely,' I don't really know what to say to her. I never really knew her that well. I go for, 'Where's your husband?'

'He's gone back. I just stayed behind to tidy the place and get it ready for a tenant. At least it means that Marcus will have some money coming in when he's, well, away. He lost his job, you know.'

'Idiots,' I say again. I take a sip of coffee. It's rotten.

'They'll regret it,' she says.

'Let's hope so.' Then I ask, 'What are your plans? Are you going back to Wales?'

She gives a brief smile. 'Yes. Most of Marcus's stuff will stay in storage. I'll get back to visit him in that place.' Her voice wobbles and impulsively I reach out and squeeze her hand. 'Don't mind me,' she says, shaking her head. 'I'm a mess since he was put in there.'

'Me too.'

'I blame myself. If I'd been any sort of a mother, he'd have told me.'

'No, he wouldn't.' I know that for definite.

'But—'

'Trust me, he wouldn't have.'

She looks grateful. 'Thank you.'

'It's the truth.'

A pause. Then, 'He liked you a lot.'

I dip my head. 'It was a long time ago.'

A pause as she digests this. She nods slowly before patting my hand. 'I'll get the box for you.' As she stands up, I think how elegant she is. Even in her jeans and white T-shirt, she moves with the grace of a dancer. 'It looks as if it's been in his attic for years,' she goes on with deliberate cheeriness. 'Poor Alan was black with dust after he'd hauled it down.'

She disappears into another room and I hear her rummaging about.

I take in the kitchen in all its flashy glory. I can see Marcus living in this place, I decide. It's so him. Shiny and cool. I think of the cottage I had with Paddy with its large garden, falling over with wildflowers, and the few miserable vegetables that I tried to grow. I think of its brick fireplaces and thick stonework. I remember the smell of old timber from the floorboards and the damp patches on the walls. It was quaint and cute and had history but it was always more Paddy's kind of place than mine. Who was I kidding, I think, in a stark moment of insight. I was no politician's wife, no country girl. Marcus had seen straight through me when he'd met me that awful day in Malahide. I'm a flashy-kitchen, cool-gadgets kind of girl. This apartment is my ideal. I wander over to the floor-length window and look out and there is a view right to the sea that takes my breath away. Blue sky, blue sea, white wispy clouds, white tops on the waves. Coloured roofs.

If Hanratty had never happened, my life would be so different now, I think, in a blast of clarity. I would never have fallen for safe, dependable Paddy. I would never have stayed in Applegate. I probably wouldn't have failed college.

The life I lost shimmers before me, out of focus and out of reach.

'I almost couldn't find it in the mess inside.' Thelma startles me as she returns with a small cardboard box, which she dumps on the table. She arches her back to stretch it, though the box doesn't look that heavy. 'Damn thing was buried under a load of boxes and papers and magazines which I'm putting into the recycling tomorrow.'

The box smells a bit damp. On one side it has the words '20 bottles of Jif', so it's a really old box and whatever is inside must be pretty old too. Black masking tape seals it shut. I run my hand over it, curious now as to what it holds.

'Did you come in a car?' Thelma asks. 'It might be awkward to carry on a bus.'

'Yes, I parked my car in a visitor's space outside.' I don't mention Paddy.

There is a lull then, neither of us quite sure what to say next. Then we both speak together.

'You first,' I say to her.

'Just … I … well, thank you.' A pause before she adds, 'I'm sure we'll bump into each other again.' Her voice is too bright, like the sun before the rain. Her eyes slide from my face; she knots her fingers together.

'I won't forget him,' I tell her. 'I will visit.'

She brings her gaze to mine. Then she swallows hard. Her eyes are shiny.

I pick up the box. It isn't heavy and whatever is inside slides about a bit. 'Thanks for coffee.'

She can't seem to speak, instead she smiles briefly and turns to stare out the big kitchen window.

I leave as quietly as I can.

Paddy drops me off at my apartment in Wicklow town around six. We had a nice lunch in Malahide followed by a walk along the seafront. But I couldn't stop the memory of the day I met Marcus from side-swiping me. With every step, I could see Marcus just a tiny step ahead of us. I had to ask Paddy to keep repeating himself and I knew that, until I discovered whatever was in the box, I wouldn't stop thinking about Marcus. Paddy sensed it because he didn't ask to come inside when he dropped me home.

He leaned over and kissed me, cupping the side of my face in his palm. Paddy is a great kisser – it's what had hooked me when he'd come calling soon after I'd moved back to Applegate having failed college. Each weekend, he'd turn up at my door, a bunch of wildflowers in his hands, and ask me if I wanted to grab a coffee in the village. I liked him best back then, when he was teacher training, when he had hardly any money, when he wore jeans and sweatshirts. When he smiled, looking a little bashful, as if he couldn't quite believe I'd go out with him. Paddy, despite all his achievements, was a humble guy.

The only times he surprised me, the times I didn't feel I knew him, were when he was on the GAA pitch. Suddenly he went from the gentleman I knew to being a complete thug. He had a gift for flattening players from the opposing team. His dad's shouts of 'Well done, son' and 'Get your fucking retaliation in first!' rang across the pitch whenever he played.

But his smile when they won a match would light up the gloomiest day and his arms about me made me feel safe.

And then, someone suggested that he'd make a great local councillor because people followed him, and Paddy gave it a go and he got elected by a massive margin and then it was on to the Dáil. And suddenly our lives were taken over by Charles Hanratty and publicity and doing things for the media and handing out leaflets and begging for votes. I hated it. I hated smiling when I didn't want to, though I'd been doing it since I was fifteen, or being referred to as Paddy Jones's partner. I hated Charles Hanratty being in our lives. I made a lot of excuses to get out of meeting him but it was never enough: he was always there with his smile and his suaveness and his money.

My stomach was never right in those days.

'I'll give you a shout later,' Paddy says, finally breaking the kiss.

'Do.'

He looks sort of lost as I take the box from the car so I blow him another kiss and he smiles a little. I only turn to go when he drives out of sight.

I unlock my apartment door one-handed, the box balanced in the other. Kicking the door closed, I carry the box to the table. I'm nervous, which is weird. Maybe it's because whatever is inside is something Marcus brought me from Applegate and I wonder how he thinks anything from that time can possibly be a good thing. I run my fingers cautiously over the masking tape, knowing that one firm pull will tear it off easily. Before I give myself time to think, I yank the tape and it rips off in one smooth motion all along the top of the box.

The flaps pop open. Pushing them apart, I inhale a huge amount of dust and spend the next few seconds coughing my guts up. When I've recovered, I peer inside. There is an oblong parcel wrapped in old newspapers and twine. I pull it out and brush off the top layer of dust before getting to grips with the twine. It won't open and so I tear off the newspapers, pulling them out from underneath the twine. I stop abruptly when I see what it is. My hand stills, emotion punches me hard and I think, no way.

An unexpected tear slides down my face.

He's kept all the *Batman* magazines I was too cowardly to collect from the newsagent's. Saved them for me, wrapped them for me and now, fifteen years later, given them to me. That he knows me so well, even after all this time, floors me. I run my fingers along the front page of the first one, half afraid of touching it, before picking the bundle up and holding the comics tight to my chest. I close my eyes. I breathe in the stale smell of them, inhaling and exhaling, loving them. These magazines are who I was, what I liked, what made me different. Marcus remembered while I forgot.

It's like meeting my younger self once again.

Still holding the small bundle, I find a scissors and cut the twine.

I start to read the first one as tears of release plop onto the pages.

Lana

Sash comes home for the weekend. She hasn't been back in Applegate much since Marcus got sent to prison because she wanted to work hard at her job because her boss was so nice to give her two weeks off for the trial. And then two more weeks off after that. So, to make up, Sash worked late on Saturdays and her boss was very pleased and so she told Sash that she could have Monday half-day off and so Sash drove down to Applegate in her little car on Sunday morning.

Paddy didn't come with her because he says he is never coming back to Applegate or his dad ever again which Sash says is sad but I don't know why. Who would want to come back to their dad when they are treated so bad by him?

I didn't say it but I'm glad Paddy didn't come. He's OK but I find him hard to talk to. No one else does but that's because he talks to them like they are normal and he talks to me like I'm not.

When Sash arrives, Mona runs out to meet her and hug her and make a big fuss of her. Dad claps her on the back and says she is welcome. They ask her if she is OK and how did her counselling go and Sash holds up a comic and tells about Marcus keeping it for her and Mona says she never heard anything so lovely.

Is that lovely? I don't know. It's a smelly old comic. Then they all sit down and chat and Mona shows Sash all the pictures of where she thinks she might like to get married. I've seen these pictures loads of times and Mona keeps asking me which place I like the best and I tell her that I don't mind,

I just don't want anywhere too noisy, and Mona says she can't control the noise in a place and then I say that I want them to get married at home because she can control the noise here and then she gets cross and says asking me is a waste of time anyway, which is rude.

I watch as she and Sash look over all the brochures and Sash asks her why she hasn't considered Hanratty's Hotel and they have a good laugh about that for some reason. And then Sash says, 'Seriously, I like the one in Donegal,' and Mona says that she does too and then Dad says that if they both like it that's where they'll get married.

It won't be in a church because Mona says that's just being a hypocrite and, anyway, her and Dad have already been married in a church so it's time for something new. Mona likes new things. I don't.

Sash tells us about Paddy and how she meets him for lunch some days and how he brought her out for dinner a couple of times. She says that he is very busy working in his school and that he even stays late in the evening to plan classes, as they expect him to work hard, so she sees him only twice a week. Dad wonders if she is thinking of getting back with Paddy and Sash says she's not sure.

I hope she won't.

Mona says that Paddy is a grand lad, that he can't help who his father is and that his mother was a lovely woman.

I ask if his mother ever fucked Hanratty. Mona and Dad draw in big breaths. Dad says saying 'fucked' is disgraceful language. Sash explains then what I mean and Mona and Dad are agog that that was the gossip at the time. They never heard it. They said Brian Jones would hardly be on Hanratty's side if it was true. That makes sense.

Then Mona goes yammering on about Paddy again. She says it was bound to be a shock when Paddy found out about what happened to Sash with Hanratty and that maybe he didn't handle it too well but that at least he turned up at the trial and defied his dad and was brave and Sash says that she knows that.

I think Sash is annoyed then.

Mona makes a face at Dad and he makes a face back and they shrug and Sash pretends not to see.

I see everything because they think I don't notice but I do. I see the detail and can never understand the story.

In bed that night, Sash can't sleep. She stares up at the ceiling, her hands behind her head. Our window is open and a breeze is coming in and the shadows on the ceiling flicker because of it. I find it like being in a boat, rocking about.

'I can't understand it,' she says into the dark.

I don't know if she's talking to herself.

'Can you?' she says then.

'Are you talking to me?' I'm curled on my side, looking at her.

'No, I'm talking to the ceiling,' she says.

I think about that. You can't talk to a ceiling. I think she's being sarcastic. 'That's not true,' I say.

'Yes, I'm talking to you,' she says. She turns on her side and faces me and she is smiling. 'It was a joke.'

She doesn't seem to mind that I didn't laugh.

I wonder will she tell me a story now. When Mammy was living with us, Sash would tell me a story in a whisper in the dark, lying on her side and facing me. Downstairs Mammy would be talking to Daddy and their voices would rumble up the stairs and under the door and into the room. Now Dad and Mona's voices do, only most of the time it's the TV as well. Mona likes Dad to be quiet when she is watching the quizzes.

'How do you think,' Sash says, 'Marcus's fingerprints got on that picture?'

'Because he touched it,' I say.

'He says he didn't.'

'Then he's a liar,' I say. Like, how else can it be?

'He isn't lying,' Sash says. She sounds a bit cross. 'OK, I'm going to tell you a story, right?'

I say nothing. I don't know if it is right.

'I'm going to give you the story and you have to try to figure out what detail is missing, OK?'

That sounds a bit hard.

Then, and this is boring, she says, 'A man walks up a driveway.'

'What is he wearing?'

'All black.'

'OK.'

'He goes into a house.'

'Does someone answer the door or does he have a key or is the door open or—?'

'Someone answers the door.'

'OK.'

'Then another man walks up the driveway. He is in black too and he doesn't go into the house. He posts a letter in. Then in the house, the first man murders the man who lived in the house—'

'Why?'

'I don't know.' Sash's voice sounds cross. 'Look, Lana, just listen to what I do know, OK?'

'You said a story, that's just details.'

'Forget it.'

She turns away from me.

'I can't forget it. How can I forget it?'

She goes stiff, then turns back. 'I'm going to tell you the details,' she says then, all calm. She takes a deep breath. 'Some of them are missing but it's all I know. I want you to figure the rest out. It's like a mystery, OK?'

I don't know what she means but I just nod.

She starts the story again. Then she says, 'This first man, the one in the house, he kills the man who lives in the house. Then he smashes a picture on top of him, scatters the pieces of paper that the second man posted in in the envelope and leaves without being seen. Then the police come, find the murdered man and blame the second man because they find a hair belonging to him and also his fingerprints are on the frame of the picture lying on top of the body, and the second man says he never was in the house or saw that picture. How come?'

'That's like what happened Marcus.'

'It *is* what happened Marcus. Only I want you to think,

Lana. You're good at details. Say the second man, who is Marcus, didn't do it. Just say. So what else could have happened?'

I think and think and think. I wonder if she left out any other details.

'Did you leave out any other details?'

'No, nothing important anyway.'

All details are important, I think.

'Just go on what I told you,' Sash says.

I think again, then say, 'The first man wasn't spotted because he found a key and let himself out a back door and locked the back door.'

'Yes. Only they traced all the keys in the house.'

'Maybe he was in the house before this and had a spare made.'

'That's good. So it had to be somebody who was in the house before or broke in before or something?'

'I guess.' I don't believe this at all but, anyway, it makes Sash happy.

'Then how did the second man get his fingerprints inside the house on the picture frame?'

'The first man made him hold it some time?'

'The second man says he never saw that picture in his life.'

I think and think and think. 'I don't know,' I say.

Sash sighs.

'The only logical thing is that Marcus did kill him.'

'No,' Sash says. 'And do you honestly think he'd have made it so obvious?'

'Maybe he didn't mean to kill him, just scare him, and he ended up dead?'

'Marcus didn't do it, all right?'

She is real mad now.

'I believe him when he says he didn't.'

'All the details point to—'

'Stop.' She turns away. 'If he killed him, he'd admit it, I know he would.'

Then a detail pops into my head. Tiny. Small. 'Unless,' I say, 'he saw the frame before but not the actual picture.'

'For God's sake,' she starts to say, and then, 'Holy fuck.' She sits straight up in bed. 'Jesus, Lana.' She sounds like I gave her a fright.

'Or,' I start to say, 'maybe there were other—'

'No,' she says, and she sounds like she might be sick. 'I think you're right. It's not the picture that matters.'

'That's good so.' I pull my blanket up and try to get back to sleep.

Sash keeps me awake, tossing all night.

Marcus

On Tuesday, a prison guard arrives at my cell and I think it's to bring me to the visitors' room, as Dessie is coming in this week – though, when I look at the time, I see it's too early for him.

'It's your barrister,' he says gruffly. 'Come on.'

I'm led through a maze of corridors before finally being escorted into a small room where Melissa is perched on a table. Her laptop is open beside her and she has a huge smile on her face.

'Sit,' she says.

Her teeth are back in braces. 'What's with the teeth?'

'Fucking never used my retainer,' she says as she slides off the desk and into her chair. 'Like who does?'

'Everyone?' I volunteer.

'Not the answer I want,' she says, though she's smiling through her mouthful of metal. 'Anyway, sit.'

'How's the appeal going?'

'Pretty damn fucking brilliant.' She swivels the laptop around to me with a flourish. 'We've had a bit of a breakthrough, thanks to your friend Sash.'

I haven't seen Sash since last week and she said nothing about a breakthrough then. 'What sort of a breakthrough?'

'You could be free soon,' Melissa says, and I've never heard her so chirpy. 'Let me tell you what we do know.'

It sounds too good to be true. I brace myself.

Sash

I've never been to Paddy's apartment before and I shouldn't be here now. But he'd rung me this morning to say he wanted to talk to me, that he had a confession to make. I had to come because I owe him that much. I hate the thoughts of the police hammering down his door as they will in the next day or so, once they check everything out.

I just need to see that Paddy is not a monster. Maybe try and understand why he did what he did.

Part of me wonders why he's decided to confess now. Has he heard that I reported my suspicions to the police? But how could he have? I've told no one only my father.

When Lana said what she did, my first instinct was to run away from it. I couldn't sleep, telling myself that there had to be a mistake and yet knowing that the only way Marcus's fingerprints could have got onto that frame was if he'd handled it before. And the only way he could have handled it before was if someone had planted it there. And Paddy had a frame exactly like it, or he had once upon a time. Our picture, that he'd had commissioned from the photographer who took the mountain view photograph of Applegate for Hanratty, had hung in an identical frame.

And when I figured it out, grief for Paddy overwhelmed me. The boy of those long-ago Applegate days was gone and in his place was this confused man, a man who would let someone do time for him. A man so determined to keep everyone happy that he'd killed to achieve it. The minute Lana said what she said, everything clicked into place. I had worked it all out. Paddy had killed Hanratty because he knew what Hanratty had done because, despite throwing Marcus out, he believed him that day in his office. Deep down he knew that Hanratty was not a good man. Maybe that stuff about his mother and Hanratty was true; maybe Paddy knew all along and chose to ignore it. That's the way Applegate was. Don't talk about it and it won't be true. He'd never actually told me that his mother hadn't been with Hanratty, only that Jennifer was angry when she'd said it. And he was able to ignore it until Marcus had come along and told him that Hanratty had assaulted me. He'd killed Hanratty rather than stand up to him, rather than have me stand up to him, because this was Hanratty after all. The saint of Applegate, the giver to charity, the man who paid for operations for his neighbours. He'd also known that once Hanratty was dead the whole town would be determined to elect him. He'd waltz into office. I don't know why he framed Marcus — maybe he was jealous or something.

The one thing Paddy probably hadn't banked on was Marcus totally freaking out and asking me to testify, which derailed all his election plans and forced him to choose between me and Applegate.

'Hiya.' Paddy, oblivious, greets me with a smile as he pulls open his door and leads me inside his place. It's bigger than mine, but only just. It's clean, though, and I get the feeling he tidied it up for my benefit — Paddy was never the best housekeeper in the world. Our cottage in Applegate was always a bit of a mess. I feel sad that he's made such an effort.

'It's not much,' he says, observing me as I look about, 'but I'm getting there.' He turns to fill the kettle. 'Sit down, I'll get you a cuppa.' He's wearing black jeans and a bright blue shirt that brings out the darkness and smoothness of his skin. He looks like the Paddy I once knew and I want to weep.

He had so much going for him and he threw it away.

'What's this confession about?' I say it as lightly as I can.

'You might need a cup of tea first.' He turns and flashes me a rueful grin.

I say nothing else as he goes through his tea-making

ritual. Paddy loves tea, he's addicted to the stuff, and he has a particular way of making it. Heating the pot, using tea leaves, not using water straight from the boil, things I used to tease him about.

He told me once that the ritual of it keeps him calm.

I take the opportunity to glance around the kitchen a little more. It's a typical man pad, functional and a bit boring. Lots of gadgets for making things, a juicer and sandwich toaster, then beside the window there is some weird-looking piece of equipment – I've no idea what it's for.

'What's that?' I can't resist asking.

Paddy groans. 'It's a yoke I got from Lidl. It's for making bread.'

Despite my unease, I chortle. 'No way.'

He gives a self-deprecating shrug. 'I was on a bit of a healthy drive for a while. I thought, you know, fresh bread out of the oven first thing in the morning.'

'It was a nice idea.'

'It was a bizarre idea.' He carries the teapot to the table and hands me a mug. 'Put some milk and sugar in and I'll pour the tea,' he says.

I do and he grins at my four spoonfuls. Finally, when we've two great steaming mugs of tea in front of us, he sits opposite me. The grin he'd worn since I came in has disappeared. My heart whumps at what's coming.

'I haven't been honest with you,' he says, staring right at me and surprising me with his bluntness. His eyes look tired. In fact, I think suddenly, the guy is exhausted.

'What's up?' I can't even lift the teacup in case my hands

shake. It's weird, I'm not afraid of him, just afraid of what he's going to say.

'I've been putting it off,' he says, 'talking to you, telling you things, but I figure I kind of have to now.'

'Now?'

'If we're going to have any kind of a life, if you want me in your life.'

I'm frozen in his gaze. He's let an innocent man go to jail.

'You might hate me after this,' he says, 'but I have to be honest.' A pause. 'I've let you down, Sash, I know that. I should have stood up to my dad that day in the kitchen, I should have been firmly on your side and like I was, it was just,' he gulps, 'kind of messed up.'

'Messed up?'

'I hated letting him down.' A pause. 'I hate letting anyone down. All my life, right, I've given people what they want: it's hard to quit.'

'You didn't give me what I wanted.'

The pause is longer this time. 'I know. I was angry at you.'

I open my mouth to say something but I realise I don't know what to say. This isn't the confession I came for but it hurts.

'I couldn't help it – like, I knew you were right, I knew sticking by you was right, but it was like you were going ahead anyway and you didn't care about me. About my dad. About anyone in Applegate. I loved that place, Sash.'

'I did care. I told you I'd let you go.'

'And what? Make me feel shit for going for election

anyway?' He stands up, faces the window, his back to me. 'It was a no-win for me. Or at least I thought that at the time. I know now I was wrong. Losing you, that was the worst.'

'You didn't just lose me, though,' I say softly. 'You lost your dad anyway and Applegate.'

He bows his head. 'They weren't worth keeping. They only liked me when I was winning, when I was toeing the line.'

'No.'

He turns around. 'Yeah. And you know what else? What the real irony is?' He doesn't wait for an answer, just goes on, sounding bitter. 'I figured out that I never even wanted to go for election in the first place. Isn't that crazy? I was just doing it to please everyone.'

'You should have said.'

'Yeah.'

'If you'd only told me.'

He flicks a glance at me. 'There was a lot we didn't tell each other.'

I flinch.

'Sorry,' he mutters.

'It's the truth,' I agree.

Not talking, I think, does more damage than anything. Paddy must think the same because he says, 'I have something else to tell you.'

'What?' My voice is a whisper; I'm not sure I want to hear it now.

'I don't regret it,' he says then. 'I'd do it again for you but I'm sorry I lied.' He looks at me from the far end of his small kitchen. 'I should have told you earlier, but anyway …' He trails off then adds, 'I'm hopeful it'll sort itself out.'

'Hopeful? How?'

'I'm applying for other jobs.'

My world tips. 'Sorry? What?'

'I lost my job,' he confesses. 'They wouldn't let me take time off for your case so I walked out. I shouldn't have let you think I was still teaching.'

My phone rings. 'Can I?'

'Sure. I'll be in here.' He thumbs to a room off the kitchen.

I answer the phone and gabble out, 'Hi, Dad, I'm grand. I'll talk to you in about ten minutes, OK?'

He says something but I hang up on him and follow Paddy into a small sitting room dominated by an over-large red sofa and a coffee table. There is a TV in the corner.

'Not my choice.' Paddy thumbs to the sofa with a grin.

'You lost your job,' I say, just to be clear.

'That's why I've been working late. I've been giving English grinds to kids. I have a few interviews lined up.'

My eye is suddenly caught by a picture on the coffee table.

My legs go weak.

Marcus

'We were stupid,' Melissa says. 'We kept asking you if you'd seen the picture before. No one, bar Lana, thought to ask if you'd seen the frame before.'

She presses a button on the laptop and a photograph pops

up. The frame with its fingerprints that caught me out. Silver. Ornate. Expensive.

'Have you seen that frame before?' Melissa asks.

I don't know what's going on only that it's good news. I stare at the picture. Have I seen that frame before? I'm not sure what I should say. I feel a little uneasy so I think it's best to say nothing.

'Marcus?' Melissa is looking at me optimistically.

'Why do you need to know?'

'Look carefully. Forget about Hanratty's house. Is there any other time you saw that frame before?'

And it clicks, like a flash going off. 'It looks a bit like the one I saw in Paddy's office about a year before Hanratty was killed.' I remember it because it was unusual.

Melissa whoops. It's as if I've just won her a million euro. 'You beautiful man.' She gives me a wink. 'Did you touch that frame?'

I try to remember. 'I think so – there was a picture of Sash and Paddy in it but—'

'Marcus,' she says, and her eyes are all shiny, 'that you touched that frame is a very good thing indeed.'

Sash

'Are you OK?' Paddy is at my side. His arm curls about my waist as he leads me to the sofa, which, despite my shock, I notice is very scratchy. 'Water?' Paddy asks.

'Yeah. Please.'

I need a breather from him. As he leaves, I inhale deeply.

He's back in a second with a glass, which he hands to me. He hovers anxiously as I take a sip.

'You OK?'

'That picture.' I nod towards it. 'It was weird seeing it.' It's the one of us. The one that Paddy had mounted in a frame identical to Hanratty's. Now, though, the picture is in a plain black frame. I though he would have switched his frame with Hanratty's? Did he not do that?

Paddy flushes. He turns the picture face down on the table. 'Sorry.'

'It's OK.'

'I keep it there because I like it,' he says, and he sounds kind of sad.

'What happened the original frame?'

It's a ham-fisted, maybe a stupid thing to ask, but Paddy doesn't flinch. 'Bloody thing broke,' he says. He sits at the other end of the sofa and angles his body towards me. 'That TY student, remember her? Well, she knocked it off my desk by mistake when she was getting a file for me.'

'Janice?' She'd been the kid of a customer of mine in the salon. Paddy had done me a favour taking her on. She'd been with him for a week in his constituency office and he'd never stopped moaning about her.

'Yeah, that was her name. Bloody useless. She broke my favourite mug too.'

'She broke the frame?'

'She was in bits. I was too. Bloody thing was expensive but it cracked right up the side. I told her to throw it out. She bought me this one instead.

'Janice broke the frame and threw it out and she bought you a new one?'

'Yes.' He's looking at me in amusement. 'I had no idea you loved it so much.'

Janice was in that office ages before Hanratty was murdered. At least a good year or so. It would have been the frame with Marcus's fingerprints on it that Paddy got rid of. And Paddy couldn't be making the story up because all anyone would have to do would be to check with Janice.

'I think I should go,' I blurt out, standing up, thinking, I have to ring Melissa. Ring the police.

Paddy looks surprised. 'OK. I thought—'

'I have to go.'

'Will I see you again?'

'I have to go,' is all I can say.

Marcus

Melissa lays it out before me, like a magic carpet that I just have to ride to get out of here.

'You see, when you called to his office that day, Marcus, you touched that frame. On the night of the murder, he carried that frame into Charles Hanratty's and swapped it for Charles's one, making it look as if you were there.'

'Why would he do that?'

She doesn't answer, instead she goes on. 'We've checked and he was away the night of the murder, at a GAA match in Dublin. He had motive in that, though he says he didn't believe your story, he still knew about it. Sash also said there was a rumour that his mother was having an affair with Charles Hanratty. So, who's to say he didn't confront Charles over those things that night?'

'I don't think—'

'I know. He doesn't seem the type.' She leans in towards me. 'There is no type.'

It'd be so easy. The evidence all stacked against Paddy Jones, my main rival. I'd knock him out again, just like I had that day in Applegate. Only back then, he hadn't prosecuted me. In fact, no one knows this, but he'd called to my house, he'd shoved out his hand, he'd told me not to worry. He said that though his dad was going mad over it, he wasn't going to say anything.

Then he'd asked after my ma.

I hadn't minded him and Sash being together after that because, though there was something a little needy about him, he was a good guy.

And though I hate it here and though I want to get out, I can't let them blame him. 'He didn't do it,' I tell Melissa.

'We haven't compiled a full list yet but—'

'I handled that frame myself, in Hanratty's house.'

The silence that follows that statement is like the silence which follows the lock being turned on my prison cell at night. Melissa glances at the policeman who's watching us. 'Say that again?'

I hate letting her down, hate the fact that now she'll view me with suspicion, just like everyone else. 'I was in Hanratty's house. I lied.'

'You fucking lied?' Her voice is low.

'In my initial statement.'

'You fucking lied.'

'Yeah. I lied when I said I was never in the house. I was scared and I couldn't take it back. I already had to take back the bit about Sash – how would it have looked if I lied about two things?'

'Better than it does now,' she spits, and I don't know if it's the braces or her anger. We both ignore the saliva on the table in front of us. She leans in towards me and her eyes pin me to my seat. Very slowly she asks, 'I want an honest answer here: did you kill that man?'

'No, I didn't.'

'I want a bloody honest answer!'

'I *am* being honest.' I rub my hands over my face. 'I broke into his house, OK? About a month before the murder.'

'You broke into his house?'

'Yeah. You don't do it as a teenager and then forget how to, you know?'

'I wouldn't know.'

Her tone cuts me. 'I set off his alarm a few times,' I explain, 'and then he just didn't switch it back on. I had a key that I'd lifted from him way back, before he realised I was stalking him. And in I went.'

'You broke in.' She sounds like she needs to be tranquilised.

'I've always thought that breaking into people's places was like looking at their souls and I had to see what his soul was like then.'

'Did you wear gloves?'

'Nope. The only thing I really touched was that picture. It made me so mad. And maybe the door. I just wanted to walk around, get a feel for the place.'

Melissa says nothing. Instead, she reaches over and pulls her laptop back towards her. She flicks it off and flips it closed.

'I'll let the cops know.'

'What? That I lied?'

'Yes, Marcus,' she says, 'that you lied.' With barely a glance at me, she indicates for me to be brought back to my cell.

So near and yet further away than ever.

Sash

I call Melissa as soon as I leave Paddy's. It's becoming a habit, I think, me telling everyone that the men in my life are innocent all the time.

'He didn't do it,' I blurt out as soon as the phone is answered. 'I was over there today—'

'I told you not to.' She sounds totally pissed off.

'Yeah, well, I had to.'

'You and Marcus, you deserve each other,' she snaps, and I think, that's not very professional. 'I know he didn't do it because Marcus admitted that he was actually in Charles Hanratty's house before. And he wasn't just in it, he broke into it.'

'But I thought—'

'Me too. Seems Mr I'm-So-Innocent is a liar.' She sighs.

'Sorry, Sash, that's very unprofessional of me. I just had such hope.'

'At least he didn't let Paddy sink,' I say, thinking that must have been hard for him.

'There is that in his favour, I suppose,' she says grudgingly. 'Anyway I'd better go, I've a client coming in soon. Sorry it's worked out this way.'

I can't reply to that, because if Marcus had got off, Paddy would be in.

She hangs up abruptly, her mind already on whoever else she is representing. I feel incredibly let down by Marcus and yet, sort of proud of him too.

Lana

Mona doesn't even care when I ask to borrow her laptop. Usually, she gives it to me with a list of instructions of all the things I can't do on it. I can't load stuff if I don't know where it comes from, I can't open suspicious emails, even though none of them say that they are suspicious, and I can't go into any of her files and I should never read her letters.

Today, she just passes it to me because she is in love with my dad and all they talk about is the wedding, the wedding.

I think it is weird that Mona will become my stepmother.

I bring the computer up to my bed and plug it in – that's another thing I have to do because the battery is not running right. The computer flicks on and I go onto the Internet.

I key in 'Marcus Dillon' and 'trial' and 'evidence'.

Marcus is pretty famous now. Loads and loads of sites

come up. I'm looking for reports from the beginning of the trial because, even though Sash said that the other evidence didn't matter, if Marcus isn't guilty, then all the evidence matters, because some of it mustn't point to him. And the bits that don't point to him are the important bits. They will point you in another direction, where the truth is.

I read and read and read. Most of the sites say all the same things I know already. Then, on page three, fourth result down, there is a news segment about the trial. I go onto the website and see lots and lots of reporting from the trial. I go back to the first one and start working my way through. Finally, I find one on the six o'clock news. The reporter is standing outside the court with a huge microphone. The wind is blowing her hair and she is squinting into the camera, like the wind is blowing into her eyes. She has a crimson coat on. And white gloves. And she should have worn a hat.

'Today in the trial of Marcus Dillon, the cartoon artist accused of murdering businessman Charles Hanratty, David Long, forensic investigator for the prosecution, introduced evidence placing Marcus Dillon at the scene of the crime. A hair from the defendant was found near the body, as were fingerprints on a number of cartoon images. Fingerprints from the defendant were also found on a picture frame which had been broken over the body of the businessman. We learned that Mr Hanratty died as a result of a number of blows—'

I leave that page. Nothing here.

Two hours, three minutes and fourteen seconds later, I find

it on page nine of the search results. A regional newspaper reports that also found on the body were fibres that were traced back to a school Charles Hanratty had visited earlier that day. That is the only other bit of evidence. I think that if the rest of the evidence is pointing one way and it's wrong, this is the bit that points in the right direction.

I google 'Charles Hanratty'. He is even more famous than Marcus. Then I think if he visited a school there must be a picture of him on the Internet somewhere.

I remember in my school, when I was ten, we had a visit from a goat. They took a picture of us standing beside the goat and put it in the local paper. It was a brown and white goat and it bit one of my friends.

Schools put everything online now.

I key in 'Charles Hanratty' 'school visit' and also the month. I press on images.

Lots of images. He sure liked visiting schools. Loads of pictures of him smiling with kids and teachers. I look through them all, thinking that there has to be one from the date he died, and I find one from Ballytemple Community School.

Charles is in the picture surrounded by loads of students. A few teachers are in the background, smiling.

The caption says, *The late, great Charles Hanratty with some of our students. RIP.*

They don't think he was a bad man.

I ring Sash with the news.

'Hello, Wicklow's Beauty Spot,' she says.

She sounds very important on the phone. I like talking on

the phone because you're not expected to know everything that's going on with people because you just have their voices to go on.

'It's Lana.'

Sash groans, which means she is tired or just being rude. 'What's wrong? I'm in work.'

'Nothing is wrong. Or maybe it is. I don't know.'

'Thanks, Justine,' Sash says, and she's not talking to me but to a customer. Then she is back to me. 'What is it?'

'I was thinking about that story you told me and the details?'

'Don't think about it,' Sash barks. 'Forget it.'

I guess she's cross because she nearly thought Paddy did it.

'I can't just make myself forget, I told you that. I have a theory.'

'Lana, just leave it now.'

'So you think he's guilty?'

'I didn't say that. I just don't think we should be running around trying to figure it out.'

'Well, I think we should because if he's not guilty someone else is and it might be someone from the school because that's the only detail that doesn't fit with Marcus.'

'What school?'

'He visited a school the day he died.'

'So?'

'There were fibres at the scene. It says so in the *Ballymacknock Gazette* on page nine, result four of a Google search on Marcus Dillon, trial and evidence. Maybe someone from the school left the fibres and it wasn't because Hanratty was at the school.'

A big puff of a sigh.

'It's the only detail left.'

She thinks about this. Well, either that or she is having a petit mal seizure but she doesn't suffer from epilepsy. 'It's a stretch, Lana.'

'Not if Marcus is innocent, it isn't.'

More long pauses. 'I'll need to find out the school.'

I tell her which one it was.

She calls me Little Miss Industry and I can't figure out if she's serious or not. Or being sarcastic or not.

Anyway, I'm done now.

Sash

Lana has emailed a grainy picture to my phone. I can make out Hanratty and a load of kids and some blurry teachers and very little else. I close it and wonder if it's worth pursuing. I'm sure the police ruled it out but then I think of what Lana said. If Marcus is innocent, and despite his lies I know he is, then this is the only piece of evidence that doesn't fit so it has to lead somewhere. The other evidence was easy to pin on Marcus, and yet he has explained it all now, even his fingerprints on the frame.

I stare at the picture again and reluctantly open my laptop. I'll google the school, see if I can locate a better picture.

As my laptop loads up, I make a coffee. I could probably

drink four coffees by the time it's finished whirring and clanking. I need to get a new one but so far I haven't bothered. Though I have a Facebook account and a Twitter account, I rarely use them. And I never use Google. My phone buzzes. It's a text from Paddy. *Any news?* is all it says. It's accompanied by a smiley.

I haven't called him at all since that day in his apartment. I think part of it is that I need to get used to the fact that I didn't know him, not really. I suppose that's how he felt about me in the beginning too.

I text him back, *All quiet. Talk soon.* And a smiley.

He doesn't respond.

My laptop pings, ready for action.

I go to Google and key in the name of the school.

A website pops up. I click on images and find the one Lana sent me. It won't enlarge and whoever took it obviously had the shakes, it's so blurred.

There are no other photographs of the visit.

I sigh. I click on a list of teachers. I run through their names quickly. Nothing that I recognise.

I sit back, thinking that it's a bit of a wild-goose chase. Thinking that maybe I should let it go. And yet, Marcus is in prison and everyone else seems to have let it go.

I scroll through the rest of the site, just to feel that I've done everything I can. There are news stories of various successes for the school in the Young Scientist, debating, athletics, all followed by pictures.

And it's in one of the pictures that I see her, only she's called Mrs Gilhooley now. She's got her arms around some of her students, who are holding aloft a cup, and her smile is wide and proud.

I sit back, shell-shocked, thinking no way. She couldn't have. And why? Why would she have? For firing her mother?

I don't know what to do now. I can't ring Melissa again. I certainly can't ring the police. What if I'm wrong again?

I google Jennifer, under her maiden name first.

There are a few sites which name her as a discus champion. I find a website for her strength and conditioning classes. Clicking on it, I see her in a pair of black shorts and a vest top, much like she wore to athletics training when I was running. She is posing, her arm flexed. She looks like she has serious upper-arm strength. She could have knocked Hanratty out easily.

I google her along with Applegate. The only thing that appears is a death notice for her mother.

Lucy Ryan (née Philips), late of Applegate and Ballyfermot, died suddenly at her home. Sadly missed by her loving daughter Jennifer.

No mention of a husband.

The date on the notice is two weeks before Hanratty was killed.

I google her under her married name. Nothing bar what appears on the school website.

Why didn't she tell anyone that she had seen Hanratty on the day he died? And if the police had interviewed the staff of the school, did she mention to them that she once knew him? Did she tell them that he'd stood by as her mother was fired? Obviously not.

But Jennifer? The woman who had apologised for bullying

me? Who had looked so upset in the courthouse? And yet, she had a temper. I still remember her stomping on my hand that time as I lay on the ground.

I pick up the phone and call my dad. There is no way I'm doing this alone.

Marcus

Melissa again. She scrutinises me as I arrive into the interview room.

'So soon again,' I say.

She doesn't bite. Instead, she eyeballs me. 'Your friend Sash is a very tenacious woman.'

'Is that good?'

'Here.' She hands me an oblong envelope. White. Inside, something flimsy. Then she smiles, just a bit, so I think, this must be OK. 'Go on, open it. I haven't looked inside, but I think I know what it says.'

I wonder uneasily if I'm being set up.

I tear open the flap and pull out a sheet of copybook paper with blue lines and neat precise writing. I look at Melissa and she nods.

Dear Marcus,

What can I say only sorry. If you've got this, it means they came looking for me and found everything. When I told you I wasn't coming back to visit you, I meant it. I'm somewhere nice now. Somewhere new, somewhere that is not a constant reminder of my old life.

I did it, Marcus. I killed him.

By now the police have the murder weapons. By now they know that I took a key from his keyring when he visited my school, had it copied and left the original behind in the house that night after first cleaning it for prints.

I never meant to murder anyone. I'd spent years putting distance between me and him. In the end I wanted to move because seeing his picture in the papers tortured me. I'd planned to move abroad where I'd never see him again. I was just about to tell the school I worked in that I was taking a career break when my mother died. It shattered me, not just because she was my mother and she was dead, but that she had died without ever knowing what that man had done. She died without ever knowing that she'd been branded a thief because of something I'd done. It had haunted her all her life, the shame of it. I don't think she ever truly believed me when I said I knew she was honest.

I wish I had told her. I wish I had told her that, in order for my dad to keep his shop and for her to have her job in the hotel, Hanratty did to me what he did to you and Sash. Only more often. The day I refused to take it anymore was when he set her up as a thief.

But how could I have told her that? I mean, which was worse for her to live with?

After she died, I put my travel plans on hold until I could bury her and get a gravestone. And then, two weeks later, after the funeral and the tears, Hanratty visited our school. He didn't know me: my name had changed (a broken marriage) and I'd aged. Or maybe he did know and he didn't let on? One certain thing is that I knew him. My stomach rolled as he put his arm about the children, as he patted their backs. And the rage that I'd buried for so long just seemed to consume me. It swallowed me up and, without stopping to think, I took one of his keys from his coat in the staffroom. It was the patio door key. I left work early, had it copied, changed into black clothes and then parked away from the school and followed him home.

I meant to kill him. It was like I was in a fog, it was like a compulsion. It was like one part of me was watching the other part of me. He answered the door, smiled and I stabbed him. Marcus, it felt good. I remember you knocking on the door, only I didn't know it was you. But I can't even remember throwing your cartoons on top of him. I can't remember writing 'Cluck'. I do remember telling him that all his chickens had come home to roost, though. That's what he used to say to me – that all my chickens would come home to roost if I didn't do what he said.

I cried afterwards. I don't know why.

I got out through the patio with my spare and left the other key back on his keyring.

The next day, it was like I dreamed it. I was back in the fog of existing, the way I'd been in Applegate.

Next thing they were charging you and I couldn't leave until I was sure you'd get off, only you didn't.

And you've always been good to me. So I owe you this.

I told you not to lose hope.

Jenny.

I have to re-read the letter about three times, while Melissa watches me, her chin in her hand. 'Sash and her father went out to the school,' she says. 'They heard that Jenny hadn't been in for a few days and when the school wouldn't give out her address, they informed the police, who tried to contact her and couldn't, so in the end they got into her apartment. Like she says in the letter, they found a full confession along with the murder weapons.'

'Jenny?' I think of that girl, shy, uncertain, and yet a memory surfaces: her stomping hard on Sash's hand that day. I'd been shocked.

'Congratulations,' Melissa smiles, 'you're finally free.'

And while the relief is extraordinary and I think I might start acting like a wuss, I can't help thinking that it takes more than being let out of prison to be free.

ONE MONTH LATER

Lana

Melissa has promised me a year's supply of Jelly Babies. She even said, and I don't know if it was a joke or she was serious, that I can work on her team if I like.

Maybe I will. No one else wants me to work for them.

Sash is still pretty upset over Paddy. I always thought Sash was good at understanding people but she is no better than me. She had to tell Paddy that she wasn't going to get back with him and that she really, really likes him but she will never love him.

Paddy was upset, she said, but he took it on the chin. Which is weird.

Sash said that when she was with Paddy she only saw what she wanted to see and he said the same about her. They never really knew each other.

I only see what I see.

Only that's not right all the time either.

Life is confusing.

Mona and Dad are staying in Applegate. Dad says it will be hard in the beginning but that it's good to stick around to remind people of what happened. Mona agrees. Dad says that Brian Jones is a broken man. He even came up to Dad in Lidl when Dad was buying a telescope and offered his hand for Dad to shake. Dad shook it.

Mona said Dad should not have bought a telescope and that he should have told Brian Jones to get stuffed.

Dad said he did what he did. He said Brian Jones has to live with the knowledge that he was happy to see an innocent man go to jail and that he accused an innocent woman of being a thief. That's hard to live with, Dad said.

Mona said if our mother walked in would Dad just shake her hand.

Dad said he would.

Mona was in a bit of a huff because she crossed her arms over her chest and did a big sniff.

Dad said, I would shake her hand and I'd thank her for leaving because if she hadn't I'd never have met you.

Mona told him to go on out of that.

Then she smiled.

I can't wait for my Jelly Babies.

Marcus

I'm two weeks out today and the publicity has largely died down. I'm stuck in a bit of a crappy bedsit as my apartment is leased for a year, but I'm out. And in the papers again. For the past two weeks, I've lain on my bed in the mornings, the curtains wide open, the window wide open, and I've let the fresh air pour over me.

I never realised that the world smells as good as it does.

Today, though, I'm up early and dressed in a fleece and jeans with a pair of Timberland boots. Outside, it's cold, the sky grey with darker grey clouds. It'll rain any time. I pull on a beanie and drive to the prison.

As I pull into a parking space, a couple of rough young lads stare in awe at the car. It's so the wrong car for around here but it's the only one I have. I jump out and slam the door, locking it, and as I walk away, I pretend not to see them creeping over to peer inside. Normally I'd have asked them if they wanted a look, but my face is too familiar now and I'm afraid they'll recognise me.

That trial changed my life and I had done nothing, well, aside from stalking the guy, for which I despise myself. But I hadn't asked to become one of the most hated faces in Ireland, I hadn't asked for my background to be torn wide open for everyone to pore over, I hadn't asked that Sash sit on the stand and tell everyone what she'd been through. I hadn't asked for my mother to have to face her past in such a cruel way.

In a way, all that attention was worse than the trial.

But we survived it. My ma stayed off the drink; Alan stuck by her through everything, believing her when she told him that her son was innocent. That man barely knew me, but he held us both up. And Sash, she's faced the past just like I have and we're sort of friends again. I hope.

We can talk again now.

I move into the queue and am the only man in a sea of women. One woman up the top seems to be doling out cakes. I turn my face away as she starts coming down the line. She runs out two people before me and calls apologetically, 'I'll make more for next time.'

Someone up the front says, 'Mel, don't be mad. Them lazy feckers down the back just need to get up earlier. Be first in the queue.'

People laugh.

I keep my head low as we're ushered in. When I get into the visitors' room, Louis hasn't been brought in yet. Some of the other lads from my landing are there and one or two of them nod a silent greeting to me.

Louis finally arrives. 'Marcus, my man,' he grins widely, 'how's it going?'

We sit opposite each other.

'I dropped in some comics for you,' I tell him.

'*Batman?*'

'Yeah.'

'And, eh, I sent you a signed *Slam Man*. Keep it and keep the next two I'll send because come a year or two, when you get out, you can sell them and make a fortune.'

'Aw, I wouldn't sell them,' he says. 'No way. They're beautiful.'

I like him for saying that.

'Did they catch that girl?' he asks me.

'Nah. I hope they don't.'

'But it means that you're not a real murderer?'

'I'm afraid not.'

'I should have beaten the shit out of you.'

I laugh.

'Seriously,' Louis nods, 'you go now and don't ever come back. You don't belong here.'

I stand to go. 'No one belongs here,' I say.

He shrugs and I tell him to look out for the comics.

I don't look back.

When I get out, my car is untouched, the lads still walking around it. I watch them for a bit, enjoying the way they rub their hands reverently along the sides as they try to peer in the window.

'She's beautiful,' one of them says as I approach.

'D'you want to see inside?' I unlock the car and open the door for them.

'Man,' the taller kid says, 'you are so lucky.'

For the first time in my life, I know what he means.

Sash

I'm waiting in the place I waited for him the very first time. It's dark and it's coming into winter and I think it might snow. The trees are bare and the orchard looks dead, as if it will never bear fruit again, but come the spring, the trees will be pollinated and blossom and apples will grow. Though the gardening group in the town are thinning out the trees now in the hope of a better crop. Lana is taking charge of it. She says, and I quote, sometimes you have to lose all the crap to make things better. Lana, who hates change.

There's hope for us all.

I am sitting on a rug on the ground, my back against the tree that bears the scars of our names. It's dark and quiet and I can't see the sky through the tangle of branches. I'm wearing jeans and boots and a fleece, a big woolly hat pulled over my ears. Mona made me wear it.

She and Dad are staying in Applegate and I think it will be better for them now. The town is still in shock that Jennifer Ryan, whom most remember as a great thrower, is guilty of murder. I hope they never catch her.

'Are you ready for a bit of a trip down memory lane?' Marcus's voice startles me. I look and there he is, striding through the gloom of early evening. He's dressed almost the same as me.

'What?'

'Come.' He motions with his head and the years fall away as I stand up and walk in his shadow towards the edge of the orchard.

Soon we're standing opposite Hanratty's house and I know what he's doing before he says it.

He jangles a set of keys. 'I got Dessie to ask Tommy for them. Come on.'

His walk is loose-limbed, athletic, and I follow. Unlike before, we walk up the driveway and Marcus slots the key in the front door. It swings wide.

'No alarm?'

'Nope. Applegate hasn't changed that much,' Marcus says.

We're whispering, for some reason.

I hesitate on the threshold but Marcus takes my hand and together we enter the house. It smells clean and fresh. He pulls me gently towards the front room, looks at me and I nod. He presses down the handle and pushes the door open.

The room is white. The furniture bright and cheerful. Pictures on the wall show sunsets and seascapes. The wall is knocked into the kitchen so it's a wide space. I breathe in. Beside me, Marcus does the same. I feel the tension I didn't know I held inside leave me, uncurling like a cat and stretching out before dissolving.

'It's just a room,' I say into the stillness.

'Yep.' Marcus moves towards the kitchen as I follow. We go upstairs, banishing the ghosts in our heads one by one. I feel my younger self looking over my shoulder as I do so, clapping, cheering me on, moving closer to me.

Later, in the orchard, he sits beside me on the rug.

His leg along the length of mine, his arm brushing mine. He reaches into the pocket of his parka and pulls out a joint. 'Too old?'

'Never.'

He lights it and takes a long, slow drag. He still has that way of smoking that turns my heart to butter. He passes it to me and our fingers touch.

I inhale deeply and feel it spread inside me.

Then, like when we were young, he slings an arm about my shoulder and pulls me near.

The scent of apple fills my nostrils, even though the ground is bare of them.

He lays his head on top of mine.

'Do you think we'll ever get over it?' I ask.

He heaves a sigh and I feel his chest move. 'Nah. We'll just live with it. It'll be grand.'

I think it will too.

'Everything is different now,' I say.

'In a good way?'

I think about that. 'Yeah, because everything is true now, you know.'

'I love you, Sash.' I don't think he meant to say it. I think the words just came out. 'Well,' he says, 'if you want stuff to be true, I've got to say it. Some things are just meant to be.'

'What?' I smile. 'Like Batman and Robin?'

'Yeah, and Superman and Lois.'

'And me and you?'

'Marcus and Sash.' He nods, runs his hand over our initials on the bark of the tree. Then he turns, takes out a penknife and I watch as he carves out a beautiful 'forever' in the shape of a heart around the letters.

Then he turns and faces me.

And we kiss.

ACKNOWLEDGEMENTS

This is my twentieth novel; it has been a wonderful journey, made more wonderful by the following people:

My lovely family and extended family.

My friends, of whom I am fortunate to have loads – I won't name anyone in case I leave people out. But childhood friends, school friends, college mates, work mates, running mates, writer friends, actor friends and friends I made through my children – you all know who you are.

My publisher – Hachette Ireland. Thanks to Ciara, Joanna, Breda, Ruth, Bernard and Jim. Thanks to Emma Dunne for her excellent copy-edit and for putting me straight on cartoon terminology.

Thanks to anyone who gave me publicity ever but most especially Aideen and Vincent of *The Liffey Champion*.

A big thanks is due to everyone who helped research this book – Julian Shanaher, Tony Joyce and most especially to John O'Shea for his criminal lawyer experience. All mistakes are most firmly mine!

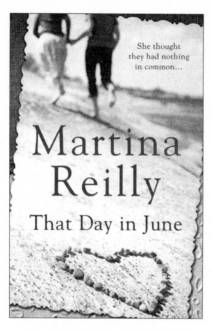

She thought
they had nothing
in common...

Martina
Reilly

That Day in June

Eight years ago, Sandy ran away from home, and has done her best never to look back. Now, the best part of her day is a morning visit from Max, a handsome and successful businessman, who's always ready with a smile. So when he suddenly disappears from her life, Sandy is worried. What has happened to him? And why did he act so strangely the last time they spoke?

As Sandy tries to track Max down, she begins to realise how little she really knows about him – his family, his job, or why his life has started to fall apart.

And when she finds him, she comes to understand that they have more in common than she'd ever thought possible. Will they learn to trust each other with the secrets they've kept hidden, and finally move on?

Also available as an ebook

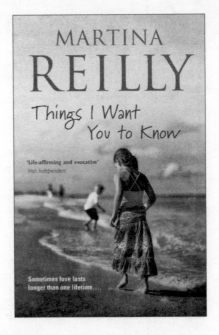

MARTINA REILLY

Things I Want You to Know

'Life-affirming and evocative'
Irish Independent

Sometimes love lasts
longer than one lifetime....

How do you pick up the pieces after the worst has happened? When Nick Deegan's wife, Kate, dies, leaving him with two small children to raise alone, he has no idea how he'll manage. But on the day of her funeral, he discovers a book Kate left for him, *Things I Want You to Know*. Her instructions for raising Emma and Liam without her give him comfort, but her other plans for him seem much more daunting ...

Five dates with five different women. Nick isn't sure his heart is in it ... but as he tries to follow Kate's careful instructions, he slowly realises that it's not romance Kate wanted him to find, but something far more important. Will Nick find the courage to take a second chance?

Also available as an ebook